COMING HOME

THE TREADING WATER SERIES, BOOK 4

MARIE FORCE

Published by HTJB, Inc.
Copyright 2011. HTJB, Inc.
Cover design by Kristina Brinton

ISBN: 978-0615824444

All characters in this book are fiction and figments of the author's imagination.

marieforce.com

The Treading Water Series

*To all the readers who asked me
to finish Reid & Kate's story...
This is for you.*

CHAPTER 1

The darkness came faster this time, too fast to prepare before it was upon her. Bright lights, the roar of the crowd, the band behind her… One minute, Kate Harrington was in the middle of a show. The next minute, she was in an ambulance being rushed—again—to the emergency room. This was the third time she'd passed out since a bout of pneumonia had weakened her, but it was the first time she'd done it on a stage in front of twenty thousand screaming fans.

As the paramedics started an IV and put an oxygen mask over her face, her sister Jill watched the proceedings with big, frightened eyes.

Kate couldn't remember where they were. There'd been so many cities, so many hotels, so many venues, so many crowds over the last ten years that they'd begun to blend together into a panoramic muddle of images. When she thought about the media coverage this incident would garner, she held back a groan.

The paparazzi followed her every move like a band of rabid dogs. Passing out in the middle of a concert would make for a big story.

She pushed the mask aside. "Call Mom and Dad so they don't hear it on the news," she said to her sister, who doubled as her manager and attorney.

"Okay," Jill said, pulling out the phone they called her Siamese twin because she was permanently attached to it.

As the ambulance sped through the night in the city she couldn't remember, Kate could only imagine what they'd say this time. She'd been accused of everything under the sun, from cocaine addiction to secret pregnancies to mistreating her staff. Nothing was off-limits. No lie was too big or too preposterous. Such was life in the celebrity fishbowl.

Though she'd gone looking for a career in country music, her "cross-over" appeal had made her a huge star—much bigger than she'd ever hoped or wanted to be. She'd sold more records in the last decade than any other female performer in the world, and along with that success came rabid interest in her every move.

The speculation about her personal life had been worse than ever since pneumonia forced her to cancel two weeks of shows, which was why she'd resumed the tour so soon, hoping to put an end to the vicious rumors. They'd said she was back in rehab, drying out from years of drug abuse. Her plan to go back to work and shut down the rumors had been working well until she passed out on stage. Now the gossip would be worse than ever.

If it hadn't been such a nuisance to deal with, the buzz would've amused her. She was, without a doubt, the most boring celebrity in the history of celebrities. She never went anywhere that didn't involve work. After a few spectacularly public romances fizzled, she'd sworn off men, especially well-known men. When she wasn't working, she holed up at her farm in Tennessee with her horses, her family and her close friends—few as they were.

Of course, boring didn't sell magazines, so they made up most of what they said about her. To the outside world, she was just another pill-popping, dope-snorting, pampered princess who'd had too much success far too soon. The people closest to her knew the truth, but sometimes she suspected even her own family wondered if any of the rumors were true.

They arrived at the hospital, and as they whisked her inside, she heard someone mention Oklahoma City and remembered arriving at the hotel suite with Jill and the sound check at the Chesapeake Energy Arena. She recalled asking Jill if they could tour the memorial at the Murrah building, and Jill saying they didn't have time to arrange the security she'd require for such an outing. Kate had been to every major city in America and countless others overseas, but she'd rarely gotten to see anything while she was there. She was always too busy working—or too insulated by the security required to go anywhere.

This late-fall tour had been the idea of her mentor, friend, producer and fellow superstar, Buddy Longstreet. He and his record company, Long Road Records, had made her a star, and there wasn't much she wouldn't do for Buddy when he asked for a favor. That was how she found herself coming off a summer tour and heading right into a second tour that was due to wrap up on New Year's Eve at Carnegie Hall.

Since she could barely lift her head at the moment, the idea of performing at Carnegie Hall in a few weeks seemed as daunting as climbing Mount Everest. Her chest hurt, her eyes were so heavy she could barely keep them open, and she felt like she could sleep for a year.

The piercing pain of another needle being jammed into her hand forced her eyes open as a team of doctors and nurses swooped in on her. Outside the cubicle, she saw Jill on the phone, pacing back and forth in the sky-high heels and power suit that was her uniform. As she rarely saw her sister dressed in anything else, Kate liked to tease her about sleeping in a suit.

Truth be told, she didn't know what she'd do without Jill to manage all the details, to hammer out the contracts, to fight the battles and manage the team that made it happen. Thanks to Jill, all Kate had to do was show up and sing. Worries that her sister was sacrificing her own life to run hers was something that nagged at Kate more often than she'd care to admit. But since existing without Jill at her right hand was unimaginable, Kate stayed mum on the subject, and Jill certainly never complained.

She worked like a dog and collected the big salary Kate paid her, but Kate wondered if she ever spent a dime on anything other than suits and heels and the latest and greatest in smartphone technology. The sisters were never home long enough to spend any of the money they'd made over the years.

As she watched her beloved older sister swipe at a tear, Kate reached her breaking point. Jill didn't cry. Ever. Jill was a pillar of strength and fortitude. The pressure was getting to them both, and it was time to step off the treadmill for a while.

The medication they were pumping into her made Kate's tongue feel too big for her mouth, but her thoughts were clear. Enough was enough. Images of the huge log-cabin-style house she'd built five years ago on her sprawling estate in Hendersonville, Tennessee drifted through her mind, making her yearn for home.

Kate must've dozed off, because when she awoke, she was in a darkened room. She blinked a few times to clear her vision and saw Jill standing at the window, staring out into the darkness.

"Hey," Kate said.

Jill spun around to face her. "You're awake."

"How long have I been asleep?"

"A couple of hours. They admitted you because you're dehydrated. That's why you passed out."

"I'm really thirsty."

Jill helped her to take a few sips from a cup of ice water on the table.

"Where are we?"

"St. Anthony's Hospital."

"Is the press going crazy?"

Jill shrugged. "I haven't looked."

"Yes, you have," Kate said with a small smile. "Don't lie to me."

"They're flipping out, as usual where you're concerned. This time they're saying it was a combination of pills and booze."

"I wish I had half as much fun as they think I do."

"I wish both of us did."

"It's probably high time we had some fun, don't you think? Let's stop the madness and go home."

Jill's eyes widened, and her mouth fell open. "What're you saying?"

"I've had enough, Jill. We've been everywhere, done everything, made a fortune. Now it's time to live a little. How many nights have you spent in your place since it was finished?" Kate had given Jill three acres of property and a "gift certificate" good for the house of her choice. After her initial reluctance to accept such an extravagant gift, the house had been built to Jill's exacting specifications.

"I don't know. A month, maybe two?"

"And it's been done for a year. That's ridiculous. What're we trying to prove? Who're we trying to prove it to?"

"You have contracts, Kate. Obligations. Buddy will freak if you bail on the tour."

"I can get a note from my doctor," she said with a playful smile.

"You're apt to be sued. It's no joke."

"I'm not joking. Let them sue me. I need a break. A real break. I want months at home. I want the family in Tennessee for Christmas. I want to see Mom, Dad, Andi, Aidan, the boys and Maggie and spend *real* time with them, not twenty-four rushed hours between tour stops. Don't you want that, too?"

"You know I do, but it's not feasible right now. We've got thirty dates left on the calendar before we're done." She didn't mention that they'd get only a few days off before they were due in the studio to record Kate's sixth album. After that, it was back on the road for another tour. "How am I supposed to get you out of all those obligations?"

"If anyone can do it, you can. I should've done this after I was sick. Instead, I went back too soon and collapsed in front of an arena full of people, giving the press enough fodder to last for weeks. I'm done, Jill."

"For now or forever?"

"I don't know yet. For now, definitely. I'll let you know about forever after I've had a break."

"There could be big trouble over this, bad press…"

Kate released a harsh laugh. "What other kind is there where I'm concerned?" She reached for her sister's hand and held on tight. "We're twenty-eight and twenty-nine years old, and we've spent the last five years working ourselves into early graves. We have millions in the bank, gorgeous homes that we pay people to keep clean for us, nice cars sitting unused in the garage, horses we pay people to ride for us, and five little brothers who are growing up far too fast and barely know us."

Jill nibbled on her bottom lip, seeming stressed as she listened to Kate.

"You haven't had a real vacation since you graduated from law school and came to work for me. I haven't had one in so long, I think the last one was Christmas break of my senior year of high school. It's time to *live* a little. What good is all the money in the world if we never do anything fun? Don't you want to have *fun*, Jill?"

And there was something else Kate wanted to do, something she should've done a long time ago, but that was her secret and hers alone. It wasn't something she could share with anyone, even her sister and closest friend.

"Our work *is* fun," Jill said. "I enjoy it, and you do, too, when you're feeling well."

"I haven't enjoyed it in a long time—long before I got sick." Saying the words out loud was somehow freeing. "I feel like I'm on a treadmill with every day exactly the same as the last. The only thing that changes is the city and the venue."

"What about the band and the roadies and all the people your show employs?"

"We'll give the roadies and the tour people a nice severance package and pay the band to give us six months before they sign on with anyone else. You think they won't welcome some time at home with their families? Some of them have kids who barely recognize them on the rare occasion they're actually home."

Jill nibbled on her thumbnail as she mulled it over. Her mind worked a mile a minute, which made her such an asset to Kate. After several minutes of mulling and nail biting, Jill glanced at her sister. "Let me see what I can do."

Damn, it was good to be home, Kate thought as she took her horse, Thunder, on a slow gallop through the woods that abutted her home twenty minutes outside Nashville. At thirteen, Thunder was showing no signs of slowing down and hadn't lost his enthusiasm for outings with Kate.

"We'll be spending a lot more time together for the next little while, boy," she said, stroking his neck as his hooves clomped along the well-worn path.

He nickered in response to her, as he always did, drawing a smile. She swore he was a human stuck in a horse's body, and the comfort of being with him filled her with joy.

As they often did when she rode Thunder, her thoughts strayed to the man who'd given her the horse after their ill-fated romance blew up in their faces. It was impossible, she'd discovered, to spend time with Thunder without thinking of Reid and the magical months they'd spent together.

Kate didn't believe in regrets. She was pragmatic enough by now to know that life could be incredibly sweet and just as incredibly painful. More than ten years had passed since the last time she saw Reid, the awful day he flew her home to Rhode Island after her sister Maggie was badly injured.

But not a day had gone by that she hadn't thought of him, wondered where he was, what he was doing, if he was happy. One night, about six years ago, during a lonely moment on the road, she'd searched for him on the Internet and discovered he'd sold his business and left Nashville shortly after they broke up.

She'd been unable to find a single other reference to him online in the ensuing decade. It was like he'd dropped off the face of the earth, which was why she was about to ask something of her sister that she'd hoped to handle on her own.

Kate brought Thunder to a stop outside Jill's two-story post-and-beam house. She slid off his back and tied the lead to the railing. Rubbing her hand over his flank, Kate said, "I won't be long, pal."

His nicker and nuzzle made her laugh. Sometimes she felt like the horse she rarely saw these days knew her better than any of the people in her life, except for Jill, of course. Since they were young girls, Jill had known her better than anyone, which was why Kate was so certain her sister would balk at what Kate was about to ask of her. But she was determined to ask anyway.

She rapped lightly on the front door and stepped inside. "Hello?"

"In here," Jill called from the kitchen.

Kate strolled into the kitchen, stopping short when she saw Jill dressed for business, bent over her latop with papers strewn across the table. A steaming cup of tea sat ignored next to her. "Okay, what part of *vacation* didn't you get?"

Jill glanced up at her. "You might be on vacation, but I'm still trying to keep your ass from getting sued."

Kate glanced over her shoulder, pretending to look at her ass.

"Stop being funny. It's no joke. Buddy is furious with you, and Ashton is, too."

"What else is new?" Kate asked of Reid's son, who'd given her the cold shoulder every time she saw him over the last ten years. Since he was the chief counsel for Buddy as well as Buddy's superstar wife Taylor Jones and Long Road Records, their paths crossed more often than Kate would like.

"Regardless of his ongoing feud with you, he's also moving heaven and earth to prevent a slew of lawsuits."

"He's not doing it for me. He's doing it for Buddy and the company."

"Who cares why he's doing it? The end result will save you millions."

Since Kate had been focusing on rest and relaxation since they got home two days ago, the last thing she wanted to hear about was the threat of lawsuits. "Remember those jeans we bought in the Mall of America? You must still have them around here somewhere."

"I still have them."

"So you can only be productive in a power suit."

"I have a meeting in the city in just over an hour."

Kate helped herself to a diet soda. "With who?"

"Ashton."

Here's your chance, she thought, as flutter of nerves invaded her belly. *Just say it.* "So, um…"

Without looking up from what she was doing, Jill said, "So um what?"

Kate dropped into a chair across from her sister.

Jill took off the gold-framed glasses she used for computer work and sat back in her chair. "What's on your mind?"

"I was wondering… While you're with Ashton, um…"

"Will you spit it out? I'm on a schedule."

"You're supposed to be on vacation."

"Speak. Quickly."

How to sum up years of longing and regret in one sentence?

"Is something wrong, Kate?"

Hadn't something been wrong every day that she'd spent without him? Hadn't every man she'd been with since him failed to live up to him? Hadn't she been disappointed time and again when she'd tried and failed to fall in love again? "Will you ask him for his father's contact info?"

Jill's mouth fell open, and then she quickly closed it. "You're serious."

"Yes."

"Why?"

"Because there's something I need to speak with him about. Something personal."

"And you think Ashton, who's never forgiven you for hooking up with his father in the first place, is going to just hand over that info?"

"That's where you come in. Your powers of persuasion are legendary."

Jill shook her head. "I don't feel comfortable asking him that. Our relationship is professional, and that's a very personal topic."

"I know I'm asking a lot. I know I always ask a lot of you, but I need to talk to him."

"And you won't tell me why?"

Kate shook her head.

"It's been over with him for a long time, Kate. I don't know what you're hoping to accomplish—"

"I need some closure."

Jill crossed her arms and studied her sister. "Closure."

"That's what I said." After a long pause, Kate asked, "Will you ask him?" While she awaited Jill's reply, her heart hammered. She had a feeling she was making this into too big a deal, but the need to see him, to hear his soft drawl, to feel the way she had when they were together, was getting bigger by the day. No doubt he was long over her and rarely spared her a thought. Kate told herself if that were the case, she would put the past where it belonged and get on with her life. But if there was even the slightest chance that he thought of her as often as she thought of him… "Jill?"

"If I get the chance, I'll ask him, but no promises."

"That's fair enough."

"Are you sure you want to venture into that hornet's nest again?"

"It was only a hornet's nest at the end. The rest of the time…" She met her sister's gaze. "The rest of the time it was magic."

Jill drove into the city an hour later in the white Mercedes coupe Kate had given her for Christmas last year. Her sister was endlessly generous and appreciative of everything Jill did to make her life run smoothly, but sometimes she asked too much. Like this morning… Kate had no way to know that the last thing in the world Jill would ever want to do was mention the ill-fated love affair between Reid Matthews and her sister to the man's ridiculously handsome and endlessly irritating son.

She always dreaded her one-on-one meetings with Ashton, which were far more frequent than she'd like, thanks to the fact that Kate and the attorney for her record company didn't speak to each other. So it was left to Jill to run interference between them. Sometimes she had half a mind to sit them down and tell them to stop acting like children, but she was wise enough by now to know that some hurts weren't made better by time. Some hurts were too deep to ever heal.

Ashton's office was in Green Hills, a trendy area that Jill might've preferred if close proximity to her sister didn't make her life much less complicated. Plus, she knew Kate liked having her nearby. Kate needed someone around who she could always count on—and trust. Most of the time, Jill was happy to be that person.

This was not one of those times.

She pulled into a parking space behind the restored Victorian Ashton used as an office and turned off the car. She took a moment to collect herself and gather the calm, cool façade she preferred for business dealings. No matter how much time she took to affect that cool façade, however, she could count on Ashton Matthews to have her rattled and furious within five minutes.

"Just get through this and you can be on vacation," she said out loud as she grabbed her briefcase and went inside.

"Hi, Jill," Ashton's assistant, Debi, said. "He's waiting for you in his office."

"Thank you," Jill said with a smile for Debi. She went up the stairs and took a right, heading for the huge office at the end of the hallway. Jill had been here a hundred times and had the same reaction every time. By the time she reached the closed door to Ashton's office, her heart beat hard, her palms were sweaty and her stomach fluttered with nerves. Why did the thought of seeing him always undo her? It was positively maddening!

Jill took one last moment to prepare for battle and raised her hand to knock.

"Come on in."

Oh, that voice. That accent. It was positively lethal. Jill opened the door and stepped inside, closing the door behind her. When she ventured a glance at the desk, she found him sitting back in his chair, eyeing her with what seemed to be a mixture of amusement and annoyance. Good, at least they were both annoyed.

He got up slowly and came around the desk. "Jill. Nice to see you as always."

She surreptitiously rubbed her sweaty palm on her skirt before she returned his handshake. It was appalling, really, the way she wanted to lean in for a better sniff of his cologne. He wore his blond hair short, and his dark suit had been cut to fit his broad shoulders.

"Something wrong?"

Jill snapped out of her visual perusal to realize she was still holding his hand. She released it quickly and searched for her missing composure. "Of course not."

"Have a seat. Can I get you anything to drink?"

"I'm fine."

Rather than sit behind his desk, he took the chair next to hers and crossed his long legs.

Jill's mouth went dry as she watched him move like a big cat on the prowl.

"Your sister has put us in one hell of a fix," he said in that Tennessean drawl that made her go stupid in the head, but only when it came from him. She heard that accent a hundred times a day from others, but no other voice was quite like his.

"She feels bad about it."

"Is she really sick or in need of a vacation?"

The implication that Kate was lying made Jill see red. But then she remembered the enmity between Kate and Ashton and quelled the urge to jump to her sister's defense. "She's yet to fully bounce back from the pneumonia. She went back to work too soon."

"The company's PR people are working around the clock to deal with the fallout."

"It's not Kate's fault that the press is convinced she's strung out on drugs, and besides, that's not what this meeting is about. The fact is, she wants a few months off, and it's our job to make that happen."

"It's your job to make that happen. My job is to keep Buddy's company from getting sued because your client is a flake."

"That's completely unfair and unwarranted, Ashton, and you know it. She's one of the hardest-working performers in the business, and she is *ill*. I'd like to see you try to put on a two-hour concert when you can barely breathe."

"Fine," he said begrudgingly. "If you say she's sick, she's sick. I'll do what I can to keep her from getting sued, but no promises."

"I hope you'll do as much for her as you'd do for any of Buddy's artists."

At that, his expression hardened. "What's that supposed to mean? I treat all our artists the same, but my job is to protect Long Road Records from exposure. Your sister has exposed us to tremendous liability."

"I'm going to keep saying it until you *hear* me—she is *sick*. If anyone tries to sue her for breach of contract, we can provide documentation from the hospital in Oklahoma City."

"I'd like to have that for the file."

"Fine, I'll fax it to you when I get home."

"Fine."

His sleepy-looking green eyes took a perusing journey over her that left Jill feeling naked and exposed. What the hell? "What're you looking at?"

"You."

"Why are you looking at me?"

"Because you're the only other person in the room."

He had such a way of making her feel stupid. He made her want to tell him that she'd graduated at the top of her class from both Brown University and Harvard Law, but she didn't say that. Rather, as she often did in his presence, she squirmed in her seat, sending the message that he was making her feel uncomfortable. That was probably his goal.

"And because I wonder if you ever loosen that top button and let your hair down."

Aghast, Jill stared at him as heat crept into her cheeks. "What business is that of yours?"

"Absolutely none."

"Then why would you say such a thing to me?"

His shrug was casual, as if this conversation was a normal part of their business routine. It most definitely was *not* normal. "I wonder. That's all."

She didn't want to ask. She absolutely did not want to know what he meant by that. "Wonder about what?" Clearly, her mouth was working ahead of her brain.

"I wonder what you're like when you're not playing barracuda protector for your sister. What do you like to do? What do you look like in a pair of jeans? What kind of music do you like? Who's your favorite author? That kind of stuff."

Jill had never been more shocked in her life. He wondered about *her*?

"Close your mouth before the flies get in there," he said, amusement dancing in his eyes.

She needed to get out of there before she said something she'd regret—such as, *I wonder about you, too.* "Are you…"

He waited a long beat before he said, "Am I what?"

Jill's mouth had gone totally dry. "Flirting with me?" The words came out squeaky and rough, and she immediately felt like a total fool. She was almost thirty years old, for crying out loud. She'd had her share of boyfriends, although none lately, not when she was so damned busy she didn't have time to do her laundry, let alone date. Why was her reaction to this man so different from any other?

"What if I am?"

"Why?" She said the first thing that came to mind, and damn him for laughing.

"Why not? You're a beautiful woman, or I bet you could be if you…unbuttoned…a little bit."

"Is that supposed to be flattering?"

"When was the last time you did something just for you that had nothing to do with your sister?"

"It's been a while," she said truthfully.

"You wanna have some fun?"

He was so gorgeous, far more gorgeous than any man had a right to be, and that accent absolutely undid her. "What kind of fun?"

"Any kind you want," he said in a suggestive tone that made her nipples tighten with interest. Thank God she was wearing a suit coat so he couldn't see them.

"With you."

"Yes," he said, laughing again, "that was kind of the idea."

"And how long have you been wanting to have 'fun' with me?"

"Awhile now, if I'm being truthful."

Jill couldn't believe what she was hearing.

"Nothing to say to that?" he asked, arching an eyebrow.

"Oh." *Brilliant, Counselor. Positively brilliant.*

"So what do you say? Want to get together while you're on vacation?"

Jill's mind raced as she considered all the implications, including what her sister would have to say about it.

"Don't think about what Kate would say. Think about what Jill wants."

His insight only rattled her further. All she thought about was what Kate wanted. When was the last time she gave the first consideration to what *she* wanted. Longer than she could remember. "I, um…"

"Take your time." He folded his hands behind his head. "I've got an hour until my next meeting."

"Wouldn't it be a conflict of interest for us to see each other outside of work?"

"Since we're usually on the same side, I wouldn't say so."

He was a much more seasoned attorney than she was, so she took his word for it.

"I need a favor," she said, diving in before she lost her nerve. They needed to get this issue out of the way before she could consider his very tempting offer.

"What kind of favor?"

"A personal favor that's going to make you mad."

"I'm listening."

Jill couldn't seem to form the words that would have the effect of gas thrown on a fire. Not when he'd just asked her out. She wanted to go out with him, which was the sad part. The minute she passed along Kate's request for contact info for his father, the date would probably be off the table.

"Jill?"

"Kate would like to contact your father."

He froze, staring at her with contempt stamped into his expression. "You can't be serious."

"I'm only the messenger, so don't shoot me."

"There's no way in hell I'm revisiting that issue." His hands dropped to his lap, and he stood. "The first time was more than sufficient, thank you very much."

"She only wants to see him for a minute," Jill said, making it up as she went along. "Apparently, there's something she needs to tell him."

"The last thing he needs is to hear from her. She ruined his freaking life and nearly destroyed my relationship with him. She has a lot of nerve thinking I'm going to help her get in touch with him."

"I understand," Jill said, and she did. It was a sore subject for all of them. "And for the record, I told her I was uncomfortable asking you."

Hands in pockets, he stared out the window. "Typical Kate to think of herself first and everyone else second."

"You don't give her enough credit, Ashton. She's very generous and good to the people in her life."

"I don't expect you to see her faults."

"I see them, but I love her enough to look past them."

"You'll forgive me if I don't love her that much." He turned to face her. "Tell her to leave it alone. A lot of people were hurt by what happened between them. My dad has a good life now, a life that satisfies him. I'd hate to see him hurt by her again."

"He hurt her, too."

"Maybe so, but I only saw his side of it, and it wasn't pretty. Trust me on that."

Jill nodded, sorry she'd broached the subject. She picked up her briefcase, stood and started for the door.

"Jill?"

She turned back to him.

"You never answered my question."

"Oh. I thought you were mad."

"I am mad, but not at you. I don't believe in shooting the messenger."

"Could I think about it?"

"Sure. Take all the time you need. You know where I am when you make up your mind."

Jill nodded and left, taking the stairs on wobbly legs.

"Have a good day, Jill," Debi said.

"Thanks, you too."

Jill nearly dropped her keys in her haste to get in the car. For a long time, she sat there, staring out the windshield, trying to process what'd happened. Ashton Matthews had asked her out. Her sister's sworn enemy was interested in *her*. What would she tell Kate?

Nothing, she decided. She'd keep it to herself for now.

CHAPTER 2

Kate forced herself to wait an hour after Jill's car came down the driveway before she headed for the winding path through a wooded area that separated their two homes. All morning, her nerves had been sharply attuned to the importance of Jill's meeting with Ashton. Kate didn't care about threats of lawsuits. She'd been threatened before—hell, she'd been sued before—and Jill always took care of it before it escalated. And whether he hated her or not, Ashton watched her back on behalf of Buddy's company.

No, she wasn't worried about lawsuits or breach of contract actions. She had far more important matters on her mind as she knocked on her sister's door.

"It's open," Jill called.

Kate stepped inside. "Well, hallelujah! You do own jeans!"

"Very funny."

Standing in her kitchen, wearing faded denim, a white linen blouse, her hair in a ponytail and her feet bare, Jill looked much as she had at twenty. Kate was relieved to see her sister out of the suit, sipping a glass of iced tea and finally looking relaxed.

"Drink?" Jill asked.

"No, thanks." Kate slid onto a barstool. "How'd it go?"

"Fine. You know Ashton. Always your biggest fan."

Kate snickered. "At least he's consistent. So I take it he wasn't willing to tell you where I might find his father?"

"Correct."

"Hmm. Well, I guess I'll try plan B, then."

"Which is?"

"B is for Buddy—and Taylor."

Jill started to say something but then stopped herself.

"What?"

"I was thinking on the way home," Jill said hesitantly, "that maybe some things are better left alone."

Kate took a moment and chose her words carefully. "That may be true—and you're probably right that I should leave it alone. But over the last few months, I've had an overwhelming need to see him, to talk to him, to...apologize to him."

"For *what*?"

"For the way I handled things at the end. After everything we shared, I owed him more than to walk away the first time things got tough."

"He went behind your back and did something you specifically asked him not to do," Jill reminded her.

"He went behind my back and saw to it I had the career I'd always dreamed of."

"At the time, you resented him for not hearing you when you asked him not to pull strings for you."

"I know. Believe me, I've been over it and over it a million times in my mind. I still wish it'd happened differently, but I've had an amazing career that he made possible. And I treated him badly."

Jill sat on the stool next to Kate's. "You've certainly changed your tune on that incident, and, I might add, you've had an amazing career because of *you* and your talent."

"If he hadn't told Buddy about me, who knows if I ever would've made it in this business?"

"You were too good to fail."

"You have to say that. You're my sister."

"You would've gotten there eventually. I have no doubt about that."

"Regardless," Kate said with a shrug. "He made it easier for me, and for a long time I've regretted the way I treated him when I found out about it."

"Why don't you write him a letter or something? Why do you have to see him to apologize?"

This is the sticky part, Kate thought. The apology wasn't the only reason she wanted to see him. "I told you—I need some closure," Kate said, going for generic over specific.

Jill eyed her shrewdly. No one knew her better than her older sister. "I don't like it. Tearing the scab off a healed wound is never a good idea."

"If I'm being completely honest, the wound never healed entirely."

Jill gasped. "God, Kate! How long have you felt this way?"

"All along, I suppose."

"Is this why it didn't work out with Clint or Bobby or Russ?"

Kate winced at the reminder of the failed affairs that had marked the years since she left Reid. "Maybe."

"So none of them ever stood a chance because you never stopped loving *him*? And you knew the whole time you were still in love with someone else?"

Kate held up a hand to stop her sister. "It's not that simple. I thought about him, about Reid, a lot. That never stopped."

"But?"

"It took a while—and a couple of failed relationships—for me to realize I'd been foolish to think that kind of love was going to come along again. I'd been foolish to think... I'd been foolish. That's the bottom line."

"I had no idea," Jill said, slumping into her chair and looking at Kate in amazement. "I spend twenty hours a day with you and had no earthly idea you were still pining over him."

"How would you know? I never talk about it—about him—to anyone."

"And yet you've thought about him."

"Every day." After a long pause, Kate said, "I need to see him. I need to know if there's any chance at all that what we once had is still there."

"And if it isn't? What if he's moved on with his life and married someone else? What happens then?"

"Is he?"

"Is he what?"

"Married to someone else? Did Ashton tell you that?"

"All he said is his father is happy and has a life that satisfies him. He said it took a long time for his dad to move on after what happened with you."

"And he didn't say where he'd moved on to?"

"Nope."

"It's like he disappeared off the face of the earth. I've tried everything I can think of to find him, but there's nothing. I saw that he sold his business, but there's no mention of him anywhere since then."

"What about his house in town?"

"Closed up tight."

"And you know this how?"

Kate flashed a sheepish grin. "I might've gone by there the last time we were home."

"What if you go to Buddy and tell him you want to get in touch with Reid and he says to leave it alone?"

"I'll go to Miss Martha," Kate said of Buddy's elderly mother, who'd once been Reid's housekeeper.

"Um, didn't she quit because she disapproved of you two?"

"That was a long time ago, and I'm not eighteen anymore. If all else fails, I'll hire a private investigator to find him. Hopefully, it won't come to that." Kate waited for her sister to fire back with another question, but she didn't. "What're you thinking?"

"I'm worried about what happens if you find him and he's not interested. What if he's gotten over it—and you—and moved on?"

"Then I'll have to accept that and move on myself. But I can't do anything until I know for sure it's really over with him. Can't you see what I mean?"

"I do, and, strangely enough, I even understand. A little. That doesn't mean I'm not worried. You've been so sick, and you're finally starting to recover. I'd hate to see you have another setback."

Kate leaned forward to hug her sister. "I love you for worrying about me, but I'll be fine."

Jill returned the embrace with equal fervor. "Promise?"

"I promise."

"No matter what happens with Reid?"

"No matter what happens." Kate pulled back from the hug. "Speaking of stuff happening, anything I need to know about from the meeting?"

"We're working on getting you freed up for this vacation you want so badly."

Kate got up to leave. "I'll leave it in your capable hands, then." At the door, she turned back to face her sister. "Try to enjoy the downtime, will you?"

"Only if you do, too."

"Oh, I will."

The next day, Kate drove her Jeep out to Buddy and Taylor's house, planning to crash Sunday dinner. The crisp autumn day reminded her of home. While nothing could top a New England fall, Tennessee was no slouch when it came to foliage and clear blue skies.

She'd lived here so long now it felt like home, but her heart would always belong to the house on the coast where her mother and stepfather still lived with their sons, Max and Nick.

Her cellphone rang, and Kate put it on speaker to take the call.

"Hey, it's me," her sister Maggie said.

"Hey, Mags, what's up?"

"I heard you were back on drugs, so I figured I'd better check on you."

"You know me, a different day, a different fix. Where'd you hear it this time?"

"On the radio at lunchtime. The DJs were talking about you like they know you. You're really, okay though, right?"

"I'm fine. I went back to work too soon after the pneumonia and passed out on stage. Anything else you hear is pure fiction."

"I know that—everyone who knows you knows that. Are you feeling better now?"

"Better every day. It's good to be home."

"Have you talked to Dad?"

"Not in a week or so, why?"

"You'll love this. The boys are letting everyone know that they want to be called John and Rob now that they're in fifth grade. Apparently, Johnny and Robby are baby names."

As her hair blew in the breeze, Kate let out a ringing laugh. "That's awesome. Thanks for letting me know. I'd hate to get in trouble the next time I call home."

"No kidding. Those two are a piece of work. They're playing in a big baseball tournament this weekend on the Cape. Dad, Andi, Mom, Aidan and all the O'Malleys are there watching them. Dad said they got the biggest turnout of all the kids on either team—including the home team."

Kate loved that her parents continued to share a warm friendship even though they were long divorced. "Can't you picture Grammy O'Malley in the middle of it, bossing everyone around?"

"Totally." The mother of their stepfather, Aidan, was an adored extra grandmother to the Harrington girls. "How's work?"

"Interesting this week. I'm signing for a deaf juror in a murder trial. Gruesome business. I'll have nightmares for weeks."

"Ugh, that sounds awful."

"It's a paycheck. How's Jill?"

"You won't believe it, but I finally got her out of her suit and into jeans. Don't look now, but I think she's actually taking a vacation."

"Shut the front door! How'd you manage that?"

"It wasn't easy, but I convinced her we both need a break—her as much as me. She works way too hard. I worry all the time that she's sacrificing her life to run mine."

"She loves every minute of running your life, and you know it."

"She does seem to love the job, but I want her to have her own life, too."

"You know Jill—she doesn't do anything she doesn't want to do."

"True."

"Well, I'd better get back to the Texas Chain-Saw Murder trial."

"Oh my God, they used a *chain saw*?"

"Hacksaw."

"Are you kidding me?"

"Yes," Maggie said, laughing. "It was a run-of-the-mill stabbing."

"That's sick. You're spending too much time in courtrooms."

"Seriously."

"Hey, Maggie, do you get time off at Christmas?"

"A week. Why?"

"Will you plan to spend it here with me? I'll send you a ticket."

"I'd love to."

"Great. I'll talk to you soon."

"Love you. Later."

Talking to her younger sister always left Kate smiling. Maggie was the same ball of energy she'd always been, zipping from one topic or task to another without so much as a pause in between. Kate wouldn't change a thing about her, and the idea of spending a whole week with her baby sister filled her with joy.

Taking the break from work had been the right thing to do. It had been so long since she'd felt anything other than exhausted, she thought, as she pulled into the driveway at Buddy and Taylor's two-story brick Colonial in Rutherford County. As Kate walked to the door, the wind whipped off the lake behind the house.

Kate thought about the first time she'd visited here, the day she learned that Reid had gone to Buddy on her behalf. She'd give everything she had, every ounce of success she'd known since then, to get back the few hours that followed those revelations.

With years of hindsight and maturity, she could see that she'd handled it all wrong. What might've been different, she wondered—and not for the first time—if she'd gone home and talked to him civilly rather than throwing her things in a bag and storming out of his house as if what they'd shared hadn't meant the world to her?

The quest to right the wrongs of the past might seem foolhardy to Jill. Hell, at times it seemed foolhardy to Kate. But it had become increasingly clear to her that she was stuck on what had happened all those years ago, and until she made peace with the past, she wouldn't be able to get unstuck or move forward.

With that in mind, she rapped on the door and stepped inside the comfortable, cozy home her superstar friends shared with their three daughters. Their son, Harrison, was in college at Texas A&M. "Hello," Kate called. "Anyone home?"

Georgia Sue, the youngest of the Longstreet sisters, came running around the corner from the kitchen and slid to a stop just short of crashing into Kate. "Hey, are you here for dinner?" she asked, hugging Kate.

"If your mom made enough."

Georgia rolled her eyes like the teenager she'd soon be. "She always makes enough to feed an army, or so she says."

"Your dad and brother eat like one."

"That's true." Georgia took Kate's hand and tugged her into the kitchen, where Taylor Jones, biggest female country star in the world, stood watch over a pot of something on the stove as she conducted an animated phone conversation. "She's multitasking as usual."

Taylor flashed Kate a warm smile and held up a finger to ask for one more minute on the phone.

"She's my idol," Kate said to Georgia.

Georgia laughed. "Want a drink?"

"I'd love one."

As Kate was a frequent visitor, Georgia got her a diet cola and a tall glass of ice without having to be told what Kate wanted. "Thank you, ma'am. How's school?"

"Boring as usual."

"I thought fifth grade was fun. My brothers are in fifth grade, and they love it."

"They're probably dorks, then," Georgia said with the sly grin that was all Buddy.

"Hey! My brothers aren't dorks!"

"Mine is."

"Yeah, he kinda is."

"I can say that, but you can't."

"Sibling handbook," Kate said, charmed as always by Georgia. "Rule 101—I can speak poorly of my siblings, but you may not."

"Exactly!"

Taylor hung up the phone and came over to hug Kate. "Are you here for dinner, I hope?"

"If it's no trouble."

"You know you're always welcome. Georgia, go finish your homework before dinner."

"But Kate just got here!"

"She'll be here awhile, right, Kate?"

"Absolutely. If you finish your homework, we can go for a walk by the lake, just you and me."

"Really?"

Kate tugged on the silky dark ponytail that was so much like Taylor's. "Yes, really. Now scram. Your mom and I need some girl time."

"I hate to point out that I *too* am a girl," Georgia said on her way out of the kitchen.

"Scram!" Taylor said in a tone that only mothers could pull off. "Sheesh! That one is full of beans. Good thing she came last and not first, or she might've been an only child."

"You know I love all your children, but she gets to me every time."

"She's always had you—and everyone else in her life—firmly wrapped around her little finger. Her father is absolute putty in her hands."

"In yours, too, if I'm not mistaken."

"In mine, too," Taylor said, blushing. They were still wildly in love after nearly twenty years of marriage, four children and more number-one records between them and together than Kate could count. Taylor returned to the stove to stir and tend. "What's this about girl talk?"

"Is Buddy home?"

"Not at the moment, but I expect him soon. He's over at his mama's house, checking on her."

"How is Miss Martha?"

"Slowing down more all the time, but don't try to tell her that. We've had absolutely no luck in convincing her to move in with us, but the day she's no longer feisty and independent is the day I'll really start to worry about her."

Kate chuckled at the image Taylor painted. Ms. Martha was nothing if not feisty and independent.

"Do you need to talk business with Buddy? You know you can always call him."

"I know, but it's not about business. Jill and Ashton have all of that covered, at least for the moment."

Taylor poured herself a glass of tea and gestured for Kate to have a seat at the table. "Then what is it, honey? I can tell you've got something on your mind."

"My sister says I'm tearing the scab off an old wound, but I told her the wound never really healed."

"You're talking about Reid."

Surprised that Taylor had gotten to the heart of the matter so quickly, Kate nodded. "I've never stopped thinking about him."

"And you have regrets."

Kate stared at her friend. "Do you have ESP or something?"

Taylor tossed her head back and laughed. "Nothing so dramatic. I know you. I've known you a long time, seen other men come and go, but nothing ever sticks. I've wondered if there was some unresolved business with Reid that was holding you back."

"That's exactly it. The thing is, I have no idea where he is. Jill asked Ashton, but he refused to tell her, so I was hoping you might know."

"I do know where he is. Buddy talked to him just last week." The two men had grown up under different circumstances in Reid's family home in Brentwood but were as close as brothers. "We spent last Christmas with him."

Kate's heart beat hard as she waited for Taylor to tell her where she could find Reid.

"You know I'd do anything for you, right?" Taylor asked hesitantly.

"Of course. That works both ways." Buddy, Taylor and their children had been Kate's Nashville family.

"It's just that I don't feel comfortable telling you where he is without talking to Buddy first."

"Talking to Buddy about what?" the man himself said as he swaggered into the kitchen, still handsome as the devil at nearly fifty. He bent to kiss his wife and then Kate. "What're you two lovelies up to?"

Taylor nodded to Kate, encouraging her to tell Buddy what she wanted. For some reason it was harder to say the words to him than it had been to tell Taylor. "I'd like to speak to Reid about something, and I need to know where I can find him."

Clearly, Buddy hadn't been expecting her to say that, because he went perfectly still. For a long moment, Kate was certain he'd say no to her.

Buddy opened the fridge, took out a beer and cracked it open. "What do you need with him?"

"It's a personal matter."

"You wouldn't happen to be revisiting ancient history, would you?"

"So what if I am?"

"Ah, darlin', nothing good ever comes of that."

"Ever?" Kate asked, raising an eyebrow, hoping to coax a smile from her friend and mentor.

Buddy shook his head. "You remind me of my daughters—and my wife. I can never win in a war of words with you women."

"We've repeatedly encouraged you to quit trying," Taylor said.

Buddy scowled playfully at his wife.

"Unless you have a good reason not to, you should tell Kate where he is and let them work out whatever it is they need to work out," Taylor said.

"I can tell when I'm outnumbered," Buddy said with a sigh. "He lives on St. Kitts."

Kate jumped up to hug and kiss Buddy. "Thank you so much."

He returned her embrace. "Don't make me sorry I told you that."

"I won't. I promise. Will you write down his address for me?"

Buddy hesitated for a moment before he reluctantly got up and walked out of the room.

When they were alone, Taylor flashed Kate a big grin. "This is so romantic," she whispered, clapping her hands. "I want every detail when you get back."

"Don't jinx me," Kate said, although it had been a long time since she'd been this excited about anything. She'd never forgotten the heady excitement of first love and how he'd made her feel..

Buddy came back into the kitchen and slapped a piece of paper on the counter. "If he's not happy to see you, I had nothing to do with telling you where he is. You got me?"

Kate laughed and hugged Buddy again. "The secret is safe with me." She released him and grabbed her purse off the table. "I've got to go."

"I thought you were staying for dinner," Taylor said.

"Can I take a rain check?"

"Of course you can."

"And will you tell Georgia I owe her a full day of shopping at the mall of her choice?"

"I will absolutely *not* tell her that," Taylor said. "She's already unmanageable."

"Fine, then you think of something that's not as extravagant that I can do with her very soon to make it up to her."

"I'll think of something."

"Could I ask one more favor?" Kate said, glancing at Buddy. "Would you not tell him we had this conversation?"

Buddy shifted from one foot to the other.

"I'd never ask if it wasn't really important." Kate wanted to gauge Reid's reaction to seeing her again without the benefit of Buddy tipping him off that she was coming.

"I guess," Buddy grumbled.

"Thank you." Kate hugged him one more time, kissed Taylor and headed for the door. "Love you guys!"

"Love you, too," Taylor called. "Good luck!"

CHAPTER 3

It was, Kate soon discovered, a lot more difficult than it seemed to sneak out of town without anyone knowing. For one thing, she hadn't the first clue how to reach the pilot who flew them to concerts. She also had no idea where her passport was, which meant she had to involve Jill.

She knocked on her sister's door just after nine in the morning but had no doubt Jill had already been up for a while.

When Jill didn't answer, Kate wandered inside and found her on the elliptical machine in the bedroom she used as a gym. After exactly one attempt, Kate had declared the elliptical a torture device, even though Jill swore it was the only aerobic exercise that actually worked. Kate much preferred horseback riding.

"What's up?" Jill asked between gasps of air.

"I need my passport. Do you have it?"

"Where're you going?"

"Somewhere."

"Kate…"

"If you must know, I'm going to see Reid."

"So you tracked him down."

"Yes."

"How're you getting wherever you're going?"

Kate had prepared herself for her sister's disapproval, so she was surprised by the practical question. "I'm still working that out." Since there was no way she could fly commercial in light of the current media feeding frenzy, she planned to charter a plane. Unfortunately, she was lost when it came to basic logistics. Jill or another member of her team usually saw to all the details on her behalf. Kate had never felt like more of a useless celebrity than she did at that moment.

Jill pressed the Off button on the machine and reached for a towel to dry her face. When she left the room, Kate followed her.

In the kitchen, Jill downed a bottle of cold water and reached for her phone. "Levi," she said, "Kate needs the plane. How soon can you be ready?" Jill listened for a moment and then held the phone to the side of her mouth. "Where to?"

"St. Kitts."

Jill relayed the information to the pilot and nodded. Her brows furrowed as she processed whatever he was saying. "She'll be there. Thanks." She ended that call and scrolled through her contacts. "This is Jill Harrington. I need a car for my sister in one hour, going to Nashville International. Can you do it?" After a pause, she said, "Great, thank you." As she talked, she went into the office off the kitchen, rooted around in a file cabinet and came back with Kate's passport.

"Have I ever told you that you're amazing?"

Jill shrugged off the compliment. "Just doing my job."

Kate went to her sister and hugged her.

"I'm all sweaty!"

"Thank you," Kate said. "For this and everything else you do for me. I don't know where I'd be without you."

Jill gave her a squeeze. "Probably in rehab."

"Shut up."

"I hope you get whatever you need from this trip. And I hope you come back in one piece."

"I will. I promise." Looking to lighten things up, Kate said, "Have some fun while I'm gone, will you? Let your hair down. Go a little wild. Skip your workout. Don't take your vitamins. Get drunk. Get *laid*."

Jill rolled her eyes at Kate. "With whom? Gordon the horse groomer?"

"Hey, he still has a pulse."

"Get outta here. The car is picking you up in an hour, and Levi is meeting you at the airport."

"Thanks again, Jill. You're the best sister anyone could ever hope to have."

"You're not so bad, either."

"See ya in a couple of days."

"Good luck."

It was as close as they ever came to getting schmoopy with each other, and it warmed Kate from the inside out as she jogged home to shower and pack.

After Kate left, Jill headed for the shower, taking her time for once and enjoying the heat of the water on her tired muscles. She had no plans for the day beyond cleaning her closet and maybe going into town to do a little shopping. It had been so long since she'd had a day with nothing scheduled that she wasn't entirely sure what to do with the time.

She'd finished drying her hair when her phone chimed with a text message. Expecting it to be Kate in need of more last-minute help, Jill was stunned to realize the text was from Ashton.

You know how to make a guy suffer.

She stared at the screen on her phone for a long time, reading and rereading the single sentence and trying to think of a suitable reply. Did she go for witty or caustic or serious? And how did he manage to get her into such a jumble with a one-sentence text? After what seemed like an endless internal debate, she went with coy.

Is that so?

Are you doing it on purpose?

Doing what?

Making me suffer...

Naturally.

I thought so.

By now she was laughing as she typed, enjoying the sparring match.

Put me out of my misery and go out with me. Today.

Don't you have to work?

I own the company.

Jill bit her lip and pondered what she should do. And then she remembered what Kate had said—have some fun, let your hair down, go a little wild, have some sex. That last part wasn't happening, but the rest of it actually sounded a bit appealing after months of nonstop work. She pressed her fingers to the keyboard.

What do you want to do?

Leave that to me. Pick you up at two?

You're actually going to venture into enemy territory? As far as Jill knew, Ashton had never come within ten miles of Kate's estate.

Two o'clock? Yes or no?

Why did it seem that so much rode on her one-word answer? After a long moment of internal debate, Jill typed her response.

Yes.

Excellent. Wear jeans. Tight jeans preferably.

She refused to dignify that comment with a response. Rattled by the conversation and the date she'd just agreed to, Jill went into her closet and sorted through a stack of jeans she'd hardly ever worn, looking for the pair that Kate once told her did wonders for her ass.

If there was ever a time for jeans that did wonders for her ass, this was it.

"Oh my God," she whispered to the clothes hanging in her closet. "What the hell did I just agree to?"

The minute the plane took off for the three-and-a-half-hour flight to Basseterre in St. Kitts, Kate began to regret her impulsive decision. So much had happened since that awful January day when Taylor accidently divulged that Reid had told Buddy about her.

Buddy's "discovery" of her, his signing of her to his record label and his invitation to join him and Taylor on tour that summer—none of it had been the happy accident Kate had thought it was.

She thought back to when she and Reid were first together, when he told her he knew people in the business, and she told him that wasn't how she wanted to get her start. She didn't want anyone giving her a leg up. She wanted to get there on her own merits. Thinking about that now, Kate had to laugh. No one made it in the music business without a leg up at some point.

Years of maturity and hard knocks had shown her what a fool she'd been back then to think it all would've happened without help.

Kate had been so shocked by Taylor's revelations that she'd vomited by the side of the road on her way home to Reid's house where she'd confronted him. Reliving those ugly minutes that tore apart their love affair could still make Kate feel sick even all these years later.

If all this trip accomplished was the opportunity to apologize for her behavior that day, it would be enough for her. Or so she told herself hours later as the drumstick-shaped island came into view below.

In truth, she hoped it accomplished much more than that. She hoped that maybe, just maybe, they might get a second chance. She hoped he might look at her and feel again the way he had during that long-ago autumn and winter when everything had seemed a tad bit magical.

Whenever she felt particularly lonely, which was far more often than anyone would suspect, she let her mind to wander back to the day she met him and all the days that followed. She remembered their horseback rides on his estate, flying in his plane to Memphis when they'd visited Graceland and then were stranded by bad weather. They'd made love for the first time that night, and Kate could still remember every detail of that amazing experience. It stood out in her memory as the single most important event of her life, and he remained one of the most important people to ever cross her path.

She needed to tell him that. Even if nothing else came of this trip, he needed to know that much.

It was late afternoon by the time the plane touched down at the Robert L. Bradshaw International Airport, just north of Basseterre.

"You got a nice warm day to visit the island, Ms. Kate," Levi said over the PA as he taxied the plane toward the terminal. "Eighty-five degrees."

Kate stared out the window into the bright sunshine. She couldn't think of anything other than seeing Reid again. What would he say? What would she say? Would he even want to see her after the way they'd left things? Would he think her horribly selfish for showing up in his piece of paradise without warning? She thought back to the day, weeks after their breakup, when he'd flown her home to Rhode Island after Maggie had been badly hurt in an accident.

She'd been so focused on getting to her sister that they hadn't talked about what'd happened between them. And when he'd delivered her to the hospital, there hadn't been a chance to say a proper good-bye. Thus, everything between them had felt unfinished ever since.

While it might be selfish, coming here to see him was the right thing to do, she told herself as she let Levi help her down the stairs and into the heat. The sun was so bright Kate was temporarily blinded as her eyes adjusted.

"Any idea how long you plan to stay?" Levi asked as he rolled her suitcase into the terminal.

"I'm not quite sure yet. If you need to get back, I can call you when I'm ready to go home."

"I think I can find a way to entertain myself here for a couple of days," Levi said with a wide smile as he led the way to the taxi queue. "You've got my cell number for when you're ready to leave?"

"Yes, I'll call you as soon as I know what my plans are."

"Take your time, Ms. Kate. I've got nowhere to be."

"Thank you very much, Levi," Kate said as she handed the first driver in the line of taxis the slip of paper on which Buddy had written Reid's address.

"That's over in Half Moon Bay on the Atlantic side of the island," the driver said in a lyrical voice that was part British, part Caribbean, part reggae.

"Half Moon Bay," Kate said, instantly curious about the place Reid called home. She shook hands with Levi. "I'll be in touch."

"Have a good time."

"You, too."

"I'll try," he said gravely, which made her laugh as the driver helped her into the cab.

During the ride, Kate watched the scenery go by—lush greens, the bright blue of the ever-present water, rundown shacks and million-dollar homes. It passed in a blur of color and activity and contrast. The driver kept up a steady stream of chatter, giving Kate a windshield tour as they drove. She tried to pay attention to what he was saying, but it was hard to hear him over the roar of her heart beating so hard and so fast she worried she might pass out or hyperventilate. In a few minutes, she would see Reid. Or at least she hoped so.

What if he wasn't here? What if he was away on vacation or somewhere else? Maybe he was in Nashville. How funny would that be? She'd come all this way, and he probably wasn't even here. Why hadn't she let Buddy tell him she was coming? That way she'd at least know he was definitely here—or not.

By the time the driver brought the car to a stop outside a home along a strip of sand dotted with beachfront cottages, Kate was on the verge of a full-scale meltdown.

"Miss?" The driver had gotten out of the car and was holding Kate's door open for her. "Are you all right?"

"Yes." Kate shook off the panic and forced her legs to carry her out of the car. "Would you mind waiting? I'll pay extra."

"Of course," he said, eyeing her curiously.

"I don't know how long I'll be."

"I'll wait right here for you. Take your time."

"Thank you so much."

"You're sure you're all right? Your face is terribly pale."

Kate's hands covered her cheeks. "Is it?"

The driver nodded.

"I'm nervous about seeing the man who lives here."

"Ahh, I see." A smile lit his face. "I like to tell my daughters that any boy they date is lucky to be with them, and they should remember that." He glanced at the house. "Whoever he is, he's lucky to have a pretty lady like you nervous about seeing him."

"That's very kind of you to say," Kate said, returning his friendly smile, "and exactly what I needed to hear right now."

"My pleasure. Good luck to you."

"Thank you."

He closed the door behind her and went around to get back into the driver's seat.

Kate studied the house, which was made of dark wood. It had a thatched roof and a comfortable front porch. Wind chimes hung from the porch roof, tinkling gently in the light afternoon breeze. The only other sound was the waves crashing on the beach and the squawk of seagulls.

An aura of peace and serenity surrounded the home, which gave her the courage to step through the gate in the picket fence that surrounded the tiny front yard.

The gate slapped shut behind her, making her jump from the unexpected noise.

As she took the three stairs that led to the porch, her legs felt watery and unsteady, the way they had after her bout with pneumonia. She stood there for a long time, marshaling the fortitude to see this through to whatever finish fate had in mind for them.

Kate felt like she was outside herself, watching someone else raise her arm and knock on the open screen door. The inside door was open, so someone was here... She could hear each beat of her heart echoing in her ears as she waited a long moment before footsteps sounded through the house.

An attractive, dark-haired woman wearing a colorful cotton dress came to the

door. Her long hair was piled in a messy bun on the top of her head. She had dark eyes and a wide, welcoming smile. "Hi there. May I help you?"

The appearance of a woman threw her off-stride. Kate realized in that moment that she hadn't actually believed he'd have someone else, although she knew she should have. He was a gorgeous, successful, thoughtful man. Why wouldn't he have someone else after all this time? "I..." She'd come too far now to leave without at least seeing him, so she cleared her throat and forced the words to come. "I'm looking for Reid Matthews. Does he live here?"

"He sure does. He's down on the beach working on his boat." She pushed open the screen door. "Come in. You can get to the stairs from the deck out back."

"Thank you." Kate followed her through a cozy living space that was colorful and comfortable. She wanted to stop and take a look around, but she followed the woman to the deck that overlooked the Atlantic. "What a great place."

"We love it."

The three small words conveyed a world of meaning. They were a couple. They lived here together. She slept with him and made love with him and ate dinner with him.

"I can see why."

She pointed to a distant figure on the beach. "Reid is down there, working on his beloved boat."

He had a beloved boat. Kate wanted to know all about it, but she didn't ask. She had no right to ask anything of the woman he shared his life with. Were they married? Kate shook off that thought as fast as she had it. "Thank you."

Feeling somewhat deflated as she took the long set of stairs to the beach, she felt the eyes of the other woman on her back. Kate wanted to apologize for showing up uninvited into their piece of paradise. She wanted to assure the woman that she was no threat to her, but she didn't do any of those things. Rather, she stayed focused on the dot on the beach, the man she'd thought about every day for ten long years.

At the bottom of the stairs, she kicked off her sandals and walked barefoot through the warm sand, making her way to him as if in a dream. *If it is a dream,* she thought, *please don't let me wake up until I've actually spoken to him.*

He was sanding the bottom of an old skiff and was so focused on his work he didn't see her coming.

She approached him tentatively, not wanting to startle him. When she was six feet from him, she stopped and feasted her eyes. He wore only a pair of khaki cargo shorts. His skin was very tan, his body still lean and fit. Silver streaks ran through his dark hair, and perspiration made his back glisten in the bright sunshine.

Kate watched him for a full minute before she cleared her throat. "Reid."

He froze and then straightened, turning slowly to face her. The shock registered in his expression and the rigid way in which he held himself. "Kate?" he said in a hoarse whisper. "What're you doing here?"

The sound of his voice transported her right back to the first time she'd ever heard him speak, in the drawing room of the vast house he'd once called home, the day her dad had brought her to meet his old friend from Berkley.

Say something! Don't just stand here and stare! "I, um… I needed to see you."

He glanced up at the house before returning his focus to her. "Why?"

"I…"

"You've been ill."

"You hard about my flake-out on stage, I take it."

"It made the papers—even down here."

"I had pneumonia and went back to work too soon. The media said it was drugs, but that's not true."

His smile was just as she remembered—slow, sexy, sweet, and she absolutely melted. "We're not so far from civilization down here that the rumors don't reach us."

Kate shrugged. "I don't give them much to work with, so they make up most of it. I hope you didn't think—"

"I knew you weren't on drugs, Kate."

"Oh, good," she said, surprised by how important it was that he not think poorly of her, despite having given him plenty of reason to think poorly of her.

"Why did you need to see me? Has something happened?"

All the words she'd rehearsed in her mind for weeks and months were gone now that she stood before him, needing to explain why she'd suddenly reappeared in his life so many years after she'd ended their relationship.

"Kate?"

Hearing her name in that honeyed Southern accent sent shivers down her spine the same way it had when they were together. He'd liked to call her *Katherine* when they made love. That memory sent a flood of heat rushing through her veins.

"I wanted to apologize to you."

He crossed his arms and leaned back against the boat. "For what?"

"For the way I ended things between us. It's bothered me for a long time, and I wanted you to know that."

"Oh. Well…"

"What you did, telling Buddy about me—"

"It was wrong of me to do that after you specifically asked me not to."

Kate shook her head. "Everything I have, everything I've accomplished, goes back to you telling Buddy about me."

"That's not true. You are amazingly talented, and everything you have goes back to that."

"That's part of it, but I don't think I ever would've had this career without Buddy's involvement—or yours."

"I disrespected your wishes. You had every right to react the way you did."

"I disrespected *us* by acting the way I did. I've regretted it for a very long time, and I wanted you to know that."

"Kate..." As if he needed something to do with his hands, he ran his fingers through his hair. "I don't know what to say."

"You don't have to say anything. I understand that too much time has gone by and we've both moved on, but it was important to me that you know..."

"That I know what?"

Kate swallowed hard and forced herself to meet his gaze. Those brown eyes... They still got to her the way they always had. No one else had ever looked at her in that particular way and *seen* her the way he did. "I've never forgotten you. I've never forgotten. Any of it."

He let out a tortured groan. "God, Kate, what am I supposed to say to that? Am I supposed to tell you that I've never forgotten either? Because I haven't. How could I? But I've got a new life here—a good life that satisfies me. I have a wonderful relationship that works for me."

Her heart was heavy when she said, "I understand."

"No, you don't." His tone was so sharp that she gasped. "It took me a long time to get here after you. A very long time."

She held up her hands to stop him from saying more. "I'm not asking for anything. All I wanted was the chance to tell you I regret how I behaved. I regret letting you think for all this time that I wasn't grateful for what you did for me, because I was. I *am*. I'm grateful. That's all I wanted to say."

His demeanor softened all at once, and he more resembled the Reid she remembered so well. "Are you happy, Kate? Does the big career fulfill you the way you thought it would?"

"I'm content. I still enjoy performing, meeting the fans, that kind of stuff. There's a lot of it I could do without, especially the media speculation about my rampant drug abuse."

"I'm sure that gets old after a while."

"What about you? Are you happy here in paradise?"

"I'm content," he said, using her word.

She was painfully aware that there was a lot of empty space between content and happy, but Kate chose not to point that out to him, because he probably already knew. "I'm sorry to just show up this way, but I wanted to tell you, in person. I wanted…"

He pushed off the boat and took a step toward her, and her heart began to gallop the way it did when Thunder flew her over the open fields behind her house. "What did you want, Kate?"

She forced herself to smile. "It doesn't matter now."

"Yes, it does."

"You're with someone else. It's a moot point."

"Tell me anyway."

If he came any closer she wouldn't be able to resist the urge to touch him, to lay her hands on his chest the way she used to, as if she still had a right to.

"If you were free, I might've asked you—"

"What? What would you have asked me?"

She looked up at him, imploringly. "Don't make me say it," she whispered.

His jaw pulsed with tension as he stared out at the water. "Where were you six months ago? Where were you before I decided to take a chance with someone else?"

"I'm sorry. I shouldn't have come. I never meant to make things worse."

"You haven't made anything worse. But she's been good to me. Good *for* me."

"I understand. Please, don't say anything more. I'll go."

He rested his hands on his hips. "I'm glad you came."

"I am, too. This is a beautiful place. I can see why you love it."

"It sure does beat the rat race in Nashville," he said with his trademark slow, sexy grin.

"I'm glad you were able to make it happen. Take care of yourself, Reid."

"You do the same. Say no to drugs."

That made her laugh. "I'll try." She glanced up at the house. The woman in his life was nowhere to be seen, but Kate had no doubt she was watching them. "Is there a way out that doesn't require going through your house?"

"Take that path."

"I was thinking I might stick around for a day or two, since I've never been here and it's so beautiful. Where do you recommend I stay?"

"My friend Desi owns the Sunset Point Resort over in Frigate Bay. I'll give him a call and ask him to set you up with something private."

"That'd be very nice. Thank you."

"No problem."

"I'll let you get back to work. I'll see you."

"Bye, Kate."

As she ventured up the path he'd pointed out to her, she felt him watching her. Only when she reached the top and saw her waiting cab did she allow herself to breathe again. It hadn't gone exactly the way she'd hoped, but she'd gotten the closure she needed. She'd have to be satisfied with the partial victory and find a way to go on without him.

CHAPTER 4

Reid watched Kate go up the path and disappear into the road. For a long time after she was out of sight, he stood there, staring at the path, his mind reeling after the conversation, the surprise, the reaction. To deny he'd reacted to her as strongly as he always had would be disingenuous.

Seeing her again had been like a punch to the gut. Even though his back had been to her, the instant she said his name, he'd known it was her. No one had ever said his name the same way she did. No one had ever electrified him just by looking at him the way she did. No one had ever set him on fire with need the way she had.

"Damn it," he muttered, turning away from the path and resting his hands on the upturned bottom of the boat he'd been restoring for months now. He'd been perfectly content with his life on the island, his life with Mari, and now... Now he knew Kate still thought of him, that she'd never forgotten him or what they'd shared, that she felt bad about the way things ended. How was he supposed to go on with his contented little life knowing all that?

For a brief moment, he was angry with her. How dare she come here, to his home, and upset his well-ordered life by saying all those things to him? How dare she make herself feel better at his expense? But then it occurred to him that it had probably taken a tremendous amount of courage for her to work up the nerve to first find him and then come to see him, especially after the way they'd left things.

Their relationship had been doomed from the start. No one in their lives had approved of the twenty-eight years between them. Hell, he hadn't approved, but he'd been powerless to resist falling in love with her sweetness, her innocence, her angelic voice and beautiful face.

She was even more beautiful at almost thirty than she'd been at eighteen. She'd grown into her coltish body, but the long, thick blonde hair and stunning blue eyes were exactly as he remembered. He'd never seen eyes quite like hers, and he'd never forgotten what it had been like to have those eyes look at him with love and affection and desire unlike anything he'd experienced with anyone else.

"Reid?"

Mari's voice jarred him out of his musings. He turned to find her looking at him warily, as if waiting for him to confirm that a bomb had just dropped into the middle of their peaceful lives. What did he say to her when he wasn't even sure what to make of it himself?

"Hey."

"That was Kate."

"Yes." He'd once told her about Kate in a moment he now wished he could take back, because she would fully appreciate the importance of Kate's reappearance. When he'd told her, he'd expected to never see Kate again. It had never occurred to him that she would seek him out.

"And?"

"Nothing. She had something she wanted to tell me. She told me." He shrugged, hoping to convey that everything was fine and not sure if he succeeded. "Nothing more to it than that."

Mari tipped her head and looked at him with wise, knowing eyes. "Is that right?"

"Uh-huh. Are you ready for some dinner? Where do you want to go?"

"So we're going to act like nothing happened? That's how you want to handle this?"

"Nothing did happen. How else would you have me handle it?"

"Maybe you can lie to yourself, but you can't lie to me. I know you too well. Seeing her had to rock you."

"I was surprised to see her. I won't deny that, but it's nothing to worry about." He stashed his tools in a bucket under the boat and brushed sand off his hands. "I'm starving. Are you?"

"I could eat something, I suppose."

Hoping to reassure her, he put his arm around her and drew her in close to him as he walked them to the stairs, comforted by her familiar scent and the easy, stress-free bond they'd had from the beginning.

Their relationship had often reminded him of what he'd shared with his late wife. With both women, he'd known friendship, companionship, familiarity and satisfying, if not earth-shattering, lovemaking.

With Kate, there'd been fire and drama and intensity and earth-shattering lovemaking. And magic. It was that last part he'd missed the most after she left. He told himself he was better off without the fire and the drama, and he could live without the magic. The peaceful existence he knew now was the tradeoff. No one got everything. He firmly believed that. His new life with Mari satisfied him, and he wouldn't do anything to endanger that.

Magic was beautiful until it wasn't anymore. And then it was painful. He'd learned that the hard way and had no desire to go there again. Once had been more than enough.

Apparently, Reid had some major connections with the owner of the Sunset Bay Resort, because Kate found herself in a beachfront bungalow with an amazing view of the moon rising over placid water.

"Is this to your liking, ma'am?" asked the young woman who had escorted Kate from the resort's check-in area.

"This would be to anyone's liking." Kate smiled and gave the woman a twenty-dollar tip. "Thank you very much."

"My pleasure. If you'd like, I could have some dinner sent to you. I can wait for you to make your selection or press nine on any of the house phones to place your order."

"I think I'll wait a bit." Kate couldn't imagine eating right now, not when her nerves were still in such a jumble after seeing Reid.

"As you wish, ma'am. Enjoy your stay with us, and let us know if we can be of service to you."

"I will, thank you."

A few minutes later, the bellman arrived with Kate's suitcase and set it in the master bedroom. And then she was finally alone. Kate couldn't remember a time when she'd wanted to be alone more than she did right now. The last time had been the week after she broke things off with Reid. She'd holed up in her Green Hills condo to lick her wounds until Buddy forced her back to work by threatening legal action.

He'd done her a favor by playing hardball, and over time she'd gotten past the hurt and shock of losing Reid and moved forward with her life. Except, she'd never moved forward romantically. She'd been stuck on him all this time. Seeing him today had brought that home for her far more than a series of failed relationships or the passage of time ever could have.

Now that she had her answer, it was time to find a way to get unstuck. They'd had their moment. Their time had come and gone and was not to be repeated. He had someone else and was happy. There was no place for Kate in his new life, and now she had to accept that and go on.

She walked onto the balcony that abutted the beach and leaned against the rail to watch the moon rise. This was such a beautiful place. She could see why he loved it here.

For the next few days, she would love it here, too. She would take some time to accept what had happened before she went home and figured out the next chapter in her life. If everything went as planned, she'd have her family to Nashville for Christmas and resume touring after the first of the year. That would give her plenty of downtime to come to peace with the past and map out a future that didn't include the only man she'd ever loved.

She shook off that thought. If she went there, she'd lose the tiny bit of composure she was clinging to as it set in that there wouldn't be anything more with him. All she had left were beautiful memories, and they were more than some people got in a lifetime.

Since she'd decided to stay a few days, she sent Levi a text to let him know.

Take your time, hon. This place is amazing.

Kate smiled, pleased that Levi was enjoying himself. They all worked far too hard and deserved some time off that didn't include jetting to the next venue, sound checks, rehearsals, recording studios or screaming crowds.

She perused the room-service menu and ordered a bottle of wine, a salmon entrée and a tossed salad. "Wait," she said as operator signed off. "Toss in the chocolate mousse, too."

"We'll have it to you in thirty minutes, Ms. Harrington."

"Thank you."

While she waited for her dinner to arrive, Kate showered and changed into a pale blue silk nightgown and robe Jill had given her for her birthday. She was brushing her hair when her phone dinged with a text from Jill.

How'd it go?

Not so great, but I'm okay.

Really?

Really. I'll tell you about it when I get home. What're you up to?

You wouldn't believe me if I told you.

Are you relaxing?

Trying…

Try harder! Talk to you in a couple of days.

Call me if you need to talk. I'm always right here.

I know. That's one of the many reasons I love you.

:-)

Kate put down the phone and stared out at the water until a knock on the door announced the arrival of her dinner.

Jill hated herself for knowing that Ashton drove a silver Jaguar with his AJM initials on the license plates. She hated herself for waiting for that silver car to come down the long lane to Kate's estate. She hated herself for being excited to see him, for wanting to know where he was taking her, for caring more than she should about this whole thing.

For the thousandth time in the last hour, she ran sweaty palms over her jeans, wishing she'd never agreed to this date, or whatever it was. "This is ridiculous."

To pass the time, she sent off the text to Kate to see how she'd made out in St. Kitts, and now she was worried that her sister really wasn't fine but was acting like she was so Jill wouldn't worry.

"You're off the clock," she reminded herself, though one could stop being an attorney and manager, but one never stopped being a sister. "She said she's fine, and she's a grown adult. If she wasn't fine, she would've said so."

Despite Kate's assurances Jill had no doubt that her sister must be devastated, which made Jill want to cancel her own plans and fly to St. Kitts to be with Kate. She was reaching for her phone to call Ashton when a black stretch limo came down the lane.

Jill's mouth fell open. "What the hell?"

The car came to a stop outside her home, and the driver alighted. Jill knew this because she was staring out the window. Even so, when the driver knocked on the door, she startled.

As she pulled open the door, she said, "I think you have the wrong place."

"Are you Jill Harrington?"

Nodding, she stared at the car.

"Mr. Matthews sent me to pick you up."

"And bring me where?"

"I'm afraid I'm unable to disclose that information. I'm told it's a surprise."

Jill stewed that over for a moment, unsure how she felt about him managing her this way. She was used to doing the managing.

"He said you might protest, but he promises you'll enjoy his plans for the evening. Oh and he said to bring a jacket. Just in case."

Jill eyed the driver warily, wanting to ask in case of what. "Anything else?"

"No, that was about it."

She thought about Kate alone in St. Kitts. She thought of the endless months on the road, day after day without so much as an hour to call her own. Kate had told her to relax, to take some time off, and as much as she might've hated herself, she was extremely curious to know what Ashton had planned.

"Ms. Harrington? Are you coming?"

"Yes." Jill grabbed a denim jacket and her purse on the way out the door. "I'm coming."

Reid's dinner with Mari was unusually quiet and awkward. He did his best to make conversation, but all he could think about was how surreal it had been to see Kate again. Over and over, he relived their brief encounter on the beach until he'd analyzed every word and every expression, trying to find the deeper meaning.

Did she say she wanted him back? And why did his heart skip a beat at the thought that maybe she did? What did it mean?

"Reid."

He snapped out of his ponderings to find Mari looking at him across the table, clearly annoyed by his inattention. "I'm sorry. What were you saying?"

"It doesn't matter." She signaled the waiter for their check.

"Don't you want dessert?" She always wanted dessert.

"Not tonight." Rather, it appeared she wanted out of there—and quickly. He always insisted on paying whenever they went out, but tonight she beat him to it, signing the credit card receipt before he was even aware that their check had arrived.

She put down the pen, took her card and was heading for the exit before he had the napkin off his lap.

Reid chased after her. "Mari, where're you going in such a rush?"

"Home."

If he wasn't mistaken, he heard tears in her voice, but he was afraid to look over at her as he drove the short distance to the house she'd recently moved into with him. Once there, she bolted from the car and went into the bedroom. He found her tossing clothes into a bag, her movements jerky and erratic—and reminiscent of the day Kate had left him. He didn't like to think about that day. It was still painful all these years later.

"What're you doing?"

"I'm going."

"Wait. Going where?"

"Anywhere but here."

"I don't understand. Something happened today that caught me by surprise. I don't even get one night to process it?"

She turned to him, and her tear-ravaged face tore at him. "If I gave you a month or a year to 'process' what happened today, would it change that fact that you're still in love with her?"

"*What?*" He stared at her, incredulous. "Where's that coming from? I haven't seen her in *ten* years!"

"And those ten years disappeared the minute she showed up here, didn't they?"

When she went into the bathroom that adjoined their bedroom, he went after her. "Mari, listen to me. Please."

She turned to him, seeming to summon an almost ethereal calm that was in sharp contrast to the emotional firestorm. "We always promised each other we'd stay together for as long as it worked for both of us, right?"

"Yes."

"I can't compete with the woman you never stopped loving, and I'm not about to try."

"How do you know I never stopped loving her? Even I don't know that."

"In all these months together, you've never once said you love me. I always suspected there was someone else, someone who had your heart. I was watching you today when you saw her for the first time, and I finally got some answers. I saw everything I've never seen directed my way."

"You're not being fair! I was surprised. I had no idea she was coming here. How would you have me react when someone I loved a decade ago appears out of the blue?"

"Look me in the eye, right here, right now, and tell me you don't love her anymore."

Reid intended to do exactly as she'd directed, because he didn't want to lose her. He liked what they had. It was easy and comfortable and peaceful. It was everything his relationship with Kate hadn't been, but he couldn't look at this beautiful, sweet woman who'd been so good to him and lie to her.

"I don't know how I feel. I wish I could tell you what you want to hear, but I'm all mixed up inside. Seeing her again has thrown me. I won't deny that. I need some time to figure out what it means."

"Take all the time you need." She picked up her bag and headed for the door. "I'll send for the rest of my stuff."

"Mari, please. You don't have to go. It doesn't have to be this way."

"Yes, it does, because I happen to love you, and I won't sit on the sidelines and watch you leave me."

"*Leave you?* You're the one who's leaving!"

"You left me the minute you saw her." This was said so quietly that Reid almost didn't hear her.

"Mari—"

"Please, don't do this. Don't deny what we both know is true. We had a lovely time together, and I don't want to watch it die a painful death while you pine for the one who got away. Don't do that to us, or to me."

Before Reid could piece together a coherent response to that, she was out the door and in her car. He slammed the door shut and pounded his fist on the wood. How had this day spun so far out of control from when he'd woken up in the morning to make lazy love with Mari to watching her storm out the door as their relationship came to a sudden, turbulent end?

"I'll tell you how it happened," he said, fuming as he grabbed his car keys. "Kate Harrington is how it happened. Once again she's turned my entire life upside down, and this time she's not getting away with it."

After dinner, Kate took what was left of her bottle of wine to the beach patio and stretched out on one of the wide lounge chairs. It wasn't lost on her that the chairs were made to accommodate two people, and as usual, she was alone. Normally, being by herself didn't bother her. But here, in paradise, she felt lonelier than she had in a long time.

Of course it was because nothing had gone as she'd hoped today. Now that she'd seen Reid again, Kate was able to admit that she'd expected to find him single and as lonely as she was for what they'd once had. But he seemed to be happily settled with the dark-haired beauty he lived with.

Thinking of her, the petite woman with the dark eyes and curvy body, Kate experienced an emotion that was all new to her—jealousy. Was he with her now, in bed, making love to her? Or were they looking at the same moon on their deck, talking about his long-lost girlfriend who'd come to visit today and laughing about how misguided she'd been to show up that way, expecting to pick right up where she'd left off with Reid so long ago?

"Ugh," she said to the moonlight, scrubbing a hand over her face as if to erase the memories of the other woman Reid loved now. It wouldn't do her any good to think about them and what they might be doing.

The house phone inside rang, jarring her out of her musings. Kate got up to answer it.

"Ms. Harrington," the operator said. "My apologies for disturbing you, but you have a visitor. A Mr. Matthews. He's quite insistent on seeing you."

Frozen with shock, Kate held the phone to her ear and stared at the wall, trying to formulate a coherent thought. Reid was here. And he wanted to see her.

"Ms. Harrington?"

"Please send him down."

"Very well."

Since she didn't have time to change before he got there, she retied her robe and ran her fingers through her hair. What was he doing here? She could barely think by the time he knocked—or rather pounded—on her door a minute later.

Before she could get to the door, he pounded again. "Open up, Kate!" What the heck had gotten into him?

She opened the door and started to ask him what was wrong when he pushed past her into the living room.

"I hope you're happy."

"What... I... What're you talking about?"

Watching him pace around the small room like a caged tiger, Kate was reminded of the long-ago night when he'd come to her place, intending to end their relationship. Rather, they'd gone to Memphis the next day and ended up in bed together.

"Mari has left me. Happy?"

"She... Why?"

"Because of you! Because you showed up and ruined everything, just like before!" The sleepy-looking brown eyes she'd adored from the start were shooting fire at her as he spoke. He wore a white shirt that offset his dark tan, and his hair was mussed, as if he'd been pulling at it. He was fifty-five now but didn't look a day over forty, and Kate still loved him as much as she ever had.

The realization sent her reeling, making her heart beat erratically and her mouth go dry. "I...I'm sorry. I never meant to ruin anything for you. I only wanted to see you, to tell you... I'm sorry."

His gaze moved over her slowly and intently, which put her already frazzled nerves on alert. "Are you?" he asked in that slow Tennessean drawl that got her every time.

"Am I… Am I what?" She hated that he turned her into a stuttering fool, but being this close to him when he was obviously enraged with her had fried her brain cells.

"Are you sorry she left me?" He stepped closer, forcing Kate to back up—right into a wall.

"I, um…" What was she supposed to say to that?

His face was now an inch from hers when he asked again, more slowly this time. "Are you *sorry* she left me?"

Since she didn't dare try to speak, Kate shook her head.

"Why?" He zeroed in on her lips, which made them go dry.

Kate licked them and watched his eyes darken with what looked like desire. His eyes had always gotten darker and sexier when he was turned on.

His hands landed on her hips, fingertips digging into her skin through the silk and setting her on fire. "*Why?*"

"Because I want you." With him standing a mere inch from her, with him touching her for the first time in a very long decade, it suddenly wasn't difficult at all to tell him the truth. "I've always wanted you. Even when I wasn't supposed to want you."

And then he was devouring her. There was simply no other word to describe the way he kissed her, as if he'd been saving up for this moment for as long as they'd been apart. He consumed her with his lips, tongue and teeth.

Kate wound her arms around his neck and held on as tightly as she could, kissing him back with everything she had. She had no idea how long they stood there, pressed against the wall, kissing each other with years of pent-up passion and desire fueling their embrace. It was unlike anything Kate had ever experienced, even with him. And still his hands never moved from her hips. He held on so tightly, as if he was afraid she might get away if he let go.

Wanting more of him, Kate arched into his embrace, encountering the hard press of his erection against her belly. When she gasped, he broke the kiss and turned his focus on her neck.

"This is crazy," he whispered between open-mouthed kisses that made her melt in his arms. "What're you even doing here?"

"I came for you." She fisted a handful of his hair, remembering the way the dark silky strands had felt between her fingers the first time they were together. The feel of his hair on her skin was something she'd thought about long after they broke up. "I couldn't stop wanting you. I tried for so long to stop, but I couldn't. I never stopped."

His groan was nothing less than tortured. "I never stopped, either. I thought of you every day. I listened to your music whenever I was in the car alone. It made me feel closer to you."

"I'm sorry," she said, a sob escaping from her lips almost against her will. "I was horrible to you, and you helped me so much."

He quieted her with another deep, searching kiss that made her want to beg for more of him. "I was wrong to go behind your back the way I did. You were exactly right when you said I'd disrespected you."

Kate shook her head. "Everything I have is because of what you did. I was an idiot to think the career would've happened without someone helping me."

"I have no doubt at all it would've happened with me or without me." As he said those words, his hands finally left their perch on her hips and moved up to cup her breasts. "You're more beautiful than ever, if that's possible. When I saw you on my beach today..." He shook his head. "I thought I'd dreamt you."

"I didn't come here to mess things up for you. I didn't know you had someone else. I swear. I never would've come if I had known that."

"Mari is a lovely woman, and she was very good to me, but she isn't you. There's never been anyone else quite like you."

Kate ran her fingers over the prominent cheekbones she'd always been so captivated by. "For me either."

"Not even Clint What's-his-name?" he asked with a raised brow.

Kate laughed at the expression on his face. "More rumor than truth."

"I was consumed by jealousy. Every time I read you were with someone new, I wanted to find them and beat the hell out of them and tell them you were mine. Mine." He kissed her. "Always mine."

"Yes," she whispered. "I was always yours. From the very beginning. I've never wanted anyone else."

"But there've been others…"

"None that mattered."

"Kate…" He wrapped his arms tight around her. "I can't believe you're here and I'm holding you and telling you these things I've kept secret all this time."

"I can't believe it, either. I've spent so many nights on my tour bus, watching the world go past my window, wondering where you were and if you were happy, if you thought of me at all. So many nights. Almost every night."

"We've wasted so much time."

Kate looked up at him. "What about… What about Mari?"

"I care for Mari," he said, a pained look occupying his handsome features. "She's a lovely person, but I never made her any promises."

"Were you together a long time?"

"Six months."

"Do you love her?"

"I love her, but I'm not *in* love with her."

"Oh. You aren't?"

"I couldn't be."

"What do you mean?"

"How could I be in love with her when I never stopped being in love with you?"

Kate stared up at him, wondering if he'd really said that or if she'd wanted it so badly she'd imagined it.

He framed her face and tipped her head back to receive his kiss, which was gentle this time, as opposed to wild. "Don't cry," he whispered. "Please don't cry. It'll be okay now."

Kate hadn't realized tears were flowing from her eyes until he swept them away with his thumbs. "I want to believe it'll work out the way we want it to, but all I can think about are the many reasons it wasn't okay last time."

"That was a long time ago. A lot has changed since then."

"Not everything. Your son still doesn't speak to me, for one thing."

"That's his problem, not ours."

"It's not that simple. There're so many things to consider."

"And none of them have to be considered tonight," he said, kissing her. "Or tomorrow." Another kiss. "Or even the next day." As he spoke, he backed her away from the wall and guided her toward the bedroom. "Do you want me to go?"

Shaking her head, she said, "I want you to stay forever."

His grin lit up his face as he came down on top of her on the bed.

Kate ran her fingers through his hair, over and over, relearning every feature of his gorgeous face. "What happened here?" she touched her finger to a new scar that ran through his right eyebrow.

"A tropical storm blew through a couple of years ago. I was helping a friend replace a window at his house when a piece of the broken one caught me just so."

"Ouch. Did you need stitches?"

"Three."

Kate brought him down close to her and pressed three kisses to the scar, making him smile.

"You've been ill," he said, tracing his finger over the dark circles under her eyes.

"Pneumonia. Hit me hard."

"I read about what happened in Oklahoma City."

"That was pretty scary."

"You're pushing yourself too hard."

"I don't have anything else to do. My work is my life."

"Ah, Kate… I've learned the hard way there's so much more to life than work." He shifted off her and propped himself up on an elbow.

Filled with questions she was dying to ask him, Kate turned to face him. The questions, she decided, were more important than the passion. "Do you miss your work?"

"Not at all. I do exactly what I want all day, every day. I get asked to consult on a lot of what goes on around here. If I feel like it, I do. If I don't, I say no. I've overseen the building of affordable housing here, which is very rewarding. It's a heck of a lot more fun than working twenty hours a day, that's for sure."

"Don't you ever get bored?"

"Nope. There's so much to do. I love to sail and scuba dive and fish. Fishing is so relaxing. I had no idea."

"I haven't been fishing since I lived at home."

"Did you like it back then?"

"I did. I was kinda good at it, too."

"You should do it again sometime. I also like to mess around with old abandoned boats, like the one I was working on today."

"What do you do with them after you fix them up?"

"I give them to local kids, who use them to fish." He twirled a lock of her hair around his finger. "I used to dream of the life I have now, you know? I'd be flying off to Chattanooga or Memphis or Knoxville to check on jobs, and all the way there I'd dream about living in the islands in a small place on the beach with nothing to do all day other than what I felt like doing."

"You worked hard for a long time to be able to do this."

"Yes, I did."

"My life is in Nashville," she reminded him.

"When you're home."

"When I'm home."

"How's Thunder?"

The mention of the beloved horse he'd given her after they broke up made her smile. "Wonderful—and human—as always. I swear he understands me better than most of the people in my life do."

"He always did get you, right from the very beginning, remember?"

"I remember everything. I remember every single minute we spent together, because I've relived every one of them a million times. The night you took me riding in the snow… I've never done anything more amazing."

"I think about that night a lot, too. It was so perfect." He continued to twirl the lock of hair around his finger, again and again. "That was the night you gave me the song you wrote for me."

"'I Thought I Knew,' still my biggest hit. I end every show with it."

"I know."

"How do you know?"

Half his face lifted into a small smile that lit his eyes.

"Oh God, have you *been* to my shows?"

"Maybe. Once or twice. Four times, actually," he said with a sheepish grin.

"Oh, Reid! Why didn't you ask to see me?"

"I didn't think I'd be welcome after the way we left things."

Kate closed her eyes and let go with a deep, pained sigh. "It was all my fault."

"No, it wasn't. We made a mess of things together, and we can both take a share of the blame. Something you said to me that last day has stayed with me all this time."

She opened her eyes and met his gaze. "What?"

"You said everyone thought I was too old for you and how funny it was that you'd been the adult in our relationship."

Kate grimaced at the reminder of that hurtful comment. "And I acted like such an adult that day."

"You were right, though. You very specifically asked me not to call in any favors for you, and I did it anyway. I loved you so much. I wanted you to have everything you'd ever dreamed of."

"I know that now, and I should've known then that the only reason you did it was because you loved me and wanted me to succeed."

"The way I went about it was wrong, though. I regret that. I've always regretted it. I should've told you I knew Buddy and Taylor, and introduced you to them and let you decide whether or not you wanted their help. I wish you knew how many times I've wanted to go back and rewrite that chapter of my life. I also never would've lied to my son. That, too, was a very big mistake I paid for dearly."

Kate reached for his hand and linked their fingers. "You two are okay now, right?"

"We're great, but it took a long time. A very long time."

"I hate that I was responsible for the falling out between you two. I've had a lot of regrets about that and my role in it."

"You weren't responsible, darlin'. I was the one who lied to him. Not you."

"Still…"

"How about you and your daddy? All your fences mended?"

"A long time ago. After Maggie got hurt, we put it all aside. I hate that it took such an awful thing to bring us back together, but I was glad to clear the air with him. I also think about that day at the hospital and the way my Uncle Jamie treated you after you'd been good enough to fly me home and get me to the hospital. I hated that. I always wanted you to know. I had a big argument with him over it after Maggie was better. It wasn't his place to treat you that way."

"Sure, it was. I'd had a sexual affair with his eighteen-year-old niece. He had every right to feel the way he did."

"Still, it was my business and yours, not his."

"Maybe so, but I never begrudged him for the way he reacted to me that day."

"I begrudged him enough for both of us."

Reid laughed.

"How about Miss Martha? Do you see her?"

"She comes to visit for a week every February. She *loves* to fish, and she's crazy good at it."

"Why can I so picture that?"

"She's a pistol."

"So many people got hurt," Kate said. "We might be better off leaving well enough alone."

"Is that what you want, darlin'?" He looked at her with concern etched into his face. "Because it if is, I'd certainly understand. I'm still way too old for you, no matter how you cut it."

"You were never too old for me. People spend their whole lives looking for what we had. The age difference wasn't a factor for us. Everyone else was upset about it, but we never were."

"No, we weren't, but I'll always be twenty-eight years older than you, and you have a right to a young husband and a family and a long life with the man you love."

"You're the man I love. You're the man I've always loved. That's one of the simple facts of my very complicated life."

He cupped her cheek and leaned over to give her a lingering kiss. "I'm going to go now."

Startled, Kate said, "Why?"

"I woke up this morning in bed with someone else. I never expected to see you again. I think we both need to sleep on this and make sure we're making clear-headed decisions and not heat-of-the-moment decisions."

Though Kate wanted him to stay and had expected him to, what he said made a lot of sense. "When will I see you again?"

"How about I come for breakfast? Would that be soon enough?"

"Yes," she said, drawing him into another passionate kiss.

"Keep that up and I'll forget all about my big plan to sleep on all of this."

"You could sleep on it here."

"If I stay here, we won't sleep and you've been sick. You need your rest."

"Do you promise you'll be back?"

"I promise," he said with another kiss. He leaned his forehead against hers and stared into her eyes. "Come on, time to get comfy." He pulled back the covers and tucked her into bed. "Now close your eyes and have sweet dreams about tomorrow."

She did as she was told. "And the day after."

"And the day after." He kissed her once more. "I'll see you very soon."

Kate heard the door click shut behind him. She was afraid if she opened her eyes, she'd discover it'd all been a lovely dream. He still loved her. He'd never stopped loving her. He'd thought about her and come to her shows and remembered all the moments that had made their brief months together so special.

She was nearly asleep when it occurred to her that she still had his number programmed into her phone, if it was even still in service. He'd probably changed his number years ago when he moved to the island. Thinking about their late-night phone calls after they first met, she reached for her phone. After scrolling through her address book, she found his number right where it had always been, and pressed send.

Kate waited to hear that the number was no longer in service.

Instead, she heard his soft chuckle. "You still have my number, darlin'?"

Apparently, he still had hers, too. "I couldn't bring myself to get rid of it."

"Neither could I."

"God, we're a couple of hopeless cases, aren't we?"

"I don't know about you, but I feel a little less hopeless after today. In fact, I'm feeling positively *hopeful*."

"So am I."

"Why do I hear a 'but' in there?"

"I keep thinking about my parents and Ashton and Ms. Martha and all the people who didn't get it before. Why would they feel any differently now?"

"For one thing, you're no longer eighteen, and for another, clearly whatever we had came with some staying power if we both still feel the same way we did then."

"That's true."

"Don't worry about it tonight, darlin'. It'll all work out the way it's meant to." After a short pause, he said, "You know what I've missed?"

"What?"

"Listening to you sing to me while I drive home. Will you sing my song for me?"

"I'd love to."

CHAPTER 5

Jill peered out the back window as the limo traveled down a long driveway lined by white split-rail fences. Rolling meadows stretched as far as she could see. They drove past a small Tudor-style home, as well as buildings that might've been stables and then, at the top of the hill, a massive stone house.

She expected the car to stop outside the house, but it proceeded around the house to a dirt road that led to another building in the distance. Out the back window, she tried to get a better look at the house, but trees obscured her view.

What was this place?

The car came to a stop, and through the window, Jill saw Ashton leaning against a red pickup truck. Wearing faded jeans, a yellow Vanderbilt T-shirt and cowboy boots, he looked nothing at all like the successful lawyer he'd been in the office the other day. Here he looked like a country boy—an extremely appealing country boy.

Ashton opened the door and held out a hand to her.

Jill wiped her hand once more on her jeans before she accepted his help out of the car.

He closed the car door, and the limo drove away.

Jill watched it go, wondering where she was and what he had planned. "What is this place?"

"My childhood home. Been in my family forever and a day."

"You don't live here anymore?"

He shook his head. "I live in town, but we still board and breed horses here, so I come out to ride as often as I can."

Jill took a second, more detailed look and noted there wasn't another house in sight. "Is that a runway?"

"Sure is."

"That's right. I remember Kate saying your dad flies. He flew her home when our sister got hurt." *Stop babbling*, she thought as she linked her fingers because she didn't know what to do with her hands. For a horrifying moment, she wondered if she'd annoyed him by mentioning his dad and Kate in the same sentence.

"We both fly."

"Oh. You do?"

"Uh-huh. My dad taught me to fly before he taught me to drive."

Jill began to get nervous about where this was heading.

He leaned back against the truck, eyeing her and smiling at her in that sexy, devilish way he did so well. "You wanna go for a ride?"

"In the truck?"

Grinning, he shook his head. "In that." He pointed to the open doors of the hangar, where an airplane nose peeked out. How had she missed that?

"Um, where would we go?"

"Buddy has a house in Malibu that he bought off one of his friends who was flirting with bankruptcy. No one's using it right now, so he said it's all mine for as long as I want it."

Jill stared at him, trying not to be swayed by his stunningly gorgeous face. "You want me to get in a plane and fly to *Malibu* with you? I thought we were having dinner!"

"We are." He pointed to some bags in the backseat of the pickup. "We'll take it with us."

Jill shook her head. "I can't go to Malibu. I have things…to do."

He raised an eyebrow that was more teasing than mocking. "I thought you were on vacation?"

"I am, but I have—"

"Things. Right, well here's a big idea. How about you do your 'things' when we get back?"

"And when will that be?"

He shrugged. "Whenever we feel like it."

"Don't you have to work?"

"I took some time off."

"This is crazy! I can't just get on a plane with you and go to…to *California* because you… you…"

"Asked you to?"

"Yes! I don't have anything with me. You didn't say anything about going out of town!"

"If I had, would you be here?" Before Jill could form a response, he said, "I didn't think so. Let me remind you we'd be going to a place that has stores where we can get anything you can't live without for a few days. So what do you say to some sand and sun? Doesn't that sound good?"

It did sound good. It sounded amazing, actually. But the practical lawyer in her had questions, and damn it, she was going to ask them. "Is getting me into bed the goal of this trip?"

"Hell, *yeah*," he said in that sexy drawl that made her blood boil. "That's definitely one of several goals."

Unaccustomed to such bold-faced honesty from a man, Jill licked lips that had suddenly gone dry.

Ashton's gaze zeroed in on her lips.

"What are the others?"

"Other what?" he asked, still fixated on her mouth.

"*Goals.*"

He tore his gaze off her lips and looked into her eyes. "I want to see you relaxed, for one. I want to get to know you better, for another—and not just in bed." Pushing off the truck, he took a slow, lazy step toward her and reached out to release the second button on her shirt. When she attempted to slap his hand away, he grasped her fingers and held on tight. "I also want to see you let your hair down and have some fun." As he said the words, he used his free hand to release the clip holding her hair.

Jill uttered a squeak of protest as her hair tumbled free.

"I knew it," he said, running his fingers through the long strands. "Thick and soft and very, *very* fragrant."

"Ashton, I don't think—"

Jill hadn't even figured out how she planned to end that sentence when he was kissing her. His arms were around her, one of his hands was buried in her hair, and the hard wall of his body was pressed against hers. In her right mind, she would've pushed him away, but her right mind seemed to have deserted her. As their tongues mated and dueled, he tightened his grip on her hair.

After several long, desperate, passionate minutes, he broke the kiss and pressed his lips to her cheek, jaw and ear. "Come away with me," he whispered, sending a tingling sensation rippling through her body. "Take some time just for you. Let me take care of you for a few days." His hands moved over her back, down to cup her bottom, bringing her in tight against the hard proof of his arousal.

With his muscles pressed against her softness, Jill couldn't seem to think of anything other than what it felt like to be in his arms, to be surrounded by his appealing scent, to know he wanted her, that he'd gone out of his way to arrange this getaway for her.

"Jill?"

She closed her eyes and counted to ten. "Okay."

His hands slid down her arms and curled around hers, gripping her tightly as he smiled at her. "I promise you'll have fun."

"I'm still not convinced this isn't a massive conflict of interest."

"You're not here because of Kate. I'm not here because of Buddy. It's not a conflict." He released her hands. "Stay here while I get the plane ready."

As he walked away, Jill zeroed in on the way his faded jeans hugged his exceptional ass. The thought that she might be able to touch him there or anywhere else she wanted—soon—made her feel a little lightheaded. Was that what she wanted? Did she want to touch him and kiss him and have sex with him? Yes! God, yes, she wanted all of that. She wanted *him*. She'd wanted him for a long time, if she were being honest.

Her phone chirped with a text from Kate. *Reid came over to where I'm staying and we talked and it looks like it might be back on… You won't believe what happened today. Call me when you can.*

Jill's stomach fell as she watched Ashton roll out the plane. Would her sister's rekindled romance derail whatever was happening between her and Ashton? He surely wouldn't be happy to hear his dad was back with Kate. He'd probably be equally unhappy that Jill had known about it and hadn't mentioned it.

Was it selfish of her to want to find out what might be possible with Ashton before she told him his dad might be getting back together with her sister? Probably. Was it even her place to tell him? Before she could further contemplate the dilemma, he smiled and waved her over to the plane.

Jill decided that for once she was going to be selfish. The problems would still be here when they got back. She'd deal with them then.

Following a restless night, Kate was up long before the sun rose over the crystal blue water. She contemplated a shower but decided to wait to see what Reid had planned for the day. If they were going to the beach, there wasn't much point in showering.

In the tiny kitchen, she brewed a pot of coffee and was thrilled to find a container of half-and-half in the fridge. You had to hand it to the five-star resorts, she thought. They sure knew how to take good care of their guests.

Coffee in hand, she went out to the patio to watch the sun crest the horizon, wondering what this day would bring. She felt giddy and excited and…happy. For the first time in years, she was truly happy to know that today she'd see him, spend time with him, hold him, kiss him—and maybe more.

That he now knew how she'd felt all along was a huge relief and a load off her mind. She'd wanted him to know for such a long time that she'd hated the way things ended between them and had regretted it every day since. No matter what happened now, he knew the truth, and that had somehow freed her from the past.

She was beginning to wonder how long she had to wait to see him when a knock on the door had her scurrying inside. She tugged open the door and found him leaning against the doorframe looking relaxed and well rested and freshly shaven. He looked so good. So very good. After thinking about him for such a long time, to have him close enough to touch was seriously overwhelming.

They stared at each other for a moment charged with energy and desire.

"Come in," she said, breaking the long silence.

"I'm glad you didn't change yet."

She turned to find him taking a slow, leisurely look at her in the matching nightgown and robe. "I was about to shower," she said, undone by his intense attention.

"Not yet."

As he came toward her with intent in his gaze, Kate's heart hammered. She wanted to cry from the sweet relief of being with him again, but this wasn't the time for tears. This was the time for happiness and joy.

He put his arms around her and lifted her into his kiss.

Kate held on tight as he walked them into the bedroom.

They landed on the bed in a frenzy of arms and legs and lips and tongue.

"Did you think about what you want?" he asked between kisses.

Kate nodded and ran her fingertips over his smooth jaw. "I want you. I've always wanted you. Did you think about what you want?"

"I want what I've always wanted, since the day you sang 'Crazy' in my dining room and made me fall in love with you."

Amused, Kate raised a brow. "I *made* you?"

Nodding, he came in for another kiss. "I had no choice. I was as powerless to resist you then as I am now."

"Make love to me, Reid."

"Are you sure, honey? I'm an old man. You could have anyone you want—"

"I'm with the one I want, and I'm tired of yearning for what used to be. That gets exhausting after a while."

"Yes, it does." Hovering above her, he combed the hair back from her face and kissed her so softly she almost didn't feel it. "I can't believe we get to be together like this again. I want to do it right this time."

"I want that, too." Kate smoothed her hands over his back, looking for the hem of his shirt. As her fingers skimmed his lower back under his shirt, he gasped in response to her touch. "There were some things we always did right," she added with a coy smile that made him laugh.

"Indeed there were. As I recall," he said, dipping his head to drag his tongue over her neck, "we did this pretty well." He punctuated the statement by rolling her earlobe between his teeth.

Kate shivered. "Very well. I've never had better."

"I hate to think of you doing this with anyone else."

She pushed his shirt up over his chest. "I didn't particularly like it, if that makes you feel any better."

Ducking his head to help her remove his shirt, he said, "Only a little better."

Her gaze fixated on his splendid chest as she relearned every inch of him with eager hands. Other than a touch of gray mixed into his dark chest hair, he looked exactly as she remembered. "At least you didn't have to *see* any of my others."

When his lips set in a grimace, Kate regretted reminding him of the breakup with Mari.

"I hate that I caused her pain."

"I hate it, too. I certainly know what it feels like to want something I can't have."

"I can't help how I feel about you."

"She knows you didn't hurt her intentionally. I was the one who showed up unannounced, so I'm sure all her anger is directed at me."

"Which isn't fair."

Kate shrugged. "I'm a big girl. I can take it." She raised her hands from his chest to his face, using her fingers to smooth away his frown.

He tugged on the belt to her robe, spread it open and pressed his lips to the valley between her breasts. "I wouldn't have thought it possible, but you're even more beautiful now than you were back then."

Seduced as much by his words as the gentle press of lips to sensitive skin, Kate wrapped her arms around him, holding him against her chest as tears slipped from the corners of her eyes.

When he looked up and saw the tears, he kissed them away. "What is it?"

"I'm so happy to be with you again. I feel like I might explode or something."

"Mmm, that sounds promising, darlin'."

Her tears turned to laughter, which became a moan when his hand landed on her leg, raising the nightgown as his fingers moved from her knee to her core.

He seemed surprised to find no barrier to stop him from sliding his fingers through the moisture between her legs.

Kate arched her back, needing to get closer to him. She fisted her hand in his hair as he made her crazy by tugging on her nipple through the silk gown with his lips while stroking her with his fingers. The combination had her on the verge of coming, and he'd barely touched her. It had never been like this with anyone else, and she was wise enough now to know it never would be. He was it for her. *The one.* The only one she needed. "Reid, please... Don't make me wait. It's been so long."

Her plea seemed to break what was left of his control. Showing none of the finesse she'd come to expect from him during their brief time together, he freed himself and plunged into her.

She cried out from the sheer pleasure of the incredible feel of him inside her again after such a long, lonely time.

"Ah, hell," he said through gritted teeth. "Did I hurt you?"

"No. *Please don't stop.*"

"Why is this so much better with you than it's ever been with anyone else?" he asked as he held perfectly still.

Kate moved her hands from his shoulders to his backside to keep him inside her. "I don't know." She raised her hips, seared by the "rightness" of their undeniable connection.

He met her gaze. In his eyes, she saw his love shining down on her. "I need to move."

She released her tight hold on him.

Their coupling was fast and frantic and everything she wanted and needed. It was just as she remembered, and she couldn't seem to get close enough to him. She wanted all of him, everything he had to give her and then some. With her arms now linked around his neck, Kate held on tight through the first peek and then through a second, more powerful release that claimed him, too. He threw back his head and cried out as he surged into her before collapsing on top of her.

Kate hugged him to her, loving the feel of his heart pounding in time with hers. For the first time since the last time with him, she was exactly where she belonged. As that realization settled over her, something eased, and the tight ball of pain she'd carried in her chest since that last awful day finally released its grip on her.

"I love you," he said. "I'll always love you."

"I love you, too."

He raised his head to look into her eyes as he pressed a kiss to lips. "How about we try that again, with some finesse this time?"

"In a minute," she said, setting his head back on her chest. For right now, she was content to hold him while he continued to throb inside her. She wrapped her leg around his hips.

And that's when it dawned on her that they'd had unprotected sex. "Aw, shit."

"What is it, honey?"

"We probably should've talked about this before…"

He looked up at her, his eyes wide with shock. "Christ have mercy! I never gave it a thought."

"That makes two of us."

"You're not—"

"On the pill? Not anymore. I haven't been in any kind of relationship in a long time."

"So we should, probably, you know…"

"Not worry about it?" she asked, smiling at him.

"That's easy for you to say. You're young and spry."

She pressed her hips tighter against him and was rewarded with a throb deep inside. "You seemed pretty spry just now."

"Maybe so," he said with a low chuckle, "but a baby…" He shook his head as if the notion was too big to get his mind around. "You should be with someone your own age, darlin', someone who can give you babies and be there to watch them grow up."

Kate knew he was being serious, but she was so thrilled to be back in his arms that she didn't feel like being serious. "Where do you plan on going?"

He poked her ribs, making her laugh. "You know what I mean."

"All I know is I've spent most of my adult life yearning to feel like I did for three beautiful, all-too-brief months when I was eighteen. There's nothing you can say or do that would scare me away or make me not want to be with you. If we just made a baby, then we'll have a baby. That baby will be loved and appreciated and cared for. That baby would be *ours*. Yours and mine, for as long as we both live."

He finally withdrew from her and shifted onto his back, bringing her into his embrace. "You're so very calm about it."

She shrugged. "It would hardly be the end of the world for either of us. It's not like we don't have the means or the ability to take care of a baby."

"True."

When he was quiet for a long time, she glanced up at him. "What're you thinking?"

"Ashton is thirty-five. He'd be horrified if I told him he's going to be a big brother at his age."

"He'll be horrified anyway, the minute you tell him you're back with me. What's a little more horror on top of that?"

"I'm outmatched by you," he said, smiling. "You have an answer for everything."

"I always was the adult in this relationship," she reminded him.

He replied with a playful scowl. "In that case, you can figure out where we're going to get some condoms. We're going to need quite a few of them, in fact."

"Why? Are you feeling spry?"

He cupped her breast and tweaked her nipple between his fingers. "Very spry."

"In that case, we're in luck. When you stay at a five-star resort, they think of everything. Half-and-half in the fridge, and condoms in the bathroom."

"Seriously? Remind me to send my friend Desi a thank-you note."

She leaned in to kiss him. "Don't go anywhere."

With his arms crossed under his head, he said, "Wouldn't dream of it."

Acutely aware that he was watching her every move, Kate went into the bathroom to retrieve the box of condoms she'd noticed in the closet along with a wide assortment of other toiletries—anything a guest could want or need. She returned to the bedroom and straddled his thighs, watching with amazement as he hardened before her eyes.

"That's one heck of a sight, darlin'," he said as his sleepy eyes took a long, slow perusal from her shoulders to the juncture of her thighs and back up to her breasts.

Emboldened by his obvious appreciation, she shifted over him and bent to take his erect penis into her mouth.

His sharp inhale filled her with enthusiasm as she set out to drive him mad with lips, tongue and the gentle drag of teeth. At the same time, she tightened her hand around the base and stroked him the way he'd once taught her to. The combination had his eyes closing and his lips parting. She kept it up until he was panting and raising his hips as he thrust into her mouth. After taking him to the brink of release and then backing away three times, she released him and sat up.

His eyes flew open as he tried to gauge her intent.

Using her teeth on the wrapper, Kate removed the condom from the foil and took her own sweet time rolling it on.

"Are you trying to kill me, sweetheart?" he asked as he cupped her breasts.

"Who? Me?" She positioned him between her legs and slid down, one inch at a time, drawing out her descent for maximum impact.

"God, that's good," he whispered as he rested his hands on her thighs.

It was so very, *very* good. Nothing had ever been better or felt more right. He was the other half of her, her soul mate, the love of her life. Knowing now what she wished she'd known way back when fired her passion as she rode him to an explosive finish.

When she collapsed on top of him, his arms came around her and his lips skimmed her forehead. Surrounded by his love, Kate closed her eyes and relaxed into his embrace. For once, everything was right in her world.

And then it dawned on her that Jill had never called.

Sun streaming through an open window woke Jill from the deepest sleep she'd had in ages. She had no idea where she was, only that the room was big, painted white and looked out on an endless expanse of blue ocean. The roar of the surf hitting the beach reminded her of home.

She sat up and pushed the hair back from her face, taking a better look at the view.

Then it started to come back to her—Ashton, and *the kiss*, the flight, eating the picnic he'd brought as they soared high above the plains. They'd talked for hours. He'd never heard about the accident that changed her life—and that of the rest of her family—when she was fifteen. Her mother had been hit by a car and left in a coma that she recovered from three years later.

Ashton had been shocked to hear about the awful dilemma her parents had faced when her mother awoke to learn her father had fallen in love with someone else. Although her parents were still close friends and had long been happily remarried to Andi and Aidan, it wasn't a story Jill told often or to just anyone. However, it seemed natural to share it with him.

He'd talked about losing his mother in a car accident when he was barely two years old. It had pained her to experience his dismay over having no memory of the woman who'd given birth to him and to realize they shared an awful bond of car accidents changing both their lives.

The cocoon of the cockpit and the isolation of soaring through the sky had given their conversation a level of intimacy that wouldn't have been possible anywhere else.

Reliving it now, Jill tried to remember how she'd gotten from the plane to the house.

"Ah, you're finally awake," Ashton said from the doorway as he came in holding two mugs of coffee. His hair was wet from the shower and his face freshly shaven.

Noticing that he wore a T-shirt and shorts had Jill realizing she was wearing only a T-shirt of his and a pair of panties.

"You conked out on me," he said.

"Did I?" she asked as she took a mug from him.

"Totally. I didn't know how you liked your coffee, so I guessed on the cream and sugar."

"Perfect." She glanced at him, embarrassed to know he'd undressed her and put her to bed. "Care to explain how I lost my clothes?"

His sheepish grin was far too adorable. "I wanted you comfortable. You were so tired." He traced a line from her cheek to her ear, tucking a lock of her hair behind her ear.

"And there was nothing in it for you?"

"I was a perfect gentleman. When I get to see the goods, I want you wide awake and fully aware."

Jill nearly choked on her next sip of coffee. "Thanks for the warning."

"No problem."

That smile, those green eyes, those cheekbones, the thick blond hair... He was absolutely gorgeous, and all his attention was directed at her. A flutter of nerves hit her belly. What was she doing here? What had she been thinking coming all this way with him when they'd never had so much as a date before this?

"Don't do that," he said sternly.

"Do what?"

"Start second-guessing everything."

Annoyed that she was so easily read, she said, "That's not what I'm doing."

"Isn't it?"

"Maybe a little," she said, amused.

"Well, don't. We're two friends spending some time together. Nothing more, nothing less."

She glanced at him over the rim of her mug. "Nothing more?"

His eyes flared with desire. "Only if it's what you want."

"What about what you want?"

"I want to see you relaxed and rested. Anything else is a bonus."

"So you're not after a vacation fling?" Jill couldn't believe she was being so blunt with him.

Apparently, he couldn't, either, because his mouth fell open in surprise. "Not exactly."

"What does that mean?" The lawyer in her needed to know the terms before she agreed to the contract.

"It means," he said, combing his fingers through her tangled hair, "I want more than a vacation fling."

She hadn't expected him to say that. "With me?" she asked, hating how her voice sounded so squeaky.

"Yes, with you, silly," he said, laughing.

"I, um... well... oh."

"What exactly does that mean?"

"I'm not sure. I haven't had enough coffee for this conversation." She glanced down at the other pillow, which was smooth and not indented, and then forced herself to look at him. "Where did you sleep?"

"In the other room."

Jill bit her lip, trying to make sense of him. He hadn't been shy about the fact that he wanted her, and yet he'd slept elsewhere. He'd been a gentleman and hadn't taken advantage of an easy opportunity.

He reached for her free hand and surprised her when he placed a kiss on her palm. The gesture sent a tingle of sensation from her arm to her nipples, which were suddenly standing at full attention.

"Do you remember the first time we met?"

Confused by the sudden shift in conversation, Jill thought about that for a second. "It was right after I graduated from law school and went to work for Kate. We were negotiating her new contract with Long Road Records."

"Right. You were wearing a navy suit with a pale pink blouse. You had on these sexy, oversized beads." He used his fingertip to demonstrate exactly where the necklace had lain against her neck. "And sky-high heels that made your legs look crazy long. You had your hair in a very professional bun."

As Jill watched, astounded that he recalled every detail of what she'd worn that day, he gathered up her hair and twisted it into a bun that he pressed against the back of her neck. "Like that," he said, surveying his handiwork. "You walked into the room, and I never heard another word that was said, except if you said it. You were so gorgeous and sincere and green—very, *very* green—but you were a tiger on your sister's behalf.

"I wanted to reach across the table and tug on the pins holding your hair so I could see what it looked like down." He released his hold on her hair and watched it tumble over her shoulders. "It was all I could do to stay seated when I was so drawn to you." Nudging her hair to the side, he touched his lips to her neck. "I've wanted you, fiercely, every day since then. So no, I'm not all that interested in a vacation fling. What I want from you, Jill Harrington, goes far beyond our vacation."

Jill had been rendered speechless, which wasn't easy to do.

"Nothing to say?" he asked, amusement marking his handsome features.

"I... I didn't know you felt that way."

"For a long time I went out of my way to keep my crush hidden from you. Our families have a bit of history that I figured would be a problem for us. Every time I saw you, though, I wanted you more than the last time. After a while, I stopped caring about our family history or that your sister slept with my dad and all the crap that caused. All I cared about was getting to know you better."

Jill stared at him, astounded and amazed.

"Will you say something? Please? You're killing me."

"I... I thought it was just me."

She swore he stopped breathing for a minute, and then he recovered, took the mug from her and put it on the bedside table. With his face mere inches from hers, he said, "You thought what was just you?"

"The crush, the crazy nerves I'd get every time I knew I was going to see you, the aggravation I felt because you threw me off my game—every time."

"Jill—"

"I couldn't reconcile you with the man my sister had such animosity toward. I couldn't figure out how it was possible that I was so drawn to you when she dislikes you so intensely."

He winced and then sighed. "She has good reason to dislike me."

Jill hadn't expected him to say that either. "What do you mean?"

Ashton looked away from her, focusing on the view of the ocean. "When I found out about her and my dad, I called your dad. Not one of my finer moments."

"It must've been a big shock to find out about your dad and Kate."

"It was... That was a bad day, especially because not long before that he'd looked me in the eye and lied about not knowing who she was involved with. That hurt more than anything, and I'm not proud of the way I behaved."

She reached for his hand, which seemed to surprise him.

"For a long time after it ended between them, I wondered if he'd ever be the same. He was so sad. I hated that I'd caused that to a certain extent."

"You didn't cause their breakup."

"I know, but I didn't help anything. I was very unforgiving and intolerant."

"You'd also been lied to by the most important person in your life."

"Yeah. Still…"

"It was a long time ago. We've all done things we regret."

"I can't picture you doing anything stupid," he said with a grin, clearly trying to lighten the mood.

"I did my share of stupid things."

"Like what? Name one stupid thing you did—and don't forget, I came clean with you."

After a brief pause to consider which of her stupid things she would share, she decided on the stupidest of all stupid things. "After my mom got hurt, my dad was a mess for a long time. It was really hard to watch." Jill could still remember the pain of those early days like it was only yesterday rather than thirteen years ago. "It took him a long time to accept that her condition was likely permanent. He was out of work for a year, and when he went back, he met someone else through a job his company was managing for a Chicago-based hotel company. They dated long-distance for several months, and then they decided Andi and her son Eric should move to Rhode Island to live with us, and I…I was less than welcoming to her."

"I bet they understood how hard it was for you to see someone taking your mom's place."

"It wasn't like that, though. Andi never tried to take my mom's place. She was very considerate of my sisters and me and what we'd been through. I, on the other hand, was a monster."

"You were a kid, and you were hurting."

"We all have regrets, Ashton."

"I suppose."

"I have to tell you something, and it might upset you, but after knowing how hurt you were when your dad lied to you, I don't want to do the same thing."

Taken aback, he said, "Okay..."

"Kate is in St. Kitts."

"Oh. Huh." He rubbed a hand over the stubble on his face. "So someone told her where is."

"Buddy did."

Ashton got up from the bed and walked over to look out the window. "He's with someone else now. Mari. They've been together for more than six months."

"That must be why she said it didn't go as she'd hoped at first, but later, she said he came over and they talked. She said it seemed like there might be hope for them." Jill hesitated, but only briefly, before she got up to join him, sliding an arm around his waist. "You're upset. I'm sorry."

"No." He turned and put his arms around her, drawing her in close to him.

Her hands landed on his chest, molding to sculpted pectorals. "Talk to me. Tell me what you're thinking."

"I'm thinking that I went to an awful lot of trouble to get you here, and the last thing I want to talk about is my dad and your sister and what may or may not be happening between them—again."

"You're not mad that she's there?"

"No." Ashton looked down at her. "He was a mess after things went bad with her. In some ways he was never the same. If she's what he wants, I'm not getting in the way of it this time. It's his life."

"And hers."

"Yes, hers, too."

"If she and your dad were together, you might have to start being civil to her."

His face twisted into an expression of sheer horror. "I would? Really?"

Jill play-punched his belly. "Be careful. That's my sister you're talking about."

"Which is the number one reason I promise to be civil to her from here on out."

"You'd do that for me?"

"Yes," he said softly, his lips hovering just above hers. "I'd do it for you—and only for you."

"And not your dad?" she asked in a teasing tone.

"Something tells me he won't care much whether or not I approve this time around."

"You're probably right."

"Are you going to kiss me or tease me?"

"I thought you were going to kiss me."

"We need to work on our nonverbal communication." He closed the small space between them, resting his lips lightly against hers in an undemanding kiss that made all her most important parts tingle. Right when things were starting to get interesting, he pulled back. "Do you want to go to the beach?"

"I was sort of liking that."

His face lifted into a sultry, sexy grin that made her want to purr. "There'll be much more where that came from—after we have some fun."

CHAPTER 6

"Where do we go from here?" Kate asked over dinner on the patio. They'd whiled away the entire day in bed, emerging only when they couldn't go any longer without eating.

"I don't know exactly."

"You live here. I live in Nashville—when I'm not touring. I'm having a hard time picturing how this will work."

"How about I come to wherever you are when you're working. And when you're not working, we come here."

Kate stared at him, incredulous. "You'd do that? You love it here."

"Yes, I do." He reached for her hand and touched his lips to the inside of her wrist. "But I love it here even more."

The vibration of his voice against her skin made her shiver. "Are you sure that's what you want? You have a life here, friends and—"

"I'm very sure that's what I want."

"I've been thinking about cutting back on the touring."

"You keep a relentless schedule. I don't know how you do it."

"For so long, I felt like it was necessary to go, go, go and get out there so I wouldn't be forgotten or overlooked or some other terrible thing that would ruin my career."

"It's probably safe to assume at this point you won't be overlooked or forgotten, darlin'. Your fans adore you."

"I'm so lucky to have such faithful fans, and I feel obligated to make myself available to them."

"You have to think of your health. I don't like those dark circles under your eyes."

"They're so ugly. I hate them." Kate raised her hands to her face, self-conscious about the purple grooves under her eyes.

"You need some rest and some downtime to rejuvenate. What do you think about spending staying here with me for a while? And not just a week or two."

"*Stay* here?"

"That's what I said."

"I need to see Thunder. I promised him I'd be home, and he'll be wondering where I am."

"I could fly you home any time you want to go."

"You still have your plane?"

"I have a new one since I last saw you—a sweet twin-engine Cessna. It'll get us to Nashville in a few hours."

"So it could really be that simple? I stay here with you and go home once in a while?"

"It could really be that simple. You could rest, relax, write some new music, shop, sleep. Whatever you want."

Kate sat back in her chair and took a drink of her wine. "God, that sounds heavenly."

"Some St. Kitts therapy might be just what the doctor ordered."

"I don't know…"

"What don't you know, darlin'?"

"It'll sound stupid."

"Say it anyway."

Kate's face heated with embarrassment. "I don't know if I'd feel comfortable staying with you in the place you shared with Mari."

"Then we'll get a different place. I rent month to month. I have for years."

"Oh. I figured you owned it."

He shook his head. "I didn't want to be tied here if I decided to move on. I spent so much of my life chained to that gigantic house in Nashville. I didn't want those kinds of obligations anymore."

His words stuck a chord of fear in Kate. What if they'd conceived a child? Would he want that kind of obligation after already raising a child?

"Kate? What is it?"

"You don't want obligations, yet you're committing to this whole life with me."

"I don't want *real estate*. That's a different kind of obligation." He reclaimed her hand and kissed her palm, her wrist and the inside of her elbow. "There're obligations, and then there is joy and pleasure and peace. Finally, some peace."

"You haven't been at peace here?" She gestured to their view of paradise.

"There was always something—or I should say some*one*—missing. Our relationship was unfinished, and that left me unsettled. I was content but not entirely happy. Now I have a chance to be both, so you bet I want to be obligated to you."

Without releasing his hand, Kate got up and went to him.

Reid guided her onto his lap and put his arms around her.

"That might be the sweetest thing you've ever said to me," she said, "and if I'm recalling correctly, you said some pretty sweet things to me way back when."

His laugh rumbled through her as his love surrounded her—steady and sure and as solid as it ever was.

She rested her head on his shoulder and ran a finger over his bare chest. "My life is very different than it used to be."

"Besides the obvious, how so?"

"I can't go anywhere in public without security, for one thing."

"That won't be a problem here. No one cares about celebrities."

"That'll be nice. I miss being able to go to the Bluebird or Mabel's to hang out and visit with friends and listen to music whenever I want to. I miss going to the mall with my sisters or walking into the movies like everyone else does, rather than getting there ten minutes late and leaving ten minutes early."

"It sounds like a bit of a gilded cage."

"In some ways it is."

"If you had it to do over again, would you have wanted the big career so badly?"

Kate mulled that over. "I suppose I would, since I've never been all that good at anything else. This is what I was meant to do. I never question that. It's just that sometimes I wish it wasn't so confining, you know?"

"I can see what you mean. Definitely."

"I sound like a jerk for complaining about a career in which I get paid millions every year to do the one thing I love to do."

"You don't sound like a jerk."

"You have to say that. You love me."

"Yes, I do, but I don't have to say anything." He kissed her nose and then her lips.

"Buddy tried to tell me. Back at the beginning, he said it would be crazy—and not always in a good way. But until you're in it…"

"You can't possibly know."

"Right." She ventured a glance at him. "You sure you want to step inside that gilded cage with me?"

"I'm very sure. One of the things I loved best about the time we spent together was that often it was just the two of us at home with the fire, your guitar and that angelic voice. What more did we ever need?"

Kate smiled, remembering the idyllic days and passionate nights they'd spent together when she was too young to know that such things didn't come along every day and should be treasured. "Not much."

"I'll need to see Mari and offer the house to her if she wants it. A lot of the things there are hers."

The idea of him seeing his ex-lover struck another chord of fear in Kate. What if he took one look at the exotic dark-haired beauty and regretted his decision to leave her?

"Stop that."

Startled by his firm tone, she said, "Stop what?"

He traced the outline of her mouth with the tip of his index finger. "Stop thinking I'm going to see her and change my mind about you."

"I wasn't thinking that," she said, even as a flush of heat invaded her face, making a liar out of her.

Reid laughed and hugged her tighter. "Sure you weren't, darlin'."

"I can't help that the thought of you with someone else makes me a little crazy."

"How do you think I felt having to read about you with *Bobby* and *Russ* and *Clint*? I wanted to go find each one of them and kill them in the most painful, bloody way possible for daring to lay hands on *my* woman."

Kate's mouth fell open in astonishment as her mild-mannered lover showed his jealous side.

His sexy mouth quivered with amusement. "Didn't know I had murderous tendencies, did you?"

Zeroing in on his sensual lips, Kate shook her head. "I had no idea, and I'm truly shocked. You were always such a kind Southern gentleman."

"There was nothing kind about my thoughts toward the other men in your life."

"I'm sorry if I caused you pain. I never would've wanted that."

"With hindsight, I suppose your relationships with other people—and mine—served to show us where we really belong, so it was all part of a grander plan."

"That's very philosophical."

"It's what I told myself so I wouldn't actually find them and kill them."

Kate threw her head back and laughed. Her laughter became a moan when he took advantage of the opportunity to place kisses on her neck that made her shiver with desire. "Let's go back to bed," she whispered.

"I have a better idea." As he spoke, he gathered her in close to him and stood. He surprised her when he opened the gate that led to the sand.

"Where are we going?"

"You'll see."

The moonlight was like a mirror on the calm water. Kate's senses were filled with the scent of sand and sea and Reid's endlessly appealing cologne. She buried her nose in his neck and breathed him in. It was all she could do not to let out a giddy squeal of delight as he carried her to the beach. She couldn't believe she was finally with him again and apparently got to keep him this time. It was too good to be true.

Under the cover of palm trees, Reid put her down and ran his hands from her shoulders, down her back to her bottom where he lingered for a minute before continuing farther south. He found the hem of her cotton dress and eased it up and over her head, leaving her bare before him.

She could see him just well enough to watch his eyes flare with heat as he cupped her breasts and teased her nipples until they were hard and tingling. "Whatever are you doing, Mr. Matthews?"

"This," he whispered as he ducked his head and took one of the turgid peaks into the heat of his mouth, sucking hard as he pinched the other one between two fingers.

Kate gasped and clutched his head to her chest, wanting him all over again, wanting him forever and always. The warm air on her fevered skin, the fear of being caught naked on the beach, the heat of the sand under her feet and the silk of his hair against her chest overwhelmed her senses. She was about to beg him to lay her down right there and take her when he let go and unbuttoned his shorts.

After he dropped them to the sand, he took her hand. "Come swim with me."

Kate hesitated. Life in the bubble had taught her to be cautious. "What if someone sees us?"

"No one will. We've got this part of the beach all to ourselves. Desi assured me of that." He gave her hand a tug. "Come on."

Kate stepped into the moonlight and let him lead her into water so warm it might've been bath water.

"Doesn't it feel good?" he asked, drawing her against him.

"So good." Kate straddled him and wrapped her arms around his neck.

He tipped her backward to get her hair wet and planted kisses on her throat and chest and in the valley between her breasts. "You look like a goddess with the moonlight on your pale skin." His voice was gruff and his erection throbbed against her. "You've never been more beautiful to me than you are right now."

Kate had never felt more beautiful—or more aroused. She moved suggestively on his lap, drawing a deep groan from him.

"No condom," he said, sounding tortured.

"I don't care." And she didn't. All she cared about was experiencing this moment with him to the fullest, and to do that, she wanted him inside her—now.

"Kate…"

"Please." She reached between them and wrapped her hand around his straining member, stroking him and laughing as he got even harder.

"Witch," he mumbled.

Thrilled with herself—and with him—she guided him home to her. Kate had never made love in the water before and was unprepared for the overwhelming sensuality of him sliding into her as the water surrounded them. She released her hold on his neck and floated, stretching her arms above her head.

Reid took her invitation and bent his head to feast on her breasts.

Looking up at a sky littered with stars as he filled her and teased her, Kate realized this was, without a doubt, the happiest—and most erotic—moment of her life. The thought brought tears to her eyes as he coaxed her to a slow, rolling climax that went on for what felt like forever.

He grasped her hips and pumped into her. "Kate, God, I love you. I missed you so much. I missed you every day."

The tears spilled from her eyes as he made her come again before he withdrew, his penis pulsing against her stomach as he gathered her into his arms.

"I love you, too." Kate clung to him, thrilled and happy and content—and a tiny bit apprehensive about whether they could hang on to the magic once they left their island paradise and ventured back into the real world.

The next morning, Reid reluctantly left Kate sleeping in bed and drove into Basseterre, where he hoped to find Mari at her sister Angelique's house. He was relieved to see Mari's car in the driveway when he parked in front of the small white house where he'd been a frequent visitor in recent months.

They'd had a lot of good times together. He'd never deny that, but he also couldn't deny that his heart had belonged to Kate from the day he met her. He'd spent far too long running from that fact of his life. The twenty-eight years between them weighed as heavily on his conscience as they ever had, but after yearning for her for so long, he wasn't about to let guilt keep them apart.

She was now a fully grown woman in the prime of her life, and she'd said she wanted him, that she'd always wanted him. Since he felt exactly the same way, he wasn't about to try to talk her out of it. No, now he was all about finding a way to make a life with her.

Keeping that goal in mind, he knocked on the door to Mari's sister's house.

Angelique came to the door, frowning when she saw him. She shared exotic dark-haired looks with her sister. "What do you want?"

"I'd like to speak to her. Please."

"She doesn't want to see you."

"I know, but we have a few things we need to work out. Please, Angi, let me in."

"You've broken her heart, you know."

"I'm sorry. I never intended to hurt her, but I also never made her any promises."

"No, you didn't. You just let her think that what you had was going to last forever when you knew it wouldn't."

Reid shook his head. "I didn't know that, Angi—"

"Let me see if she wants to talk to you."

She walked away, leaving Reid on the front porch to wait.

A few minutes later, Mari came to the door, looking tired and sad, which made him sad, too, knowing he'd done that to her. "What are you doing here?"

"We need to talk."

"What's there to talk about? We've said everything we need to say."

"No, we haven't."

She seemed to think about that for a minute before she came outside, closing the inside door behind her. "Let's walk."

Thankful she hadn't slammed the door in his face, Reid went down the stairs ahead of her. In the street, she folded her arms and kept her head down, apparently waiting on him.

"We need to talk about the house."

"It's your place. I'll get my stuff out of there."

"Or you can keep it, if you'd like. I'm making some other plans, so if you don't want the place, I'll let it go."

"What other plans are you making?"

"You really want to know?"

"Sure, why not," she said with a bitter laugh.

"I'm going back to Nashville."

She let out a snort of disbelief. "I thought you said you'd never go back there. You hated it there."

Reid couldn't deny he'd said that, so he didn't. "Things changed."

Mari shook her head in amazement. "All she had to do was crook her finger in your face, and you went running back to her after she broke your heart."

Reid bit back the nasty retort that hovered on the tip of his tongue. "That's not how it happened."

"She didn't break your heart?"

"We both made mistakes that we regret, but we're past that now."

"I know who she is."

"I'm not surprised. She's very well known."

"Is that what attracts you? Her fame and fortune? Her glamorous life?"

"I loved her when she was no one in the business, and I hardly need her money."

"No, I don't suppose you do."

"I'll take care of you, Mari. You won't want for anything."

At that she turned on him, her normally genial brown eyes narrowing in anger. "I won't want for anything? How can you say that? I'll *want* for *you!*"

He immediately regretted his choice of words. "I meant financially."

"Keep your money," she said with a dismissive wave of her hand. "I never cared a fig about that, and you know it."

The only fights they'd had were over his desire to pay for everything.

"I have to say, I had no idea you liked them so young. I must've seemed like an old hag after you'd been with her."

"That's not true! You're a beautiful woman, and I always considered myself lucky to spend time with you."

"But you never fell in love with me."

He shook his head. "I'm sorry. I hate that I've caused you so much pain. I never wanted that."

"If you didn't want to hurt me, maybe you should've thought about how I'd feel about her showing up at our house to stake her claim on you."

"That's not how it happened, and you know it. I had no idea she was coming, and you're the one who left."

"Was I supposed to stick around and watch you pine for her?"

Reid didn't know what to say to that, so he stayed quiet.

"All I know is that two days ago I was living a life I loved with a man I loved, who I thought maybe loved me, though he'd never said so. Now, my whole world has been turned upside down, and I'm supposed to just accept that and go on like it never happened."

"I did love you, Mari. I *do* love you."

"But not the same way you love her."

He rested his hands on his hips and shook his head. "No. I'm sorry."

"Save your apologies. I'm glad we had this conversation. At least I know now what I need to do."

"And what's that?" he asked, slightly undone by malice in her tone. He'd never seen anything remotely like that from her, but he'd also never crushed her before.

"That's none of your business. You lost the right to know that when you chose her over me. Go have your life with your little girl lover. I hope you're very happy together."

Realizing the conversation was over, he said, "Do you want the house?"

"No."

"When would you like to get your things?"

"I'll do it this week."

"Fine."

"Fine."

"Mari—"

"If you say you're sorry again, I'll punch you."

Reid nodded, saddened to end on such an unfriendly note, but he supposed he couldn't blame her. He'd hate him, too, if he were her. "I was just going to say take care of yourself."

"Don't worry, I will."

A sense of unease settled over him as he walked to his car, wondering what she'd meant by that.

Jill emerged from the shower and toweled her hair dry, reliving the day she'd spent with Ashton. He'd produced a gleaming Harley Davidson motorcycle from the garage that Jill had eyed with trepidation.

"I've never been on a motorcycle," she'd said.

"*Never?*"

She shook her head.

"You don't know what you've been missing."

The bike was huge and shiny and daunting. "I'm okay with what I've been missing."

That made him laugh. "Trust me. I've been riding bikes since I was a little kid, and I promise you'll love it."

"Your father let you do all kinds of crazy things when you were a kid."

"I didn't have a mother to tell him not to."

The statement was made in jest, but Jill sensed the pain behind it. He would've liked to have a mother to fret over his safety. What little boy wouldn't?

He held out a helmet to her. "What do you say? Want to take a walk on the wild side?"

"If you're sure we'll be safe."

He tucked her hair behind her ear and caressed her face. "I'd never endanger you. Not when I have so many plans for you."

The softly spoken words did something to her insides, making her all fluttery. In all of her life, Jill Harrington had never been fluttery. Maybe it was about time she was. "Okay."

She couldn't remember ever having more fun than they'd had cruising through Malibu and along the Pacific Coast Highway, stopping for lunch at an out-of-the-way place that he'd been to before and loved. He'd handled the bike like a true expert, and never once had she felt unsafe. Rather, she'd felt exhilarated and free in a way she hadn't often experienced.

Anxious to get back to him after hours snuggled against his back on the bike, she brushed her hair and put it up in a ponytail before dressing in the jeans and tank top she'd bought while they were out. She went downstairs to find him tending to the grill on a deck that overlooked the Pacific. After growing up on the coast, Jill was used to exceptional views, but this was better than most.

Ashton's back was turned, and since he was shirtless, she had an even better view of his broad shoulders and muscular back.

The feelings of exhilaration and freedom from earlier ran through her mind as she stepped outside and clearly surprised him when she rested her hands on his shoulders. Who was this brazen woman who walked up to a man and touched him without being invited to? This was a whole new woman, and Jill rather liked her.

Apparently, he did, too, because his muscles quivered under her hands. She started to withdraw them.

"Don't," he said, softly but harshly. "Don't stop. Touch me."

Emboldened by his reaction, Jill massaged his shoulders.

His head fell forward, and he shuddered. "Feels so good."

"What's for dinner?" she asked, her lips close to his back, so close.

"Shrimp and salad." His voice sounded strained, which made her smile as she kneaded muscles gone tense under her hands.

"Sounds good."

A loud click caught her attention as he turned off the grill.

"Is it done?"

"Yes."

He left the skewers of barbequed shrimp on the grill when he closed the lid and turned, his eyes hot with desire that had Jill taking a step back from the almost predatory look he sent her way. His arm hooked around her waist to keep her from escaping.

"Ashton—"

Whatever she was about to say—and she had no idea what she'd been about to say—was lost when his mouth came down on hers, hard and demanding.

Her arms encircled his neck as he lifted her right off her feet and took her inside. His tongue entered her mouth in questing strokes that made her head spin and her heart pound. She'd never been kissed like this before, and nothing could've prepared her for the overwhelming need that had her pressing against him with increasing urgency.

When he lowered them to the sofa, Jill tightened her hold on his neck.

As he came down on top of her, molding his body to hers, he tipped his head and took the kiss deeper. He propped himself on one elbow and his other hand dipped under her top, pushing her bra out of the way. The heat of his hand on her bare breast seared her.

He tore his lips free and gazed down at her, devouring her with his eyes. "Tell me to stop."

Jill shook her head.

"Are you sure?"

"Yes." She reached for him. "I'm sure."

He pushed her top up and focused his attention on her breasts, licking and sucking and even biting gently as he somehow managed to remove her tank top and bra.

Jill had never experienced anything remotely similar to the all-consuming way he loved her as he kissed his way down the front of her. When he unbuttoned her jeans and tugged at them, she raised her hips to help him get them off.

And then he stopped, resting his forehead on her belly. "I didn't want it to be like this."

Jill combed her fingers through his thick hair. "Like what?"

"Fast and frantic on the sofa. I wanted to take my time and make you come so many times you wouldn't know your own name. And *then* I'd made love to you."

Her heart beat fast as she realized how much thought he'd put into this. "How about we do that next time?"

He gazed up at her. "Yeah?"

She nodded and held out her arms. "Come here."

Ashton shifted up, propping himself on his arms. "I'm here."

"Closer."

Smiling, he lowered himself, bringing his chest into contact with hers. The coarse hair rubbed against her straining nipples, making her crazy. She ran her hands down his back to dip them into his shorts.

"Jill." This was said through gritted teeth as he pressed his erection against her belly.

She curled her legs around his hips to better align them and moved one of her hands to the front of his shorts.

He dropped his head to her shoulder and seemed to freeze as he waited for her next move.

Jill decided to prolong the pleasure by skimming her fingers over his lower belly in teasing strokes that made him groan.

"Do you want me to beg?"

"I think I do. Yes."

Half laughing, half groaning, he thrust his hips in an effort to get what he wanted. "I'm begging."

Jill decided to have mercy on him and wrapped her hand around his straining member. Her mouth went dry as she learned his length and width by stroking him slowly.

"Jesus," he whispered. "You're going to finish me right off like a horny teenager."

Jill laughed at the torture she heard in his voice. "Would that be so bad?"

"Yes, it would be bad. You'll always remember that I ruined our first time together."

"You're not ruining anything." To prove her point, she tightened her hand around him and stroked him harder, taking the choice away from him.

He pumped his hips, matching the rhythm of her hand. "*Jill…*"

She turned her head and kissed him, giving him her tongue in gentle strokes that were in sharp contrast to what she was doing to him with her hand. She'd never been so brazen or forward with a man and discovered she quite liked the reactions she was drawing from him.

The arm he was resting on trembled with the effort to hold himself up as she kissed and stroked him to an explosive finish. He cried out as he spilled into her hand. By the time he'd recovered from the powerful release, she'd freed him from his shorts.

"Condom," he said. "Need one."

"Where are they?"

"Bathroom. Upstairs."

"Let me up."

"I can do it. Just give me a minute."

"Take your minute while I get what we need."

"Okay." He raised himself up and off her.

Jill got up and headed for the stairs, trying not to think about the fact that he was probably watching her naked ass as she left the room. She found an unopened box of condoms in the master bathroom closet. The fact that it was unopened made her happy, for some strange reason. The idea of him spending time here with another woman didn't sit well with her.

"You're already turning into a jealous fool," she whispered to herself, avoiding the mirror while she was in the bathroom.

Ashton was face down on his belly when she returned, and she wondered if he was asleep. She took a moment to appreciate his fine form, the muscular arms and shoulders, the narrow waist and perfectly rounded rear. He was an incredibly sexy man, and all his attention was focused on her—for now, anyway.

With that in mind, she straddled him, pressing the heat between her legs to his bottom as she ran her hands over his back.

His mumbled, "Mmmm," told her he was fully awake and enjoying what she was doing. "I want to turn over."

"In a minute." She dropped a trail of kisses down his backbone, pausing as she hovered over his ass before she took a gentle bite of one perfect cheek.

"That's it! Let me up!"

His reaction startled her as she lifted to let him turn over. "Condom." He held out his hand.

Jill avoided his hand and tore open the box, taking one out and removing the foil wrapper.

"Jill…"

"Don't be so bossy, Counselor." She smiled at the look of torture on his face as she took her time rolling the condom over his erection. "There," she said when the condom was in place.

He surged up, his fingers digging into her hips as he lifted her and headed for the stairs.

Jill let out a squeal of surprise. She gripped his neck when he ran up the stairs as if carrying her was no big deal. His strength was a huge turn-on, as if she could be any more turned on. "Where are we going?"

"I want a bed for this."

She worried that she'd pushed him too far and would pay for her sins once he got them to a horizontal surface.

In the master bedroom, he remained standing when he lowered her onto the bed and tugged at her hips until she was at the very edge of the mattress. "Did you enjoy making me crazy?" he asked, hovering over her.

Nodding, Jill raised her hands to his face, caressing his smooth jaw. "I really did."

"I could tell." He pressed his erection against her, retreating before she could align him to where she wanted him most. "Revenge is a bitch."

"I've heard that, but you wouldn't be mean to me, would you?"

His smile softened his expression considerably. "Don't try to charm your way out of this." He slid into her slowly, torturously.

Jill raised her hips, trying to urge him to hurry, but he wouldn't be rushed.

He withdrew from her, making her moan. "Patience, my love," he whispered as he kissed her belly.

His words made her heart flutter. Did he mean that? Was she his love? Did she want to be? The press of his tongue between her legs required her full attention, driving the internal debate from her mind. He exacted his revenge one lick and suck at a time, driving her up to the very edge of orgasm before backing off and doing it all again.

"Ashton..." She twisted her hips, trying to get free of him, but he'd anticipated that by laying a heavy arm across her midsection to anchor her to the bed.

"Tell me what you want," he said, sliding two of the fingers on his other hand into her.

"I want to come."

"How badly?"

"Really badly."

"Is that so?"

She moaned, frustrated and aroused beyond endurance. "Please..."

"Since you asked so nicely..." He closed his lips around her pulsating clitoris and sucked it into his mouth, running his tongue over her heated flesh and sending her into a climax that seemed to come from the very tips of her toes. She felt the effects everywhere, from the palms of her hands to the souls of her feet and the tingling of her scalp.

She came back down from the incredible ride to find him perched above her, looking down at her reverently.

"You're so beautiful." He brushed the hair back from her brow and then kissed her forehead, nose and lips. "So incredibly beautiful. Your eyes aren't quite blue, and they're not really gray. They're a different color every time I look at them." With his hand on her thigh, he wrapped one of her legs around his hips.

Moved by his words, Jill waited to see what he would do.

His next move was to thrust halfway into her before withdrawing again.

Moaning, Jill said, "I think I've been properly punished."

"I haven't begun to punish you." On the next thrust, he entered her fully but then withdrew, leaving her wanting much more.

He bent his head to draw her nipple into his mouth, sucking hard enough to cause painful pleasure. Under her, his big hands shaped her bottom, squeezing and kneading her cheeks as he surged into her again.

This time Jill was ready for him and tightened her leg around his waist to keep him from escaping. She felt him grow impossibly larger inside her and was thrilled to know she'd done that to him.

"Let me move," he said, his voice sounding taut with strain.

"Do you promise no more teasing?"

"For now."

She let her leg drop to the bed, which seemed to trigger something fierce in him.

With his feet still planted firmly on the floor, he pounded into her, gripping her bottom so tightly she had no doubt there'd be bruises. She came twice, one right on top of the other, and still he kept up the fierce possession. This, she r ealized in a single moment of coherent thought, was what she got for taking the edge off for him earlier.

He surprised her when he suddenly slowed the pace, gathering her close and kissing her softly and reverently as he moved inside her. "So good," he whispered between sweet kisses. "I knew it would be. I knew it."

"You gave this a lot of thought."

"If you had any idea how much, you'd think there was something wrong with me."

Knowing he'd wanted her so much for so long gave her heart a happy lurch that scared her. She was falling for him. To be honest, she'd been falling for him for a long time now, and to know he felt the same was exciting and little frightening, too.

"Why did you just get all worried?" he asked as he continued to move slowly.

"I didn't."

"Yes, you did." He placed a kiss on the furrow between her brows, which was how Jill realized she'd furrowed her brows. "Talk to me. What're you thinking?"

She hugged his hips with her legs. "You want to talk *now*?"

"I'm a master multitasker." He flexed his hips and made sure his chest hair abraded her nipples, both of which drew a gasp from her. "See?"

His delighted smile drew one from her, too. "I never doubted your skill for a minute."

"Something made you unhappy. Since I'm inside you at the moment, you're giving me self-confidence issues."

"You haven't lacked for self-confidence a single second in your whole life."

"I am right now. What is it, honey? Tell me."

Those words said in that accent in this moment made her melt. "I, um, I'm a little frightened by this."

"By *me*?"

She shook her head. "Not by you. By *us*. It's happened so fast."

"It hasn't been fast. It's taken forever by my count. That's how long it's been since I first wanted you. Every day, minute and second since the day I met you." As he said the words, he picked up the pace again, holding her tight against him as he made passionate love to her.

It didn't take much effort on his part to take her up again, impossibly higher this time because he joined her, thrusting into her with a cry that seemed to come from his very soul.

Jill held on as tight to him as he held her.

"So damned good," he whispered many minutes later.

"Yes."

"Don't be afraid. I waited so long for you. I have no plans to let you go."

As far as assurances went, Jill thought, it didn't get much better than that.

CHAPTER 7

Reid and Kate spent the next few days at the resort. They talked about venturing out so Reid could show her around the island and so they could find another place to call home when they were on St. Kitts. In the end, however, they ended up spending most of their time taking long walks on the beach, spending leisurely afternoons in bed and talking.

They talked nonstop.

At one point, Kate joked that they were attempting to relive every minute they had spent apart by sharing those minutes with each other. By the end of the third day, after Reid convinced her to skinny dip and make love in broad daylight, Kate was as relaxed as she could remember being since she left home as a naïve eighteen-year-old ready to conquer the world.

Other than a few cryptic texts from Jill, Kate hadn't had any contact with the outside world in days, which was fine with her.

She emerged from the shower to find Reid waiting for her in bed.

He held out a hand to her.

Kate dropped the towel and slid in next to him. "This week has been amazing," she said when he had settled her into his embrace.

"For me, too." He traced a finger under her eye. "The dark circles are starting to fade."

"Despite all your attempts to disturb my sleep, I'm as well rested as I've been in ages."

"Good," he said with a chuckle. "Then I can keep you up nice and late tonight."

"Could I ask you something?"

"There's still something you haven't asked me?"

"Uh-huh."

"Go right ahead, darlin'. I'm an open book where you're concerned."

"What happened when you went to see Mari the other day?" He hadn't said anything about the visit with his ex-girlfriend, and Kate couldn't help but be curious about what had transpired.

His deep sigh answered the question.

"You don't have to tell me if you don't want to."

"I don't mind telling you." His fingers spooled through her damp hair, loosening tangles she hadn't bothered to comb out. "She was angry."

Kate had so many questions, but she forced herself to stay quiet and let him talk.

"I can't say I blame her," he said after a long silence. "She deserved better than what she got from me. We were together one minute, and the next it was... over."

"I asked Buddy not to tell you I was coming. I wanted to see how you'd react to me after all this time had gone by."

"When I saw you there on the beach, I thought I was hallucinating. I'd been thinking about you a few minutes earlier, and then there you were."

"You were thinking about me?"

"Honey," he said with a laugh, "I always thought about you. I never stopped."

"Neither did I."

"Which is why I had no business being with Mari. It wasn't fair to make a life with her when my heart was engaged elsewhere."

"How did you meet her?"

"Through mutual friends. By then I'd been alone for nine years, and I was starting to get tired of myself. Heck of a reason to start a relationship, huh?"

"You were alone for longer than that before you met me."

"I was never lonely then, because I had Ashton to think about and a company to run. After you, I was lonely."

Kate ached at the pain she heard in his voice, knowing she'd caused some of it. "So it was better after you started seeing Mari?"

"That's the kicker. It wasn't really. Don't get me wrong, I enjoyed the time I spent with her, but I was still lonely."

Kate tipped her head back so she could see his face. "Why?"

"Because she wasn't you."

"Reid—"

He rested a finger on her lips to quiet her. "It may sound trite, and I wouldn't blame you for accusing me of feeding you lines, telling you what you want to hear. But the truth is that since we've been back together... It's the first time I haven't felt lonely since I lost you."

Filled with remorse over what they'd both lost so long ago, Kate blinked back tears.

"Don't cry, darlin'. Things happen the way they're meant to. Who knows if we could've held it together back then? Maybe you needed the last ten years to get your career off the ground. I probably wouldn't have fit into that, you know?"

"Maybe."

"The age difference was a bigger deal then, too."

"To other people, but not to us."

"You know I was never comfortable with it. I still worry about what you might miss out on being with me."

"I've had a long time to find out how it feels to be without you, and I didn't like it."

"Have you thought about what your daddy will have to say about us being back together?"

"Some, but he knows I'm a grown woman now. I make my own decisions. I hope he'll respect the fact that I choose you."

"Are you prepared for the possibility that he won't?"

A flurry of nerves attacked her stomach when she thought of telling her dad she was back with Reid.

He raised a brow. "Darlin'?"

"I won't deny that I'm nervous about telling him, but no matter how he reacts, it won't change how I feel about you."

"And how is that?" he asked with a playful smile.

"Why tell when I can show?" She raised herself up and started with kisses to his chest, working her way down in slow increments designed to make him as crazy as he made her.

"When do you have to go home?" Jill asked Ashton in the middle of the night, nearly a week after they arrived in Malibu. The time with him had been incredible, and the thought of having to go back to her regular life made Jill want to cry.

"Why? Are you anxious to be rid of me?"

"Quite the opposite."

"Oh, so my devious plan has worked?"

"What devious plan is that?"

"To make myself essential to you. I'd given it ten days, but if we got it done in seven, I won't complain."

Jill moved so she was on top of him and smiled when his arms came around her, as she'd known they would. "It only took two days, but don't let that go to your head."

"Too late." He kissed her forehead and squeezed her tighter. "We'll go back to Nashville on Sunday, if that's okay with you."

"Fine by me."

"When will you head back out on the road?"

"Not until after the first of the year, at the earliest."

"Really? So we'll have *months* together in town?"

"If that's what you want," she said, purposely nonchalant, hoping to get a rise out of him.

"Hell yes, that's what I want. Haven't I done a good enough job of showing you what I want?" To make his point, he squeezed her bottom.

"If you'd done the job any better, I might never walk again," she said dryly, drawing a guffaw of laughter from him.

"What about what you want, sweetheart? Is this it? Am I it?"

"Yes. Of course I want this." She raised her head and kissed him. "I want you."

"That's good to know, because you've got me falling head over heels in love with you. I hope you know that."

Jill stared at him, utterly astounded.

"Too soon?" he asked with a wince.

"No. Not too soon."

"Then what?"

"I just… I can't believe everything that's happened this week."

"Does that mean you might, you know, be a little head over heels with me, too?"

"I—"

Her reply was cut off by the ringing of his cell phone to the tune of "Can't Take That Back," one of Buddy's biggest hits. "Goddamn it. That's Buddy. I have to take it. He wouldn't bother me this week unless he really needed to."

Amused by his dismay, Jill slid off him so he could retrieve his phone.

"This had better be good," Ashton said into the phone, smiling at her as he stood in the middle of the room in all his glory, looking better than any man had a right to look.

Jill propped herself up on one arm to take full advantage of the view, which was how she saw his smile fade.

"You gotta be freaking kidding me. What the hell were they thinking?"

Concerned about what he was hearing, Jill sat up and tucked the sheet over her bare breasts.

Ashton began to pace the room as he listened to Buddy.

Filled with anxiety, Jill wanted to go back in time to before the phone rang.

"Yeah, I'll do what I can, but with something like this, once it gets out, it's hard to contain it." He paused before he added, "I'll get in touch with Jill to let her know." Another pause ramped up Jill's already out-of-control apprehension even further. "Right. I'll call you later. No, I'll be home tomorrow. See you." He slammed his phone onto the table, making her start. "*Fan*-fucking-*tastic*."

"What is it?"

"My dad, your sister, frolicking nude in St. Kitts. Caught on film. Apparently, it's all over the Internet already."

Kate perused the listing for the house in the Cockleshell Bay area, overlooking the island of Nevis across the narrow channel that separated the two islands. "What do we need with four bedrooms?"

"It's not about the bedrooms," Reid said. "It's about the location." He reached for her hand and tugged her down the walkway toward the house.

Her cell phone rang, but Kate ignored it, anxious to see the house. She reached into her pocket to put the ringer on mute.

The real estate agent led them through an open, airy space that called to Kate at once. "This is the best one yet."

"I agree," he said, squeezing her hand.

"You're Kate Harrington, the singer, aren't you?" the agent asked.

"Yes, I am."

The agent smiled. "I saw you on the Internet."

People usually said they'd heard her on the radio. "Oh, right. Well... "

"About the house," Reid said. "How soon is it available?"

"At the end of the month. Would you like to see the rest?"

"Sure." Reid put his arm around Kate. "We'll wander." They checked out the three bedrooms and bathroom on the lower level before walking up the stairs where the living room, kitchen and dining area were one big room that overlooked the water.

He led her onto the spacious deck. "What do you think? Would this do as a home away from home?"

"I was thinking," Kate said as she leaned on the rail to watch a sailboat head toward Nevis. "What if we made Nashville our home away from home and this was our primary residence?"

"You'd want to be here more often than there?"

"I think I might. Could we bring Thunder here?"

"I suppose we could, but he's getting on in years. He might be happier in his own home."

"That's true."

"We can be here as often as you're able to be, and when you're ready to quit touring, it'll be here waiting for us."

"I still have trouble believing we're going to make this happen. That all I had to do was come here to find you."

"Apparently, I was waiting for you and didn't even know it."

"Should we look at the other two places?"

"It's up to you. If you're happy, I'm happy."

"We probably ought to check out the master bedroom," she said with a coy smile.

"Lead the way."

The master shared the deck with the living room. Kate went through the sliding door into a large room with a thatched-roof ceiling. "Oh, look!" she said, looking up at the ceiling. "That's so cool!"

"You'll feel like you're sleeping in a hut on the beach."

"I love it." She went into the bathroom that was even nicer than the one at the resort. It had glass tile and basin sinks that sat on top of a teak countertop. The shower walls featured the same green, blue and white glass tiles. "This is gorgeous."

"I agree, and we'd have plenty of room for guests if your sisters or family want to come down."

"Do you think Ashton would visit if I'm here?"

"Hopefully."

Kate turned to him. "Would it hurt you if he didn't?"

"Don't worry about him. I'll see him, even if I have to do it on my own. I'd never allow another breach to form between us."

"I wouldn't want to be the cause of that."

"Let's not worry about him for now. Let's focus on what we want, and then I'll do my best to sell it to him. Okay?"

"Okay." Kate returned to the deck for another look at the view.

Reid followed her, slipping his arm around her waist.

The agent came out to join them a few minutes later. "What do you think?"

"We love it," Kate said. "I was wondering, though, are the owners interested in selling?"

"I could certainly check with them. Let me give them a call."

After she walked away, Reid glanced down at her, grinning. "You're full of surprises, darlin'."

She shrugged. "If we're going to put down roots, I say we go all the way."

"Only if we can go all the way together."

"You know that's my favorite way to go," she said with a chuckle.

He laughed. "I mean financially, you crazy girl."

"You'd want to buy it together?"

"I'd prefer to buy it for you, but I suspect you wouldn't go for that."

"You suspect correctly."

"I had a feeling…"

The agent came back outside. "You're in luck. The owners are willing to entertain an offer."

Kate glanced at Reid. "What do you think, Mr. Matthews? Should we make an offer?"

"By all means, Ms. Harrington."

An hour later, their offer had been accepted, and they were the proud future owners of a beach house in St. Kitts.

"That was a little too easy," Kate said as they drove away in his convertible. With the top down, the wind rushed through her hair. Kate raised her hands above her head and let out a giddy squeal.

Chuckling, Reid rested a hand on her thigh and squeezed. "Happy, darlin'?"

"Very, very happy."

"That's how I like you best."

His phone rang, and he drew it out of his shirt pocket to hand it to her. "See who it is."

Kate took the phone and glanced at the caller ID. "Ashton. Want to take it?"

"Not now. I'll call him later."

That was when Kate remembered the call she'd ignored earlier. She retrieved her phone and found six calls from Jill, two from her father and one from Maggie. "Oh God. What's going on?" Memories of the day Maggie had fallen off the ladder came rushing back, reminding her of how things could change in a heartbeat. Her hands shook as she called Jill.

"Thank goodness you called," Jill said.

"What's wrong? You called six times, and Dad and Maggie…"

"Oh, great. So they know, too."

"Know *what*?"

"Are you sitting down, Kate?"

Reid reached for Kate's hand, and she held on tight to him as she braced herself for what she was about to hear. "Just tell me, Jill."

"There's a video on the Internet. You and Reid, naked…"

Kate felt the blood drain from her head, taking all her thoughts with it. Surely, she'd heard her sister wrong. There was no way…

"Kate? Are you there?"

"Did… Did you see it?"

"Yes."

"And you can tell it's me?"

"Yes."

"Oh my God!"

"What, Kate?" Reid asked. "What's wrong?"

Kate tuned him out for the moment to focus on the conversation with Jill. "I… What should I do?"

"I'm heading home later today. When I get back to the office, I'll see what I can do about a cease-and-desist order, but I have to warn you. The damage is already done. All the entertainment websites are all talking about your sex video going viral. It's already a huge story."

Suddenly nauseated, Kate said, "Pull over. Please stop the car."

Reid brought the car to a stop by the side of the road.

Kate bolted from the car and bent in half, sucking in deep gulps of humid air that didn't do much to alleviate the nausea. She felt Reid's hand on her back and could hear Jill calling her name through the phone.

"Yes," Kate said to her sister after a minute. "I'm here."

"Are you okay?"

"Sure, I'm great. The whole world is watching me have sex. Other than that, I'm fine."

Reid's sharp gasp made her feel bad for letting him hear it that way, but was there any way to sugarcoat news like this?

"I'll do what I can on my end."

"Oh my God. Dad called. And Maggie. I'm going to be sick."

"Is Reid with you?" Jill asked.

"Yes," Kate whispered.

"You two need to stay off the radar and let the story die down. In a couple of days, something else will happen and people will forget about this."

"No, they won't. They'll never forget."

"Hang in there. I'll call you as soon as I know anything else."

"Okay." Kate clicked off the phone and stood upright, still not sure if she was going to be sick or not. "Someone filmed us. In the water."

"God, Kate, I'm so sorry. That beach is totally secluded. No one even knows you're here."

"That's not entirely true."

"What do you mean?"

"People at the hotel know. Your friend Mari knows. My pilot knows, not that he would tell anyone. People know."

"Mari would never tell anyone."

"You're sure about that? She's rather pissed at you at the moment and no doubt feeling vindictive toward me. Why wouldn't she tell people that the famous singer stole her man? It's right out of a bad country song. Maybe I should write that song." Kate could feel herself descending toward hysteria but couldn't seem to pull out of the free fall. "Wonder how much they made on their little movie. Millions probably."

Reid tried to put his arms around her, but she turned away from him. "Kate, honey…"

"Don't. Please don't. I can't right now." When she was certain she wasn't going to vomit, she got back in the car.

"Where do you want to go?" he asked.

"Do you have a computer at your place?"

"Kate—"

"I want to see it. I want to see what the rest of the world is seeing. What my parents and sisters are seeing."

"You're sure that's a good idea?"

"Yes, I'm sure."

He sighed deeply but started the car and pulled onto the road. About twenty minutes later, he cut the engine in front of his house and got out of the car without another word to her.

Kate followed him inside.

"The computer is in there," he said, pointing to a room off the main living area.

"Don't you want to see it?"

"I was there. I know what happened."

Kate wished she could be so detached, but of course he wasn't the public figure facing a nightmare of bad publicity in the coming days and weeks.

On wooden legs that trembled beneath her, Kate found the computer and slid into the chair. Her hands shook when she fired up the browser and typed her name into the search bar. "Oh my God," she whispered when she scanned the first page of results, full of the words "Sex Tape."

She clicked on one of the links and watched Reid cajole her into swimming naked in broad daylight. Her face was easily recognizable as she watched herself glance around at the desolate stretch of beach, filled with trepidation while he talked her out of her bikini top and tugged her by the hand into the water.

If there was any silver lining, unlike the first time they'd skinny-dipped in the dark, she'd left the suit bottoms on so the whole world didn't get to watch her bare ass walking toward the water. At this point, he was still clothed, too, but that didn't last long once they were in the water and wrapped up in each other.

There'd be no doubt in anyone's mind what they were doing in the water. At one point, she'd floated on her back to let him feast on breasts that bobbed above the surface of the water. If it hadn't been out there for the world to see, Kate would've found the video intensely erotic. Now, of course, it was intensely embarrassing.

The camera had caught every nuance of their private interlude, right down to the explosive finish, and Kate had never felt more violated. All the allegations of drug abuse had nothing on this, she thought as she closed the browser and slumped down in the chair to stare out at the water.

All she could think about was her parents seeing that and how they would feel. That thought finally broke the dam, and she began to sob.

Reid stepped into the room and tugged her from the chair. "Come here, honey." He wrapped his arms around her and held her tight against him. "Shh. Don't cry. I'm so sorry I put you in this position. I'm so sorry."

She wanted to tell him she didn't blame him. No, she blamed herself. She was the famous one who'd taken an awful risk with a reputation that had already taken a beating. However, she couldn't find the energy to say the words. Rather, she closed her eyes and sank into his embrace, hungry for his comfort in the storm.

On the flight home, Jill worked the phone, calling in every favor she'd accumulated since she'd been Kate's attorney and manager. After an hour, though, it became clear that all the favors in the world couldn't put the genie back in the bottle.

Anxiety pooled in her chest, making her wonder if she was having a heart attack at twenty-five-thousand feet.

Ashton reached over to place his hand on top of hers. "Take a break, baby. You've done all you can."

"I've done nothing. That video is still out there for all the world to see."

"That's not your fault. It's hers. It's *theirs*. They did this, not you."

"My job is to protect her, and I can't protect her from this."

"And that kills you. I know. But she took a foolish risk by cavorting in broad daylight, and by now she ought to know better."

Jill pulled her hand free of his. "If you're going to kick her when she's down, I don't want to hear it."

"I'm not kicking her. I swear I'm not. I'm only stating the obvious. She should've known better. They both should've."

"You're right," Jill said. "I'm sorry."

"No need to apologize for being upset, darlin'. When I get my hands on my father, I may have to punch him for this."

"Like you said, what's done is done. No point in coming to blows over it."

"He should've protected her better than he did."

"I'm sure he's beating himself up more than any of us ever could."

"Probably," Ashton conceded. "Whatever I may think of the two of them together, he was wrecked by what happened with her."

"For what it's worth, so was she."

"So I suppose after all those years of yearning for each other, they weren't exactly thinking with their brains."

That drew the first hint of a smile from Jill since the call from Buddy.

"We can relate, right?" he asked with that charming grin that sent a rush of desire zipping through her veins. Once again, he took hold of her hand, but this time he brought it to his lips.

"Yes."

He waggled his brows. "Want to join the Mile High Club?"

Jill stared at him, aghast. "Are you out of your mind?"

"Nope." He turned her hand to focus his attention on the inside of her wrist, where her pounding pulse gave away her true feelings on the matter.

"Who would fly the plane?"

"The autopilot," he said, gesturing to the dashboard. "That's who's flying it now."

"No. Absolutely not. N-O."

"You're no fun at all."

"I believe I've provided adequate proof to the contrary over the last few days."

"I love when you get all lawyerly with me. Makes me hot."

"Everything makes you hot."

"Not everything. Only you." Giving her hand a gentle tug, he pulled her over for a kiss.

Jill marveled at how he'd managed to diffuse her anxiety and take her mind off her sister's mess. She closed her eyes and fell into the kiss.

"Holy shit," he said a few minutes later when he finally pulled back from her. "For a girl who said no so forcefully a few minutes ago, that was kinda mean."

"How do you figure?"

He rested her hand over the bulge between his legs. "That's how I figure."

"That feels like it might be uncomfortable," Jill said, pushing down gently as she moved her fingers over his length.

Ashton sucked in a breath.

"Oh, sorry." Jill started to pull her hand back, but he put his hand over hers.

"Don't stop."

"Ashton…"

"It's fine. I promise we won't crash."

The sky stretched before them, vast and blue and littered with puffy white clouds. They were completely alone as the plane hurtled through space and time, infusing Jill with an unusual sense of daring as she tugged on the button to his jeans and unzipped him, drawing a hiss from him as the zipper traveled over his erection.

She released her own seat belt and turned in the seat.

His eyes went wide when he realized her intent. "Jill…"

"Hmm?"

"What're you doing?"

He'd driven her crazy more than once over the last few days, teasing her into an orgasmic frenzy until she was practically catatonic in the aftermath. Paying him back would be fun.

"This," she said, bending to tease the tip of his very hard penis with her tongue.

"Shit," he muttered, gasping. He fumbled around the far side of the seat and pushed it back a few inches, giving Jill the room she needed to maneuver.

The armrest poked her in the ribs, but she ignored that to focus on him. "Pay attention to the plane," she said, making sure her lips vibrated against his sensitive skin.

"Ah, yeah. Sure. That's all I'm thinking about."

She smiled and took him into her mouth, using her tongue and lips to maximum effect.

His fingers sank into her hair, tight enough to cause pain, not that she minded. Knowing he wanted her so badly was a huge turn-on.

The plane hit a bump of turbulence, forcing him deeper into her mouth and making him moan. "God, that's hot," he whispered.

"Mmm," she said against his shaft as she stroked him with her hand and lips.

"Maybe you ought to stop."

The note of warning wasn't lost on her as she continued to tease him with her tongue, adding a tiny bit of suction.

"Jill, baby...stop. *Stop.*"

Not in the mood to do what she was told, Jill continued until he was coming into her throat, both hands clutching her hair.

"Wow," he said, his chest rising and falling rapidly. "You're full of surprises."

"It's not fun being predictable all the time." He'd put her in touch with a lighter, playful side to herself that she hadn't known existed before him.

"Come here."

She inched closer to him and his appealing scent as his arms encircled her.

"I'm crazy about you," he whispered against her ear, making her shiver with desire and excitement at the promise in his words.

"I seem to have the same problem."

"That's convenient," he said with a laugh.

Jill pulled back from him so she could see his handsome face. "I have a feeling it's going to be completely inconvenient."

"Maybe so, but it'll be awfully fun, too."

"It already is."

With his hands on her face, he smoothed his thumbs over the fragile skin under her eyes. "You look rested and relaxed. I know this thing with Kate is upsetting, but I don't want you to make yourself sick trying to make it right for her. You got me?"

Jill smiled at him, appreciating the concern behind his words. "Yeah, yeah." She glanced down at his lap. "Need some help putting that away?"

"Ah, no, that's all right. You've done more than enough."

Laughing, Jill sat back in her seat, feeling quite pleased with herself. She'd shown him.

CHAPTER 8

Whenever something went wrong in his life, Jack Harrington went for a run. Usually the exercise helped to calm him, which led to a solution to whatever was bothering him. Some things, however, couldn't be pounded out on the pavement of Newport's famous Ten Mile Ocean Drive. Tormenting questions kept cycling through his mind. Primary among them: What the hell was Kate doing back with Reid Matthews? And how could they have been so stupid as to be caught having sex in broad daylight?

It had been a very long time since he'd experienced the sick feeling in his stomach that had been with him from the minute he'd first heard about the video. In the ten years since his ex-wife, Clare, had recovered from her coma and they'd survived the trauma of their divorce to move on with new spouses, life had been relatively calm and quiet—well, as quiet as it could be for a father of six children who ranged in age from twenty-nine to ten. He much preferred calm and quiet to turbulent.

But as he'd learned from the past, life could turn on a dime and lay down a new challenge when you least expected it. In the decade that his middle daughter had been a music-industry sensation, Jack had learned to live with the rumors and the innuendo that seemed to follow her. Kate often assured him that the rumors were part of being a celebrity in a twenty-four-hour news cycle that was always hungry for the next big scandal. She'd told him time and again that he had nothing to worry about where she was concerned. She liked to joke that if the gossipmongers had any idea how boring her life really was, they'd be extremely disappointed.

Well, he thought as he jogged through the dark, Kate had certainly given them something to talk about this time. And since there was no refuting the fact that it was actually her on the video, he doubted the gossips were disappointed. Not that he'd looked. He couldn't bring himself to do that. But his youngest daughter Maggie had told him it was indeed Kate, and Maggie had confirmed with Jill that Kate was indeed with Reid—a former friend of his who Kate had taken up with after she moved to Nashville.

He'd tried to call Jill to get her take on the situation, but Jill's phone had gone straight to voice mail. No doubt she was overwhelmed trying to deal with the mess Kate had made.

As he ran the length of the beach near his home, he told himself Kate was twenty-eight years old. No longer a child, no longer his responsibility. However, he could tell himself that over and over again, but no matter how far she traveled or how famous she might be, she'd always be his little girl. And the thought of her in pain, even if it was pain of her own making, caused him pain, too.

He arrived home a short time later and braced himself to put on a brave face for Andi and their three sons. Determined to keep his torment private, Jack came in through the mudroom and was surprised to find only one light burning over the stove in the kitchen and Andi waiting for him at the kitchen table with a bottle of wine.

"Hey," she said with the sexy smile that could still turn him to putty after more than twelve years together. "You were gone a long time. That's usually a sign of trouble."

He smiled because how could he not? She knew him so well. Better than anyone ever had. Sometimes he felt like she knew him better than he knew himself, which should've frightened him but didn't. He was in very good hands with her by his side.

"Sorry to worry you."

"I knew this news would hit you hard for more reasons than one."

Jack shrugged and ran his fingers through damp hair that would probably be even grayer by morning. He credited his six children with turning him prematurely gray.

"Come sit with me," Andi said. "Have some wine. Talk it out. Let me help."

Everything in him was drawn to her and her generous offer. "Where're the boys?"

"If they know what's good for them, the twins are taking showers, and Eric is finishing his homework. He was upset earlier. Read about it on Twitter, I guess. He's preparing himself for some razzing at school tomorrow."

"That's just great." Jack cringed at the idea of their seventeen-year-old son watching his sister have sex online. "Tell me he didn't look at it."

"He said he didn't want to know."

"I suppose that's one bit of good news."

"Clare called earlier, too. She's anxious to speak with you."

"I'll call her in the morning," he said as he dropped into a chair at the table.

Andi reached for his hand. "Talk to me, Jack. It might help to air it out."

"What's there to say? She's back with him and getting busy in broad daylight where anyone can see."

"I had a feeling that her being back with him would be the worst part for you."

"What is she thinking? She could have *any guy* she wanted. *Why him?*"

"Think about what you just said."

"Which part?"

"About her having any guy she wants."

Jack focused on the comfort of her hand wrapped around his. Being close to her always calmed him. "I can't get my head around that. I never could." He'd introduced her to his college friend when she first moved to Nashville, hoping Reid would "keep an eye" on his eighteen-year-old daughter as she tried to break into the business.

Reid had done a lot more than that, and the resulting rift between Jack and Kate had taken a long time to heal. If Jack were being truthful, things between them had never been the same since the day he caught Kate and Reid together and cut off all ties with his daughter. They'd made up long ago, but still … It was different.

"It's been a long time, Jack. Whatever they had between them is apparently still there. It seems to me that she's with the guy she wants."

"How can she want someone my age? *How?*"

"I don't know, honey, but why does anyone want anyone? Why do you want me?"

He rolled his eyes at her. "Look at you." Her thick dark curls fell over her shoulders, and her soft, brown eyes looked at him with love, always with love. "You're gorgeous and sweet and funny and… You're you, and I love you. I couldn't live without you."

She smiled as she always did when he professed his undying love for her. "Maybe it's possible that Kate feels the same way about Reid?"

Even though what she said made all kinds of sense, Jack shook his head. "That was over ages ago."

"I don't think it was."

"Why do you say that? Do you know something I don't know?"

"Of course not. I learned my lesson a long time ago on that front. I don't keep things from you. I promise. But when you think about the other guys she's been with over the years, there was never any spark."

He also couldn't deny that was true. "So all this time she's been carrying the torch for him?"

"It's very possible, and I think you need to accept that she's chosen to be with him, even if he's not what *you* would've chosen for her."

Jack drummed the fingers of his free hand on the table as he thought about what she'd said. "Am I supposed to welcome him into the family and act like I don't feel betrayed by the fact that he once seduced my young daughter and now he's failed to protect her from this latest situation?"

"She's equally culpable in the video debacle, Jack. If anything, she's more culpable."

"How do you figure?"

"After a decade in the spotlight, she certainly knows better than to do anything to feed the gossip machine—she knows better than he would how vulnerable she is as a celebrity. This was a huge mistake in judgment that she's paying for dearly."

"When you put it that way, it's very difficult for me to hate him as much as I'd like to."

Andi's soft laughter went a long way toward warming the chill that had invaded him earlier when he'd heard about the video. She stood and tugged on his hand. "Come with me."

"Where're we going?"

"Upstairs." She handed him the bottle of wine and took the glasses as she headed for the stairs. "Did you lock up when you came in?"

"Yep."

Inside their room, she took the wine bottle from him and nudged him toward the shower. "Take a long, hot one. You'll feel better after."

"Will you be waiting for me when I'm done?"

"You bet. I'm going to check on the boys, but I'll be right back."

When he emerged from the shower fifteen minutes later, she'd lit the fireplace in their room and poured them both a glass of chardonnay. He knotted a towel around his hips and went to join her in the seating area in front of the fire.

"Everyone in bed?"

"Almost. As always, Johnny was asleep the minute his head hit the pillow, and as always, Robby is fighting it."

"You'd better not let them hear you calling them by their 'baby' names."

"I know! But I can't get used to calling them *John* and *Rob*. That sounds so wrong."

"I know," he said with a chuckle. It had been hard for him, too, but their little boys were ten now and not babies anymore. "How about Eric?"

"Wresting with geometry, but he appears to be winning. I told him to get to bed at a reasonable hour."

"Which he will. He's a good boy."

"Yes, he is," she said, smiling. "He's a lot like his dad that way."

Jack loved when she referred to him as Eric's dad. He'd adopted the boy shortly after they were married and loved him every bit as much as his other five children—sometimes even more so because of the graceful way he overcame the challenges of being deaf since birth. "This is nice," Jack said, using his wineglass to gesture to the fire. "Thanks."

"I know you have to be so upset, Jack. I hope you don't think I was trying to make light of it before. Heck, I'm upset about it, and I'm only her stepmother."

"You're more than that to her, and you know it." She'd come into their lives just over a year after the accident that left Clare in a coma for three years, and Andi's bond with his girls ran deep .

"Tell me what you're thinking," she said.

"At times like this, I wish I'd fought harder against her going into the music business."

"You could've fought it all you wanted, but she was going to do what she wanted to do. You remember what she was like back then. Beyond determined and filled with so much talent she could hardly contain it. Trying to stop her would've been like trying to keep the waves from crashing onto your precious beach."

She was always so full of wisdom, his lovely wife, and she was usually right, something he'd long ago stopped trying to deny.

Andi put her glass on a table, leaned forward in her chair and placed both hands on his knees. "I know it's so hard for you to see your kid get hurt and not be able to do anything about it. Remember when that bully was teasing Eric about being deaf when he was in middle school?"

"I'll never forget that." Jack could still recall the rage he'd felt when he'd heard about what had been happening at his son's school.

"Neither will I. For a few days there, I was worried you might actually seek the kid out and give him a taste of his own medicine."

"I thought about it," Jack conceded.

Andi laughed. "I believe it. And one of the things I love so much about you is how much you love all of us."

"Come here." He held out his arms to her. "You're too far away over there."

She snuggled into his lap.

Wrapping his arms around her, he was surrounded by the fragrant scent of her hair. She'd once bought a different brand of shampoo, and he'd protested so vociferously, she gone back to her usual brand to pacify him. "There. That's much better."

"Yes, it is."

"And I feel much better than I did before, so thanks for making me talk about it."

"I didn't do anything."

"Yes, you did." He nuzzled his nose into her curls and pressed a kiss to the top of her head.

"I have one more bit of news that you need to hear."

"Oh *God*," he said with a moan. "What now?"

"According to Maggie, Kate is planning to invite everyone to Nashville for Christmas. She wants the whole family there—your parents, my mom and aunt, Clare, Aidan, their boys, even Aidan's family, if they want to come."

"There's *no way* I'm spending Christmas with Reid Matthews. No way."

"Jack…"

"What?"

"You'd really miss out on Christmas with your family—you'd make the boys miss Christmas with their sisters—because of him?"

"Yes."

"Well, we'll just have to wait and see what transpires."

"I hate that this is happening to her, and I'm certainly not thrilled to discover—especially this way—that she's back with him. But I can deal with it. I can deal with anything as long as I don't have to be around him and as long as I have you."

"You've got me, love. For better or worse, I'm all yours."

"It's been a lot more better than worse." They had recently celebrated ten years of a marriage that had brought them unparalleled joy.

"A lot more." She looped her arms around his neck and kissed him. "And this too shall pass. I promise."

Jack held on tight to her and took her words to heart. Since his gorgeous wife was always right, he'd have faith she was right about this, too.

"But I'm not going there for Christmas."

Laughing, she gave him one last squeeze before she stood and held out her hand to him. "Let's go to bed."

Across town, Clare O'Malley paced from one end of the circular bedroom she shared with her husband Aidan to the other as she waited for her daughter Kate to answer the phone. When she once again reached Kate's voice mail, she had to fight the urge to throw the very expensive phone against the wall.

"*Why* does she do this? Every time something goes wrong, she goes deep undercover and doesn't answer the phone, even when her *mother* is calling."

"Think about it from her point of view," Aidan said, always the voice of reason, which at times like this was rather aggravating. "She's got to be mortified. You're probably the last person she wants to talk to."

"I'm not going to judge her. That's not why I'm calling. I want to know if she's all right."

Aidan stood and came over to stop her from pacing by putting his hands on her shoulders, forcing her to look up at him. His green eyes were filled with love and compassion. "She's not all right, and there's nothing more you can do tonight to help her. You've left her messages. You've told her you love her and you're thinking of her. When she's ready, she'll call you."

"I hate that she won't talk to me."

"She's probably not talking to anyone."

"I bet she's talking to Jill. I should call her."

Aidan gently eased the phone from her hand and placed it on the bedside table. "Jill is probably in full-on crisis mode, putting out fires all over the place. Come to bed."

"There's no way I can sleep knowing they're going through this."

"Try."

As much as Clare hated to be managed, she allowed him to help her into bed and curled into his embrace the way she did every night.

"I know this is very upsetting, but there's nothing you can do. She knows you love her no matter what." As he spoke, he ran his hand over her back soothingly.

Clare tried to relax even as her mind raced. "I can't believe this is happening. She never even told me she was going to St. Kitts or that she wanted to see him again."

"I know you'd like to think they tell you everything, but there're some things one doesn't tell one's mother."

"My girls aren't like that. We talk about things like this."

"What if she'd gone to see him and he hadn't been happy to see her? What if they attempted a reconciliation that didn't work out? She was probably waiting to talk to you until after she saw him and had something to tell you."

Clare hated to admit that he might have a good point. "Maybe." She took comfort from the familiar woodsy scent of sawdust that clung to her carpenter husband. "Why *him* of all people?"

"Who knows? But there must be something still there if she went to see him after all this time."

"He's *so* much older than her."

"You're *so* much older than me," he said, catching her fist before she could slug him.

He was about to turn fifty, but the stinker didn't look a day over forty, whereas she felt older and more decrepit by the day, despite what he said about her when he wasn't being a smart ass. The seven years between them had never been an issue, but there was a big difference between seven years and twenty-eight years.

"That's not funny," she muttered.

"Yes, it is."

Clare couldn't contain the smile he brought to her face just by being himself. He always knew what to say to her, how to comfort her and how to make her laugh, even when it seemed that nothing was funny. "Thanks," she said.

"What for?"

"Making me laugh when I don't want to. Being here to talk me off the ledge."

"Where else would I be? You're my girl, and Kate's my girl, and if you're hurting or she's hurting, so am I. I hate that this is happening to her. I hate that she took this huge chance on going there to see a man she was in love with a long time ago and this happened to her. I hate that she's trapped by her celebrity and can't live her life in peace the way normal people do."

Clare listened, amazed by the passion behind his words. How had she ever gotten so lucky to be loved by such a man?

"But I also know all this crap is part of the life she signed on for when she left home and went to Nashville, looking to make it big. While the crap isn't fun, a lot of what she gets to do is fun, and she loves it."

"Yes, she does. You're right about that. I just hate that I can't wave my magic mommy wand and make this go away for her."

"And I hate that I can't wave my stepfather wand and make it go away."

"I love you for wanting to."

"I love you, too." He kissed her softly and sweetly, and as she always did, Clare melted into him.

"Don't try to distract me."

"Why not? It's working." With his hand buried in hair that required chemical assistance to remain blonde these days, he tipped his head and kissed her again, more intently this time.

"Aidan," she whispered against his lips.

"Hmm?"

"I'm not done ranting."

"Yes, you are."

His hand slipped under her T-shirt, and when he cupped her breast, she decided the ranting could wait. She had something better to do. Her husband was an endlessly creative lover, and tonight was no exception. He took his time driving her to distraction, which she suspected was his goal, before he finally slid into her, making her come the second he was fully seated within her.

"Oh, yeah," he said as he began to move, riding her climax.

One of the benefits of being married to a younger guy was that he had no idea he was supposed to be getting old, and his stamina was every bit as good as it had been the day she met him. By the time he made her come a second time, she was about to beg for mercy. Luckily, her climax broke his control, and he came, too.

He remained on top of her, absorbing the aftershocks, as Clare ran her hands over his muscular back. Feeling his heartbeat, surrounded by his familiar scent and his overwhelming love, Clare felt centered again for the first time since Maggie had called earlier to give them a heads-up about the video. Clare had taken her youngest daughter's advice and not looked at it, but the idea that strangers were watching Kate have sex was enough to make her ill.

"What happened?" Aidan asked, raising his head to meet her gaze. His dark brown hair was in need of a trim and had more silver highlights than it used to, which only made him better looking, if that was possible. "I had you all relaxed, but you just got tense again."

"I was wondering how many perverts are watching my daughter have sex right now."

"Clare, honey. Don't do that. Don't go there."

"It's hard not to."

"I know." He kissed her and withdrew but remained perched above her. "I wish there was something I could do for you."

She reached up to caress his handsome face, so dear to her after a decade together. "That was pretty good."

He raised his eyebrows, as she'd known he would. "Only *pretty* good?"

Her shrug was like throwing a red cape in front of a bull.

"*Pretty* good? I'll show you pretty good."

Though she was tired and distressed, being held and kissed and loved by him made everything better.

Much later, as she lay awake next to Aidan, thinking about Kate, Clare hoped that wherever Kate was tonight, the man she loved was taking care of her.

CHAPTER 9

Reid had no idea what to do for her. He was eaten up with guilt over the whole thing and wishing he could have that half hour on the beach back again. Never in a million years would he have exposed her to something like this. He'd been certain they were totally alone on the beach, or he never would've coaxed her out of her bathing suit and into the water to make love.

He wanted to kick something, break things, scream and yell, but none of that would help the situation, and it wasn't what Kate needed right now. He wished he knew what she *did* need. After viewing the video in its excruciating entirety, she'd curled up on the sofa on the sunporch and withdrawn into herself, freezing him out. He couldn't say he blamed her. He wasn't too happy with himself right now either.

The vibe between them reminded him of the horrible day in Nashville when her dad had caught them together. Jack had disavowed his daughter when she chose to stay in Nashville with Reid. After the blowup with her dad, she'd retreated into herself the way she was now, and it had taken a very long time to coax her back into their relationship.

Reid hoped that wouldn't happen again this time when they were so newly back together and so very happy. Earlier in the day, they'd been hopeful and excited about their future when they bought the house on the beach. Now he had no idea where they stood, and the uncertainty was killing him. Would she decide to go home without him? Would that be easier for her? He couldn't lose her again, not after what they'd shared since she'd come to St. Kitts. He wasn't sure he'd survive it a second time.

His phone rang, jarring him from his disturbing thoughts, and he reluctantly took the call from Ashton. "Hi, son."

"Well, this is a fine mess you've gotten yourself into."

Reid was relieved that Ashton sounded more bemused than furious, which he would've understood. How embarrassing would it be to have your fifty-something father caught *in flagrante delicto* for all the world to see? "I know. Believe me."

"What were you thinking?"

"I wasn't thinking. That's the problem. I always view St. Kitts as removed from the rest of the world. I guess I've been shown otherwise."

"This is a really big deal, Dad. Buddy's pissed."

Ashton didn't have to remind him that Buddy was the CEO of Kate's record company. "He's not talking about dropping her, is he?"

"Fortunately, he's not that stupid, but he's not happy."

"Neither are we. Trust me on that."

"So... You're back with her."

A statement, not a question, Reid noted. He glanced at the huddled form on the sofa. "Yes."

"What about Mari?"

"What about her?"

"You two had a good thing going."

"Yes, we did, but it wasn't the same as this. Nothing is the same as this." After a pause, Reid added, "I know you won't approve—"

"Dad... I have no desire to go down that road again."

"What road is that?"

"The one where you and I don't speak for months because you're dating a girl who's younger than me."

"She's not a girl anymore."

"I'd like to think we've all grown up since then."

"So you don't hate me for being back with her?"

"I guess not."

"Gee, thanks," Reid said with a laugh. He adored the boy he'd raised on his own who'd become his best friend as an adult.

"I may have some news of my own to share before too long."

"What kind of news?"

"I'd rather tell you in person. When will I see you?"

"Before all this happened today, we'd been talking about going back to Nashville for Christmas. Now I don't know."

"It might not be a bad idea to hang there for a while. Lay low for a couple of months until it blows over. Kate's not on tour again until next summer anyway."

"She's due back in the studio in January."

"So she has time."

"Can I ask you something?"

"Sure."

"Will you be civil to her?"

"I'll do my best, but I doubt we'll ever be the best of friends."

Knowing he couldn't ask for much more than that, Reid said, "I love you. I don't say it often enough, but I hope you know how proud I am of you."

"I know, Dad. You've never left me wondering about any of that."

"I'm sorry to have caused you grief with this video thing."

"If only you knew the grief you've caused me," he said with a good-natured chuckle. "But I'll tell you about that when I see you."

"I'll hold you to it. Call me if there's anything we should know."

"I will."

"Listen, Ashton, while I have you, I'd be very interested to know the source of that video. Can you to find out who posted it?"

"I'm already working on that for Buddy. Do you have any thoughts on who it might be?"

"I don't want to think that Mari could be behind it, but she was pretty pissed when I chose to be with Kate."

"I can't picture Mari doing something like this."

"I don't know if she actually did the filming, but I wouldn't put it past her to sic the paparazzi on Kate. She was extremely angry with both of us."

"I'll look into it and let you know what I find out."

"Thank you."

"Try to behave down there, will you? Keep your pants on in public."

"Very funny. I'll talk to you soon." Reid ended the call and tried to think of something he could do for Kate. Before he formed a plan, the phone rang again. This time, his friend Desi was on the line.

"I'm so sorry, Reid," Desi said without preamble. "I vow to investigate this fully and fire the ass of anyone who invaded your privacy at my place."

"Thanks, Des." Not that it would matter, since the damage was done, but he did appreciate the gesture.

"I'd like to offer you and your lady my place in Lovers Beach on Nevis. It has a live-in staff who've been with me for years, and they'll protect your privacy like piranhas. I'll have all your things moved there right away and have my boat put at your disposal to take you over on your schedule. Of course, Ms. Harrington's stay at the resort will be comped as well."

Reid thought about that for a second. They couldn't stay here because Kate didn't want to be in the space he's shared with Mari, which he understood, and they couldn't go back to the resort where the video had been taken. No doubt the place would be overrun with reporters by morning. "That's very good of you, Desi, and I'll take you up on it. Thank you."

"I hope you'll accept my apology as a friend. I'm horrified this happened on my property."

"Of course I accept your apology. It wasn't your fault. Hopefully it'll blow over before too long, and Kate can get back to work."

"That's my hope as well. Call me when you're ready, and we'll pick you up at the location of your choice for the ride to Nevis."

"I will. Thanks again."

"It's the least I can do."

"I'll be in touch." Reid ended the call and contemplated Kate on the sofa, trying to think of something he could do to make her feel better. "Tea," he said to himself. "I'll make her some tea. She used to love it. Hopefully, she still does."

With his offering in hand ten minutes later, Reid stepped onto the sunporch. "You awake, darlin'?"

"Yeah."

"I made you some tea."

She sat up and turned to him, her red eyes and nose tugging at his heart. "That's nice. Thank you."

He handed her the mug. "Milk and two sugars, right?"

"You remembered," she said with a small smile.

"I remember everything." Returning her smile, he sat next to her. "Desi called from the resort. He's beside himself over what happened."

Her face fell at the reminder, and he wanted to shoot himself for mentioning it.

"It wasn't his fault."

"That's what I told him. Still, he feels bad, and he offered us his place on Nevis for as long as we need it."

She looked over at him with those dazzling eyes, reminding him of the eighteen-year-old he'd fallen so hard for. Her vulnerability tugged at him, making him want to go out and conquer dragons on her behalf. If only he could.

"Do you think we should go there?" she asked.

"I do. It would get us off St. Kitts and away from any media who come sniffing for a story. Desi said his household staff has been with him for years, and they'll protect our privacy."

Kate frowned as she contemplated her tea.

"What're you thinking?"

"There's no such thing as privacy in my world. People could be looking at us right now, taking pictures."

Reid glanced through the big windows with the panoramic view of the water. He'd always loved that view, but now he felt exposed and could only imagine how Kate must feel. "How about we check out Desi's place and see what we think of it. We don't have to decide anything until we see it."

She shrugged, as if the effort of contemplating their options was more than she could manage. "Whatever you think. We can't stay here. People know you live here. They'll find us here in no time."

"I'll call Desi and make a plan to get you out of here." He leaned in to kiss her forehead. "Don't worry about anything, darlin'. I'll take care of it."

"Thanks."

Ninety minutes later, Desi himself drove Reid and Kate across the island of Nevis to his hideaway gated estate. Short and round with light tan skin and dark hair, Desi was a ball of energy who'd been Reid's friend for almost as long as he'd lived on St. Kitts. The two men had bonded over their shared love of flying and fishing.

Desi slowed the car and punched in a code at the gate, which swung open to admit them. "No one can get on the property," Desi assured them. "We have round-the-clock security. If anyone steps foot inside the gates, we know about it."

"Why so much security?" Reid asked. Nevis wasn't exactly known for its crime.

"My wife was once involved in a home invasion. It gives her peace of mind to know that no one can get to her. Her peace of mind is my peace of mind."

Listening to Desi, Reid began to relax a bit. Here he could protect Kate for the time being, until the story died down and they were able to return to Nashville. He was consumed with guilt over the damage he'd done to her reputation, not to mention what her family must be thinking of him. That thought didn't bear further examination.

The contemporary home was big and beautiful and isolated. Desi bustled around, giving orders to the staff that greeted them and ushering Reid and Kate into the house, where he gave them a tour and their choice of bedrooms. "Anything you want or need, you have only to ask a member of my staff."

"Thanks so much, Desi," Reid said, shaking the other man's hand.

"Happy to have you." To Kate, he said, "I hope you'll accept my heartfelt apologies for what happened at my resort. You can be assured that I'll be overseeing a full investigation."

"That's good of you."

Her dull, flat tone, so in contrast with her usual exuberance, set Reid's jangled nerves further on edge.

"For what it's worth, I'm a big fan of your music," Desi added with a shy smile.

"Thank you. That's nice to hear."

An older woman who could've been Desi's mother bustled into the room. "You're here! I'm Desi's Aunt Bertha, and I run this place for him."

Desi grinned at Reid. "See what I mean when I say my staff has been with me forever?"

"So nice to meet you," Reid said, shaking hands with Bertha. "I'm Reid, and this is Kate."

"The Kate Harrington with the voice sent straight from heaven," Bertha said, cradling Kate's hand between both of hers. "I'll take very good care of you, honey. Don't you worry."

When Kate's eyes filled with tears, Reid realized that Bertha's warmth had touched her deeply.

"Kate is so tired," he said.

"Of course she is," Bertha said. "Come along. Let's get her tucked into bed."

"I'll check on you tomorrow," Desi said as he took his leave.

Bertha led them into the master bedroom and closed the plantation shutters to block the waning light. "Can I bring you some dinner?"

"After a while," Reid said. "She needs to sleep."

"If you press the intercom button on the phone, you can reach a member of the staff—day or night. You let us know when you're ready for dinner."

"Thank you very much."

Bertha left the room and closed the door behind her.

"Do you want to change?" he asked Kate.

She shook her head and crawled up the bed to find a pillow.

He pulled a throw blanket over her. "Do you want me to leave you alone?"

"No." She reached for his hand, and he linked their fingers, grateful for the contact after so many hours of uncertainty. "I know you're beating yourself up over this, but it's not your fault either."

He turned on his side to face her. "It was my idea."

"We were both there, equal participants, and I had much more to lose than you did."

"Still… I should've thought about what could happen."

"We both should've." Her eyes fluttered shut.

Reid leaned over to kiss her forehead. "Get some rest. I'll be right here with you."

Kate squeezed his hand and drifted off.

Ashton shot the approach to the runway, pleased to see the rolling meadows of home laid out before him. Central Tennessee was particularly gorgeous with the trees turning gold and red and orange. Autumn was his favorite time of year, even more so now that he'd taken the first major step toward the relationship with Jill he'd wanted so badly. As much as he'd hated to leave Malibu—and their time alone together—earlier than planned, it was always good to be home, and he couldn't wait to see what was ahead for them.

He glanced over to make sure her seat belt was still fastened and brought the plane down for a smooth landing. As he taxied from the runway to the hangar at his family's estate, Jill wrapped up the latest in a string of phone calls to everyone she could think to reach out to, trying to stem the damage to her sister's reputation. To him, the metaphor "bailing the *Titanic*" seemed fitting, but he didn't think she'd appreciate hearing that right now.

So he kept quiet as he took care of the plane and stored their stuff in the back of the truck he preferred when he wasn't working. When there was nothing left to do, he went to the passenger side of the plane and opened the door to find her staring at the windshield.

"Jill?"

"Oh, sorry. I was just… I was…" Whatever she'd been about to say was lost in a torrent of tears that seemed to take her by surprise.

"Come here, honey." He helped her out of the plane and into his arms, holding on tight while she cried out her frustration.

"There's not a damned thing I can do."

"I know, but you tried so hard. Kate will appreciate that. I'm sure she will."

"For all the good it did." She swiped at her damp cheeks. "It's my job to protect her from crap like this, but I can't protect her. I can't."

"I know you won't want to hear it, but she did this to herself. She knows that. My dad knows it. No one's blaming you."

"There should be something I can do. We have laws—"

"And your sister is a public figure who did a stupid thing in public. The law doesn't protect her in that situation." He framed her face and compelled her to look up at him. Her gray-blue eyes were mostly gray today, flat and dull rather than vivid and bright as usual. "I have my associates trying to figure out who posted the video. If we're successful, you may be able to go after them civilly."

"That won't get the video off the web."

"No."

"So this'll stay with her forever."

"Most likely, but there are some bright sides to it."

"Like *what*?"

"First of all, there's nothing overtly dirty about the video. From the brief bit I saw, it's more sensual than pornographic. She's not screaming at him to 'do me, do me harder' or anything like that."

"That's a *real* blessing."

"Hear me out. Her fans will be happy to know she's happy. There'll be a ton of interest in her and in them as a couple. If you spin it the right way, it could turn out to be really good for her career."

Jill shook her head. "I know you're trying to make me feel better—"

"Right now, I'm talking to you as a fellow entertainment attorney, not as your lover."

His use of the word "lover" made her face flush with color, which pleased him greatly. "I've been around this business a long time, babe—a lot longer than you have. I grew up with Buddy Longstreet as my godfather. I was in the wedding party when he married Taylor Jones. I was weaned on country music. I promise you that once the dust settles, she'll be bigger than ever, especially if she's self-deprecating about the video. A couple of interviews with the right reporters, and she'll be back on top. She should play it off as a big "oops." Vacation brain. That kind of thing. Her fans will be outraged by the violation of her privacy rather than disgusted by the video."

She bit her lip as she thought about what he'd said. "You really think so?"

"I know so, but you have to act fast. Get her out ahead of the story before it spins any further out of control."

"Why are you giving me this advice when you hate her so much?"

"Aw jeez, Jill. I never hated her. I hated her and my dad as a couple, because of the age difference. But mostly because, for a very brief time, I thought I wanted her for myself, though I can see now it never would've worked between us."

Her eyes flashed with anger. At least they weren't dull or flat anymore. "Well, that's good to know. You lusted after my sister. What am I? Second best?" She started to walk away, but he reached for her arm to stop her.

"Cut it out. I had a *minor* crush on her ten years ago. What I have on you is a *major, all-consuming* crush. No comparison." With his arms around her, he brought her in close to him. "And the reason I'm giving you this advice is because I want to help *you*. Not her. *You*."

"By helping me, you're helping her."

He shrugged, amused by her logic even if he didn't let her see that. "By-product."

She surprised him when she reached up to hook a hand around his neck to bring him down for a kiss that blew the top off his head. "It's good advice," she said many minutes of vigorous tongue activity later. "No, it's *great* advice. Thank you."

"If you're going to kiss me like that, I'll give you advice any time you need it—free of charge."

Her smile lit up her face and his world. And then he remembered he'd told her he loved her right before Buddy called earlier, and she hadn't returned the sentiment. "Jill—"

She tugged on his arm. "Let's go. I have a lot to do."

This wasn't the time to push her. She had too many other things on her mind. But soon, he decided. Soon he'd get her to admit she felt the same way about him, and they'd make a plan for a life together.

Kate had no idea where she was when she woke up alone in a dark room. And then it all came rushing back to her. The video. The scandal. The move to Desi's house. Reid's guilt. The sick feeling in her stomach when she thought of strangers watching her have sex.

After all the years of rumor and innuendo, she'd finally given them something to sink their teeth into. She could only imagine what was being said about her on the entertainment websites, the magazines, the TV shows. The thought of it made her shudder with revulsion.

Tears flooded her eyes and spilled down her cheeks. She'd been so happy to be back with Reid, so caught up in the magic and the moment and the seclusion of the island that she'd let down her guard. Now she would pay for that mightily. As it occurred to her that Buddy's record company might dump her, her stomach began to ache.

And as quickly as she had that thought, she realized she didn't care anymore. Let them dump her. Let them turn her into a pariah in the business. Let them say whatever the hell they wanted about her. She'd worked her ass off for years. She'd sacrificed everything for this almighty career. She had five brothers who barely knew her, and until recently, she'd gone to bed every night alone.

For what? Another gold record? Another million in the bank? She had a wall full of gold and platinum, more millions in the bank than she could spend in a lifetime and very little else to show for all the hard work.

Enough was enough.

Filled with a new sense of purpose, she sat up and wiped the tears from her face. She'd be damned if she would shed another tear over her almighty career. Screw that. After a quick trip to the bathroom to freshen up, she went to find Reid.

He was standing on the deck, staring intently into the darkness. In the distance, Kate could hear the crashing of waves against the shore. The familiar sound—the sound of home—brought comfort and resolution as she stepped onto the porch.

He startled when she slipped her arms around him from behind. "Oh hey, you're up."

"Sorry to conk out on you like that."

His hands covered hers at his waist. "You needed the rest."

"That's not all I need." She released him and urged him to turn so she could see his face.

Brushing the hair back from her face, he said, "What else do you need, honey? I'll get you anything."

"I want to go home."

She could tell she'd taken him by surprise. "To Nashville?"

"Yes."

His face set into a grim expression. "I can't say I blame you. This hasn't exactly been the vacation you were hoping for. St. Kitts is usually a lot more restful than it's been for you."

She placed her hands on his chest and went up on tiptoes to kiss him. "In all the most important ways, it was exactly the vacation I was hoping for."

"I gotta be honest with you, darlin'. You're confusing the hell out of me."

"I'm sorry," she said, laughing.

"I didn't expect to hear you laugh tonight."

"I didn't expect to feel like laughing, but I've made a decision, and now I want to go home and make it happen."

"What decision have you made?"

"I'm quitting the business."

His mouth fell open in shock. "Wait. What?"

"I've had enough. I want to be a private citizen again. I want a life, a real, genuine life that doesn't include two hundred nights a year on the road. I want to get to know my brothers and, and…" She stopped herself from giving him the full list so as not to scare him away. "Well, there're a lot of things I want to do, and I can't do any of them as long as I continue to chase the music. I've done everything I set out to do in the business. I have almost everything I need. Now it's time for me."

"I, um… I don't know what to say. Is this because of the video?"

"That's part of it." Her entire body hummed with energy. Having made the decision, now she couldn't wait to implement it. "This has been a long time coming. My health has been shit for the last year. I'm exhausted all the time. I haven't been writing music the way I used to, which is one of the things I most love to do. I'm not doing *any* of the things I most love to do. I spend hardly any time with my family, other than Jill, my brothers are growing up way too fast. The twins are ten now. Ten! Did you know that?"

Reid shook his head.

Fueled by excitement, Kate paced the deck. "My mother and her husband have two young sons, too, Max and Nick. They're thirteen and ten, and they barely know me. I give more to my fans than I do to my own family. That's not right."

"Don't you have contracts?"

"I'll get out of them." Throwing her hands into the air, she spun around. "I feel *free* for the first time in longer than I can remember. I'm *free*. I can do whatever I want, and what I want has nothing to do with singing or performing. It has everything to do with the people I love."

He folded his arms and leaned back against the rail that surrounded the deck. Kate stopped moving and zeroed in on him. "What?"

"Nothing. I'm listening to you."

"But what is it you're dying to say?"

He hesitated, seeming to choose his words carefully. "I'm thrilled to see you so happy. Really, I am. It's just that I worry this incident with the video has upset you more than you're willing to let on, and you're making a big decision while in the midst of a crisis."

"I know you'll find this hard to believe, but the video didn't cause me to make this decision."

"You weren't talking about quitting the business before this happened."

"No, but I was thinking about it. I've been thinking about it for quite some time, if I'm being honest. The one thing that's kept me going is my sister."

"How do you mean?"

"She works for me. If I quit, what happens to her?"

"It's not like you'd walk away and have nothing to do with the business ever again."

"I might not…have anything to do with it…"

"Kate, really, I fear you're being hasty. You're upset over what happened, and rightfully so, but to make a decision like this now—"

"I didn't make it today. That's what you're not hearing. I made it in a hospital room in Oklahoma City when I said I wanted to go home. I knew then that I didn't want to come back. I was done then. I didn't realize that entirely until I came here, but I get it now. I'm done. I've had enough of being accused of doing drugs when I've never touched a drug in my life. I'm sick of a different city every day but still feeling like I've never actually *been* anywhere. There's never time to *see* anything. Do you know I've been to London six or eight times, but I've never seen Buckingham Palace? What kind of *life* is that?"

The words, one she started, poured forth in a stream of thoughts she'd had over the last few months. Saying them out loud for the first time was liberating. "I haven't told anyone this," she said with a nervous laugh. "You're the first to know."

"Come here, darlin'." He held out his hands to her.

Kate crossed the deck to take what he offered. With her hands in his, she looked up to find him watching her guardedly. "I'm here."

"I'm honored to be the first to know how you've been feeling. But I'd be remiss if I didn't urge you to sleep on it before you tell anyone else. I don't want you to make a hasty decision that you'll regret in a month or two."

"I won't regret it. I'd regret *not* doing it. That much I know for sure." She tried to calm her racing heart. "I get that you think I'm being hasty, and I get why, but you don't know how it's been."

"Then tell me. Tell me how it's been."

As she searched for the words she needed, she stared out at the darkness. "When things between us fell apart, something in me shut down. I think it was the part of me that took chances, the part that risked the odds and didn't care what anyone thought of me." She smiled. "How else would you explain why I was willing to risk everything on an affair with a man twenty-eight years older than me?"

"And here I thought all this time I was irresistible."

Kate laughed, delighted by him. "Of course you were. But after this, after us, I wasn't like that anymore. I cared too much about what other people thought. It hurt me when they accused me of doing drugs and sleeping around. I played it safe with other guys. I picked people who I knew would never break through the huge wall I'd put up around me. They couldn't break my heart because they couldn't *get* to it." She shook her head. "I'm not making any sense."

"No, you are. I get what you're saying."

"I want a *real* life, Reid. I want an authentic life. Not some glitzed-up celebrity existence where my every word and action is scrutinized by people who don't even know me. I'm tired of my whole world revolving around the next show, the next city, the next arena full of nameless, faceless people."

"You should have what you want. You went right from your daddy's house to superstardom with almost nothing in between."

"This," she said, sliding her hands to his shoulders, "was *not* nothing." She pressed her lips to his and was comforted by the familiar taste and scent of him. "*This* was everything."

"Kate, God, you have no idea what you do to me when you say those things."

"I have some idea," she said, laughing as she rubbed against his arousal.

"Not just there, but in here, too." He took her hand and placed it on top of his fast-beating heart. "You touch me everywhere."

"Will you come back to Nashville with me and help me find that real life? A real life that absolutely must include you if it's to be truly authentic."

"You want me to come with you?"

She stared at him, incredulous. "What did you think I've been saying?"

"That you were quitting the business and setting out to find your life."

Kate threw her head back and laughed—hard—which seemed to annoy him. "You silly, silly man. You *are* my life. How did you miss that part?"

"Um, ah, I don't know, but it sure is good to hear. I thought…" He shook his head. "Never mind what I thought."

"Tell me. What were you going to say?"

"I thought you were telling me you were leaving. Without me."

"God, I'm such an ass. I'm sorry. That wasn't at all what I was saying. The exact opposite."

He gathered her into his arms, holding her tight against him.

"So will you come home with me?"

"On one condition."

Kate drew back slightly so she could look up at him. "What's that?"

"If you want a real, authentic life, you're going to have to marry me. I can't see any other way—"

A squeak of surprise escaped from her lips the second before she kissed him.

He tipped his head and buried his hand in her hair, kissing her with an urgency he hadn't often shown her.

Kate clung to him, kissing him back with everything she had, everything she'd ever be. It was all his. It always had been, and now that she knew for sure where she belonged, she'd never let go again.

"Is that a yes?" he whispered, his voice husky with emotion.

"Yes. That's absolutely a yes."

"I don't have a ring, but I'll get you one. As soon as I can. I'll get you the best ring you've ever seen."

"I don't need that. I've had glitter and glam. All I want now is simple and real."

"I can do that."

She smiled, happier than she'd been since it all went wrong between them. "Does this mean we're engaged?"

"It certainly does."

"However shall we celebrate?" she asked with a flirtatious smile.

"Any way you want, my love."

She ran her fingers through his hair and brought him down for another passionate kiss. "Since we're keeping it simple and real…" She unbuttoned his shirt as she ran her hands over his chest. When she released the last button, she bent her head to press kisses to his throat and chest, loving the tremble that rippled through him, loving that she did that to him.

"Not here." He grabbed her hand and tugged her behind him as he headed inside.

Kate reclined on the bed, amused by his thoroughness as he locked the door and closed the blinds before removing his clothes. "Afraid someone is watching?"

Nodding, he helped her out of her dress. "I hope you're fond of beds, because we're never, *ever* doing it outside again," he said, leaning over her.

She looped her arms around his neck and drew him down on top of her. "Yes, we will. When people no longer give a fig about me, we won't have to worry about being watched."

"From now on, I'll always worry about being watched. It makes me sick to think I put you in such a vulnerable situation."

"You were carried away. We both were. I wish you wouldn't blame yourself."

"I can't help it. I love you so much, and when I think about people watching us—"

"Don't," she said, tugging him toward her for a kiss. "Don't think about it."

"Right." He barked out a laugh that made her laugh, too. "Don't think about it. Who's being silly now?"

"They can only hurt us if we let them. Let's not let them. Let's not let anyone else in so no one can hurt us ever again."

He pulled back from the kisses he was placing in strategic areas of her neck to look her in the eye. "We can't be real or authentic without the other people we love being part of us, honey. And for the record, your daddy may hate my guts, but I will ask for your hand in marriage."

"He'll never give it to you."

"I'm still going to ask. I'm old-fashioned that way."

She smiled up at him. "Don't use the word 'old' around me. You're timeless."

"And you, my love, are deluded."

Kate laughed, filled with love and joy and hope for the future. "I'm so excited. Are you excited, too?"

He pressed his erection into the V of her legs. "It's not obvious?"

"Not about that, although that's always exciting. So exciting you ruined me for all other men at the tender age of eighteen."

"I wish I could say I was sorry about that, but hey, I'm not really."

Smiling, she combed her fingers through his hair and over his cheek, where the first hint of whiskers had begun to appear. "I meant are you excited about all our other plans?"

"Of course I am. How could I not be?"

Kate thought about the one thing she hadn't told him.

"What? And don't say it's nothing, because your smile faded right off your face, and I saw that."

He was so tuned in to her that it was hard to hide anything from him. That was both a blessing and a curse.

"There's something else I want, and I'm not sure you want it too. I wouldn't blame you if you didn't—"

Reid kissed her thoroughly and then pulled back to meet her gaze. "Tell me."

Kate swallowed the lump of fear and emotion that had settled in her throat as she looked up at the face that had haunted her dreams for so long. "I want a baby. Maybe more than one."

"Oh, well… I'm kind of old for that, darlin'."

"I knew you'd say that, and it's okay if we don't have kids—"

"No, it's not okay." He shifted off her and stretched out next to her, looking up at the ceiling fan that moved in a slow, lazy circle above them. "You should have everything you want."

"If I had a choice of having six kids or having you with no kids, I'd choose you. I've seen what it's like without you, and I'm not interested in that life."

"It wouldn't be fair to the kids to lose their father so early in their lives. I'd be lucky to get thirty years with them."

"And how blessed would they be to have that time with you?"

"I also can't help but wonder how Ashton would feel about it."

"He's going to hate the whole thing, so a baby couldn't make it any worse."

"I don't know if that's true. I talked to him earlier."

"And?"

"He didn't seem all that surprised or annoyed to hear we were back together. He wasn't thrilled about the video, of course, but who is?"

"We've all grown up. Him, too, I suppose. And while I know it wouldn't be the same, he'd certainly be there for his brother or sisters… After." Kate shook her head. "Forget I said that. I refuse to think about a time when you're not here with me anymore."

He turned his head and reached for her hand. "You have to, Kate. You've agreed to marry a many almost thirty years your senior. Please don't pretend that you won't spend a large portion of your life without me."

The thought was so far beyond depressing, she refused to allow it in when she was otherwise overjoyed. "I get it. I really do. But I don't want to talk about it, especially not today."

Smiling, he brought her hand to his lips for a tender kiss to her palm. "Fair enough."

"Will you think about the remote possibility of having kids?"

"I'll think about it, but no promises."

She flashed him a saucy grin. "Might be too late for thinking anyway," she reminded him.

"Might be." He turned on his side and put his arm around her. "Come here. You're too far away over there, and I thought we were going to celebrate."

"We are," she said with a sigh of utter contentment. "We're going to celebrate every day we get as the blessing it is, and we're not going to spend one second worrying about the future. That'll take care of itself."

"If you say so, darlin'."

"I do. I say so. Now, about that celebration…"

His face lifted into a sexy smile that made her melt. All he'd ever had to do was look at her just like that, and she was his. Now she got to have forever with him. How lucky was she?

Determined to show him how lucky she felt, she pushed him onto his back and bent over him, kissing his chest and focusing on his nipples, which made him gasp and made her smile. Filled with her own power, she worked her way down, kissing, licking, nibbling.

"Christ, Kate," he said between gritted teeth.

"What's wrong?"

"Don't act all innocent, like you don't know what you're doing to me."

"What am I doing to you?" she asked, letting her hair tickle his straining erection.

"You know exactly what you're doing." He sounded positively tortured, which she loved.

"I'll stop if you don't like it."

He fisted her hair, keeping her right where she was, hovering over him.

"Is this what you want?" She dabbed at the head of his penis with delicate strokes of her tongue.

"Yeah."

"How about this?" She dragged her tongue over the length of him.

"That's good, too."

"What about this?" Moving lower, she cupped his balls and took him fully into her mouth.

His hips surged off the bed, and his fists tightened in her hair, almost to the point of pain, but Kate didn't care. She remembered the first time she'd done this to him, how he'd told her what he liked and showed her what to do. She'd been unable to bring herself to do it for anyone else. This, like so many other things, belonged to him and him alone.

"Kate...stop. Stop."

Surprised by his harsh tone, she looked up at him. "Did I do it wrong?"

"God, no. You did it just right. Come here."

She crawled into his outstretched arms. "What's wrong?"

"Absolutely nothing." He massaged her neck and shoulders, which felt heavenly. His erection surged against her belly, demanding she take notice. "I need to get a condom."

Kate moved off him so he could get up.

When he returned from the bathroom, her mouth went dry as she took a good long look at him in all his aroused glory. "See something you like, darlin'?" he asked, amused.

"I've never seen anything I like better."

"While I find that hard to believe, I'm very, very grateful."

"Can I go back to where I was?" she asked. "On top?"

"You can go anywhere you want."

He stretched out on his back, and Kate straddled him, leaning over to kiss him as he cupped her breasts and teased her nipples with his fingers. "Lift up a little," he said, sounding tense and strained, which made her realize how hard he was fighting to hold on to his control.

Pleased by his reaction to her, Kate did as he asked. When she felt the nudge of his erection between her legs she eased herself down on him, letting her head fall back in surrender as she took him in.

"Yes," he whispered. "That's *so* good."

"So good. Better than anything." With him growing inside her, Kate was filled with an overwhelming sense of contentment and anticipation of all they had to look forward to.

Reid sat up and arranged her legs so they were wrapped around him. His chest hair rubbed against her nipples, making them tingle and tighten. Their eyes met and held. In a moment of perfect harmony, he tipped his head and held her gaze as he kissed her gently, reverently.

Kate's heart beat so hard and so fast it made her lightheaded, or maybe he made her lightheaded. It was him. Definitely him.

His hands slid slowly down her back to grip her buttocks as he compelled her to move. And then one of his hands was between her legs, coaxing her. When his lips closed around her nipple, the orgasm crashed over her, stealing what was left of her sanity. She gasped when he dug his fingers into her bottom as he surged into her and came with a cry.

He hugged her tightly afterward.

"How did I live without you—without that—for so long?" he asked.

"I don't know how I did it either."

"I should've come after you."

"I never should've left."

"We won't make those mistakes again."

"No, we won't." Kate closed her eyes and drifted in a sea of serenity. The future stretched out before them, bright with promise. "Will you take me home, Reid?"

"What about your pilot?"

"I'll tell him he's on his own."

"We'll go home tomorrow."

"Thank you."

CHAPTER 10

Because she wanted to be in her office with her things, Ashton followed Jill's directions and drove to Kate's estate in Hendersonville. He hadn't been out this way in years and couldn't help being impressed by the home Kate had built for herself as well as the one where Jill resided.

Hers was much smaller than her sister's, but the post-and-beam house suited her perfectly, Ashton thought as he followed her inside. He'd intended to drop her off and head home, but now that they were here, he found that he was unable to leave her alone and upset.

Inside, she turned to him and gave a wary smile, as if she too was uncertain of what happened now that they were home and back to reality.

Ashton was comforted to know he wasn't the only one unsure of himself. After the closeness they'd shared over the last few days, however, he refused to allow her to put distance between them.

He glanced around at the cozy living room, the fireplace, the overstuffed sofas, the bookshelves. Her sister probably paid her a lot of money to manage her career, but nothing about Jill's home was showy or ostentatious. "I like your place."

"Thanks. I like it, too, not that I'm here very much."

He watched as she glanced at the clock on the cable box before she returned her gaze to him.

"I know you want to get to work. Do you mind if I take a look around outside?"

"Oh, so you're going to stay?"

"Is that all right?"

"Sure, that's fine. I just figured you'd have better things to do than kill time while I work."

He couldn't stand to go another minute without touching her, so he put his arms around her and kissed the top of her head. "I've got nothing I'd rather do than wait for you to get your work done so we can get back to having fun."

"I thought…"

"What did you think?"

"I didn't expect you to want to hang out, especially here. At Kate's place."

"I want to be wherever you are." Tipping his head, he kissed her so softly their lips barely made contact. When he pulled back, she leaned forward, looking for more. "Later." Smiling at her growl of frustration, he gave her a nudge. "Go get your work done. I'll be here when you're finished."

"Don't get into mischief. Kate would never forgive me."

"You're already sleeping with the enemy. What other mischief could I get into that would top that?"

"I have a feeling you're endlessly resourceful when it comes to mischief."

"That hurts my feelings."

"What*ever*." She rolled her eyes and left him laughing in the living room as she sauntered into the kitchen.

Watching her go, he took a moment to appreciate the view of her very fine ass in tight denim. He'd wanted to see her out of the prim business suits she favored. He'd wanted to see her ass in denim. He'd wanted to see her relaxed and at ease. He'd gotten all of those things, but nothing could've prepared him for the many faces of Jill Harrington—relaxed, happy, sexy, aroused, sated, amused, annoyed, undone.

That last one had been tough on him. Seeing her upset over the mess her sister and his father had made of things had been hard to watch. He left her house and headed for the path that led toward Kate's place. Knowing the diva wasn't in residence gave him the freedom to poke around a bit.

Her home was gorgeous and sprawling, with windows of every shape and size. The A-frame log cabin must've been four thousand square feet, at the very least. What one person needed with all that space was beyond him, until he remembered Buddy once saying that Kate had built a recording studio at the house so she could spend more time at home.

Behind the house was a four-stall garage and beyond that he found stables. Anxious to see Thunder, he stepped inside and let his eyes adjust to the dim light.

"Help you with something?"

The voice behind him startled Ashton as he turned. "Hi, there. I'm Ashton Matthews, a friend of Jill's."

"Gordon, the groom."

Ashton shook the older man's outstretched hand. "Mind if I say hello to Thunder? He's an old friend."

"'Course not. Make yourself at home, son."

"Thank you."

"Third stall on the left."

Ashton had already zeroed in on the dark, handsome thoroughbred that had once belonged to his father. He walked past a white horse and a chestnut roan before he got to Thunder's stall.

"Hi, old guy." Ashton held out his hand for Thunder to nuzzle. "Remember me?"

Thunder's nicker made Ashton laugh. "Yeah, it's been a while. Has Kate been taking good care of you?"

The question was rhetorical because he could see that Thunder had the biggest stall, a fresh lining of shavings, plenty of oats and water in his feed bin, and his coat shone from regular grooming.

As Thunder nuzzled his hand and then his face, a surge of emotion caught Ashton off guard. Seeing Thunder again took him right back to the dark days after his father and Kate got together, when his dad had lied to him about their relationship because he knew his son, older than the girl he was dating, wouldn't approve.

Ashton vividly remembered the day he'd put all the pieces together and stormed into his father's bedroom, catching him with Kate. He'd been blinded by anger and hurt. He'd said things his father never should've forgiven. He'd gone home and called Kate's dad to tell him what was going on in Nashville. He'd hurt a lot of people with his impulsive actions.

A couple of days later, Kate had confronted him in the parking lot of the condo complex where they'd both lived. She'd looked at him with those distinctive blue eyes, which had been large and wounded.

"Why'd you have to call my dad?" she'd asked.

"Why'd you have to screw mine?"

He winced, still ashamed after all this time that'd he said that to her. She'd been an eighteen-year-old girl and he a man of twenty-five. His father had raised him better than that, and the shame of it had stayed with him for a long time.

He'd been so angry at both of them—and so very hurt. The rift with his father had been the single most painful episode of his life. He'd been far too young when his mother died to remember the cataclysmic impact of her loss. But losing his dad, even for a short time, had devastated him. Nothing, not even the knowledge that his dad was back with Kate, could make him want to relive that dark period.

The chain of events that followed the breakup with Kate had led to his dad packing up and leaving Nashville for St. Kitts, where he'd lived ever since, far away from his only child. Ashton wondered if he'd still be an only child now that his dad and Kate were together again. She was a young woman who'd probably want kids of her own. Would his dad accommodate that? How did Ashton feel about baby siblings at his age?

"What do you think, Thunder? Should Dad and Kate have kids?"

Thunder nuzzled him, and Ashton would swear that the horse was all for the idea.

"Figures you'd take her side. You always did love her best."

"'Scuse me," Gordon said. "Thought you might like some carrots."

Embarrassed to have been caught in a conversation with a horse, Ashton said, "We'd love some." Ashton took the proffered carrots and held them up for Thunder to see. "Hungry?"

The horse snapped one of the carrots out of his hand before Ashton knew what hit him. "That was crafty," he said, laughing. "I heard you were getting old. Not too old for hijinks, I see."

Gordon laughed as he walked away. "There ain't nothin' old about that fella."

The same might be said about his dad, Ashton thought. Even though he was in his mid-fifties now, he looked and acted like a much younger man. While Ashton wasn't thrilled to hear that his dad and Kate were back together, he wanted his dad to be happy. And though the relationship had caused a lot of heartburn the first time around, standing before the horse they all loved, Ashton vowed to do his best to understand this time. He would try his hardest to be friendly to Kate and to welcome her into their lives.

Since he wanted his dad to do the same for him with Jill, how could he do any less for his dad? He fed the rest of the carrots to Thunder and ran a hand over the horse's silky muzzle. "I'll be back to see you again soon."

Ashton left the stables and took a long walk in the woods, circling back around to Jill's place more than an hour later. Not wanting to disturb her when she was working, he let himself in, took off his coat and was heading for the sofa when she appeared in the doorway to the kitchen.

"Oh hey, you're back. I thought you might've left." She looked pale and tired, which made him mad. She'd been so relaxed in California.

He went to her, put his hands on her shoulders and massaged away some of the tension. "I told you I'd wait for you."

"Still… You must have something you'd rather be doing than waiting around for me."

He shook his head.

"Oh."

"You're cute when you're caught off guard."

"Then I must be very cute, because you catch me off guard all the time."

"You're very, *very* cute, and I like to keep you on your toes." His hands moved from her shoulders to her face, and for the longest time, he just looked at her, drinking her in like the hungry, needy fool he became in her presence.

She licked her lips nervously, drawing his attention to her full bottom lip.

"Why are you staring at me?"

Still zeroed in on her enticing mouth, he said, "Because I can."

"What does that mean?"

He smiled and kissed her forehead, her nose and then her lips. "It means that for so long I had to subsist between meetings, hoping to catch a glimpse of you here or there. Now I get to look to my heart's content."

Her face heated, which pleased him to no end. Knowing he got to her, that he affected her the way she affected him… His thought process was derailed by the feel of her soft hands slipping under his shirt to make contact with his back. He went from hungry and needy to desperate the second her skin brushed against his.

"Did you get everything done?" he forced himself to ask.

"Not everything, but I made some good progress. I got a couple of interviews booked for Kate that should help to put the story into her own words. Now if she would only return my calls."

This was said with a hint of aggravation.

"She will. When she's ready."

"I hope she's ready soon. I need her to get her ass back here and deal with this."

He nuzzled her fragrant, silky hair, captivated by her scent and the way she fit so perfectly in his arms.

"Ashton?"

"Hmm?"

"What're you doing?"

"Holding you." Was it his imagination, or did she snuggle closer to him? "Do you want to go out to dinner?"

He felt her shake her head against his chest.

"What do you want to do?" he asked, hoping with every fiber of his being that she wanted the same thing he did.

She ran her hand down his arm and curled her fingers around his. "This," she said, tugging him toward a hallway that he prayed led to her bedroom.

Thank you, Jesus.

Her room was practical yet feminine with frilly curtains and a patchwork quilt on the bed. Ashton didn't waste much time taking in the décor, especially after she tugged her shirt up and over her head. Standing before him in a peach silk bra over pale, creamy skin, and her dark hair loose around her shoulders she looked like a goddess. His hands curled into fists at his side as he held himself back from grabbing her and taking her with the force of the desire that pounded through him. She tugged at the button to her jeans, and he was frozen, utterly unable to move as he watched her.

A small, sexy smile curved her mouth. She knew exactly what she was doing to him, undressing slowly in front of him. She shimmied out of the jeans to reveal a peach silk thong that matched the bra. He'd been with her when she bought the set in California, but he hadn't appreciated then how glorious it would look on her. He certainly appreciated it now.

When she reached behind her to release the bra, he finally found his voice. "Wait." The single word came out much harsher than he'd intended.

Her hands fell to her sides, and a hint of uncertainty appeared in her expression.

"Let me."

He started at her hips, his hands sliding over her ribs and up to cup her breasts through the bra. He watched, transfixed, as her nipples pebbled, and bent to suck one of them between his teeth, which made her gasp. Her fingers combed through his hair, pulling him closer.

Ashton didn't have to be asked twice. He tugged her in tight against him, releasing the bra with the snap of two fingers behind her. Nudging it off her shoulders, he kissed and licked and suckled her smooth skin. He was addicted to her scent, her taste, her smoothness.

He'd intended to take her slowly, to draw out the suspense for both of them, but the instant her breasts sprang free of the bra and pressed against his chest, all his finesse abandoned him, and the need took over. It had been hours and *hours* and hours since he'd last held her and kissed her. Thinking of the way she'd bent over him and taken his erection into her mouth on the plane sent a surge of desire to his already hard penis as he devoured her in a series of kisses that left him dying for more.

From the first instant she walked into his office, he'd known she was going to change his life. He could admit that now that he had her pliant in his arms, straining against him, using her body to tell him what she wanted. Before he'd had the opportunity to be with her like this, he'd been afraid to own up to the effect she'd had on him that first day.

He used to wonder how he'd survive if he never got the chance to show her what she did to him just by walking into a conference room, full of purpose and intent, endlessly efficient. He'd suspected all along that underneath the cool veneer was a hot, sexy woman. Now he held living proof of just how hot and sexy she really was in his hands, and he was filled with relief and excitement—and overwhelming desire.

"What're you thinking?" she asked as he lowered her to the bed and hovered over her. "Right in this second, what are you thinking?"

"That I can't believe I get to hold you and kiss you and touch you and make love with you after thinking about doing all of that—and more—for so long."

Her arms curled around his neck, and her eyes went soft with affection as she looked up at him. "You could've said something sooner."

He shook his head. "I was afraid to."

"Why?"

"I'm not exactly your sister's best friend. I figured she'd poisoned you against me, and I had no chance with you."

"I know you think she hates you, but she doesn't. It's more that she thinks you hate her."

"I don't."

"Sometimes you act like you do."

Ashton couldn't deny that was probably true. "I don't want to talk about her." His lips found her throat and neck on his way to her earlobe, which he bit down on gently. "I want to talk about you and this tiny mole, right here." His tongue dabbed at crest of her breast, making her squirm beneath him. "I want to talk about this nipple. And this one. And your skin. God, it's like silk. So soft and sexy." Once again her fingers tightened in his hair, letting him know she liked what he was doing. "I can't get enough."

"Neither can I." Her voice was husky and sexy. "Ashton…"

"What, honey?" He moved farther down the bed to press his lips to the damp patch of silk between her legs, inhaling her tantalizing scent.

Her hips surged.

He took advantage of the opportunity to slide his hands under her, cupping her supple cheeks and squeezing.

"I…I don't know what I was going to say."

Chuckling, he ran his tongue over her outer lips, using the silk of her underwear to stimulate her. After a few minutes of that, it wasn't enough for him—or for her. He retreated only long enough to remove the scrap of fabric before returning to where he'd been, using his shoulders to part her legs. Not since he'd played football in high school had he been so thankful for extra-broad shoulders.

"So pretty," he whispered as he bent his head to lick and suck and stroke her to a series of orgasms that had her screaming from the pleasure. He was like a man possessed. Giving her pleasure did more for him than taking it from any other woman ever had. His entire world was reduced to what was right in front of him, and nothing mattered more than taking care of her.

Carrying her essence on his lips and tongue, he kissed his way from her belly to the valley between her breasts to her lips. That was when he saw the streaks of tears on her cheeks. "What's this?" he whispered, dabbing his tongue over the trails they'd left behind.

"I...I don't know. I didn't know I was crying."

"Was it too much?"

She shook her head as she welcomed him into her embrace. "It was incredible."

Ashton came to his senses the second before he would've slid into her equally welcoming sex. "Condom."

Moaning, she released him.

He moved quickly to find his wallet and retrieve the strip of condoms he'd stashed in there before they left Malibu. As he returned to her, he rolled one on and was inside her two seconds later.

She gripped his ass and pulsated around him, stretching to accommodate him.

Afraid to hurt her by giving her too much too soon, he forced himself to stay still, to restrain the need that pounded through him, threatening to end this far too soon. "Jill," he said through gritted teeth. "I need to move."

"Wait." She pressed tighter against him and held perfectly still, which triggered another release for her.

Ashton had never felt anything more erotic in his life.

When she relaxed her hold on him, he finally snapped, pounding into her with all hope of finesse abandoned in a flurry of passion unlike anything he'd ever experienced. He drove into her one last time, coming with a deep, guttural groan torn from his chest. That was when he discovered he'd wrapped an arm around her leg and pushed it into her chest so he could go deeper.

"Christ," he muttered as he released the tight hold he had on her leg. "I'm sorry." Mortified by his total loss of control, he was almost afraid to look at her.

"For what?"

He finally dared to meet her gaze. "I went at you like a prisoner who's just been released after twenty years of hard time."

That made her laugh, which made her muscles squeeze intimately around him. His penis surged with interest, as if he hadn't just had the most explosive orgasm of his life.

"In case you didn't notice the four orgasms, I rather enjoyed it."

"I didn't hurt you?"

She smoothed the hair from his sweaty forehead. "No."

He stared down at her. "You make me crazy. I've never felt anything like this."

"Neither have I."

"What I said to you earlier—"

Her finger over his lips stopped him. "The phone rang before I was able to reply."

"I noticed."

Her smile was warm and sweet and loving. "Have you been twisting in the wind all this time, thinking it might be only you who feels that way?"

"Sorta."

She wrapped her leg around his hip, and her arms tightened around his neck. "It's not just you."

Until she said those words, he hadn't realized he'd been holding his breath since earlier in the day. Relief flooded through him, making his skin tingle. "I don't think I'm falling anymore."

He felt her stiffen beneath him. "You changed your mind?"

Raising he head, he met her gaze. "No." He touched his lips to hers, lingering to revel in her sweetness. A thousand emotions passed through her eyes as she watched him, trying to gauge his meaning. "I've already landed."

In the morning, Reid woke Kate with the news that an incoming storm would keep them on the island at least one more day. Since they had some extra time, he'd decided to go across to St. Kitts to deal with his belongings at the house and speak to his landlord. He leaned over the bed to kiss her before he left. "Rest, relax, and I'll be back before you miss me."

"No, you won't." She hooked her arm around his neck to bring him down for a better kiss. "You'll be back before the storm comes?"

"Long before."

As she watched him get dressed, she was struck by the memory of watching him dress for a weekend business meeting he'd wanted to skip so he could spend more time with her. "Remember the time you were going to a meeting in the city and I asked you for a ride?"

His eyes lit up with mirth. "As I recall, you made me hideously late."

She enjoyed revisiting that long-ago morning until she recalled the rest of what happened. "That was the day my dad caught us."

Returning to the bed, he sat next to her and took her hand. "Don't think about that now. It's all in the past. Think about the future. Think about what kind of wedding you want and where you want to have it. No negative thoughts. Got me?"

"I got you," she said, tingling at the mention of their wedding. "Hurry back."

"I won't be gone for one minute longer than I have to." He kissed her again. "Love you, darlin'."

"Love you, too." Kate reluctantly released him and watched him leave the room. "Don't forget to come back."

He turned in the doorway, smiling. "Not a chance."

Kate was lonely for him from the minute she heard the front door close downstairs. "You're being ridiculous. He'll be gone a couple of hours, and you have plenty to do while he's gone." Buoyed by her pep talk, Kate headed for the shower and then downstairs to find some coffee.

Bertha was in the kitchen, overseeing something on the stove. "Oh, you're up. I was going to bring breakfast to you. Mr. Matthews told me you prefer egg-white omelets and wheat toast with fresh fruit."

"That sounds lovely."

"Coffee?"

"Yes, please."

Bertha handed her a steaming mug and placed a carafe of cream and a sugar bowl on the counter. "You're welcome to have a seat on the veranda, and I'll bring breakfast out when it's ready."

"Thank you." Kate took her coffee outside where the sky was darkening with storm clouds that so far were only threatening rain.

After a delicious breakfast and a peaceful interlude on the veranda, Kate decided it was time to return the flurry of phone calls she'd received from her family over the last two days. Her recently satisfied stomach turned at the thought of speaking to her parents about the embarrassing video, but she couldn't avoid them forever.

She started with Jill, who sounded like she might've been still asleep when she answered the phone.

"Are you actually *sleeping in*?" Kate asked.

"Didn't you tell me to take a vacation?"

"I never expected you to actually *do* it."

"I only got half a vacation, thanks to your antics on the island."

"Yeah, sorry about that."

"I've been working the phones, and I've got a plan."

"You're too good to me, sis, but I've made some plans of my own."

"What kind of plans?"

"I'll talk to you about it when I get home."

"And when will that be?"

"Tomorrow. We were going to leave today, but the weather isn't cooperating."

"So Reid is coming with you?"

"Yes." Kate paused before she asked, "Have you talked to Mom or Dad?"

"Both briefly yesterday."

Kate closed her eyes and braced herself. "What'd they have to say?"

"Oh, you know, the usual. How did your sister manage to get herself caught on video having sex? That kind of thing."

"I'm glad you find it funny."

"It's not funny, Kate, but what do you think they said? They're freaking out, especially since you can't find the time to call them back."

"What am I supposed to say to them?"

"Just tell them you're okay, and they'll be satisfied. You are okay, aren't you?"

"I'm much better than okay. Reid and I are engaged."

"Oh my God, Kate! When did that happen?"

"Last night."

"I'm happy for you. I know how badly you hoped he'd still feel the same way."

"He does. We both do. It's even better than it was before, if that's possible."

"I'm glad for you."

"Are you really?"

"I want you to be happy. That's all I've ever wanted for you."

Jill had been the one person in her life who'd never hassled her about Reid or the age difference the first time they were together. "Thanks. You don't know how much that means to me."

"I think I have a small idea."

"What've you been up to?"

"Not much."

"Taking it easy, I hope."

"Uh-huh. Nice and easy, until you forced me back to work."

"Sorry again. I didn't exactly plan to get caught having sex. Have you heard from Buddy?"

"Not directly, but I did talk to Ashton. He says Buddy isn't happy, and Ashton shared a few ideas about how to get out in front of the story. That's what I want to talk to you about when you get home. I've set up some interviews for you—"

"I'm not doing any interviews, Jill."

"Hear me out—"

"Jill… No interviews."

The comment was met with stony silence from her sister.

"I'm sorry. I know you went to a lot of trouble to set them up, but I'm going in a different direction."

"Well, do feel free to share your new direction with your manager and attorney at your earliest convenience."

"I want to talk to you in person."

"Fine."

"You're pissed."

"I don't know what I am! I'm trying to do my job, but you're not making it easy."

"I know. I'm sorry."

"Stop apologizing. We'll talk when you get home."

"I appreciate all you do for me."

"I know that. You don't have to say it."

"Yes, I do. I'll see you tomorrow."

"I'll be here. Call your parents."

"Doing that now. See you."

Jill ended the call without another word.

"That went well," Kate muttered, finding her mother's number on her list of favorites before she lost her nerve.

CHAPTER 11

While Jill was talking to Kate, Ashton placed a big, warm hand on her belly.

Annoyed, aggravated and concerned after the conversation with her sister, Jill tried to squirm out of his embrace, but he pulled her in tight against him so he was tucked up to her back. "Stay. Talk to me. What did she say?"

"You heard enough to put two and two together."

"So they're engaged."

"Yes." All at once, Jill stopped thinking about herself and turned to gauge how he was feeling. His expression was completely blank. "I'm sorry you had to hear it that way."

He shrugged. "I figured they'd probably head in that direction this time around."

"Are you okay?"

"Don't worry about me." He brought her hand to his lips and pressed kisses to the inside of her wrist that short-circuited all her brain cells, making her briefly forget her dismay over Kate's refusal to do the interviews. "What else did she say?"

"She won't do the interviews," Jill said with a sigh as she reluctantly withdrew her hand. She couldn't think when he was doing that.

"I thought she might say that."

Surprised, Jill looked over at him. "Yet you advised me to set them up?"

"You did your job. What she does next is up to her." He paused and then looked up to meet her gaze. "I noticed you didn't tell her you're with me."

"I didn't think it was the time."

"It's not because you're afraid she'd going to blow a gasket over us, is it?"

"No, of course not," Jill said with less conviction than she felt.

"You're sure of that?"

"Mostly."

He smiled, but it wasn't the full-face event his smiles usually were.

"Are you hurt that I didn't tell her?"

"Not really. I haven't told my dad or anyone else about us, so why should you?"

"I will tell her. When she gets back. I'll tell her then."

"And when will that be?"

Jill turned back onto her side, and Ashton cuddled in close behind her. There was something about having his strong arms around her that made her feel safer and more secure than she'd felt with any other man. "I guess they were going to leave today, but the weather isn't great, so they're aiming for tomorrow."

He nudged her hair out of the way so he could get to her neck. "Looks to me like you have another day off."

"Looks that way."

"However will you spend all that time?"

"I'll probably go shopping or something," she said with a teasing grin he couldn't see. "I could use a couple of new suits."

He let out a growl as he slid his hand straight down the front of her to cup her sex. "That's not what you need."

Jill pushed her bottom against his erection, drawing a groan from him. "No?"

"Nope."

"What do I need?"

"This," he whispered in her ear as his fingers delved between her legs. "Me. You need me."

"Do I?"

"Mmmm."

As he set out to show her just how much she needed him, Jill's worries over her sister's career faded into the background.

"Thank goodness you finally called me back," Clare said when she answered Kate's call.

Kate winced at the worry she heard in her mother's voice. "It's been a rough couple of days."

"I can imagine."

"I'm sorry for causing you embarrassment."

"Forget that, Kate. I want to know how you are."

"Sex tapes aside, I'm very, very happy—happier than I've been in ten years. I know you don't approve—"

"Don't put words in my mouth, Katherine."

The use of her full name startled her, since her mother rarely pulled out the big guns anymore. "Sorry," she muttered. "I should've told you where I was going—and why."

"I would've liked to have known, but you're not under any obligation to report in to me about your every move."

"Still, I wish you'd heard the news from me."

"So, tell me… Tell me your news."

"We're back together. For good this time. Among other things."

"What other things?"

"I… We're… We're getting married."

"Oh, Kate… Wow. That's… Wow."

Her eyes flooded, and her throat closed tight around a wedge of emotion. "I know I don't need it, but I so want your approval."

"Oh, honey, you have it. Of course you do. You're a grown woman, free to make your own choices, and if this man is the one you want—"

"He is. He's always been the one I wanted. I never got over him."

"I often wondered if that was the case."

"You did?"

"You couldn't seem to make it stick with anyone else. It wasn't hard to put two and two together."

"Dad won't understand."

"Maybe not at first, but he'll come around."

"He can't stand Reid."

"He can't stand what Reid did ten years ago. Before that, he thought of him as a friend."

"Still…"

"The advice I'd give a friend in this situation is to follow your heart and hope for the best where everyone else is concerned."

"That's very generous advice to give a daughter who just told you she's going to marry a man nearly thirty years older than her."

"I'd like to think my daughter is also my friend."

"I am," Kate said, blinking back tears. "Of course I am."

"Does he love you, sweetheart? Honestly and truly love you?"

"Yes. He never stopped loving me."

"Then what more could any mother want for her daughter?"

"I didn't expect you to be so understanding."

"You know how I love to be unpredictable."

Kate smiled as a million memories of her mom siphoned through her mind, stopping at the fateful moment in which a car had struck her in a parking lot, changing all their lives forever. For the ten-millionth time since her mom recovered from the long coma, Kate was thankful to have her back in her life. "Mom?"

"Yes?"

"Will you bring Aidan and the boys and Grandma Anna and Grammy O'Malley and any of Aidan's family who want to come to Nashville for Christmas? I want the whole family there. Maggie's already said she'll come. I've got plenty of room for everyone." She didn't, really, but they'd make due. Somehow.

"We'd love to."

"I'm going to invite Dad and Andi, too."

"I had no doubt."

"You're sure that's okay?"

"Do you know the first Christmas I ever spent alone—"

"When you first moved to Stowe?"

"Right. All I hoped for then was that the time would come when we could all spend holidays together without it being awkward."

"You and Dad did that for years when Maggie was still at home."

"Right, but you've never been there, and it's been a long time since Jill was home for the holidays, so it wasn't quite the perfect Christmas I envisioned."

Kate had spent most of the last ten Christmases performing somewhere in the world while yearning for her family and home. The last five years, her sister had been with her, too.

"So I'd love nothing more than to spend Christmas in Nashville with you and your sisters and your father and the rest of our family."

"Do you think Dad will come?"

"It might take some cajoling, but he won't let you down."

"He never has before. I guess I'd better call him now."

"Best of luck with that."

Kate laughed at her mother's droll comment. "He never changes."

"Thank goodness for that."

"How're Aidan and the boys?"

"Good, busy as all hell. The usual. The boys are playing hockey this fall and keeping us hopping. I don't remember being this frantically busy when you girls were their ages."

"They're boys, and you're a lot older than you were when we were their age."

"Thanks for the reminder," Clare said dryly. "Speaking of the boys, I have to run to pick them up at their friend's house. Let me know how it goes with Dad?"

"I will. And Mom, thanks."

"What for?"

"For being you, for understanding, for loving me no matter what."

"I do, Kate. I'll always love you no matter what. Don't forget that, okay?"

"I never could. Talk to you soon."

"Bye, honey."

Emotionally drained after the conversation with her mom, Kate wanted to postpone the call to her dad, but that wasn't fair. He was probably frantic with worry by now. Bracing herself for his anger and his disapproval, Kate placed the call.

"Kate." The single word conveyed a world of relief. "I'm so glad you called."

The familiar sound of his voice brought tears to her eyes. "I'm sorry to have worried you."

"Tell me you're not really back with him."

She closed her eyes tight, trying to contain the flood, but was unsuccessful. "I can't tell you that."

His silence spoke volumes.

"I know it's not what you want for me—*he's* not what you want—but he's what I want." She recalled what her mother had said about wanting to know her daughter was loved. "He loves me, Dad. He really does, and I love him, too. I never stopped loving him."

"Surely there has to be someone closer to your age—"

"Maybe there is, but I spent ten years thinking about Reid every single day. That has to mean something, doesn't it?"

Again he was silent.

"Dad?"

"I guess so," he said grudgingly.

"I know this is hard for you to understand."

"It's impossible for me to understand. It always has been. I know that's not what you want to hear."

"No, it isn't."

"If he loves you so much, how could he have led you into a situation that ended up all over the Internet?"

"Dad, I'm twenty-eight years old. He didn't lead me anywhere I didn't want to go, and besides, I'm the public figure. Not him. I should've known better."

"He should've known better."

"Why? Because he's older than me?"

"Among other reasons."

Kate rested a hand over her stomach, which was rejecting the breakfast she'd recently enjoyed. "There's something else I need to tell you," she said haltingly. "I don't want you to hear it on the news."

"What?"

"He… Reid and I… We're getting married."

"You have to be kidding me, Kate! Why in the world would you want to marry a man so much older than you? You'll be a widow when you're barely married."

At that, Kate began to get angry. "That's an awful thing to say, Dad."

"Are you going to sacrifice your chance to be a mother so you can marry this older man?"

"Who said anything about not being a mother?"

"He's actually interested in having kids at his age?"

"He's considering it, and you're one to talk. Your youngest kids are only ten."

"And I'm painfully aware of how much more difficult parenthood is in my fifties than it was in my thirties and forties. This is crazy, Kate. You go down there to St. Kitts on a wild hair a couple of days and one sex tape ago, and now you're going to *marry* him?"

Kate fought to keep her cool. The last thing in the entire world she wanted was another rift with her dad. "It was hardly a wild hair. It's something I've wanted to do for a very long time."

"You know I want to support you—always. But I can't support this. I just can't."

"Mom understands. I wish you could, too."

"Maybe Mom is more enlightened than I am, but the idea of my gorgeous young daughter sleeping with a guy my age doesn't work for me at all."

"This is about how well it works for *me*! He loves me, Dad. Doesn't that mean anything? I'd think you'd be grateful to know that someone loves me as much as you do."

"No one loves you as much as I do."

"Yes, Daddy," she said softly, wiping at a stray tear that rolled down her cheek. "He does. He might even love me more than you do."

"I'm hardly going to compete with Reid Matthews for my daughter's love," he said disdainfully.

"It's not a competition. I have more than enough love for both of you, but once again you're putting me in the awful position of having to choose between you. I won't do that. I *can't* do that. I'm asking you—as an adult—to respect my choices and support me."

"I can't support this, Kate. I'll support you in any other way you need, but not this."

"I want you and the family to come to Nashville for Christmas."

"Will he be there?"

"Of course he will, Dad! He's my fiancé."

"Then I won't be there. I'm not spending the holidays with that guy. No way."

"Dad—"

"I have to go, honey. The twins need a ride to soccer practice, and they're waiting for me."

Kate didn't bother to remind him that she'd called his cell phone. "Okay."

"I love you."

"I love you, too."

"Let's leave it at that, okay?"

"Sure," she said as she dealt with a torrent of tears. "No problem."

"I'll speak to you soon."

And then he was gone, and Kate was transported back to that awful day in Nashville when he'd caught her with Reid and demanded she come home to Rhode Island with him immediately. When she refused, he'd driven away from her after forbidding her to have any further contact with him or her younger siblings.

Their relationship, which had always been close, had taken a big hit that day, and had never truly recovered. There'd been distance between them ever since, despite the fact that they spoke regularly and saw each other as often as her busy career would allow. They were always cautiously polite with each other, which she absolutely hated. But since it beat the alternative of not speaking to him, she went along with it.

"Miss Kate?" Bertha asked softly as if she was afraid to intrude on a private moment. "Are you all right?"

Kate shook her head and brushed the tears off her face, embarrassed to have been caught weeping. "Not really. Rough couple of days."

"Is there anything I can do for you?"

"No, thank you. I'm going to take a walk."

"That path over there leads to the shore."

"A walk on the beach is just what I need. I'll be back in a while."

"Enjoy." Bertha gathered up Kate's dishes and went inside.

Kate took the stairs from the veranda to the path Bertha had identified and headed for the beach. The crash of the waves became louder as she got closer, but tears blurred her view.

She supposed she'd been deluding herself to think her dad would understand her relationship with Reid this time around. After all she was no longer a fresh-faced eighteen-year-old who'd just landed in Nashville to chase the dream. She'd done a lot of living and a lot of growing up since she left home. She sat atop an empire worth hundreds of millions of dollars and certainly knew her own heart. Why couldn't he give her some credit for any of that?

Perhaps if he hadn't once been friends with Reid, hadn't trusted him to look after his young daughter in the big city and then been so betrayed by their affair...

Perhaps if Reid were any other fifty-five-year-old man, her father wouldn't be so angry about their relationship.

"Who knows?" she asked out loud. "Maybe he's predisposed to hate any guy I love, any guy Jill or Maggie loves, too."

Though the thought brought some comfort, she knew in her bones that the reason her dad was so unhappy was because she'd chosen Reid. Her dad had certainly never forgotten how he'd forced her to choose between him and her lover and been left on the outside looking in at his own daughter.

Kate and her dad and sisters had been through a lot together. After their mother's accident, the three girls had been crippled by grief and the unending horror of having to relive the accident they'd witnessed over and over again. Their equally grief-stricken dad had stepped up for them as best he could.

For years afterward, Kate would wake up in a cold sweat after dreaming about the car coming at them, out of control in a parking lot. And her mother, just standing there, as if wishing the car would hit her. Much later they learned about the rape that had traumatized their mom and the threats the man had made against her children.

Kate shuddered as if chilled, though the day was warm. Storm clouds hovered, dark and ominous. She hoped they weren't a harbinger of things to come.

Desi sent a car from the resort to meet Reid at one of the public docks. On the way to Half Moon Bay, Reid relived the last few glorious days with Kate, culminating in their engagement the night before. It had taken being with her again, being swept up in the magic they created together, to fully understand just how lost he'd been without her.

Watching the scenic island pass by in a blur through the window, Reid thought about how he'd done his best to forge ahead after their breakup. The move to St. Kitts had worked out well for him. He enjoyed his life here, especially the work he did with the local community to build affordable housing for island residents. He'd made friends here—good, genuine friends who he enjoyed spending time with.

He'd met Mari here and had tried his best to give her what she deserved from their relationship, even if he'd held back the most important part of himself. He'd done that, he now knew, because that part of him belonged to Kate and always would.

It had taken about ten seconds in her presence for it to become clear to him that for all his contentment and serenity, he'd been living half a life since the day she'd walked out of his home in a fit of fury he'd completely deserved.

There was no going back, no sense beating himself up for mistakes long in the past. The future stretched out before them, an expanse of endless possibility and adventure. His incredibly beautiful fiancée could truly have any man she wanted, and she had chosen him.

That was a gift he'd celebrate every day for the rest of his life.

She'd thrown him for a loop telling him she wanted children. He'd assumed they'd forgo a family because he was so much older than her. He should've known better than to think that a twenty-eight-year age difference would keep Kate from going after what she wanted.

He chuckled softly to himself as it became very clear to him that there was nothing at all he wouldn't do to make her happy, including becoming a father again at fifty-six or –seven—maybe both—if that was what she wanted. From the first instant she'd opened that glorious mouth and sung for him, she'd had his heart and soul.

To pretend otherwise would be less than genuine, and he'd promised her a real, genuine life. Thinking of her round and swollen with his child made his heart skip a beat. He wanted to see that. He wanted to lay his hands on her belly and feel their child moving inside her. He wanted to help her bring their baby into the world and watch her glow with the joy of holding him or her to her breast.

He wanted it all so badly he ached. Maybe he was nothing more than an old fool, but he was an old fool who was madly in love, who'd been madly in love for a long, lonely time. Now that she was back in his arms, his life and his bed, there was nothing he wouldn't do to keep her there and to keep her happy.

With that in mind, he was determined to get through the next couple of hours as quickly as he could so he could get back to her and tell her how he felt. He'd left her with the impression that he didn't want children with her, but that couldn't be further from the truth. He wanted *everything* with her—every damned thing life had to offer both of them.

The car rolled onto his street, coming to a halt behind several emergency vehicles.

"What the heck?" Reid asked as he alighted from the car and took off at a run, concerned about the neighbors who'd become his St. Kitts family.

It didn't take long to see that the activity was focused on his place. He came to a skidding stop outside the picket fence, shocked to see the windows were smashed and the front yard littered with clothing and other items he recognized as his.

A cold knot of anger and dismay curled in his belly as he approached the cops who had gathered in the street.

"Oh, there he is! Reid!" His neighbor and fellow American ex-patriot, Jeff Herbert, came running up to him.

"What happened?" Reid asked, staring at the damaged remnants of the place he'd called home for nearly a decade.

"We don't know," Jeff said. "We had the neighborhood dinner in town last night and got home late. When we got up this morning, we noticed the damage to your place. We tried to call you and Mari last night, to see where you were when you didn't show up for dinner."

"Mari and I aren't together anymore."

"Oh," Jeff said, seeming shocked by the news. "I hadn't heard that. Sorry."

"Thanks." Reid continued to stare at the shattered windows, feeling somewhat removed from the surreal sight. Was this really happening?

"You don't think she…" Jeff shook his head. "What am I thinking? Of course she didn't."

Reid wished he could be so certain.

One of the police officers approached him. "This is your place?"

Reid nodded. "I rent it."

"Any idea who might've trashed it?"

He had a few thoughts, but he refused to entertain them. He'd slept with her, made love with her, shared his life with her for half a year. Surely she wouldn't do something like this to him. Would she?

"No, I can't think of anyone."

Beside him, Jeff remained silent, for which Reid was grateful. If this was Mari's handiwork, he'd let the cops figure that out. He wasn't going to hand her over to them.

"Can I go inside?"

"Let me check with my captain," the officer said. He walked away.

"It's none of my business," Jeff said.

"But?"

"She knew we'd all be at the dinner last night. It'd been planned for weeks. There'd be no one here to report that glass was being smashed."

Jeff made a good point. A very good point. But it was too much for Reid to process. She'd professed to love him. How fast love had turned to hate.

"Mr. Matthews," the young police officer said. "My captain said it's okay for you to go in as long as one of us goes with you."

"That's fine." There wasn't much inside he needed, beyond his computer and a few photos he treasured, mostly of Ashton. His gut ached at the thought of what she'd probably done to the computer. What she didn't know was that due to some power issues they'd had in the beachfront community a few years ago, everything was fully backed up on a remote server.

These were the thoughts that spiraled through his mind as he followed the officer inside through the yard, where one of his favorite shirts had been shredded and tossed into bushes he'd planted himself. They stepped into the shattered remains of his home, where nothing remained intact. The glass covering pictures on the walls had been smashed, curtains torn down, blinds hung askew, the mattress on the bed they'd shared had been ripped open, as had the pillows, and his computer lay in a mangled mess on the floor. He noted the lamps she'd bought were gone, as were the crystal wineglasses she'd loved.

"Damn," the officer muttered. "You're sure you didn't piss anyone off?"

In a state of shock, Reid ventured farther into the room, where he found one of Ashton's baby pictures torn to pieces and sprinkled on the floor as if it were just another piece of trash. Seeing that, he no longer felt the need to protect her.

"I believe Mari Christenson did this. You can find her at her sister Angelique's house in Basseterre." Enraged, he rattled off the address.

Over the next hour, he answered the many questions the police had about his relationship with Mari and how it ended. He also talked to his landlord and offered to pay for the damage. In the same call, he let the landlord know he'd be ending the lease. He talked to his neighbors, promised to be in touch and received their hugs and support with grace, even though he felt completely numb inside.

When there was nothing left to do, no one left to talk to and all the questions had been answered to the best of his ability, he walked down the street to discover Desi's driver had waited for him. In the last hour, the storm clouds had gotten closer and the wind had begun to whip. It would be a choppy ride across the channel to Nevis.

Watching him with eyes gone wide with shock over the scene at Reid's house, the driver held the backseat door open. "Is there anything I can do, Mr. Matthews?"

"I need to do an errand in town before we head back to the dock."

"Of course."

"And thank you for waiting."

"Not a problem."

As the driver backed the car down the street, Reid thought about taking one last look at the place he'd called home for so many years. But then he thought better of it. There was nothing here he needed anymore.

Jack was in his study later that afternoon, staring out at foamy whitecaps on the Atlantic, when his wife came to find him.

"There you are," Andi said. "I've been looking all over for you. I didn't expect to find you in here on a Sunday, especially when there's football to be watched with your boys."

He'd gone out of his way the second time around as a father to leave work at the office on weekends and to spend as much time as he possibly could with his wife and sons. "Sorry. I was catching up on a few things and lost track of time. Are the boys all right?"

Andi eyed him shrewdly. "Everyone's fine. Are you?"

"Sure. What do you want to do for dinner?"

"Jack..."

He couldn't bring himself to say the words. If he said it out loud, it became real. "I talked to Kate."

"Oh good! Finally! How is she?"

"Better than expected."

Andi came around the desk, pushed some of his stuff out of the way and took a seat on the desktop. "How do you mean?"

"Apparently, she's getting married."

Andi's mouth fell open with shock, but she quickly recovered. "Oh. Well, they didn't waste any time."

"No."

He diverted his gaze to the ocean, where everything made sense to him. On windy autumn days like today, the water took on a darker grayish hue and whitecaps churned. On clear, sunny days, the water could be so painfully blue it would hurt his eyes to look at it. After living most of his life on the coast, he could predict the ocean's moods and rhythms with practiced ease. He wished he could do the same with his children, who'd proven endlessly unpredictable.

"What did you say when she told you her news?" Andi asked.

"I don't want to tell you, because you'll probably be disappointed. I already expect an earful from Clare, who's apparently all for it."

"Hmm, interesting. So you told Kate you don't approve."

"Among other things."

"You can't help how you feel, Jack, and I don't blame you for being upset about it."

"But?"

She raised a dark eyebrow in amusement. "How do you know there's a but?"

"Because I know you."

Andi bit her lip, seeming to consider whether she should speak her mind or not. Since it was unlike her to hold back any thoughts from him, watching her debate made him nervous about what she might say.

"If you're going to say I'm a horse's ass and I need to grow up and let my girls make their own mistakes, go ahead and say it. It's nothing I haven't already told myself."

"I wasn't going to say that, but now that you mention it…"

He laughed. Against all odds, she'd made him laugh. Shaking his head, he said, "You're too much, Andrea Harrington. Right when I thought I might never laugh again, there you are."

Her face lit up with delight. "Happy to help."

"So what were you going to say?"

"It might make you mad…"

"I promise I won't get mad at you. I'm mad at the situation. I'm mad at Reid Matthews but not at you. Never at you."

"Earlier today, even before I heard this latest news, I was thinking about where Kate's relationship with Reid might be heading and how you might react to it."

"So you expected me to be a horse's ass."

"I didn't say that…exactly."

Her smile warmed him as it always did, reminding him that no matter what happened, he had her to help him through the challenges.

"Do you remember when we first got together?" she asked.

The sudden change in direction took him by surprise, but she was always doing that—surprising and stirring him. "I remember every minute of it."

"So do I. It was an extremely difficult time for you. Clare had been in a coma for more than a year, you were suddenly raising three teenage girls mostly on your own, and you'd recently gone back to work after spending more than a year trying to find help for Clare."

Jack hated to think about that time in his life, even if it had led him to Andi.

"When we got together," she continued, "a lot of people supported us, despite the fact that our situation was anything but conventional. Your wife was still alive. You were still technically married but getting involved with someone else."

He thought about what she'd said, her point obvious to him even if he didn't care to admit it. "You're saying it's the same as what she's doing with Reid?"

"Not the same but *similar*. It's an unconventional situation—one you don't see every day and one that will make their life together, especially at first, a little more challenging than they'd like it to be as the people in their lives get used to them together." Pausing, she reached for his hand and held on tight. "Remember how essential it was to us to have the support of Jamie and Frannie and my friend David and our children?"

He nodded in agreement. It had meant the world to them.

"Even Clare's mother stepped up for us. Imagine how difficult and painful it must've been to see her sick daughter's husband moving on with another woman."

"Anna was amazing to me. She always was."

"Yes."

Andi let that single word hover in the air between them while he considered what she'd said—and what he'd said to Kate. One of the things he loved best about Andi was how she instinctively knew when to say nothing at all.

"I really am a horse's ass."

"No, Jack. You're a loving father who's rightfully concerned about the choices your child is making."

"She's not a child anymore. She likes to remind me of that."

"She'll always be your child, your little girl who grew up far too fast for your liking."

Wasn't that the truth? "She's going to marry him."

"Yes."

"I'm going to have to give her away. To *him*."

"Not if you don't want to. She'd never ask that of you if you weren't willing to do it."

"What father of girls doesn't think about that moment the whole time their daughters are growing up?"

Again, she held her tongue and let the silence speak for her.

"She wants us there for Christmas."

"I told you that days ago."

He glanced up at her. "What do you think?"

"It's up to you. The boys and I will do whatever you want to do. If you want to go to Nashville, we'll go with you. If you'd rather stay home, we'll do that, too."

"And you won't think I'm a horse's ass if I decide not to go?"

"Never. I meant it when I said you have a right to your feelings, even if others don't agree with them."

"You make a good point about when we were first together. I don't know what I would've done if people like Jamie and Frannie or my kids treated me like I was a monster for wanting to be with you."

"Kate might appreciate the same courtesy from you."

"Of all three girls, she was the most willing to go along with you moving here."

"Is that right? You never told me that, but it doesn't surprise me. She was the friendliest to me when Eric and I first arrived."

"*Shit*," he said with a moan. "I totally screwed this up. I said all the wrong things to her."

"You're a wonderful father, Jack, and you're allowed to screw up every now and then."

"You never do. You never screw up."

"That's because I'm the mom. We can't afford to screw up with you crazy dads around to mess things up."

"Very funny."

"You can always call her back to fix it."

"True."

"Is that what you want to do?"

"I think it might be."

She kissed the back of his hand and released it. "Then I'll leave you to it." She got up off the desk.

He stood to stop her from escaping. With his hands on her shoulders, he took a good long greedy look at her.

"What?"

"I love you so much. I hope you know that."

She rested her hands on his chest. "How could I not know when you show me every single day?"

He drew her in close to him, comforted by her unwavering love. Their bond had been unshakable from the very beginning, and he wouldn't have survived without her. He drew back from her, just far enough that he could kiss her.

"Thanks," he said many passionate minutes later.

"Mmm," she said, taking one more taste. "Definitely my pleasure."

"Can I get back to you and your pleasure at bedtime?"

"It's a date. Do you want me to stay while you talk to her?"

"You don't have to."

"I do need to make sure Robby finished his math homework."

"His name is *Rob*."

"Right. Keep reminding me." She left him with one last kiss. "Good luck, love."

"Thanks."

CHAPTER 12

The arriving storm woke Kate from a nap late that afternoon to wonder when Reid would be back. She hadn't expected him to be gone this long and suspected he'd been delayed by the storm.

She tried to call him, but his phone went right to voice mail.

Wind whipped through the trees and shook the windows as she thought about the stretch of water between the two islands. What if he couldn't get back to her? What if something happened to him?

That thought drove her out of bed and down the stairs, where she found Bertha in the kitchen, enjoying a cup of coffee and a magazine. "Oh, Ms. Kate," she said, jumping up when Kate came into the room. "I was just taking a short break."

"Please don't let me interrupt."

"Is there something I can get for you?"

"I was wondering whether Mr. Matthews will be able to get back because of the storm."

"I'm told he's on his way."

"Oh. I tried to call him, but he didn't answer."

"Probably can't hear the phone in the wind."

"That's true."

"I sent one of the cars down to meet him. They should be back any time now."

"Thank you," Kate said, relieved to know he was fine. Just running late. "Please enjoy your break. I have no doubt you've earned it."

Bertha's smile lit up her face as she sat. "I like to think so." She paused before she said, "If you don't mind my asking, what's it like to perform on a stage in front of all those people?" She stopped herself. "I'm sorry. You're on a break yourself. That's probably the last thing you want to talk about."

"I don't mind talking about it." As she slid into a chair across from Bertha, Kate said, "It can be scary, especially when you're new to it. But after a while, you get used to it and it becomes more routine."

"I can't imagine how that ever becomes routine."

"Two hundred nights a year. That's how."

"That many?"

"On a slow year."

Bertha laughed. "My lord. No wonder you're in need of some rest and relaxation. How long did it take you to get used to it?"

Settling into the conversation, Kate thought about that. "I was terrified for a full year, and now… Now it's a thrill. The highest of highs. An adrenaline rush. All those things." And she was giving it all up because she was ready for thrills of a different sort, the simpler kind.

"Your voice is simply magnificent."

"That's kind of you to say."

"My favorite song of yours is 'I Thought I Knew.'"

Kate smiled. She heard that often from her fans. "Want to know a secret?"

Bertha propped her chin on her upturned fist and leaned in. "Lay it on me."

"That song was written for Reid, ten years ago when we were first together."

Bertha's eyes widened. "The same Mr. Matthews who's staying with you now?"

"One and the same. We were together for a short time ten years ago. I wrote the song then. It's still my biggest hit."

"If you don't mind my asking…" Bertha seemed to think better of the question and stopped herself. "I'm sorry. It's none of my business."

Cocooned in the cozy kitchen while the storm howled outside and rain beat against the windows, Kate tried to keep her mind off where Reid might be and whether he was safe. Talking to Bertha helped. "Please, feel free to ask whatever you want."

"I just wondered how your mama feels about your relationship with an older man." Bertha blushed and let out an unsteady laugh. "See what I mean? None of my business."

Kate laughed along with her. "My *mama* is a lot more understanding than my *papa*."

"Ah," Bertha said, her eyes dancing with mirth. "I suppose that's to be expected."

"He and Reid were friends in college. When I moved to Nashville, he asked Reid to keep an eye on me. We became good friends, and one thing led to another. I was very much in love with him. There was quite an uproar when my dad found out about our relationship."

"I imagine so."

"We spent ten years apart, wishing every day we were together. We only recently found out that we both felt the same way." Kate placed her hands over her face, which was suddenly heated.

"That's a very sweet story. Love is so hard to find, and lasting love... Well, that's something most of us only dream about. I've certainly never found it." Bertha frowned as she said the words but rebounded quickly. "But, I have lovely children and grandchildren who absolutely adore your music. Wait until I tell them I met you. They'll be so jealous."

"Are they here? On Nevis?"

"My whole family is here."

"If you'd like to invite the kids over, I'd be happy to meet them."

Bertha's eyes bugged. "You don't have to do that!"

"I'd really love to, if they don't mind venturing into the storm."

"Are you kidding? Those kids will absolutely drag their parents over here. Do you mind if I call them?"

"Go right ahead."

Bertha scurried into the kitchen, and Kate chuckled when she heard the older woman's excited conversation. She returned wearing a huge smile.

"They insisted on bringing dinner, and the kids are beside themselves. Thank you so much, Miss Kate."

"Please, just call me Kate."

Bertha beamed at her. "They say a lot of mean things about you in the paper. I've never believed any of them."

"That's nice of you to say." Kate wondered if Bertha had heard about the video, or worse yet, seen it. Ugh, she couldn't think about that. "We'll do a little jam session, and the kids can sing with me."

"That's so very kind of you. I can't thank you enough."

"It'll be fun." And it would be, she decided.

The slam of a car door had Kate scurrying from the kitchen to the front door. When she saw Reid running through the rain, she went out to meet him. Until she saw him, hadn't realized just how fearful she'd been of something happening to him in the storm.

She bolted down the stairs and met him halfway, leaping into his arms.

He caught her, lifting her right off her feet. "You're going to get all wet, darlin'."

"I don't care," she said, kissing his face and then his lips. "I was worried about you."

"I'm fine." He tipped his face to kiss her again, more seriously this time.

With her arms tight around his neck, Kate thrust her tongue into his mouth while his hands gripped her bottom.

As the rain beat down on them, she couldn't stop kissing him. "Missed you," she said when they came up for air many minutes later.

"So I see," he said with a chuckle. "Should we go in?"

"I kinda like kissing in the rain." She nuzzled his nose. "I don't think I've ever done that before."

"I like it, too."

They spent another ten minutes outside before Kate began to shiver from the chill. She whimpered when he broke their kiss to walk them to the porch.

"You're not relapsing on my watch," he said sternly as he took the stairs.

"You ruin all my fun."

"Is that so?"

She nuzzled her cold nose against his neck. "Uh-huh."

Inside, he went straight up the stairs to their room and headed for the shower. He moved very quickly to strip them of their wet clothes and guided her into the steaming water.

"Ah that feels good," Kate said as the heat drove the chill from her bones.

He held her from behind, his hands traveling from her breasts to her belly and below.

"That feels good, too," she said, already weak in the knees.

"Put your hands on the wall." His voice was gruff and sexy.

Kate did as directed and waited to see what he would do. Her legs quivered as anticipation mixed with desire.

He kneaded her shoulders and back, working his way down to give her bottom special treatment.

She pressed back against his arousal, drawing a groan from him.

When his arm encircled her hips and lifted her, a surprised squeak slipped from between her lips that quickly became a moan when he entered her from behind. "Oh God," she muttered.

"You like it?"

He expected her to talk right now when she could barely form a thought, let alone words? "Yeah." Her mind raced as her body reacted to the new experience of being taken from behind.

Letting her feet slide back to the floor, Reid urged her to bend forward. His fingers dug into her hips as he slammed into her, making her come once and then again when he reached around to stroke her to another shattering climax.

He pushed hard into her one last time, coming himself with a groan that echoed in the shower.

Kate's legs felt like rubber as he withdrew from her. She turned into his embrace, reeling from the shockingly erotic interlude.

"Are you okay, darlin'?"

Pressed against his chest, she nodded as the warm water rained down upon them. He tended to her with almost religious reverence, washing her hair and body as if she were made of porcelain. When he was done, he toweled her off and carried her to bed.

He slid in next to her and reached for her.

Kate turned into his embrace, resting her face on his chest.

"Did I hurt you?"

"No, of course not."

"You're so quiet."

"I've never done that before."

"We did that."

"No, we didn't."

"Are you sure?"

"Yes," she said, laughing. "I'm positive."

"Was it too much?"

"I loved it."

He hugged her tightly. "So did I."

"Is there other stuff we haven't done?"

"Lots of other stuff."

"Can we do all of it?"

Laughing, he said, "We can certainly try."

"I'll look forward to that," she said kissing his chest. "How did everything go on St. Kitts?"

"Fine." After a beat of silence, he said, "That's not true, actually. It wasn't fine. I wasn't going to tell you because I didn't want to upset you, but I got into trouble before by not being honest with you, and I don't want to make that mistake again."

Alarmed, Kate propped her chin on his chest so she could see his face, which was troubled. "What happened?"

"Mari trashed our place. Everything was smashed and destroyed."

Kate gasped. "Oh my God. Are you sure it was her?"

He nodded.

"Did you call the police?"

"They were already there when I arrived. I guess the neighbors called. There was a neighborhood dinner in town last night, so Mari would've known everyone was out. I wasn't going to give them her name until…"

"Until what?"

"She ripped up one of Ashton's baby pictures. I saw that, and I didn't care about protecting her anymore."

"I don't blame you," Kate said, furious on his behalf. "She has to know what he means to you after all the time you spent with her."

"Which is why she did it. She wanted to hurt me the way I hurt her." He combed his fingers through Kate's hair. "As much as I hate to say it, I have a feeling we're going to find that she was somehow behind the video, too. She knows I would've sent you to Desi's place if you asked me where you should stay. It wouldn't have taken much for her to confirm you were there, especially if she followed me the other night."

"I'm so sorry I caused you all this trouble."

"It's not your fault, darlin'. You did me a big favor by showing up when you did. I had no idea she was capable of such malice. What she did to my house… It was… It was bad."

"Was everything of yours ruined?"

"Pretty much. I was able to salvage some pictures, and luckily my computer is backed up. Not to worry, though. They're just things. They can be replaced."

"That's an awful last memory of a place you loved."

"Yes, it was."

"Thank you for telling me. I don't want you to protect me by keeping upsetting things from me. I want to help you through them."

"You did help," he said, reaching for her.

She snuggled into his embrace and smiled when his lips touched her forehead.

"Did you talk to your folks?"

"Yeah."

"And how did that go?"

"We're batting five hundred," she said, pained when one of her dad's favorite phrases rolled off her tongue. "My mom was pretty cool, but my dad… Not so much."

"I suppose that's to be expected."

"Yeah, I guess."

"It hurt, huh?"

"Kind of. I invited him and his family to Nashville for Christmas, but I'm not sure he'll come. My mom and her family are in, and my sister Maggie is coming." She glanced up at him. "Do you think Ashton would come?"

"I can ask him, but it's hard to say. He may have his own plans for all I know."

"I hope he comes."

"Do you? As I understand it, there's no love lost between the two of you."

"I'd like to put all of that in the past. We're going to be family to each other, whether he likes it or not. I'd like for us to at least be sociable for your sake."

"That'd be nice, darlin'. I got the sense from him the other day that he's looking to mend fences, too. He said there's something else going on in his life that he's anxious to tell me about when he sees me. I wonder if he's met someone."

"How would you feel about that?"

"I'd be thrilled. I want him to know real love. There's nothing quite like it."

"No, there isn't." She punctuated her words with soft kisses to his chest.

"I bought you a present in Basseterre."

"What kind of present?"

"The really good kind."

"Where is it?"

"In my coat pocket, but you have to let me up so I can get it."

Kate kissed him, lingering despite her excitement over the present. There was nothing he could give her that was better than his kisses, his love and the promise of forever together. "I still have the locket you gave me," she said as she moved off him so he could get up. "I wear it all the time. Wearing it made me feel closer to you."

"That's very sweet." He got back in bed.

"Where is it?"

"Where is what?"

"My present."

"You have to find it," he said with a delightfully playful smile.

Kate took great pleasure in frisking him, touching him everywhere until he was hard as a rock.

"How did this backfire on me?" he asked as she stroked him.

"I can't find it anywhere."

"You're not looking in the right places. Close your eyes."

Kate did as he asked but continued to caress his erection until she felt the slide of a ring on the third finger of her left hand. She gasped, and her eyes flew open. She raised her hand so she could see the simple, elegant ring set in white gold or platinum with one large square-cut diamond. Tears rolled down her cheeks as she stared at the ring her one true love had put on her finger, making her his forever. Finally.

"Is it okay?" he asked, sounding uncertain.

Kate couldn't stop staring at it. "It's… It's perfect." It was exactly what she told him she wanted—simple and real, but also glorious.

"Oh, good. I was worried for a minute there."

Kate wrapped her arms around him. "Thank you so much. I absolutely love it."

"I absolutely love you."

With her hands on his face, bestowed a kiss upon him that was filled with all the overwhelming emotions she was experiencing—joy, love, excitement, desire and, most of all, relief. To have what she'd wanted for so long, to know that wherever she went he'd go too, to know that whatever life had in store for her, he'd be there with her…

Without breaking the kiss, he cupped her breasts, giving special attention to her nipples.

Kate raised herself up to take him in, and then held perfectly still, celebrating the joy of their joining.

His arms tightened around her, his kiss became hungrier.

She tore her lips free. "Reid…"

"What, honey?"

"We keep forgetting the condom."

"I haven't forgotten."

Kate stared at him. "What're you saying?"

"That I want what you want, no matter what it is."

"Do you mean it? You want kids? With me?"

"I want you to have everything you've ever dreamed of, and for some reason you've staked your claim with me. I'd never deny you the chance to be a mother, as long as you know you may not have me around—"

She swooped down on him, kissing that thought right off his lips. "I'd rather have thirty amazing, magical years with you than fifty okay years with someone else."

"Thank you, darlin'." His fingers pressed into her hips, and his erection lengthened inside her. "Can get back to what you started here?"

"Most definitely."

They flew back to Nashville early the next morning. The storm was long gone, and the skies were clear and sunny, with puffy white clouds off in the distance.

Sitting next to Reid in the cockpit reminded Kate of their trip to Memphis and the monumental event that had occurred there.

"What're you smiling about, darlin'?"

"I'm thinking about the first time I ever flew with you."

"Reluctantly, if I recall correctly."

"You hadn't told me you were a pilot, and then you pop it on me out of nowhere. What was I supposed to say?"

"You were supposed to say, 'Reid, I trust you with my life, and if you tell me you're a great pilot, I believe you.'" Hearing him imitate her tone had her staring at him, speechless.

"How'd you do that?"

"Do what?"

"Perfectly imitate me."

He reached over to rest his hand on her leg. "I've heard your voice in my dreams for years. I know how you sound."

Touched by his words, she said, "It's a little unnerving how well you do it."

"Now you do me."

She raised an eyebrow. "Didn't I already do you this morning?"

He tossed his head back and laughed. "I meant imitate me, though I do love how you think."

Kate thought about his challenge for a moment. "Harder, darlin'," she said in his accent. "Yeah, like that." She glanced over to find him looking at her with eyes gone hot with desire. "How'd I do?"

"Pretty good. How about you say that to me when we get home and I can actually do something about it?"

"Sure," she said, laughing. "You got it." She watched the scenery go by in a sea of brilliant blue. "So pretty."

"Yes, it is."

"Last night was fun, huh?" Bertha's family had arrived en masse with pots of chili, cornbread, salad and brownies. Kate had sung with the kids, autographed CD cases and posed for pictures with each of them.

"Sure was. Those kids will never forget their night with you."

She rested her hand over the one he had on her leg. "I'll never forget the night we officially got engaged."

"Neither will I." He squeezed her thigh. "So when do you want to tie the knot?"

"I've been thinking about that. What would you say to doing it over the holidays when my family is in Nashville?"

"That soon? You don't want to plan a big shindig?"

She shook her head. "You're the one telling me there's no time to waste, and besides, everyone I'd want there will be in town. Maybe if he knows we're getting married, my dad will come."

"And if he doesn't?"

Kate didn't want to think about the possibility of getting married without him there to give her away, but she refused to put a damper on their celebratory mood. She shrugged. "Then I guess we'll do it without him."

"I sure hope it doesn't come to that."

"So do I. He left me a message last night that he wants to talk some more, but I'm not really ready to talk to him after what he said yesterday." She glanced over at him. "Anyway, how about we get married on your birthday?"

"You remember my birthday?"

"Sure, I do. I remember that I couldn't wait to get back to Nashville the day after Christmas to help you celebrate."

"Sounds good to me."

"We can do at my house with a JP, some food, music. Nice and simple. That'd be just what I want—if it's okay with you."

"I told you—whatever you want is okay with me."

"Are you always going to be so easy to get along with?"

"Making you happy makes me happy."

She looked down at her gorgeous ring, which sparkled in the bright sunlight. "I feel very happy today, as well as lucky and hopeful."

"I'm glad."

"And also a little scared."

"Of what, darlin'?"

"Of what'll happen when we step out of the bubble we've been in. The last time we did that, it didn't go so well."

"As long as we stay focused on our relationship and honest with each other about everything, we'll be fine."

"You make it sound so simple."

"It is simple."

Kate hoped he was right, but she couldn't help but worry about what might be waiting for them at home.

Ashton woke with a sense of dread, knowing he had to leave Jill and get back to work. He'd already been gone a day longer than planned, and there was no postponing the inevitable. In the faint early morning light coming in through the blinds, he could see her gorgeous face and her dark hair on the pillow.

He'd never get tired of looking at that face. He ran a finger over her cheek, reluctant to disturb her but wanting her to know he was leaving.

Her eyes fluttered open, blinking several times. "You're awake early."

"I have to go to work."

"Oh."

"The party had to end sometime."

"I suppose so."

He wondered if she knew that the knitting of her brows gave away her worries. "Just because the vacation is over doesn't mean this is." With an arm around her, he brought her in snug against him, loving the feel of her skin pressed against his. "This," he said, kissing her neck and then her lips, "is just getting started."

She put her arm around him and caressed his back, sending shivers of sensation skittering over his skin. She stirred him like no other woman ever had, like no other woman ever would.

He held her for a long time, hating that he had to leave her even for a few hours. "See you for dinner tonight?"

"That sounds good."

"What do you have on for today?"

"I'm not sure, exactly. I guess I'll wait for Kate to get home so she can tell me this big plan of hers."

"Whatever it is, you can handle it. I know you can."

"I guess we'll see."

He drew back so he could look into her eyes. "Last night was amazing."

She nodded. "Very much so."

"I don't want to go."

Her fingers skimmed over his chest and down to encircle his straining erection. "I can tell," she said with a small shy smile. As she stroked him, Ashton forgot all about work and about the nine o'clock meeting with Buddy that had been on the calendar for weeks. His world was reduced to her soft hand on his hard shaft.

"Jill…"

She tightened her grip, stroked him harder. "Hmm?"

He shuddered. "*God.*"

Her soft laughter filled his heart to overflowing. She knew exactly what she was doing to him, and she loved it.

"You'd better stop," he said, though that was the last thing in the universe he wanted.

Apparently, she knew that because she added her other hand, working him over until he filled her hands with his release.

"There," she said, kissing his chest and then his lips. "Now you can go to work without that pesky thing bothering you all day."

He released an unsteady laugh. "That *pesky* thing, as you call it, will bother me all day because I'll be thinking about that. And you."

With one last kiss, he reluctantly got out of bed and headed for her shower, where he was unable to find soap that didn't smell like her. Oh well, he thought, as he rubbed it all over his skin, smelling like her wouldn't be any more torturous than thinking about her all day.

He emerged dressed and ready to go to find she'd fallen back to sleep. Leaning over the bed, he kissed her cheek and smiled when she murmured in her sleep.

"I love you," he whispered in her ear.

Driving away from her was one of the hardest things he'd ever done. "You're being totally ridiculous," he said to himself as he drove down the long lane that led to the main road. As he drew closer to the gate that kept Kate's property sealed off from the rest of the world, he stopped when he saw the road lined with satellite trucks and a horde of reporters.

"Shit." He banged a U-turn and returned to Jill's place. When he got to the door, he realized he'd locked it on the way out and uttered a curse. He pulled out his cell phone and called her, hoping the ringing phone would wake her.

"Hey, miss me already?" she asked in a sleepy, sexy voice that stirred his recently satisfied libido. Everything about her stirred him.

"Absolutely, but we have a little problem. The press is camped outside the gate."

"Shit," she said, sounding much more awake.

"I said the same thing."

"I need to warn Kate. They're on the way home."

"Come down and let me in."

"Oh, you came back?"

"Yeah, I came back. I don't want to leave you here by yourself with this."

"I thought you needed to go to work."

"I do, but I was thinking maybe you should come with me. You could stay at my place in town until this blows over."

"What about Kate? She's going to need me."

"If they're smart, they won't come anywhere near here when they hear about the press invasion."

"True."

"So you'll come?"

She opened the front for him as she ended the call. "Give me ten minutes to grab a quick shower and throw some clothes in a bag."

"That's about all I've got." He'd already accepted that he wouldn't have time to go home and change. Good thing his meeting was only with Buddy, who wouldn't care if Ashton met him wearing jeans. Buddy's mantra was the more casual the better.

True to her word, Jill came running down the stairs ten minutes later, wearing a sweater and jeans tucked into boots. Her hair was contained in a ponytail, and she carried a backpack. She stopped short when she noticed him smiling at her. "What?"

"You look like an eighteen-year-old co-ed."

"I was in a rush."

"I didn't say that was a bad thing, darlin'."

"Oh, that's right. The men in your family like them young."

"That's not nice," he said with a laugh as he ushered her out the door.

"Sorry," she said with a sheepish grin. "That was a softball."

He held the door to the truck for her and then walked around to the driver's side. When he was in the truck, he reached into the backseat for a jacket he kept there. "Want to put this over your head so they don't recognize you?"

"You really think that's necessary?"

"Unless you want Kate to find out we're together before you're ready to tell her, I'd say it's necessary."

As he pulled up to the gatehouse to punch in the code she'd given him the day before, Jill squirmed down in the seat and pulled his jacket over her head. The instant the gate swung open, Ashton hit the gas, propelling the truck forward too quickly for the reporters to react.

He glanced in the rearview mirror and saw a few of them giving chase, but they drove quickly out of range. "It's safe to come out."

Jill popped up and ran a hand over her hair, glancing back at the mob scene outside the gate. "Wow," she whispered. "So much for the story dying a natural death."

"You need to warn your sister that she's coming back to a hornet's nest."

Jill withdrew her phone from her bag. "Damn, it went right to voice mail," she said. "Kate, it's me. The media is camped at the gate. You might want to avoid the house for the time being. Call me when you get this message."

"Let me try my dad," Ashton said, dialing as he drove. "Great. His went right to voice mail, too. Dad, you guys might want to avoid Kate's place. I heard it's crawling with reporters. Call me when you land." He glanced over to find Jill staring out the window, nibbling on her thumbnail. "Hey."

She turned to him.

"Don't worry. I know it's easy for me to say, but this'll die down eventually."

"Will she have a career left when it's over? What if all the mothers of those devoted teenage girls won't let them listen to her music anymore?"

"I don't think it'll come to that."

"It could if she doesn't address the fact that she made a mistake."

Since Ashton couldn't argue with that, he didn't try. Rather he reached for her hand and held it all the way into town. When they were getting close to his office, he said, "What do you think about coming to my meeting with Buddy? Maybe between the three of us, we can figure out a next step for Kate."

"You'd do that?"

"Of course I would. Buddy's label has a lot invested in her. It behooves all of us to figure a way out of this."

"Oh."

Ashton pulled into the parking lot next to Buddy's Escalade. "What does that mean. Oh?"

"I thought maybe you were doing it for Kate and not because of business."

"I'm doing it for *you*, silly." He leaned over to kiss her.

"Oh."

"There's that word again." Tugging on her ponytail, he said, "She's second only to Buddy in terms of sales for Long Road Records, which makes her problems Buddy's problems—and mine. But more than anything, I want to see that worry line between your brows disappear."

She reached up to feel for the line in question. "I don't have any lines."

"Yes, you do. Let's go see what Buddy has to say about all of this."

Inside, they exchanged greetings with Ashton's assistant, Debi, who sent him a secret smile when she saw him with Jill. Debi had helped to arrange the car to pick up Jill before their trip to Malibu and had called him out about his crush on her months ago, urging him to act on it.

When Jill wasn't looking, Debi gave him a thumbs-up.

Ashton rolled his eyes at her and ushered Jill up the stairs to his office where Buddy Longstreet was sitting in Ashton's chair, feet on the desk, like he owned the place.

"Comfortable?" Ashton asked his godfather.

"Very," Buddy said, watching as Ashton held a chair for Jill and waited until she was settled before he sat in the chair next to hers. "Fine mess your sister's gotten us into."

Jill winced. "Yes."

"When's she coming home?"

"Today."

"Good. She needs to get her ass out there to defend herself."

"That's what I told her," Jill said. "But apparently she's got other plans."

"What other plans?"

"She hasn't shared them with me yet."

"Huh."

"This is all your fault," Ashton said to Buddy.

"How's that?"

"You told her where to find my dad."

"So what if I did? I never told them to get it on outside where anyone might see them."

Buddy's indignant tone made Ashton laugh.

"How was Malibu?" Buddy asked.

Ashton glanced at Jill to find her staring at a picture on the wall, her face blazing with color. He hadn't told Buddy who he was taking on the trip with him, but his arrival with Jill, both of them in unusually casual attire, was a dead giveaway. "Fine."

Buddy's golden eyes danced with delight. "I bet it was."

As he resisted the urge to clobber Buddy, Ashton's cell phone rang with a call from his dad. Saved by the bell. "Hey, are you back?"

"Just landed. Where are you?"

"At the office with Buddy and Jill."

"We'll meet you there."

"Sounds good." He ended the call and told Buddy and Jill that Reid and Kate were on their way.

"Well," Buddy said with a guffaw, settling into the big leather chair, "this is about to get mighty interesting."

CHAPTER 13

Kate didn't want to go to Ashton's office. She went out of her way to ensure their paths rarely crossed, and even now that she was going to marry Reid, she couldn't imagine Ashton would be happy to see her. If anything, the opposite was probably true. After more than a week away, all she wanted was to go home.

But that wasn't possible with the media storming the gates.

"What's wrong, darlin'?" Reid asked as he drove the car they'd rented at the airport.

"Nothing." How could she tell him that seeing his son always made her nervous and brought back that awful day in the parking lot and the ugly accusations they'd hurled at each other? They'd barely exchanged a single word since then, despite their frequent business dealings.

When Kate thought of seeing him again, this time as his father's fiancée, her stomach began to actively ache.

"I wish you'd talk to me," Reid said as he drove through Nashville traffic on the way to Green Hills.

"I'm fine. Really."

"If you say so."

"I'm mad that we can't go home. I really want to see Thunder."

"I was thinking about that. Is there another way onto your property other than the main gate?"

Kate's eyes lit up when she tuned into his thought process. "Yes, but it's through my neighbor's place and only accessible on foot or horseback."

"Could your groom meet us with horses?"

"Yes!" Thrilled with the plan, she leaned over to kiss him. "You're always thinking."

"I don't like to see you unhappy."

"I've got nothing in the world to be unhappy about, so don't worry." Well, other than her father's disapproval of her upcoming marriage, but she refused to think about that today. There'd be plenty of time to think about that later when she didn't also have to face Ashton.

Reid pulled into the parking lot and parked next to Ashton's sleek silver Jaguar and a red pickup truck. She remembered the Saab Ashton had bought right out of law school and how proud he'd been of that car. He'd taken her on her first tour of Nashville, had brought her to Mabel's, introduced her to his friends, and she'd thanked him by having an affair with his father.

Well, that was a pleasant trip down memory lane, she thought as Reid took her hand to lead her inside. Her footsteps felt wooden and heavy as she stepped into Ashton's office for the first time. All her meetings with him had taken place at the Long Road Records offices.

Ashton's assistant, Debi, greeted Reid warmly, but her eyes bugged when he introduced Kate as his fiancée.

Debi jumped up and tripped over her desk chair in her haste to shake hands with Kate, who reached out to catch the younger woman before she fell.

"Wow, that was embarrassing," Debi said.

Laughing, Kate released her hold and shook hands with Debi. "Pleasure to meet you."

"I'm such a huge fan. Maybe even your biggest fan."

"That's nice of you to say. Thank you."

"Do you think…" Debi shook her head and gestured to the stairs. "Ashton is waiting for you in his office."

"Could I sign something for you before we go up?"

Again, Debi's eyes nearly popped out of her head. "You'd do that?" She hustled around her desk, banging her leg—hard—on the corner but never missed a beat as she handed Kate a note pad.

"How about a pen?" Kate asked, amused.

"God, I'm a mess," Debi drawled. "I see Buddy Longstreet all the time and never act like this much of a dork around him."

"I'm much more famous than Buddy," Kate deadpanned, making Debi and Reid laugh. She wanted to thank Debi for taking her mind off the meeting with Ashton. The butterflies in her stomach had calmed while they talked to Debi. Kate wrote, "To Debi, it was a thrill to meet you. Thanks for listening to my music! All the best, Kate Harrington." She handed the pad back to Debi.

"Thank you so much. I'm going to frame this. Heck, I'll make copies for home, work, my car and anywhere else I can hang it up. Wait till my friends hear that I met you. They'll be so jealous."

"Debi!" Ashton called down the stairs. "Quit playing fan girl and send them up."

Debi's face turned bright red. "Right this way."

"Don't listen to him," Kate whispered. "I never do."

Debi giggled and stepped aside so they could head up the stairs.

"That was nice of you, darlin'," Reid said when they were out of Debi's earshot. "You made her year."

"She and people like her made my career," Kate said with a shrug. "Where would I be without them?"

"It's fun to watch you with your fans. I've never gotten to see that before."

Kate hadn't thought about what it might be like for him to experience her fans for the first time with Bertha's family and now with Debi.

His hand on the small of her back fortified her as they stepped into Ashton's office.

Jill rushed over to hug Kate, who held on to her sister for dear life. She'd been fine until she saw her sister, and then the roller coaster of emotions she'd experienced over the last week had tears flooding her eyes as Jill's familiar fragrance filled her senses.

"Good to see you," Kate said, blinking back tears.

"You too." Jill drew back to study her. "You look good."

"So do you."

"Vacation agrees with us," Jill said. "Scandal, on the other hand…"

"I know, believe me. This is Reid. Reid, my sister Jill."

Jill shook his hand. "Nice to finally meet you after all this time."

"Likewise. Thank you for taking such good care of Kate when I wasn't around to do it."

"Oh," Jill said, seeming surprised—and charmed. "It was certainly my pleasure."

"Sorry about the mess at home," Kate said.

"Buddy was just suggesting we send some of his security guys over there to move them away from the gate," Jill said.

Kate sent her mentor and friend a grateful smile.

Buddy got up and came over to give her a hug. "Every time you come within five feet of this guy, you get yourself in trouble." Buddy released her to hug Reid.

"That's why we figured we ought to get married," Reid said.

Kate watched as he sought out his son across the room.

Ashton was standing, watching them warily.

Reid went over to hug his son.

Ashton returned the embrace with equal enthusiasm, which was a relief to Kate.

"So what're we going to do about this fine mess you've gotten yourself into?" Buddy asked as he returned to his post behind Ashton's desk.

"Are you a guest in your own office these days, son?" Reid asked Ashton.

"It appears that way," Ashton said dryly.

Buddy sent them one of his famous shit-eating grins.

Reid and Kate settled into chairs that Ashton got for them. She appreciated that Reid sat right next to her and reached for her hand the minute they were settled.

All eyes landed on her.

"I've made some decisions in the last few days," Kate said haltingly. She glanced at Jill. "I should probably talk to you privately before I tell everyone else."

"It's fine," Jill said. "Your plans affect all of us, so it would save us some time if you told us at the same time."

Grateful for her sister's clear, unemotional thinking, Kate steeled herself to say the words, to step away from the career that had defined her life. Perhaps for good.

Reid squeezed her hand and smiled at her, filling her with strength and determination. For him, for *them*, she was willing to do whatever it took to ensure they had a somewhat normal life. With that in mind, she met the golden gaze of Buddy Longstreet and said, "I'm done."

Buddy sat up a little straighter, but his feet remained planted on Ashton's desk. "With?"

"The music. The business. The career."

"Wait a minute," Jill said.

Ashton crossed his arms and shook his head, seeming disgusted and annoyed at the same time. Kate expected nothing less than both from him.

"Hear her out," Reid said, his gaze never leaving Kate as she struggled to find the words.

She tried to stay focused on her goal of a real, authentic life. "I've given this career everything I've had to give for a very long time. I've sacrificed any semblance of normal life, and you have, too, Jill. I don't enjoy it anymore, and I haven't in a very long time." She paused and looked at Reid. "I did it because I didn't have anything better to do. Now I have other things I want to do. I want a home and a family and the simple things most people take for granted. I want out of the whirlwind, off the treadmill, off the stage."

Buddy stared at her as if she were speaking a language he simply couldn't understand.

"I'm sorry to disappoint you," she said, looking again at Buddy. "You've done so much for me. You've made everything possible. But this is the right move for me now. I really believe that."

A pervasive silence hung over the room.

"Please," Kate finally said, glancing between Buddy and Jill. "Say something, will you?"

"You're the boss," Jill said flatly. "Whatever you want is what I want."

"I think you're a goddamned fool," Buddy said in a tone Kate had never heard from him before.

"Buddy…" Reid's voice held a note of warning.

"This isn't personal, Reid, so don't get your knickers in a twist."

Kate could tell that Reid was dying to respond to that, but he held his tongue.

"This is business," Buddy said, addressing Kate now. "Big business. It's the kind of business all the young ingénues and wannabes would give their right titties for. Hell, I remember a time—not all that long ago—when you'd give *your* right titty for it."

"Just for the record," Kate said, "I was never that desperate."

Ashton snorted with what might've been a laugh.

Buddy slammed his fist on the desk, making them all jump. "It's not funny! I've busted my ass making you into a star. It's what you told me you wanted. I gave you everything, and I'll be goddamned if I'm going to let you walk away at the peak of your career all because you want to get laid."

"Buddy!" Reid said. "You will not talk to her that way!"

Kate tightened her grip on Reid's hand to keep him from launching out of the chair to beat the crap out of his best friend. "While I appreciate your candor, Buddy, this really has nothing at all to do with sex, although as you and the rest of the world now know, the sex is pretty damned good."

That made Ashton laugh out loud, which spurred nervous laughter from Jill.

A warm look of camaraderie and—maybe something else—passed between them. But before Kate could examine the vibe more closely, Buddy was launching into a tirade about contracts and schedules and tours and other words that had once defined Kate's life. Not anymore.

"I'm sorry you're upset," Kate said. "But my decision is final. I want out."

"For how long?" Buddy asked.

"I don't know."

"So we're not talking about a vacation?"

"No. We're talking about a *life*. I want a *life*. I want a family. I want to know my little brothers and see my parents for more than a rushed dinner every couple of months. I want to actually live at the house I spent so much time and money building. I want to ride the horse that isn't going to live forever, as much as I might wish to believe otherwise." She stopped, glanced at Reid, who was gazing up at her with love and pride. Tearing her eyes off him, she looked at Buddy. "I'm sorry. I know this isn't what you want to hear, but I can't help how I feel."

"And I can't help thinking you're making an impulsive decision in the midst of what's been a rough stretch for you, between the pneumonia, the fainting, the video. No one would blame you for being sick of it. Hell, a big part of *me* doesn't blame you. Don't you think I get sick of the demands on my time, the rigors of running a business while trying to be creative, the endless string of nameless, faceless venues that all run together in one big blur of stage lights? Do you think I don't get sick of being away from my wife and kids?"

"I don't know," Kate said. It had never occurred to her that Buddy didn't love every bloody minute of it. No one did a better job of balancing a career and family than Buddy Longstreet.

"I do. I get goddamned sick of it. But I have a shitload of people depending on me for their livelihood. I don't have the luxury of walking away, and you know what? I hate to be the bearer of bad news, sweetheart, but you don't have that luxury either. While you were out becoming a big star, you might not have noticed that you employ a lot of people. What about them? What becomes of them?"

A pervasive sense of guilt filled Kate as it occurred to her that beyond Jill, she hadn't given much thought to what would become of the rest of her employees.

Ashamed, she forced herself to look at Buddy. "I assumed I could give them severance packages—"

Buddy's scoff ended the sentence prematurely. "And then what do they do?"

"You're not being fair, Buddy," Reid said. "The music business is the backbone of this city. Don't make it sound like they won't be able to get other jobs."

"Sure, they can get other jobs. But there's a big difference between being a roady for Kate Harrington and hauling speakers for John Q. Up-and-coming singer—and you know it. You're acting like they don't matter at all."

"Of course they matter to me," Kate said. "You know they do."

"Then don't do this to them. Don't do it to yourself. If you need a break, take one, but to completely walk away is not only irresponsible, it's downright mean to your fans and your employees."

When it came to laying down guilt trips, Buddy Longstreet had written the book. He had her questioning everything she'd so recently decided.

"Surely," Ashton said, startling Kate, "there's something in the middle between going full tilt and quitting entirely."

Intrigued, Kate forced herself to look directly at him for the first time since she entered the room. She half expected him to be looking back at her with acrimony, but rather she saw something far more conciliatory. "Like what?" she asked.

"What if you confined your touring to summer months only and spent the other nine months of the year at home. You've got the studio at home, so you could work on new music the rest of the year. That way you wouldn't have to quit or fire your employees, but you could have the normalcy you seem to crave."

"That's a fine idea, son," Reid said. "What do you think, darlin'?"

"I sort of had my heart set on not working at all," Kate said.

"And you really think you could do that?" Jill asked. "When you're not performing, you're composing. If my phone is my Siamese twin, your guitar is yours. Sometimes I wonder if you sleep with it."

That drew a laugh from everyone and went a long way toward easing some of the tension that had crept into the conversation.

"She's right," Buddy said. "I can't picture you without the music, and I can't picture music without you."

"Ashton's idea does have merit," Kate said. Though she felt somewhat begrudging about admitting that, she kept it out of her tone in deference to Reid.

"I agree," Jill said. "It would allow you to have the best of both worlds."

"And if we have children," Reid said, "they could tour with you in the summer so you'd never have to be away from them."

Kate really liked that idea.

"Kids?" Ashton said. "Seriously?"

Reid sent him a sheepish grin. "What can I say? The girl wants a baby."

"And *you* want that? At your age?"

"Watch it," Kate said. "He's not exactly senile—yet."

"Like Jill," Reid said, smiling at her, "I want what Kate wants. She's convinced me that our children would be lucky to have whatever time I've got to give them, and she'll finish the job for me if it comes to that."

"Which it won't," Kate said. "I appreciate everything y'all have said, and I promise to think about it before I do anything hasty."

"Well," Buddy said, sagging into his chair, "that's a goddamned relief."

"I thought Taylor had broken you of your swearing habit," Kate said.

"*Shit*," Buddy guffawed. "That'll be the fuckin' day."

They all busted up laughing, filling Kate with relief. They'd figure something out where her career was concerned, but she'd just taken a huge first step toward the life she wanted so badly. And it seemed that she'd broken the ice with Ashton, which was also a welcome development.

She turned to Reid. "I'd really like to go home."

"Before you do," Buddy said, "we need to talk about this video and what you're going to do about it."

Kate felt her good mood start to evaporate. "Do we have to?"

"Yes, you have to," Buddy said sternly. "Ashton and Jill have put their heads together to come up with what I think is a dynamite idea."

"Ashton and Jill did," Kate said. "Is that right?" Was it her imagination or was Jill refusing to make eye contact with her?

"Hear them out," Buddy said. "They're on to something."

With some input from Ashton, Jill proceeded to lay out their plan for a series of high-level interviews with some of the top names in the business—all people who were guaranteed to keep their claws sheathed.

"We think you need to take a mea culpa," Ashton said, "an 'aw shucks, shit happens' standpoint. It would also be an opportunity to announce your engagement and make your fans a part of your excitement."

Kate thought about that for a minute. "What about you? Are you going to be a part of my excitement?"

She'd clearly caught him off guard with the question.

"I want what my dad wants. It seems that perhaps he's always wanted you, so who am I to get in the middle of that?"

For a second, Kate wondered if she was hearing him right. And then it registered that he wasn't going to hassle them. He was genuinely happy for his father. Apparently, she wasn't the only one who'd grown up in the last ten years. "Thank you," she said softly.

"Yes, thank you, son," Reid said. "That means a lot to both of us."

Kate watched, intrigued, as Jill bequeathed a warm smile on Ashton, who seemed pleased by her approval.

What the heck was going on?

"So, what's it going to be, Kate?" Buddy asked.

Kate glanced at Reid, who nodded with encouragement. Bolstered by his support, she said, "I'll do one interview with Nancy Ferguson, and only if she comes here. I'm not traveling anywhere. And I'll think about the summer tour idea."

Buddy seemed relieved by her decision. "Good enough. I need to get home, but keep me posted on everything."

"We will," Ashton and Jill said together.

Jill's face turned bright red. Yes, something was definitely up.

Buddy shook hands with Reid and Ashton, and cuffed Kate on the chin. "Stop giving me heart attacks, will ya?"

Kate looked up at the man who'd meant so much to her as a friend, surrogate big brother and mentor. "I'll do my best."

After Buddy left, Kate said, "I'd like to speak to my sister for a minute, if that's all right."

"Of course, darlin'," Reid said. "Take all the time you need."

"I'll buy you a coffee in the break room, Dad," Ashton said, leading his father from the room.

When the door closed behind them, Kate took a good long look at Jill.

"What is going on with Ashton?"

"Let me see your ring."

"I asked first," Kate said. "Spill it."

"What makes you think there's anything going on?"

"Oh please, Jill. Who knows you better than I do?"

Again, her unflappable sister's face turned bright red.

"Are you *sleeping* with him?"

"Um, well, maybe?"

"Jill! Oh my God! When did this happen?"

"Recently."

Kate stared at her sister as her mind whirled with shock and questions and disbelief.

"Say something, will you?" Jill said after a long moment of uncomfortable silence. "Are you mad?"

"I'm stunned. I had no idea you thought about him that way."

"I didn't want to think about him that way. I know you hate him, and he's the last guy on earth you'd want me to date, let alone sleep with—"

"Whoa, Jill. Wait a minute. I don't hate him. I never hated him. I disliked something he did a long time ago that caused me a lot of trouble."

"He regrets that."

For the second time in five minutes, Kate was stunned. "He does?"

Jill nodded. "He wishes he had it to do over again, along with the conversation in the parking lot. He's been ashamed of what he said to you ever since."

"Wow, I never would've guessed that he felt that way."

"Well, he does."

"And what about you? How do you feel?"

"I…I like him. I've had a bit of a crush for a while now that I barely admitted to myself because of your issues with him. But then he asked me out, and we went to Malibu and—"

"You went *away* with him?"

Jill squirmed under Kate's intense scrutiny. "Maybe."

"This is huge! I can't believe you didn't tell me!"

"I thought you'd be mad."

"Are you happy, Jill? Does he make you happy?"

"He's amazing, and yes, I'm happy. Very much so."

Kate hugged her sister. "That's all I've ever wanted for you. I wanted you to know what that was like, and I was so worried you were giving up your own chance at happiness to run my life."

"Because of running your life, I might've found my happiness."

Kate pulled back to look her sister in the eye. "Are we really going to end up with a father and son?"

"I don't know about that, but it looks like you're ending up with the father. Show me the ring. Now."

Laughing, Kate held out her left hand.

"Oh, Kate. It's beautiful and so perfect for you."

"I thought so, too. He did good."

"Have you talked to Dad?" Jill asked.

"Some. He's upset that Reid and I are back together. He left me a message last night that he wants to talk some more about it, but I haven't called him back yet."

"I'd hate to see you at odds with him again over this."

"Me, too, but what am I supposed to do? I can't not be with Reid because Dad doesn't approve. I'm twenty-eight years old, and I spent years mourning the loss of this relationship. But I love Dad so much. . ."

"I know that, Kate, and so does he."

"No matter how much I love him, I won't let him ruin this for me."

"Maybe you should call him back. See what else he has to say."

Kate shrugged. "Maybe. I don't want to fight with him."

"When's the wedding?"

"The day after Christmas."

Jill's eyes bugged. "Jesus! You don't mess around."

"Haven't we waited long enough?"

"Yes, I suppose you have. Well, since we won't be going back out on tour in January, I'd better get busy sucking up to the promoter so he doesn't sue your ass, and we've got a wedding to plan."

"You'll be my maid of honor, right?"

"Duh. Of course I will. I'd have to kill you if you asked anyone else."

"There's no one else I'd ask besides you and Maggie. I'll probably have Buddy's girls as junior bridesmaids. For the longest time I've thought of them as the kids I'd never have. And now I might get to have some of my own." Kate's eyes filled, and she closed them in a failed attempt to contain the tears that leaked from the corners. "I want to pinch myself to believe this is really happening."

"One thing is for sure, good looks sure do run in their family."

"I know, right?" Kate said with a laugh.

"So you two picked right up where you left off, huh?"

"Pretty much. If it hadn't been for his psycho ex, it would've been a perfect week."

"What do you mean?"

As Kate was about to fill Jill in on what had transpired with Mari, a knock on the door stopped her. Ashton and Reid came back in, both looking grim.

"What's wrong?" Kate asked, immediately on edge.

"I had one of my associates look into the video and where it might've come from," Ashton said.

"They've been able to prove that one of Mari's cousins, who works at the resort next door to Desi's, took the footage," Reid said.

"So she must've told him I was there."

"Yes," Reid said. "I'm so sorry, darlin'. I didn't want it to be her."

"It's not your fault."

"What recourse do we have?" Reid asked Ashton with a hard edge to his voice that was wildly out of character for him. It told Kate just how furious he was at his ex-girlfriend.

"With your permission, we'll turn over what we uncovered to the local authorities in St. Kitts," Ashton said. "We can also file a civil suit against her and the cousin."

"She doesn't have much money."

"At the very least, you can make her life almost as uncomfortable as yours has been since the video went public," Jill said.

Reid looked at Kate. "What do you want to do?"

"Whatever you think is appropriate."

He looked at Ashton. "Put the screws to her."

Ashton nodded. "I'll have one of my people take care of it."

Kate looked up at Reid. "I'd really like to go home, if that's okay."

"The media is all over your place," Ashton reminded her.

"We've got a plan," Reid said with a smile for Kate. "Let's get going."

"I'm, ah, going to stay in town until things die down at home," Jill said.

Kate glanced at her and then at Ashton, before zeroing in on her sister's red face. "I can't say I blame you. I'll give you a call in the morning."

"Sounds good."

On the way past Ashton, she squeezed his arm. "Take good care of my sister."

"You have my word on that."

Kate nodded and preceded Reid out of the office and down the stairs.

When they reached the car, Reid stopped her from getting in. "What was that all about with Ashton just now?"

"He and Jill are seeing each other."

"Really? He never said a word!"

"He was probably waiting for her to tell me."

"What do you think of them together?"

"I don't know what to say. I've barely had a chance to get my head around it."

"I know you don't think too much of him—"

"That's not entirely true. My feelings where he's concerned have been complicated. But Jill just told me that he regrets calling my father about us, and he regrets what he said to me after he found us together."

"What did he say? You never told me."

"It's not worth repeating, and it's so far in the past it doesn't matter now. I'm glad to know he regrets it. That matters to me."

"So you approve of her dating him?"

"I want her to be happy. I don't think she's ever been in love before, and it always made me sad to think she might miss out on love because she was taking care of me."

"You and your sister with a father and son," Reid said with a grin as he started the car. "Now there's a hit country song waiting to be written."

Kate busted up laughing. "So true. What do you think of them together?"

"Well, I only just met Jill, but if she's anything at all like her sister, my son is a very lucky man."

"Aww, you're very sweet to say that. She's like me in some ways but nothing like me in others. The differences make us a good team, but I've always thought that any guy who ended up with her would be very lucky."

"Then I'm glad for him—and for her."

Kate withdrew her cell phone from her purse and called Gordon. He agreed to bring Thunder to meet them on the road that ran from her neighbor's property to hers. A quick call to her neighbor gave her permission to access the road from their side.

"We're in," she told Reid when she was done with her calls.

"I can't wait to see Thunder. I sure have missed that old boy."

"Having him helped me through a rough time, so thank you again for that."

"That's good to hear, darlin'. He was meant for you."

Kate leaned her head on his shoulder and wrapped her hand around his. "So were you."

He squeezed her hand. "Our little family. Back together again."

Despite the worries about her dad and what to do about her career, Kate smiled all the way home.

CHAPTER 14

Gordon was waiting for them with Thunder when they emerged from the woods on Kate's property. The groom eyed Reid suspiciously, and Thunder whinnied when he recognized them.

Kate released Reid's hand and broke into a run, delighted to see her horse.

Thunder rewarded her hug with a horse kiss to the cheek that made her laugh.

"Gordon, this is my fiancé, Reid Matthews."

"Good to meet you," Gordon said gruffly.

Reid shook hands with the other man. "Same here."

Kate couldn't get enough of Thunder and his nuzzling. "Look who I have with me, pal. Your old friend."

Reid stroked the horse. "Hi, there, bud. Looking good, old man."

Kate leaned in close to the horse's mouth. "What's that you say? He says same to you."

Reid laughed and put his arm around Kate.

Gordon cleared his throat. "Will you be set from here, Ms. Kate?"

"We'll be fine. Thanks again, Gordon."

"Any time." With one last suspicious glance at Reid, Gordon mounted the other horse he'd brought and headed back to the stables.

"Chilly around here," Reid said with a shiver.

"Sorry. My staff is protective of me."

"He's probably wondering what a gorgeous young woman is doing with an old man like me."

"Let him wonder. If he says it out loud, he'll be looking for a new job." She raised her foot into one of the stirrups and hoisted herself up onto Thunder—one of the few places on earth she ever felt truly at home. Extending a hand to Reid, she said, "Let's ride."

"Are you sure the old guy can handle both of us?" he asked as he swung his leg over Thunder's back and settled behind Kate.

"He says to tell you he can still outrun you."

Laughing, Reid said, "I don't doubt that." He gathered up her hair and moved it to one side, baring her neck for his kisses. "Just like old times, huh?"

Kate snuggled into Reid's embrace and gave Thunder his head. "The best of old times."

Thunder took them the long way home. Kate pointed out the creek that ran through the south border of her property, took him over the bridge she'd had installed where the creek bisected her land and showed him the grazing field that had once been full of trees. "We used all the trees we removed to build the house."

"I love that."

"And then we planted a bunch of new trees to replace the ones we had to take out."

"Sounds like you put a lot of thought into it."

"Everyone told me not to buy it. They said it was a wreck and would require too much work to make it habitable, but it was exactly what I had in mind when I set out to find the perfect place. So I made it work."

"Sure looks that way to me."

"I almost called you."

"When?"

"Before I bought it. I wanted your opinion so badly. That was the closest I came to reaching out to you."

He groaned and hugged her even closer to him. "God, I so wish you had."

"So do I. Would you have approved?"

"Absolutely. You didn't need me to see the potential."

"I really wanted your approval, though, and for you to tell me it was perfect."

"Well, I can tell you now. It's perfect—for you, for me, for us."

Kate tipped her head back so she could see him. "You haven't even seen the house yet," she said with a smile.

"Do you live there?"

"Um, yeah. You know that."

"That's all I need, baby."

Those words, that accent… Kate wondered if she'd ever get so accustomed to hearing his lyrical voice that she wouldn't be moved by it anymore. She sure hoped not. "So you'd be okay living here?"

"I'd much rather live here than in the mausoleum my family called home. There's nothing warm or inviting about that place. I only keep it for the airfield that Ashton still uses and for the stables."

"I wonder if there's something we could do with that house so it isn't sitting there empty."

"Like what?"

"Maybe it could be a place for women and children who've fallen on hard times to get back on their feet," Kate said, thinking out loud. "We could hire counselors and help them with career stuff and housing advice and teach the kids to ride—"

"I love it. That's absolutely brilliant."

"Really? You think so?"

"I do. I enjoyed working on the affordable housing initiatives in St. Kitts. It's very satisfying to know you're helping people who've been less fortunate. I was born into a lot of money. I've never known any other life until I started getting down in the trenches with people in need. I liked the feeling that came with knowing I'd helped to make a difference for them. So yes, I love your idea. I'd need to run it past Ashton, but I'm sure he'd be all for it, too. He does a ton of pro bono work for needy causes in town."

Kate was a little ashamed that she was truly surprised to hear that Ashton gave back to the community. She'd spent far too much time thinking poorly of him to accommodate such a possibility. "I didn't know that."

"I'm hoping the two of you can get to know each other better and discover there's a lot of good stuff you don't know about each other."

"I hope so, too. I appreciated his input today. What he said made a lot of sense to me."

"Did it?"

She nodded. "I suppose I'd be a fool to walk away entirely, but I'm determined to cut way back. He made it sound like that's totally doable. What do you think of summers on tour?"

"Sounds fun to me. Would we get to sleep in one of those narrow bus bunks that are made for one person?"

When she laughed, he took advantage of the opportunity to slide his cold hands under her sweater.

Not wanting to startle Thunder, she forced herself to stay still as the chill quickly turned to heat. "How about we go home and I show you the incredible bed I had custom built?"

"Now that I'd like to see."

"Thought you might say that." She directed Thunder to the stables, where she turned him over to Gordon for grooming. They fed him some carrots to thank him for the ride before they walked to the house.

"I swear you'd probably sleep with that horse if you could find a way to make it happen," Reid said.

"You know it. It's so not fair that dogs can live in the house but horses can't."

"Do you have dogs?"

She shook her head. "I'm away too much, but I want them. A whole bunch of them. The bed is big enough for all of us."

"No way am I sharing you with anyone else in bed."

"You're showing your age."

"Call me a fuddy-duddy, but I have my limits. No dogs in the bed."

"All right. If you're going to be that way about it."

Reid's cell phone rang. "I gotta take this. It's Ashton. Hi, son." As he listened to what Ashton was saying, he stopped walking and frowned. "I suppose that was to be expected." He listened some more. "Thanks for letting me know. I'll call you tomorrow."

"What's wrong?"

He hesitated, and Kate could tell that he was deciding whether or not he should tell her.

"Just say it. Whatever it is, we'll deal with it."

"Apparently, the media have figured out who I am, and they're digging into my life. They're making a big deal about the age difference between us. Ashton recommended we ignore it, which is good advice."

Kate's first thought was about her dad seeing the coverage and having it make things worse.

"It was inevitable that they'd figure out who was with you in the video," Reid continued.

"I'm sorry. I hate that they're dragging you through the mud, too."

"Don't be sorry. I knew what I was getting into, and I've gone into it fully aware of the possible fallout." He put his arms around her and drew her in close to him.

Resting her head on his chest, Kate closed her eyes and took comfort from his embrace.

"No matter what happens, no matter what they say or how intrusive they may be, there's nothing they could say or do that would make me not want you. That would make me not want this life we're figuring out for ourselves. Got me?"

Kate nodded and held on to him, her anchor in the storm.

"The next few months are apt to be rough, darlin'. You've chosen an unconventional path by agreeing to marry a guy my age. People are gonna talk, and some of it will probably be vicious. I'm a big boy, and I can take it. There's no way they'll drive me away, so don't spend one second worrying about that, okay?"

"Okay," she whispered.

"Now how about you show me this incredible house we're going to call home?"

"I'd love to."

"What did your dad say about the media reports?" Jill asked as Ashton drove them to his place. She'd spent the afternoon at his office, making calls, arranging the interview and dealing with the firestorm surrounding Kate, Reid and the video.

"Not too much."

"Hopefully, he'll take your advice and not look."

"I hope so."

"I feel sort of sorry for them," Jill said. "Here they've missed each other all these years and when they finally get back together, this happens. It's not fair."

"Well, they should've been a bit more circumspect in St. Kitts."

"True, but they thought they were alone."

Ashton reached for her hand. "Let's forget about them for a while. What do you want to do tonight?"

"Is it okay to say not much? I'm so tired. Thinking about all of this is exhausting, and now there's a wedding to be planned."

"They've set a date?"

"Your dad didn't tell you?"

"We never got around to talking about that."

"You should probably let him tell you."

"Come on," Ashton said, laughing. "Just tell me."

"December twenty-sixth."

"On his birthday."

"Oh, I didn't realize that was his birthday."

"Uh-huh."

"How do you feel about that?" she asked.

He stared straight out the windshield. "Fine. I guess."

"You don't sound fine."

"I'm sure he'll ask me to be his best man."

"You don't want to do it?"

Ashton glanced over at her and then returned his attention to the road. "It's hard to talk to you about this. My future *stepmother* is your sister."

"She's not exactly going to be your stepmother, Ashton. As funny as that would be."

"I'm glad you think so." He paused. "I don't want to sound like a jerk, because I am happy for him—for both of them. Hell, I've lived long enough to know that what they seem to have doesn't come along every day. It's just that she's younger than I am, you know?"

"It's weird for you."

"A bit. Yeah. See? I sound like a jerk."

"No, you don't. Maybe he could ask Buddy to stand up for him."

"He could, but he won't. He'll ask me, and I'll do it because it's him asking."

"But you won't really want to."

"No," he said with a sigh. "I don't want to."

"Maybe you should tell him that before he asks you to spare you both the awkwardness of it."

"I could never say that to him. It's hard to explain what we've meant to each other over the years. My mom died such a long time ago. Our family was me and him, with the Longstreets thrown in there, too, of course. Since everything happened the first time with Kate, I've often wondered if I would've been pissed no matter who he ended up with."

"Probably a little. You'd had him all to yourself for a long time."

"Yeah."

"Want to know what I think?"

"I really do."

Jill smiled at his earnest tone. "You've already been very supportive of a relationship that once caused you a lot of pain. You wouldn't be out of line to draw some boundaries if you need them."

"I suppose you're right." He drove into a parking lot in the middle of a cluster of town homes. "Here we are. Home sweet home. Stay there." He got out of the car and came around to open her door.

"There's a lot to be said for dating a Southern gentleman," Jill said, charmed by his manners.

"Guys up north don't open doors for their ladies?"

"Not with any level of reliability."

"Then they weren't raised right."

"I'm beginning to think you're right about that."

"Kate used to live over there," Ashton said, pointing to a building across the parking lot from his.

"I remember her saying you guys were neighbors."

"Yeah, she moved out as soon as she could—probably because I was here. I like the place, so I stayed put." He led her into a nicely decorated home that was clearly occupied by a guy, with leather and chrome and a gigantic flat-screen TV in the living room. "I have my needs," he said when he caught her staring at the TV. "Football, baby. Lots and lots of football."

Jill wrinkled her nose at the mention of a sport she'd always hated. "That might be a deal breaker."

He seemed stricken. "No… You probably need a better understanding of the game so you can appreciate it."

"I understand the game just fine, and I'll never appreciate it."

He honestly looked like he might cry. "I thought you were the absolute perfect woman for me, but now I'm not so sure."

Jill bit her lip to keep from laughing. "If it's too much for you," she said, backing toward the door, "I could leave now before this goes any further."

"Or," he said, following her with intent in his eyes, "you could think of some way to make it up to me."

"Make it up to you?"

"You are the only girl I've ever dated who doesn't like football as much as I do."

"Is that right?" By now she was backed up to the door and he had surrounded her with his arms propped over her head.

"Uh-huh." He pressed his body against hers, and Jill had to restrain herself from pulling him even closer.

"So whatever will we do about this significant difference of opinion?"

"I suppose," he said, dipping his head to kiss her neck, "we'll have to come to some sort of compromise."

Jill tilted her head to give him better access. "You don't have to give up football for me. Really, I'd never ask that of you." The next thing she knew, she was hanging over his shoulder as he ran up the stairs. She let out a squeak of surprise and protest. "Put me down!"

He dropped her with an ungraceful plop in the middle of his big bed.

"That was very undignified."

"I like you this way—with your hair all messed up and ruffled."

Jill started to fix her hair, but he required her full attention when he came down on top of her, propping himself on strong arms. "Did today feel very, *very* long to you?"

Jill nodded and raised her hands to grip bulging biceps. "Very long."

He never broke eye contact as he brought his lips down to claim hers in a deep, sweeping kiss full of pent-up desire. "I was thinking," he said when he came up for air, "since Kate is going to be cutting back, you might have some extra time on your hands. Maybe you could come to work with me."

She stared at him, agog. "You can't be serious."

"I'm very serious. You're extremely good at what you do, and I have other clients who'd benefit greatly from what you've learned running Kate's career."

"But you and me, working together?"

"Why not?" He kissed her again, scrambling a brain that was trying to focus on his offer.

She turned her head to break the kiss. "Don't toss out something like that and then try to distract me."

He nudged at her belly with his erection. "I like distracting you. And if we worked together, I could distract you whenever I wanted to."

"And that's supposed to be a selling point?"

"I thought so."

"Rather full of yourself, aren't you?"

"I'm rather hoping you like me as much as I like you. I'm rather hoping that this is the start of something important for both of us. And I'm rather hoping you might want to be my partner at work as well as at home."

Flabbergasted, Jill stared up at him.

"I can see that I've taken you totally by surprise." He moved off her and put his arm around her, urging her to turn on her side to face him. "Stop looking at me like I just told you I believe in aliens."

"Sorry. I didn't mean to do that, but you did catch me by surprise."

"It must seem like I'm moving way too fast since we got together, but I feel like I've waited such a long time for you, and now that I have you..."

"What?" she asked breathlessly.

"I want everything, and I want it now."

"God, you don't mess around, do you?"

"Never."

Jill knew there was a world of sincerity behind that single word, and she appreciated the double meaning. "I...um... I don't know what to say. I don't do things like this. I'm not impulsive. I'm a planner. I make lists and spreadsheets and more lists."

He smiled indulgently as she described herself. "Can I ask you something I have absolutely no right to ask this soon?"

"Okay..."

"Do you love me?"

"Yes," she said without hesitation. "I suspect I have for quite some time."

"That's really good, because I love you, too. I have since that first day you walked in the room and wiped every reasonable, logical thought right out of my head just by *walking in the room*. I knew right then and there that you were the one for me, and you hadn't yet said a word to me."

Overwhelmed by the torrent of emotion his sweet words aroused in her, Jill had no idea what to say. "Ashton…"

"I know I wasn't in your plans or on your spreadsheets, but I hope you can make some room for me, Jill."

She reached for him. "I can definitely make room for you."

He put his arm around her and held on tight. "Will you think about the job offer?"

"You don't have to do that. I'm sure Kate will still keep me plenty busy."

"I'm not being entirely altruistic with this offer. I'm reaching the point where I'm going to have to take on a partner anyway. I choose you."

"You're serious."

"Hell yes, I'm serious." He nuzzled his favorite spot on her neck again. "I've waited such a long time for you. My whole life. I don't want to waste any more time."

"You're overwhelming me."

"I'm sorry." He leaned his forehead on hers, closed his eyes and took a deep breath. "I don't mean to. I don't want to mess this up."

Sorry to have caused him distress, Jill caressed his face, following her hands with kisses. "You're not messing it up. I need some time to think about what you've offered. It's not in me to jump in with both feet and think later. I think first."

"Don't think too hard." As if the control he'd been clinging to had suddenly given out, he moved quickly to get rid of their clothes, found a condom in the bedside table and was inside her while she was still processing everything he'd said. The second he entered her, however, she stopped thinking about anything other than how amazing it felt to be loved by him.

"Nothing that feels this good can be bad," he whispered in her ear.

Jill wrapped her legs around his hips, which seemed to make him a little crazy.

"God, Jill." He kissed her ravenously, as if he might never get enough of her.

She hoped he never would, because he was right. Nothing had ever felt quite like this, and she wanted to hold on to it forever. With that in mind she put her arms around his neck and buried her fingers in his thick hair.

He met her gaze and held it, slowing the movement of his hips and driving her crazy with slow, deep strokes that took her to the edge of climax.

Shuddering, she gasped. "Ashton…"

"What, honey?"

"I need… I want…"

He kissed her softly as his chest hair rubbed against her nipples. "What do you want? Tell me."

"I need to come." She felt her face heat with embarrassment. She'd never spoken so bluntly to a man in bed.

As he swelled and throbbed inside her, he smiled and kissed both cheeks. "Don't ever be embarrassed to tell me what you want."

"It's embarrassing."

"No, it's sexy." He began to move again, faster this time.

When he pressed his fingers to her core, she went off like a rocket. She might've even screamed from the pleasure that shot through her. Opening her eyes, she found him watching her intently and realized he was still hard and still moving inside her.

"Very sexy," he said, kissing her again.

"Did I scream?"

His smile was full of masculine pride. "Yep."

She gripped his backside and made him gasp. "Your turn."

"Do I get my choice of how I want it?"

"Um, sure. I guess."

Before she knew what hit her, he'd turned them over so she was on top without losing their connection.

"Nice move," she said.

"You like that?"

Nodding, she rolled her hips, drawing a deep groan from him.

"Yes." He combed his fingers through her hair. "You're so beautiful. I wish you could see yourself the way I do."

"Ah, no thanks."

He laughed and moved his hands lower to cup her breasts.

Jill's head fell back as she gave herself over to the power they generated together. She couldn't believe it when another orgasm swept over her without warning, taking him this time, too. She slumped down on top of him, his arms around her and his lips brushing over her hair as he whispered sweet words of love that she could barely hear. She didn't need to hear exactly what he was saying. He'd shown her, repeatedly, how devoted he was to her, and she wanted everything he'd offered—and then some.

"I want to work with you," she said.

"What about your plans and your spreadsheets and your checklists?"

She propped her chin on his chest and met his gaze. "The best laid plans go out the window when the right one comes along."

His eyes widened with surprise and his lips pursed, as if he was going to say something.

Laughing, Jill said, "Did I finally render you speechless, Counselor?"

"Yeah," he said, framing her face with his hands. "You take my breath away, Jill Harrington."

Deeply moved by his softly spoken words, she said, "Do you think I still will when we're working together?"

"I know you will."

Jill cuddled into his embrace, completely content for once to throw the best laid plans out the window.

CHAPTER 15

Kate stood before the mirror in the master bathroom, trying to tame her hair into something resembling submission. She had hair-and-makeup people on her team, but she liked to do her own whenever possible.

She hated this whole thing. The idea of going on national TV to talk about her relationship with Reid as well as the sex tape the whole world had seen by now had left her feeling nauseated for days. As they'd settled into a new routine, she'd gone out of her way to hide her growing torment from Reid, knowing it would upset him.

If only the interview hadn't been hanging over her head, she would've been happier than she'd ever been in her life. Being with Reid again, especially here in the home she loved so much, was amazing. They just had to get past today, and then Kate would be able to truly relax and enjoy their new life.

"Hey, darlin'. I thought you could use some coffee."

She turned to find him freshly shaven, his hair still damp from the shower. He must've used one of the guest bathrooms so she could have the full run of theirs. "That's just what I need," she said, as she took the mug from him. "Thank you."

"Are you nervous?"

"A little. Mostly I'm pissed that I have to do this at all."

His hands landed on her shoulders and his chin on the top of her head as he met her gaze in the mirror. "I know, but for what it's worth, I think you're doing the right thing."

"It's worth a lot, but it feels like such a huge invasion of our privacy."

"Don't tell them any more than you have to."

"I think about my dad watching the interview…" She shook her head. The thought had tormented her for days.

"Maybe if you returned his calls you could clear the air with him."

"If only I thought we'd clear the air and not make things worse, I'd call him back."

"You're going to have to talk to him eventually if you want him here for the wedding."

Kate wondered if her dad would even come, another thought that had been plaguing her lately. "I'll call him after the interview."

"You're sure you don't want me there with you?"

"That would make me more nervous, worrying about what you're thinking. I'd rather you not even watch it."

"Whatever you want, darlin'." He kissed her cheek and squeezed her shoulders. "Speaking of your daddy, there's something I need to tell you in the interest of full disclosure."

Kate couldn't imagine what it could be. "What's that?"

"You know how we promised completely honesty this time around?"

"Yes."

"Normally, I'd prefer not to tell you what I'm doing today while you're tied up, but because we're being honest, I'm telling you that I'm flying to Rhode Island to see him."

Kate stared at him in disbelief. "Whatever for?"

"I'm an old-fashioned kind of guy, darlin', and when a man plans to marry another man's daughter, he asks permission. That's just how it's done."

"He'll never give you permission. You know that."

"Maybe so, but I'm still going to ask."

"You don't have to do this."

"Yes, I do."

Kate rested a hand on her stomach, which had begun to ache.

"I don't mean to make you more nervous than you already are, but I wanted you to know where I'll be today."

She looked up at him. "It might make things worse."

"How? How could it make anything worse?"

"He might punch you or something. He's wanted to for a decade now."

"If that's what he feels he needs to do, so be it. That won't change how I feel about his daughter or that I plan to marry her very soon." He put his arms around her. "I'm probably wasting my breath by telling you not to worry, but please don't. It'll all be fine."

"I'm glad one of us is so sure of that."

"Nothing can come between us unless we let it. I have no plans to let anything or anyone come between us. Do you?"

"No, you know I don't."

"Good," he said, kissing her. "Whenever you're ready, the car Jill sent for you is here."

"Okay." She took a deep breath and let it out slowly. Then she finished the coffee, brushed her teeth and took one last look in the mirror.

"You look gorgeous as always."

"You have to say that."

"No," he said, laughing, "I don't."

"Yes, you do."

"No."

"Yes."

"No." He stopped her rebuttal with a passionate kiss that reminded her of how much he loved her.

"*Yes.*"

"Always have to have the last word, huh?"

"You bet." The playful exchange had helped with the nerves, and Kate felt ready to face whatever this day might bring.

"I'll keep that in mind." He walked her out to the black sedan with the polarized windows that would make it impossible for anyone to see who was in the car.

"You'll be careful flying?"

"You bet."

"Call me when you're on your way back?"

"I will." He kissed her one last time and held the door for her. "Knock 'em dead today, darlin'."

"I'll try."

She slid into the car and forced a smile for him. "See you later."

He leaned into the car and kissed her again. "I love you."

She caressed his face. "I love you, too."

Reid closed the door and then slapped the roof to tell the driver to go.

As the car pulled up the long lane that led to the main road, Kate thought about him going to see her dad and what might transpire between them. She knew she ought to call her dad and warn him that Reid was coming, but then she decided the element of surprise might work in Reid's favor.

The two men had once been close friends. Perhaps that history might inspire some civility in her father. She could only hope so. While she appreciated Reid's honesty and knew it was critical to their relationship, she sort of wished he hadn't told her his plans. It was one more thing to worry about in a day already full of worries.

The car drove past the media still gathered outside her gate, and though they strained to peer inside the car, Kate took comfort in knowing they couldn't see her.

What a way to live, she thought, trapped in her own home. On the way into town, she went over the answers she and Jill had rehearsed to the most probable questions. Jill had made it clear with the segment producer that Kate would not directly address the sex tape but would speak about her relationship with Reid and their engagement. She was prepared to talk about their age difference, the possibility of children and some vague thoughts about her career. Jill had encouraged her to hold off on any big career announcements until they had time to make a concrete plan.

Jill met her at the Hermitage Hotel on Sixth Avenue in downtown Nashville, where a suite had been secured to film the interview. Nancy Ferguson, one of the top stars in celebrity news, had flown in to interview her. Nancy had treated her well in the past. Kate hoped she treated her well this time, too.

On the sidewalk outside the hotel, Kate hugged her sister. "Back in the suit, huh?"

"I thought it was appropriate for the day's agenda."

"Back in jeans after this, you hear me?"

"Yes, ma'am." Jill took a perusing look at the brown sweaterdress they'd chosen for Kate. "You look great. I love that color on you."

"Thanks, now let's get this the hell over with."

Laughing, Jill linked her arm through Kate's and led her into the hotel.

They attracted a few stares and a couple of murmurs on the way through the lobby, but they'd chosen the Hermitage intentionally, hoping the staff and clientele could be counted on for discretion. Jill had suggested she come in via the loading dock, but Kate had refused to do that. At some point, she'd have to show her face in public again, and as far as she was concerned, there was no time like the present.

Nancy Ferguson's assistant met them on the top floor with handshakes and effusive thanks for giving Nancy the exclusive.

"No problem," Kate said, even though it was a huge problem.

The hair-and-makeup people descended the second they were in the suite, undoing all of Kate's efforts in record time. While she wanted to protest, she let them have their way because arguing about it would take time she could better spend at home.

When she was ready, they brought her into the main salon, where cameras and lights had been erected around two chairs.

Nancy came in a minute later, drinking from a mug and talking a mile a minute. A petite blonde, Nancy had built her career on probing celebrity interviews. She was known for getting stars to divulge information they wouldn't tell their own mothers. If Nancy tried that crap today, she would leave disappointed.

"Kate!" Nancy said, deftly handing her mug to one of her lackeys. "It's so good to see you again!"

Kate returned Nancy's embrace because she was expected to, not because she was particularly happy to see the woman.

"Thank you so much for this," Nancy said. "I can't tell you what it means to me that you picked me out of everyone who wanted this interview."

"No problem."

"Have a seat. Get comfortable."

Sure, as if that was going to happen. Kate took the seat that Nancy designated for her and sat still while microphones were adjusted, hair was fussed over—again—and bronzer was reapplied. While they did their thing, Kate thought about Reid and their rides on Thunder and Saroya, one of the other horses in Kate's stable, a gorgeous white mare with a gentle disposition. Kate had insisted that Reid ride Thunder, even though he'd protested that the horse was hers now and he didn't feel right taking him away from her.

"It makes me happy to see you on him," Kate had said, which was all her fiancé had needed to hear.

"Whatever makes you happy," he'd said.

Kate smiled, thinking of the afternoon they'd spent exploring every inch of the property and the picnic they'd enjoyed by the creek. The unusually warm autumn weather had provided the perfect backdrop for yet another exceptional day together. The more time she could spend exactly that way, the happier she would be.

They'd also made plans for his unused home, which Ashton had agreed would make an outstanding place for women in need to get back on their feet. He'd also offered to handle all the legal work involved in the project.

"Kate?" Nancy asked, drawing Kate out of her musings. "Are you ready?"

"Sure, whenever you are."

Before Kate's eyes, Nancy morphed into her on-air personality, launching into an elaborate intro scripted on cue cards that were held by a man standing to Kate's right.

"Kate, we're so very pleased to welcome you to the Nancy Ferguson Show today for an exclusive interview."

"Happy to be here." Could the whole world tell she was lying? She hoped not.

"This has been an eventful couple of months for you, between the bout with pneumonia, the fainting incident on stage and now your highly publicized new relationship with a much older man. Would you describe the last few months from your point of view?"

Yeah, Kate wanted to say, *a lot of it has sucked, but the last part has been pretty great.* Of course, she couldn't say that. "It's been kind of crazy. I was really sick for a while there. Until you've had pneumonia, you can't fully appreciate how it totally wipes you out. I was anxious to get back to work and made the mistake of going back too soon, thus the fainting incident in Oklahoma City. And just to clear up any misconceptions, I wasn't in rehab. I've never spent a single day in rehab of any kind."

"That rumor seems to stick to you. Why do you think that is?"

"Who knows? I've never touched a drug in my life. I've never even smoked pot. I have an occasional glass of wine with dinner. I'm about as boring a celebrity as you'll ever find, so I have no idea where those rumors keep coming from. There's not a shred of truth in it, not that anyone will believe me." Kate shrugged to show that she didn't care if they believed her or not.

"I believe you, Kate," Nancy said, resting a hand on Kate's knee.

"Glad someone does," Kate said with a laugh.

"What your fans really want to hear all about is the new man in your life." This was said in a conspiratorial girlfriendy tone that made Kate want to barf.

"Reid is... Um..." How did one describe the love of one's life? "He's wonderful, and we're very happy."

"That's so nice to hear," Nancy said, sounding sincere. "How did you meet?"

"We knew each other years ago. He was a friend of my dad's."

"You said was a friend of your dad's. Are they no longer friends?"

God, I walked right into that, Kate thought, furious with herself for giving Nancy the easy opening. "They haven't seen each other in recent years."

"Does your dad approve of your relationship with a man his age?"

"He's not thrilled about it, naturally, but I think he wants me to be happy, and I am very happy. Happier than I've ever been."

"Speaking of the age difference between you and Mr. Matthews, can you tell us your feelings on that?"

"I have no feelings on it. I love him. He loves me. Other people are hung up on the age difference. We're not."

"A woman your age must give occasional thought to children, no?"

"Very occasional. I've been a little busy the last few years."

"Indeed," Nancy said with a smile that seemed forced. Apparently, it was sinking in that Kate wasn't going to roll over and play dead. "Are children in your future plans with Mr. Matthews?"

"Could be. We're not ruling anything out."

"I understand you're engaged."

"That's right."

"Care to show us your ring?"

Not really, Kate thought, but she extended her left hand anyway.

"It's gorgeous. Congratulations."

"Thank *you*."

"When's the big day?"

"We haven't set a date yet, but we hope it will be soon." No way was she giving up that information.

"As one of the top female singers of your generation, naturally your fans want to know what your personal plans mean for your career."

"I'll be cutting back on the touring, for one thing." She could almost sense Jill's wince as the words rolled out her mouth. That was definitely not part of the plan for the interview. At some point over the last few blissful days at home with Reid, she'd made a decision. "I'll be touring in the summer and spending the rest of the year at home with my family and working on new music."

"That's a substantial change in what you've done in recent years."

"Yes, but it's time to come home from the road. I can't continue to tour two hundred days a year and have any kind of life, too. I'm ready for some balance, and this plan seems to give me the best of both worlds."

"I don't mean to sound condescending, but you appear to be that rare performer who's completely grounded in reality. Is that a fair statement?"

"I'd like to think I keep it real. The last ten years have been amazing. I'm so grateful to my fans and to my dear friend Buddy Longstreet, who's been such an amazing mentor and supporter, and all the folks at Long Road Records who've worked so hard on my behalf. But I've started to feel lately that life was passing me by a bit, and it was time to step out of the public eye for a while. That didn't work out exactly as I planned," Kate said with a laugh, making a vague reference to the infamous sex tape, "but I know it's the right thing for me to do."

Kate could tell that Nancy was absolutely dying to ask about the video. "So your fans can still expect plenty of new music?"

"Oh absolutely," Kate said, relieved that Nancy hadn't crossed the line and stayed within the boundaries Jill had set ahead of time. "I'm always writing music, and I've got a full recording studio at home that I plan to make good use of in the next few years. As soon as we have the plans for the summer tour locked in, we'll let the fans know."

"Kate, it's been an absolute pleasure to spend this time with you today. I hope you know that the Nancy Ferguson Show is a huge fan of your work, and we'd love to have you on again any time."

"Thanks, Nancy. I appreciate that."

"That's a wrap," the director announced.

Kate let out the deep breath she'd been holding during the half-hour interview.

"Thanks very much," Nancy said, extending a hand.

Kate shook her hand. "Thank you. I appreciate the fair treatment."

"Sure thing. Keep in touch, okay?"

"I will. When is this due to air?"

"Day after tomorrow. We're rushing it through to get it on the air as soon as possible."

That gave Kate two days to tell the rest of the people who mattered to her that she was engaged—and invite them to a day-after-Christmas wedding.

Reid passed the three-hour flight to Rhode Island thinking about all the many ways this mission could blow up in his face. While he was adamant about following tradition when it came to his fiancée's father, he was well aware that he was far from welcome at the office where Jack worked with his brother-in-law, Jamie Booth.

Once upon a time, the three men had been close friends at Berkley where they'd studied architecture together and formed a bond that had been blown to smithereens when Reid had an affair with Jack's eighteen-year-old daughter.

As a father himself, he could certainly understand Jack's anger. He'd experienced his share of shame over the feelings he'd had for Kate, right from the first minute he met her. Despite the years between them, though, their connection had intensified every time they were together.

Being with her again was nothing short of miraculous. For the rest of his life, he'd never forget the sight of her walking toward him on the beach in St. Kitts. His heart had nearly burst from his chest when he heard her voice. Over the years, he'd thought about going after her, but she was the one who'd ended their relationship, and he'd tried to respect that decision.

Now he knew he'd been a fool to stay away from her, and he was determined to make sure that whatever time they got together was as peaceful and happy as he could make it. She deserved nothing less. *They* deserved nothing less, thus the effort to reach some sort of accord with her father.

He landed at T.F. Green airport outside of Providence, Rhode Island, and rented a car for the thirty-minute drive to Newport. Before he left Nashville, he'd looked up Jack's office online and written down the address that he now punched into the car's GPS.

Although the ride over the bridges that led to Newport was scenic, Reid barely noticed as he followed the directions to the offices of Harrington Booth Associates. Once there, he sat in the parking lot and stared at the building where Kate's father worked. What if Jack wasn't even here after he'd come all this way to see him?

Reid laughed at that thought and shook his head. Wouldn't that be just his luck? He hadn't wanted to call ahead because he'd been certain Jack would refuse to see him. Hopefully, showing up in person would make a difference.

His cell phone rang, and he checked the caller ID to find the number unknown. Because it might be Kate calling from someone else's phone, he took the call.

"Reid."

Crap, it wasn't Kate. "What do you want, Mari?"

"Please... They arrested me." She spoke so softly he almost couldn't hear her.

"What do you want me to do about it?"

"Tell them it wasn't me! Tell them I couldn't have done this!"

"But you did do it. You trashed my place and shredded pictures of my son."

"You can't prove that!"

"The police can—and they will."

"If you tell them it wasn't me, they won't charge me."

"Why would I do that when you told your cousin that Kate was at Desi's place and he filmed us having sex? Are you the one who posted it on the Internet, or did you let him do that for you, too?"

"No! I'd never do that!"

"Don't make it worse by lying, Mari. I hope you made enough off the video to pay for a lawyer. Sounds like you're going to need one."

"Reid, *please*. All you'd have to do is make a call. People respect you here. You know I don't have the money for a lawyer."

"You should've thought of that before your vindictive streak kicked in. I'm already paying the landlord for the damage you did. I'd say that more than makes us even."

"What about *me*? We were happy together until she showed up!"

"She did me a huge favor by showing up when she did. I had no idea you had this kind of nastiness inside you."

"I didn't mean to hurt anyone, and I'm so sorry about Ashton's picture. That shouldn't have happened."

"You're damned right it shouldn't have happened."

"Are you going to marry her?"

"As soon as I can."

She let out a whimper of distress. "Did you ever feel anything for me?"

"Yes, but I don't anymore. Please don't call me again, or I'll change my phone number. We have nothing left to say to each other." He pressed the End button and gripped the phone tightly as he took a series of deep breaths to calm down. That call was about the last thing he'd needed right now with the confrontation with Jack looming.

He stashed the phone in his pocket and got out of the car before he lost his nerve. Inside, a receptionist directed him to Jack's office, where his assistant was on the phone.

"Hi there," she said a few minutes later, after she ended the call. "Sorry about that. Crazy busy today. What can I do for you?"

"I'd like to see Jack Harrington, if possible."

She studied him with shrewd green eyes. "Is he expecting you?"

"Ah, no," Reid said with a laugh, "he is most definitely not expecting me."

"Your name?"

"Reid Matthews."

Her eyes widened for an instant before she recovered her professional demeanor. "Please have a seat, and I'll see if he's available."

As she scurried into Jack's office and shut the door behind her, Reid took a seat in the reception area to await the verdict.

Lost in his own thoughts, he didn't see Jamie Booth approach Jack's office.

"What the hell are you doing here?"

Kate's uncle was tall and blond and clearly furious. "Hello to you, too. Nice to see you, Jamie."

"Answer the question."

"I need to speak with Jack."

"He has nothing to say to you."

"That's fine, but I have something to say to him."

"You've got a lot of nerve showing up here after you've ruined Kate's life—again."

"Kate's life is hardly ruined."

"You selfish bastard."

"I'm not here to fight with you. I'd like to speak to Jack, and then I'll be on my way."

With a last furious look for Reid, Jamie went into Jack's office and slammed the door.

When Quinn came in and shut the door, Jack looked up from the plans he'd been reviewing. It was unlike her to come in without knocking. He'd long ago told her to quit knocking, and she'd refused, which was one of their many ongoing jokes. He was prepared for her to razz him about his perpetually messy desk, but she seemed rattled. "What's wrong?"

"He's *here*," Quinn whispered.

"Who is?"

"*Him*. Reid Matthews."

Jack stared at her, wondering if he'd heard her correctly.

Jamie stormed into the room, slamming the door behind him. "Can you even *believe* this guy? Showing up here like he'd be welcome by any of us? That takes some kind of balls."

Jack's mind raced as he tried to process what Jamie was saying while still trying to get his mind around the fact that Reid was *here*. Then he realized Jamie and Quinn were watching him, waiting for him to say something. "Did he say what he wanted?"

"Only that he'd like to see you," Quinn said.

"You don't have to do it, Jack," Jamie said. "You don't owe him anything."

While Jack tended to agree with Jamie, Andi's voice echoed in his mind, reminding him of their conversation a few days ago. "I'll see him."

"Jack—"

"Kate's going to marry him," Jack said. They'd gotten the official word the day before, along with an invitation to a wedding the day after Christmas. He'd been asked to pass the word to his sister Frannie and her husband, Jamie, but this was the first he'd seen of either of them since Kate's call.

Jamie's entire body went rigid with rage. "You gotta be freaking kidding me! She could have *any guy she wants*!"

"Exactly." He let the word hang in the air between them, the same way Andi had done to him. Some of the starch seemed to leave Jamie's pose as Jack's point registered.

"For Christ's sake," Jamie muttered as he went through the bathroom that adjoined their offices and slammed another door.

"Should I show him in?" Quinn asked tentatively.

"Yes, please."

"Do you, um, do you want me to stay?"

"Thanks for offering, but I've got this."

"Okay."

Steeling himself, Jack stood, ran his fingers through his hair in a show of nerves, and then propped his hands on his hips.

Reid came in, looking much the same as he had the last time Jack saw him on that awful day in Nashville when he caught his friend fooling around with his daughter. His ex-friend, he should say. Reid walked over to Jack's desk and extended his hand.

Jack eyed Reid's hand for a long, *long* moment before his manners kicked in and he shook Reid's hand.

"Thanks for seeing me."

"Um, yeah, have a seat." Jack was grateful to sink back into his desk chair, because his legs had begun to feel rubbery and his hands had curled into fists that were dying to make contact with something. Reid's face was a little too handy.

When he was settled in one of Jack's visitor chairs, Reid propped his elbows on his knees and leaned forward. "I'm sorry to show up without an appointment, but I really needed to see you, to tell you, to ask you…"

Jack stayed quiet. He refused to make this easy for Reid.

"I'd like to marry your daughter."

What the hell was he supposed to say to that? "So I've heard."

"Kate told me I didn't have to come here, that I don't need your approval or your blessing."

Reid rubbed a hand over his jaw in a gesture Jack recognized as nerves. Good. At least he wasn't the only one who was exquisitely uncomfortable. The thought of his gorgeous daughter sleeping with this guy… He pushed that thought far, far into the back of his mind.

"But I wasn't brought up that way," Reid continued, "and even though this is difficult for both of us, I wanted to do the right thing by her. And by you."

"It's a little late to show respect for me or our former friendship, isn't it?"

"Yes, I suppose it is," Reid said with a sigh. "Here's the thing, Jack. I love her. I've loved her from the very beginning. I never stopped loving her during all the years we were apart, and I'm three thousand percent sure I'll never stop loving her for the rest of my life. There's nothing I wouldn't do to make her happy, nothing I wouldn't give her… Whatever it takes. All she has to do is ask, and it's done."

Listening to Reid's speech, Jack had to wonder if that lyrical Southern accent wasn't part of the draw for Kate.

"I know I'm not what you would've chosen for her."

Jack let out a grunt of laughter. Wasn't that the understatement of this century and the last one, too?

"However," Reid continued, seeming determined to present his case in its entirety, "I'm the one she seems to want, and it would mean a great deal to her—and to me—if you and I could somehow reach an accord. That would make someone we both love very happy indeed."

With nervous energy zinging through his veins, Jack could no longer stay seated. He got up and jammed his hands into his pockets to ensure they wouldn't go rogue on him and end up plowed into Reid's handsome face. He turned to look out the window at one of his favorite views of the beach and was quiet for a long time as he tried to figure out what he should say. And then he knew exactly what he needed to say to the man who wanted to marry his daughter.

"When Kate was a little girl, she used to be crazy about the *Wizard of Oz*. Most little kids, including her sisters, were scared to death of the witch and the monkeys, but Kate loved them. She was fearless. She gave her mother fits by doing cartwheels into the pool and riding her bike with no hands. We had this one particularly intense storm, and Clare found Kate out on the deck, soaked to the skin, watching the lightning like it was a movie rather than something to be afraid of." Jack paused for a moment, lost in the memories of a tiny blonde girl with the heart and courage of a lion king. "And then she grew up far too quickly and told me she wanted to go to Nashville, to find her way in the music business. I remember thinking how scared I would've been to be alone in a strange city where I didn't know anyone—as an eighteen-year-old. But Kate wasn't scared. She was thrilled to be following her dreams." He turned then to face Reid. "She's never been afraid of anything, which is what makes her so supremely vulnerable to being hurt."

"I'd never hurt her. Ever."

"You did once before."

"Did she ever tell you why we broke up?"

"Ah, no. We've gone out of our way to not speak of that time in our lives—ever."

"Do you remember the day you and Kate arrived at my house and you and I went for a walk while Ashton took Kate into town?"

Jack nodded, curious despite his intense desire not to be.

"I told you then I knew people in the business."

"And I said I didn't think she'd want anyone pulling strings for her. She was quite determined to make it on her own."

"Right. She told me the same thing." Reid looked up at Jack, seeming to force himself to make eye contact. "I grew up with Buddy Longstreet. He's my best friend and the brother I never had."

Suddenly, a lot of things made sense. "So you told Buddy about her."

Nodding, Reid said, "Against her express wishes. When she found out what I'd done, she left me."

"And then she went on to have a blockbuster career, thanks in large part to Buddy's support."

"Yes."

"I didn't know you'd played a role in that. I suppose I should thank you for helping her to get a start."

"It was wrong of me to go against her wishes, and I learned a very painful lesson about what happens when you disappoint Kate Harrington. When she came to find me in St. Kitts, she said she too had learned a valuable lesson in the last decade."

"And that was?"

"That no one gets somewhere in her chosen field without help. I regretted disrespecting her wishes. She regretted the way she reacted when she found out about what I'd done. We both had a lot of years to wallow in the regrets—and a lot of years to grow up."

"I didn't know any of this."

"What I really want you to know is that despite the difference in our ages and the disapproval of people in both our lives, other than the day we broke up, every, single minute we spent together was nothing short of magical. We had the kind of connection that people spend a lifetime looking for and often never find. Since we've been back together, it's been just like that again. We're both older and wiser this time around, and we're very determined to make it work."

Jack felt his resistance crumbling under the weight of Reid's compelling arguments. "What about kids? She's a young woman who'll want a family of her own someday."

"Remember when I said there's nothing I wouldn't do for her? I meant that."

"So you'd have more kids *now*?" Jack couldn't fathom the idea, but then again he'd been managing young kids for the last decade and Reid had not.

"If that's what she wants."

"And she knows this?"

"We've talked about it."

Jack's mind raced as he tried to process everything Reid had told him.

Reid stood. "I've taken enough of your time, and I've given you a lot to think about. You don't have to say anything now, but it would mean a great deal to both of us if we could be married with your blessing. It would mean everything to Kate if you were with us for Christmas and the wedding we plan to have the day after. We won't ask anything more of you than your presence."

Reid extended his hand and held it out for a long, awkward moment. Jack could tell that Reid was about to withdraw it when Jack stood and shook his hand.

"I'll think about it." That was the best he could do.

Reid nodded. "Appreciate that. Hope to see you in Nashville for Christmas."

Jack kept his gaze fixed on Reid's back as he walked out of the office, closing the door behind him. He thought about everything Reid had said, especially the insight he'd provided into why he and Kate had broken up. He hadn't known that Reid had been so instrumental in helping Kate to have the career she'd always wanted.

Thinking back to headstrong, eighteen-year-old Kate, he could only imagine how she'd reacted to learning Reid had gone behind her back to connect her to Buddy Longstreet.

Quinn came into the office through one door, Jamie through the other.

"What'd he say?" Jamie asked.

Right in that moment, Jack made a decision. He might not fully approve of her choices, but no child of his was getting married without him at least there to watch it happen. "Looks like we're going to Nashville for Christmas."

Chapter 16

Winter was slow in arriving, as Indian summer lingered well into November, past Thanksgiving, which Reid, Kate, Ashton and Jill spent with the Longstreets. There was, however, nothing slow about the frantic pace at which Kate and Jill planned a family Christmas and a wedding.

Soon after inviting her entire extended family to Nashville for Christmas, Kate realized she didn't have enough room to house everyone between her house and Jill's.

"We'll build something," Reid had said matter-of-factly at the beginning of November.

"*Build* something? Between now and Christmas? Are you crazy?"

"Darlin', do you *know* who you're talking to?" He'd rolled his eyes and told her not to give it another thought.

Only because she was so busy with all the other details of the wedding did she let him take over the project he was calling "The Bunkhouse." He'd chosen a spot behind a copse of trees that blocked the view of the site from her house and told her to stay away until it was done. For once in her life, Kate did as she was told, because it seemed important to him that she not see it until it was finished.

The property was overrun with cement mixers, construction vehicles and a team of men he'd recruited from somewhere. A decade after he shuttered Reid Matthews Development, he apparently still had sway in the local construction community.

He'd also been occupied with the renovations to his house, which was taking shape as the shelter they'd envisioned for women and children in crisis. After the first of the year, they planned to begin looking for a director.

The interview Kate had done with Nancy seemed to diffuse the rabid interest in her. When it became clear that she'd meant it when she said that interview would be the only one she'd give—and when it became clear that she had found other ways on and off her property—the reporters left their post outside her gate. Kate was thankful the siege seemed to be over—for now anyway.

"When do I get to see this so-called Bunkhouse?" she asked Reid over breakfast a week before the family was due to invade.

"Soon."

"How soon is soon?"

"If you keep asking me, it'll be longer."

"What if I don't like it?" she teased as he downed the rest of his coffee and stood.

He leaned over to kiss her on his way out. "I promise you'll like it. See you for lunch."

Kate was tempted to follow him and satisfy her curiosity, but she certainly had more than enough on her own to-do list. She and Jill had labored over every detail of the long weekend with the family, from where everyone would sleep to meals to entertainment to wedding plans.

She was poring over Jill's latest sleeping arrangement suggestions when her cell phone rang. Kate happily took the call from her stepfather's mother.

"Grammy Colleen! What an awesome surprise!"

"Hello, love," Colleen said warmly. To hear Aidan tell it, her Irish brogue was thicker today than it'd been when she left the old country. "Have I caught you at a bad time?"

"Of course not. I'm always happy to hear from you. How are all the O'Malleys?" She and Colleen had become e-mail buddies over the years, and Colleen's cheerful dispatches full of amusing anecdotes about her sprawling family were a source of great entertainment to Kate, especially while she was on the road.

"Everyone is doing well. The grandkids are growing like weeds. But the reason I'm calling is I have some bad news. I can't make the trip to Nashville for the wedding as much as I'd absolutely love to be there. I've been having an awful time with my arthritis, and getting on and off planes would be next to impossible."

"Oh, that's too bad! It won't be the same without you. Dad and Aidan are chartering a plane to bring everyone, but if that doesn't work for you, I could send Reid to pick you up at the Cape so you don't have to drive to Providence. I know he'd be happy to do it, and he's a great pilot. You'd be perfectly safe."

Colleen's delicate laughter came through the phone line like wind chimes. "That's very sweet of you to offer, love, but I'm sticking closer to home these days, where I'm most comfortable. Getting old is no fun."

"Is there anything I can do to help you feel better? Are there specialists we could call who might be able to help? There has to be something. I hate to think of you in pain."

"Brandon and Colin took me to Boston last month to see a rheumatologist. I'm on some new medicine that's bothering my stomach—of course it's helping the arthritis. But I didn't call to be a killjoy. I want you to know how truly delighted I am for you and your Reid. We all are. Mike is heartbroken to miss the wedding because of the school trip to Europe that was booked a long time ago for Christmas vacation. She was so excited to be invited."

"Of course she was invited. She's my biggest fan! Tell her I hope she has a wonderful trip, and I want to see tons of pictures when she gets back."

"I'll be sure to tell her. She's sixteen now, if you can believe it, and learning to drive. Apparently, she landed them in the neighbor's yard a week or so ago. Brandon was fit to be tied telling me about it."

Kate laughed. "I can imagine."

"I hope you know all the O'Malleys will be there in spirit, wishing you well and sending lots of love. Aidan has a few gifts from me."

"You shouldn't have done that."

"Yes, I should have. You know I love you and your sisters like my own grand-children, right?" Colleen asked, her voice thick with emotion.

Moved, Kate said, "You've always been so good to us, and we love you, too."

"You girls and your mother saved my son's life. You have no idea…"

"We love him, too. I never would've thought that so much good could come from my parents' divorce, but my sisters and I ended up with a lot more people who love us and who we love, too."

"You can never have too many people who love you. I'd give anything to see you walk down the aisle to meet your new husband."

"We'll come to you, as soon as we can."

"Oh, honey, I know how busy you are. Please don't worry about me. Your mom has promised me lots and lots of pictures. Enjoy every minute of your big day."

Kate wiped a tear from her cheek. "I will, Grammy. Thank you so much for calling."

"Love you, honey."

"Love you, too."

Reid came in through the back door and stopped short when he saw her wiping away tears. "What's wrong?"

"I just talked to my Grammy O'Malley. She's not feeling too well, so she's going to stay home."

"I'm sorry, honey. I know you were looking forward to seeing her."

"I told her maybe we could go see her sometime soon."

"I'd love to meet her. She sounds like a real character."

"Oh, she is."

He came over to the table and put his arm around her.

Kate leaned into his embrace, comforted by the scent of fresh air and sawdust and his distinctive cologne. "What're you doing back so soon?"

"Forgot my phone." He pressed a kiss to the top of her head. "You know what would cheer you up?"

"What's that?"

"A first look at your Bunkhouse?"

"Now?"

"Right now. Get your coat."

Kate's tears were forgotten as she scrambled from the kitchen to get her coat. She was back ten seconds later.

"That's more like it," Reid said of the smile she greeted him with. "I don't like to see tears on that gorgeous face."

"I'm apt to be a bit of a waterworks for the next week or two."

"I'll allow that, but then only smiles and laughter. Got me?"

"That sounds good to me." They headed out the door toward the path he'd worn in the grass between their house and the new bunkhouse. Just as they reached the tree line, Kate was felled by a wave of nausea. She stopped walking and took a few deep breaths of air that had finally gone cold in the last week.

"What is it, darlin'?"

"The usual this time of day." The nausea arrived with infuriating regularity at about nine thirty every day.

He rested his hand on her back. "Do you want to go back?"

She shook her head and took a couple more deep breaths, trying to battle through it.

"Isn't it about time you had a doctor confirm what we already know?"

"I have an appointment tomorrow."

"I hate to see you suffering."

"You do know there's nothing the doctor can do about the nausea, right?"

He put his arm around her to continue along the path. "Nothing at all?"

"Nope. I have to suffer through until it lets up."

"I hope it lets up soon. We have lots of plans to see to."

They came around the final bend before the clearing where the Bunkhouse now stood.

Kate stopped and opened her mouth to say something, but the words got stuck in her throat. "Oh, Reid… Oh my God!" He'd built a mini version of her log-cabin house, complete with the A-frame roof and deck.

"Told you you'd like it," he said close to her ear, sending shivers down her spine.

She threw herself into his arms. "It's absolutely perfect. Thank you so much." She took advantage of his close proximity to plant a passionate kiss on him, which he returned with equal fervor.

The construction workers stopped what they were doing to offer catcalls and whistles.

Reid was smiling when he pulled back from her. "I love the way you say thank you, darlin'." He kissed her forehead and then her nose. "Come see the inside."

Kate took his hand and followed him into the cozy living room/kitchen/dining area that boasted a huge stone fireplace. A bedroom suite was located off the kitchen.

"That'll be perfect for my Harrington grandparents," Kate said. "They have trouble with stairs these days."

"I remember you telling me that."

Her fiancée paid attention when she talked to him, which was just another reason to love him beyond all measure.

They went up the stairs to find four more bedrooms and two bathrooms. In her mind, Kate began assigning rooms to her dad and Andi, Jamie and Frannie, Jamie's parents…

"Check this out," he said, leading her up another set of stairs to a loft. "I thought the kids might like to sleep up here."

"Yes," Kate said as a grin stretched across her face. "Yes." He'd given her exactly what she needed without having to be told exactly what she needed. She hugged him and sighed when he returned the embrace. "How did I live without you for so long?"

"I have no idea how either of us managed without the other. Luckily, those days are over now."

"Thank God." A thought occurred to her. "We have to order furniture and appliances!"

"Jill took care of that weeks ago."

"Of course she did," Kate said laughing.

"It's all due to be delivered on Friday."

"I can't believe you went to all this trouble."

"I figured you might want to make Christmas in Nashville an every-other-year tradition."

"I'd love to do that."

"We needed more beds," he said with a shrug, as if it had been no big deal to make this miracle happen in six short weeks.

"I love you so much."

"I know you do, darlin'. I love you just as much. Maybe even more."

She followed him down the stairs to the first floor. "No way. That's not possible."

"You don't know that."

They continued the "argument" all the way home. Kate shed her coat and turned to him. "Do you have to go right back to work?"

"I have a lot to do today to be ready for the deliveries on Friday. Why?"

She let her cold hands wander inside his coat and under his sweater. "I was just wondering."

He gasped when cold met warm. "Katherine..."

She'd always loved the stern way he said her full name. "Yes?"

"Don't act all innocent like you don't know what you're doing to me."

"What am I doing? I only asked if you have to go right back to work."

"You know exactly what you're doing, you little witch." With his hands on her bottom, he brought her in tight against him to demonstrate the effect her cold hands on his back had had on him.

"I hate to let that go to waste, but you do have to work, so..."

"Not so fast."

Venturing a glance up at him, she found fire in his eyes as he looked at her with thinly veiled intent. Oh. My. "I'd hate to keep you from your work."

He laughed as he bent his head to kiss her. "I suppose you're going to say this was my fault, right?"

"You did come back for your phone," she said, the picture of innocence.

"That I did." When he let out a growl, turned her around and marched her toward the stairs Kate dissolved into laughter, thankful once again that she'd had the courage to go after what she wanted most. One thing she knew for certain, she'd never let him go again.

The invasion began on the twenty-second of December with Maggie's arrival on a commercial flight from LaGuardia into Nashville International. Kate rode along with Jill to pick up their younger sister.

"Thanks for everything you did to make this weekend happen," Kate said.

"I enjoyed it, and it'll be great to have everyone here. The Bunkhouse is amazing, Kate. I can't believe Reid pulled that off so quickly."

"Neither can I."

"He's good at what he does, that's for sure."

"Yes, he is."

"I really like him. I want you to know that. I'm glad I've had the chance to get to know him better in the last few weeks."

"I'm glad, too. It means a lot to me that you like him."

"I like you two together. I'll admit that I wondered what you'd possibly see in a guy Dad's age, but after spending time with you two, I get it now."

"I appreciate that more than you could ever know." Kate glanced over at her sister, who was focused on the road. The forecasters had warned of black ice and snow showers over the next twenty-four hours. They'd also mentioned the possibility of a white Christmas, but Kate refused to get her hopes up. "What about you? What's up with Ashton?"

"We're having fun, hanging out, you know."

"Nothing serious?"

"I didn't say that."

"Okay, do tell."

"We talk about the future. Sometimes."

"What about the future?"

Jill sighed with exasperation. "About spending it together. That kind of thing."

"Why do I get the distinct impression that you're totally holding out on me?"

"You've got enough going on this week without worrying about what's up with me."

Kate turned in her seat to get a better look at her sister. "Are you waiting to make plans of your own until my wedding is over?"

"Maybe…"

"Don't do that! Don't wait on me. I'm sick of being responsible for holding you back."

"You've never held me back. Don't give yourself that much credit."

"You know what I mean. If you want to make plans, make them. I'm more than happy to share the spotlight with you, of all people."

"That's very nice of you, but we're not quite there yet—at least I'm not. He's a bit ahead of me."

"I want you to be happy."

"I *am* happy. There is one thing I wanted to talk to you about, though."

This was said with a hint of hesitation that put Kate on edge. "What's that?"

"Ashton asked me to be a partner in his firm. Since you're cutting back on the career commitments, I thought there might be some extra time in the schedule to try some other things, but if you don't want me to—"

"It sounds like a great idea. How do you feel about working with him?"

"I'm not sure. He keeps telling me it'd be great, but I have my doubts."

"There's only one way to find out."

"That's what he says, too."

"I want you to do whatever you want, Jill. Working with me was never intended to be a lifetime indentured-servant kind of thing."

"I'm hardly indentured, and I love working with you. You know that. If I do this with Ashton, you'd still be my number-one client—always."

"Could I tell you something that I'm not going to tell anyone else until after the wedding?"

"Absolutely."

"I'm pregnant."

Jill looked over at her and then back at the road to correct the swerve. "Oh, Kate! That's amazing news! You must be thrilled."

"I'm beyond thrilled. I had no idea it was possible to be this happy."

"When are you due?"

"Late June."

"So no summer tour this year."

"Right."

"We'll deal with that after the holidays."

"That's what I hoped you'd say."

Kate's phone chirped with a text from Maggie. "Her flight got in early. She's waiting at the curb." Kate's heart beat fast with excitement. She couldn't wait to see her "baby" sister.

They reached the airport a few minutes later only to confront a maddening traffic jam at the arrivals level.

"Is that her?" Jill asked of the figure jogging toward the end of the line.

"Yes!" Kate jumped out of the car to wave at Maggie, who darted through other cars to get to them. Right there in the middle of the lane, Kate hugged her sister. "Dad wouldn't approve of you playing in traffic."

"Dad wouldn't approve of a lot of my favorite past times," Maggie said with a cheeky grin as she got into the backseat. A perfect combination of their parents, Maggie was the tallest of the three sisters, with Jill's sleek dark hair and Kate's bright blue eyes.

"That sounds interesting," Jill said, turning her face to accept a kiss from Maggie in the backseat. "What've you been up to in the big city?"

"Oh, you know. Some of this, some of that."

"Any boyfriends?" Kate asked.

"A few, but nothing serious."

"Typical Maggie," Jill said. "Breaking hearts from coast to coast."

"Mostly on the east coast, but I've met a few from out west recently. What about you, Jill? Any good boys in Nashville?"

"Oh, you know," Jill said in a teasing tone. "Some of this, some of that."

"Tell her the truth," Kate said.

Sensing good gossip, Maggie leaned forward so she was between the two front seats. "Spill it, sista."

"Put your seat belt on!" Jill said.

"After you tell me the scoop."

"I'm not telling you anything until you're buckled in."

"God, you're just like Mom," Maggie grumbled as she returned to her seat and put her seat belt on.

"Thank you."

"I'm buckled, Mom, now tell me your news."

When Jill hesitated, Kate filled in the gap. "She's doing the horizontal bop with Reid's son, Ashton."

"Kate!"

"What? It's true!"

"Shut the front door!" Maggie said. "*A father and son?* What about me? Is there one left for me?"

Jill and Kate laughed. "We've got them all," Kate said. "Sorry."

"You two were never very good at sharing."

"Don't pout, Maggie," Jill said. "There's a whole crop of Southern boys waiting to meet you."

"Except Dad is going to be here, and he loves to ruin my fun."

"Mine, too," Kate said, wondering if he was going to ruin her fun this weekend. She sure hoped not. They'd spoken a few times in the last few weeks, sticking to neutral, nonconfrontational subjects. He'd agreed to spend the holiday in Nashville and attend the wedding. Kate was trying to be satisfied with the partial victory but hadn't dared broach the subject of him giving her away.

"When can I see my dress?" Maggie asked.

"As soon as we get to my place," Jill said.

"And when do I get to meet my future brother-in-law?"

"In the morning," Kate said. "We're having a girls' night tonight while he puts the finishing touches on the Bunkhouse."

"What the heck is the Bunkhouse?" Maggie asked.

"Just you wait and see," Jill said.

With the help of Ashton, Buddy and Buddy's eighteen-year-old son Harry, Reid got the furniture distributed in the Bunkhouse. When Buddy decided the place needed a woman's touch, he called Taylor, who promised to be right over with Ms. Martha and the girls.

They arrived a short time later with pizza, beer and soda, and Reid had to admit they truly saved the day. They'd taken all the items Reid and Kate had bought in a shopping frenzy and put them together to make a warm, cozy, inviting space for Kate's family.

"It looks awesome," Harry declared over pizza when the work was finished.

"I can't believe how fast you built this place," Buddy said.

"That's what he does," Ashley reminded her father.

"Thank you, Ash," Reid said, thankful that Buddy and his family had been frequent visitors in St. Kitts. He would've hated to be a stranger to his best friend's kids.

"Are you nervous?" Taylor asked Reid. "With all the in-laws coming and the holiday and the wedding?"

"Not really. I'm looking forward to finally being settled with Kate."

"Been a long time coming," Buddy said, holding up a beer bottle.

Reid clinked his bottle against his friend's, sharing a smile. "Yes, it has."

"I'm so very happy for you and Kate, Reid," Martha said. "I know I wasn't always happy for you two, but she's a grown woman now who clearly knows her own heart."

"Thank you, Martha. It means a lot to me that you approve."

"All my friends think it's really cool that I get to be a junior bridesmaid in Kate Harrington's wedding," Georgia said.

"Don't they know who Mom and Dad are?" Harry asked his youngest sister.

"Sure, but they're nowhere *near* as cool as Kate is," Georgia said with a sly glance at her parents, who were, as always, sitting close together on the sofa.

They also spoke as one in protesting. "*Hey!*"

Georgia laughed at the faces they made at her. "Well, it's true."

"Sheesh," Buddy said. "You give these kids your heart and soul, and they grow up to be rotten brats."

"Yes, they do," Martha said with a pointed look at her son.

"Wow," Ashton said, laughing. "Rough crowd."

"You know it," Buddy grumbled. "I'm abused in my own home."

"Not by everybody, baby," Taylor cooed at him.

"Thank God for you," Buddy said, kissing her right on the lips in front of their four disgusted children.

Reid laughed, amused as always by the Longstreets.

"We'd better get home," Taylor said. "One more day of school before vacation."

The girls let out enormous groans.

"Not for me," Harry said, grinning from ear to ear and looking more like his father with every passing day. "Yet another benefit of college life. A whole month off at Christmas."

"Shut up, Harry," Chloe said in a sinister tone that shocked Reid. He wouldn't have thought sweet Chloe was capable.

"All right, citizens," Taylor said in the no-nonsense mom voice that worked every time. Reid was never quite sure how she managed to pull that off. "Let's go before this descends into all-out Longstreet warfare."

Reid walked them to their cars, where Harry wisely chose to ride with his dad while the girls and Martha went with Taylor. "Thanks a million for all the help."

Taylor gave him a big hug. "We're so thrilled for you and Kate. We can't wait until the wedding."

"Thanks, Tay. Love you guys."

"Love you, too." She kissed him full on the lips, patted his face and got into her car.

"I saw that," Buddy grumbled.

"*She* kissed *me.*"

"Uh-huh." Buddy surprised the hell out of Reid with a hug. "Enjoy all this, brother. Don't let the haters get you down."

Leave it to Buddy to say what everyone else was thinking. "I won't."

"Anything I can do—you know where I am."

"There is one thing…"

"What's that?"

"Well, I know Kate asked you to walk her downstairs to the wedding, but if you could maybe be my best man, too, I'd be mighty grateful."

Buddy glanced at the Bunkhouse and then at Reid. "I thought you'd ask Ashton to do that."

Reid would never admit to how much it pained him that he didn't feel comfortable asking his son to stand up for him. "Don't want to push my luck."

"Right. Yeah, probably wise. Of course I'll do it."

"Thanks—for that and everything."

"You have no idea how glad I am to see you guys back together and happy as hell. I beat myself up for a long time over what happened the first time around."

"You shouldn't have. It was all our doing. You got caught in the crossfire."

"Still… Feels like we're righting a wrong or something, you know?"

"I sure do, and I'm so glad you and your family will be a part of it."

"So are we. We'll see you for Christmas."

Reid was incredibly thankful that his "family" would be present for the holiday. He needed all the friends he could get with Jack Harrington and Jamie Booth coming to town. "See you then."

He went back inside where Ashton was cleaning up the beer bottles, soda cans and pizza boxes. "Thanks for the help tonight, son."

"Sure, no problem."

They'd been cautiously polite to each other in the weeks since he and Kate had been back in town. Neither he nor Ashton had any appetite for trouble in their relationship, and for that Reid was profoundly grateful. But he would give almost everything he had to feel that his son was even slightly happy for him and Kate. He wanted that more than he'd realized, until it became clear that Ashton wasn't going to say the words he longed to hear.

It was enough, Reid told himself, that his son was participating, that he'd come to help with the Bunkhouse when Reid asked him to. Except it wasn't enough. It wasn't anywhere near enough. At some point, Reid needed to tell him about the baby that was on the way, but he'd yet to find the right time to broach a subject that might upset his son.

"Are you going to head home?" Reid asked when all the work was done and the living room had been straightened after the impromptu gathering.

"I was thinking about crashing the hen party," Ashton said with a devilish gleam in his eyes. "Want to come along?"

"Kate was pretty adamant about wanting some time with her sisters."

"So was Jill."

Their eyes met in a moment of lighthearted unity that made Reid feel like there might be hope after all.

"Are you in?" Ashton asked.

"Sure, why not? But if it goes bad, it was your idea."

Ashton laughed as Reid locked up the Bunkhouse and they headed for the well-worn path that led to Jill's place.

Reid felt like a kid sneaking out to perpetrate a prank with his favorite partner in crime. The air was brisk and cold. Snow flurries danced in the air, a promise of things to come over the next few days. Kate had refused to get too hopeful about a white Christmas, but all reports indicated snow on Christmas Eve.

"Colder than a well-digger's ass," Ashton muttered.

"Sure is."

The lights were on at Jill's, and an inviting wisp of smoke curled from the chimney.

Ashton marched right up the front stairs as if he had every right to be there and rapped on the door.

Jill answered a minute later, surprise registering on her face. "What're you doing here?"

"My dad wanted to see Kate." He stepped aside so she could see that Reid was with him.

Reid let out a bark of laughter. "He lies. This was all his idea."

"We're freezing our agates off," Ashton said. "Are you going to let us in?" When Jill hesitated, he said, *"Pretty please?"*

"Oh, all right."

"She can't resist me," Ashton said to his father as they went inside.

"Don't push your luck," Jill said, even though Reid could tell she was delighted to see his son.

Ashton truly pushed his luck by stealing a kiss from her.

Wanting to give them a minute alone and hungry for a glimpse of his fiancée, Reid looked around the family room, which was empty. He followed voices to the kitchen, where he found Kate with Maggie.

Kate's eyes lit up with delight when he walked into the room. He hoped she would always be that happy to see him.

"What're you doing here?" she asked.

"Ashton wanted to see Jill and dragged me along."

"I'm so glad he did." Kate came over to hug and kiss him. Over her shoulder, he noticed Maggie watching them. With an interesting combination of their features, she was as gorgeous as her sisters.

He pulled back from Kate's embrace but kept his arm around her. "You must be the mysterious third Harrington sister."

"That'd be me." Maggie stepped forward to shake his hand. "Great to finally meet you."

"You, too."

"I owe you a long-overdue thank-you," she said.

Reid looked down at Kate, who seemed equally baffled. "Whatever for?"

"I understand you flew my sister home to Rhode Island after I fell off the ladder."

"Oh, that. Well, it was no problem."

"I was really happy to have her there."

"We're really happy to have you here," Reid said.

Maggie smiled at him, and he relaxed a bit when it became clear that she had no beef with him marrying her sister.

Ashton came in with Jill, who introduced him to Maggie. Reid noticed his son's face was flushed with color that couldn't be completely attributed to the cold. He had a dazzled, stunned look about him whenever he glanced at Jill, which was often. To see his son truly in love for the first time was an amazing thing.

"Since you two have officially crashed our party," Jill said dryly, "what can I get you to drink?"

"Beer works," Ashton said. "For both of us."

Jill rolled her eyes at him and got the beers.

Ashton leaned on the center island, making himself right at home with the chips and dip. "So, ladies, what'd we miss?"

CHAPTER 17

The all-out invasion occurred at high noon the next day, when three limos started down the lane to the house.

Kate had been vibrating with excitement since she woke up at five and bounded out of bed to greet the day on which her family would finally arrive. She'd wanted to go to the airport to meet them, but Reid had convinced her to spend the morning at home to get through the hours of nausea she battled each day.

Since the nausea had been particularly intense today, she was grateful for his foresight. How in the world was she going to keep the secret about her pregnancy if she turned green at exactly the same time every day?

As the limos got closer to the house, she decided she'd worry about that tomorrow.

"Ready?" she asked Reid, who'd been quieter than usual all morning. He had to be nervous about her family arriving, knowing some of them were less than pleased about him and the wedding.

"As ready as I'll ever be."

"In case I forget to tell you later, I love you for a million reasons, but I especially love you for welcoming my family into our home for the holiday and our wedding. I love you for building that amazing Bunkhouse practically overnight, and I love you for going to see my dad when you knew you wouldn't be welcome."

"That's a whole lotta love, darlin'," he said with a warm smile.

"I want you to remember how much I love you no matter what happens in the next few days."

"I will."

"Promise?"

Nodding, he planted a lingering kiss on her lips.

It was the last moment of peace or quiet as people poured out of the limos. Kate stayed close to Reid, introducing him to everyone and not giving anyone a chance to say or do anything untoward. She noticed her dad and Uncle Jamie went out of their way to say as little as possible to Reid, even though both of them shook his hand—somewhat begrudgingly, it seemed to Kate.

Her mom, Andi, Aunt Frannie and all her grandparents—real and adopted, in the case of the Booths—hugged and kissed Kate and Reid, which she appreciated. The six kids—the Harrington and Booth twins along with the O'Malley boys—were running and screaming in the yard after being cooped up all morning on the plane.

Kate spent the next hour getting everyone settled. Her dad's family, his parents and the Booths—senior and junior—took possession of the Bunkhouse, while her mom's family and her grandma Anna settled in Kate's house. Maggie had decided to stay at Jill's where it was "safe."

"Everything is beautiful, honey," Kate's mom, Clare, said of the Christmas decorations Kate had labored over the last few weeks.

"I'm so glad you think so." Kate hugged her mother again. "I can't believe you're all here and that we actually pulled this off."

"I know. It's amazing. I remember the first Christmas after Dad and I got divorced, and I hoped that someday we might have a Christmas just like this one, all of us together with the people we love most."

Kate blamed pregnancy for putting her every emotion on full alert. She blinked back tears. "That's what I wanted, too. I wanted it so badly. It's been such a long time since I was able to be with you all for Christmas."

Clare embraced her daughter. "We've missed you, honey."

"Hey, Clare, do you remember where I put my phone charger?" Aidan asked as he came in, stopping short when he saw them hugging. "Oh, sorry." He started to back out of the room.

"No," Kate said, holding out a hand to him. "Don't go."

He came in to take her hand, and they added him to their hug.

"I'm so happy to see you," she said to her stepfather. "Thanks for coming."

Aidan planted a kiss on Kate's forehead. "Our pleasure, honey."

"Have you had a chance to talk to Dad at all?" Kate asked her mom. "About the wedding?"

Aidan and Clare exchanged glances that set Kate's nerves on edge.

"Some," Clare said. "He's doing the best he can."

"He's here," Aidan added. "That's something."

"Yes," Kate said softly. It was something, but it was nowhere near enough.

"I know for certain that he wants you to be happy," Clare said. "That's all we've ever wanted for you."

"I'm so happy. I've never been happier."

"Let him see that for a few days," Aidan said. "He'll come around."

"What about Jamie?" Kate asked.

"He'll follow your dad's lead," Clare said. "You know how they roll."

Kate laughed, because she did in fact know how they rolled—as a unit. They always had, and they always would.

"It means a lot to me that you guys support us," Kate said.

"I've learned that life can be very unpredictable, and we're far better off when we go with the flow rather than trying to fight our way upstream," Clare said.

Aidan smiled at his wife. "Well said."

"Plus," Clare said with a devious grin for him, "I've learned that being married to someone *much* younger has its challenges, but they can be overcome with patience. A lot of patience."

"Oh, that's very funny," Aidan said, swatting her on the rear. "Now what the heck did you do with my phone charger?"

***

Kate had refused to hire any help for the weekend but had yielded to Reid's pleas for caterers for the wedding. With the help of her mom, Andi, Jill, Maggie, Frannie, Grandma Anna, Grandma Madeline, Mary Booth and Frannie's daughter Olivia, they managed to get everyone fed and outside for a huge game of football on the lawn.

Even though she wanted to play, Kate was mindful of the new life growing inside her and wisely decided to hang out with the seniors on the porch who were watching the action on the lawn as it turned from touch to tackle. Her Grandpa John and Neil Booth made a wager they thought no one else noticed, but Kate did and somehow refrained from laughing at their predictable antics.

The game came down to a last-minute touchdown that Ashton completed despite Jill cutting him off at the knees just short of the end zone.

Her face flushed from exertion, Andi jogged over to Kate. "What's up with Jill and Ashton?" she asked.

"Why do you ask?"

"Because Jill hates football, and that was one hell of a tackle."

Kate wilted under Andi's stare. "Um, well. . ." Her relationship with Ashton was, after all, Jill's news to share when she saw fit.

"I knew there was something," Andi said smugly.

"Why don't you ask her?"

"I believe I will." She leaned in closer to Kate. "She's not the only one keeping secrets, is she?"

Kate stared at her beloved stepmother. "What're you, some sort of witch or something?"

"I know my girls. That's all."

Kate smiled at her, a flood of memories assailing her from the most difficult time in her life after her mother's accident and the long coma that took her away from them for three years. Andi had come along during those years, offering friendship and warmth and support to Clare's daughters that none of them had ever forgotten.

Kate enveloped Andi in a spontaneous hug. "Don't tell anyone, okay?"

"I wouldn't dream of it, honey. I'm so happy for you."

"Thanks. I wish Dad was, too."

"He'll get there. Give him some more time. Be patient with him."

"I will." Kate happened to look up at the football game to see Jamie and Reid having an intense conversation off to the side of the yard. "Excuse me," Kate said to Andi and walked over to the two men. She didn't bother to listen to what was being said. Rather, she took her uncle by the arm. "Take a walk with me."

"I'm not done talking to him," Jamie said.

"Yes, you are." She ventured a glance at Reid and found his face tight with tension that made her ache. Wrapping her hand around Jamie's arm, she led him away from the gathering. They walked toward the stables in silence as Kate thought about what she wanted to say to him. Since the words weren't coming, she took him inside to see the horses and introduced him to Thunder.

"He's a beauty," Jamie said, extending a hand to caress the horse's soft hair.

"Reid gave him to me."

Jamie withdrew his hand.

Kate turned to face the man who'd been her father's best friend since before she was born and her uncle since he married Aunt Frannie eleven years ago. "Do you know what my first memory of you is?"

Jamie jammed his hands in the pockets of his jeans and shook his head. He was tall and blond and handsome—and pissed. That last part was patently obvious. Despite his anger, Kate pressed on.

"The time you brought me ice cream after I had my tonsils out. Remember that?"

Jamie looked at her, incredulous. "I can't believe *you* remember that. You were like two or three."

"I was almost four, but I remember it vividly. I remember that and so many other things—pool parties, holidays, first communions, graduations, vacations, sailing, swimming, your wedding to Frannie, your twins being born, the way you and Frannie propped us up after my mother's accident. You've been a part of my everything, Jamie, and I've been a part of yours."

He stared down at the ground, kicking at the dirt with the toe of a well-worn running shoe.

"I've loved you as much as it's possible to love anyone."

"Shit, Kate," he muttered, and she was stunned to see tears pooling in his eyes. "Don't do this to me."

"I know you think he took advantage of me the first time we were together. I need you to hear me—one adult to another—when I tell you that couldn't be further from the truth. Every single thing that happened between us happened because I wanted it. Sometimes I think I wanted it more than he did."

"He should've controlled himself. He was a forty-five-year-old *man*, Kate. You were just a kid."

"I stopped being a kid the day that car hit my mom right in front of me, and you know it. You were there. You know that's true."

He shrugged and shook his head. "Still…"

"I'm asking you to put aside what happened ten years ago and focus on what's happening right now. I'm about to marry the only man I've ever loved, and I want my Uncle Jamie to be happy for me. I've never asked you for anything, but I'm asking you for that."

"You're asking an awful lot."

"I know." Because he seemed to know she needed it, Thunder nuzzled her neck and let out a gentle nicker. Kate rubbed his nose, grateful for his unwavering love.

After a brief period of silence, Jamie reached out to stroke Thunder's nose. "For the longest time, I was convinced I'd never have kids of my own, but I was okay with that because I had you and your sisters. You were my kids."

"And we always knew that. Always."

"It was hard for me when a man I once considered a good friend did what he did with you. It was a bitter pill, especially because I was the one who suggested your dad reach out to him when you decided to move here."

"Then I owe you a debt of thanks."

"Really, Kate," he said with a laugh. "You're as exasperating at twenty-eight as you were at ten."

Taking advantage of the lighter moment, Kate rested a hand on his arm. "You know how much you love Frannie?"

"Yeah."

"That's how much I love Reid. Not one day passed when we were apart that I didn't think of him or wish I were with him or wonder what he was doing or if he was happy. Imagine what it was like to find out he felt the same way. I know we might only get twenty or thirty good years, but I'll take every one of 'em. I'll take every minute we get and be thankful I'm spending that time with the man I love."

Jamie sighed deeply. "I guess I owe him an apology."

"I'm sure he'd appreciate that. I know I would."

"I *am* happy that you're happy, Kate. Of course I am. How could I not be? It's just…"

"What?"

"I wish it wasn't him."

"Well, it is, so I need you to put aside all the old animosity and draw upon all that love you've always felt for me."

"You don't play fair," he said gruffly as he pulled her into a hug.

"I need you to love me more than you hate him."

"Aww, honey, I do. I love you that much and more."

"Thank you."

"Sorry to be an ant at the picnic. I don't want to ruin anything for you."

"Then don't. Help me to celebrate and be happy for me. That's all I need."

He kissed her cheek and hugged her again. "Okay."

***

Buddy, Taylor and their kids joined them for dinner that consisted of lasagna Kate had made herself. Afterward, the group migrated to the great room, where the twelve-foot-tall Christmas tree sparkled with white lights and a roaring fire filled the stone hearth. Clare suggested a sing-along featuring Kate on the guitar and Aidan on the piano. Kate had always loved playing with her stepfather, and this time was no different. It took considerable cajoling to get Buddy and Taylor to join them, as they didn't want to intrude on a family event.

"You *are* my family," Kate said simply, which seemed to win them over.

"I'm feeling a tad bit intimidated," Aidan said to laughter from the entire room.

Turned out he could more than hold his own with three superstars, and Kate was glad Maggie was videotaping their "show" on her phone. It was a memory Kate wanted to be able to revisit often in the future.

She ended the sing-along alone with her guitar, singing "I Thought I Knew" for Reid in front of everyone they both loved, declaring her love for him to anyone who might still harbor doubts.

I thought I knew
what love was,
but then there was you…
I thought I knew
how it would be,
but now I see,
And now it's true…
I didn't know
until there was you…
Until there was you…
Until there was you…
I thought I knew
And now it's true…

I thought I knew
what peace was,
then there was you...
I thought I knew
what dreams were,
then there was you...
I thought I knew
how it would be,
but now I see...

A hushed silence hung over the room as Kate created a moment she hoped they wouldn't soon forget. She had a surprise for her fiancé—a new verse she'd recently written.

I thought I knew
What love was
But then I lost you
Then I lost you
And now I know what love is
Because I found you
Because I have you
Because I love you

Reid stared at her, clearly moved by the new addition to the song that had defined them so long ago.

Kate pushed through the rush of emotion to finish the song.

I thought I knew
what love was,
but then there was you

Then there was you...

***

In the back of the room, Jack stood alone and watched his daughter serenade the man she loved. He couldn't deny the obvious love and devotion between the two of them. He'd watched them closely since arriving earlier and noticed that they were never far from each other. If they were together, they were holding hands, sharing smiles or otherwise glowing with happiness.

He who had never expected to spend another minute in Reid Matthews's presence now had to concede that the man seemed completely smitten with Kate, and vice versa.

As if he needed further proof, Kate's song cemented the deal. He hadn't known she'd written "I Thought I Knew" for Reid. Or he supposed he'd never bothered to think about where the song had come from. Now it made sense that her biggest hit had come from her greatest love.

"Excuse me, Jack."

Rustled out of his musings, Jack said, "Hey, Ashton." He'd been surprised to see Ashton at Kate's house, knowing there'd been no love lost between the two of them after Ashton alerted Jack to the affair between Kate and Reid.

"I, um, I wondered if I might have a word with you? In private?"

Oh God, Jack thought. *What now?* "Sure." He followed Ashton into the kitchen, which had been abandoned after dinner.

Ashton held up a bottle of bourbon. "Drink?"

Suspecting he might need the fortification, Jack nodded.

Ashton poured them each a couple of fingers of the amber liquid and handed one to Jack.

That was when Jack noticed a slight tremble in the other man's hand. "What's on your mind?"

"Jill."

Okay, he sure as hell hadn't seen that coming. "What about her?"

"I'm in love with her. I have been for a very long time, and I'd very much like to ask her to marry me."

"You… You love Jill."

Ashton never blinked. "I love Jill."

"She's never mentioned you."

"I'm sure she hasn't," he said with a laugh as he ran his fingers through his hair. "It's relatively new. The relationship, that is. The feelings—not so new."

"I had no idea."

"I think your wife knows. She's been watching me like a hawk all day."

That drew a laugh from Jack. "I have no doubt she tuned in to whatever is going on about five minutes after we got here. I have to run to keep up with her."

"I know I haven't given you much reason to respect me—"

"Why do you say that?"

"After what I did, calling you about Kate and my dad…"

"I appreciated that. They probably didn't, but I did."

"That call caused a lot of heartache for everyone involved, you included, I'm sure. If I had it to do over, I wouldn't have done it. My dad was very unhappy after he and Kate broke up. I bore a big part of the blame for that unhappiness." Ashton seemed to make an effort to shake off the unpleasant trip down memory lane. "Anyway, I hope we can get past all that because I'd very much like to marry your daughter. I love her more than anything, and there's nothing I wouldn't do to ensure her happiness."

"Does she want to marry you?"

"I sure as hell hope so, but I guess we'll find out when I ask her."

Jack was intrigued to realize Ashton honestly didn't know what to expect from Jill. "She won't make it easy on you."

"Ah, believe me," he said with a laugh, "I know. May I count on your blessing?"

"Yes," Jack said, shaking Ashton's hand. "Yes, you can."

"Thank you, sir. I appreciate that."

"Don't call me sir. Makes me feel ancient."

"Right, sorry. Thank you, Jack. I'm going to, um, go back to the party."

As Ashton hightailed it out of the kitchen, Jack took a moment by himself to absorb the new blow. His daughters were long grown and out of the house, living on their own and thriving in their chosen careers, but they'd always be his little girls. And now two of them would soon be married, or so it seemed likely.

Jamie came in to get another beer and closed the fridge, startling when he saw Jack there. "Shit, you scared the crap out of me."

"Sorry."

"What're you doing in here all by yourself?"

"I wasn't by myself." He told Jamie about the conversation with Ashton.

"Holy double whammy, huh?"

"Yeah."

"What'd you say to him?"

"What could I say? He said he loves her, he'll always love her." Jack shrugged. "I gave him my blessing."

"Reid said those same things, didn't he?"

"Yeah, but this is different."

"I know."

Jack glanced at the man who'd been his best friend since their first day of college, his business partner for most of his adult life and his brother-in-law for eleven years. "What?"

"I had a talk with Kate earlier."

"I saw you two go off together."

"She hauled me away before I could take a swing at her fiancé."

"Did he say something to you?"

"No. Mostly he stood there and let me rage at him. And then Kate hauled me away and took me to meet her horse." Jamie pause for a second. "She really loves the guy, Jack."

"Yes."

"I mean, really, *really*."

"I know."

"She said she's going into it knowing they might only get twenty or thirty years. But she wants to spend every second of that time with him. She..."

Jack looked over at him, surprised to see Jamie wrestling with his emotions.

"She asked me to love her more than I hate him."

"Ouch."

"No kidding. I think we both need to do that, you know? It's none of my business, but if I was butting in, I'd say you probably owe Reid the same courtesy you just gave Ashton."

"It's your business, and you're not butting in. And besides, I happen to agree with you."

"Really?"

Jack nodded. "He's what she wants. At the end of the day, that's all that matters." He paused. "Do you know that before today I'd never seen them together, other than the time I caught them in the car? I'd never seen them as a couple. I only had the vision of one bad day upon which to frame my entire point of reference where they were concerned."

"They do seem devoted to each other."

"Indeed. And what more could any father want for his daughter than a man who is utterly devoted to her?"

"Nothing, I suppose. Are you going to tell him that?"

"As soon as I get the chance."

Reid was already in bed by the time Kate got there just after midnight. She'd gone around one more time to make sure everyone knew where the extra blankets, pillows and towels could be found. In the living room, she'd discovered her brother Eric sacked out on the sofa. She covered him with a blanket and then planted a kiss on his cheek because she could.

He'd gotten so grown up since she last saw him. According to Andi, he was shaving and had a girlfriend at home, not that Kate was allowed to ask him about either of those things.

"What're you thinking about?" Reid asked as he gathered her in close to him.

"My brother Eric. He became a man when I wasn't looking."

"It happens. Did you have a good time tonight?"

"It was wonderful. Everything I'd hoped for, and then some. How about you?"

"Much better than expected. And the song… Wow, Kate. You blew me away with the new verse."

"I'm glad you liked it."

"I loved it."

"Let me turn over so I can kiss you."

He released his tight hold on her, but only for the time it took her to turn to face him. Then she was right back in his arms again.

She found his lips in the dark, running her tongue over his bottom lip, teasing and cajoling until he allowed her in. Their tongues mated and tangled as his hands found their way under her shirt.

Wanting him desperately, Kate arched into him, tightening her arms around his neck.

Reid drew back from the kiss, eliciting a whimper of protest from her.

"It was just getting good."

"It's always good."

"Then come back."

"I can't make love to you when half your parents are sleeping upstairs."

She wrapped her hand around the erection that made a liar out of him. "Yes, you can."

With his hand over hers, he stopped her from stroking him. "No, I can't."

"Seriously? You're going to make me wait days and days and days?"

"It's only two days, and you'll survive. It's enough that I'm sleeping with you while they're here."

"Of course you're sleeping with me. You *live* here."

"Let's wait, baby. It's only two days, and think about how amazing our wedding night will be if we wait."

She squeezed him, drawing a tortured groan from him. "I don't want to wait."

He peeled her fingers off his erection. "Katherine…"

"Oh my God!" She flopped onto her back. "You're serious!"

"Yes, I'm serious. It's also because you're running around here like a crazy woman seeing to their every need. You, my pregnant love, need your sleep."

"You're not the boss of me."

He laughed, as she'd hoped he would. "Now you sound like a five-year-old."

"You aren't going to deny me what I want just because I'm pregnant, are you?"

"I'll never deny you anything—after we're married and as long as the doctor says it's safe."

"Fine."

"That's my girl. Now go to asleep."

Kate was already well on her way.

The next afternoon, Kate took Jill, Maggie and their mom to see the home for troubled women they were creating at Reid's family estate. The nausea had taken a much-needed day off, and Kate was enormously grateful to not have to hide her condition from her family while fighting the need to vomit.

She walked her mother and sisters through the downstairs, which had once boasted heavy velvet curtains and elaborate works of art that were now in storage. While the graceful bones of the old house could never be downplayed, Reid and Kate had decided to simplify the decorating to make it cozier and more welcoming to women in need. In the dining room, she smiled as she remembered Ashton asking her to sing "Crazy" for them the day she met them. Reid always said he'd fallen in love with her the minute he heard her sing, right here in this room.

Maggie asked no fewer than a thousand questions as they toured the kitchen where the women would be encouraged to share communal meals, the downstairs bedrooms that would be converted to counseling rooms and the suite where Martha had once lived, which would be made available to the program director if he or she chose to live onsite.

"This is very impressive, honey," Clare said. "I can picture it from how you describe it."

"Thanks, Mom. We're really excited to start interviewing for the director. A lot of what happens here will depend on who we get."

"Where are you with licenses from the state?" Maggie asked, running her hand over the mahogany banister.

"Ashton is handling all that. Once we had the idea of how we could put this place to good use, we didn't want to wait to get it moving."

She showed them through the upstairs bedrooms that had been converted to accommodate mothers and their children. Some rooms could hold up to five people, while the smaller rooms were outfitted for only two. "We've also got the horses and can give the kids riding lessons."

"Have you given any thought to offering therapeutic horseback riding?" Maggie asked.

"I'm ashamed to say I don't know what that is," Kate said.

"It's the use of horses and horseback riding to help people with a variety of disabilities. Teaching them to ride horses helps them to overcome a number of challenges and gives them a sense of satisfaction and self-worth. I took a class on it in college."

"I thought that was only a horseback-riding class," Jill said.

"It was a *therapeutic* horseback-riding class," Maggie said, sticking her tongue out at her sister.

"And here I thought you were looking for three easy credits," Clare said, sharing a smile with her youngest daughter.

"It's a really intriguing idea, Mags. Reid and Ashton board horses here that mostly belong to their friends, but I bet we could include them in our program. Somehow."

Kate took a good look around the room that used to be Reid's bedroom, where they'd spent so much time together the first time around. Back then everything had been difficult and unsettled. Now the path ahead stretched before them filled with promise and joy. She couldn't wait to get back to him. As she had that thought, the floor swayed beneath her feet, and she reached out to grab hold of the wall.

"Kate?" Her mother rushed over to her. "What is it?"

"Nothing. I just felt dizzy for a second there."

"Sit down," Maggie said, directing Kate to a chair.

Clare felt Kate's head for fever. "You're pale as a ghost."

Kate met Jill's gaze above their mother's head.

Jill tipped her head as if encouraging Kate to tell the others her news.

"Do you think you're coming down with something?" Clare asked. "I'd hate for you to be sick for your own wedding."

"I'm coming down with a baby," Kate said. "In about seven months."

Maggie let out a shriek and hugged Jill.

"Why didn't you say something?" Clare asked, still squatting before Kate.

"I was going to after the wedding. I figured we'd take it one step at a time."

"Oh, honey, such wonderful news," Clare said, hugging her. "But you're really going to make me a grandmother? Aidan will have a field day with this."

Kate and her sisters laughed at their mother's dismay.

"I'm kidding," Clare said. "Congratulations. I'm so thrilled for you. I wasn't sure you wanted to be a mom."

"I wasn't either, until I was back with Reid. Then it was all I wanted—along with him, of course."

"Are you feeling all right? In general?" Clare asked.

"The nausea has been tough and the dizziness is new, but other than that, I feel great. Oh, and my boobs. They hurt sometimes."

"Mine hurt with all three of you," Clare said.

"Ewww," Maggie said to laughter from the others.

They waited until they were sure Kate was feeling better before they left the house to take her home to nap. Under normal circumstances, Kate would protest that plan. But right now, a nap sounded like heaven.

CHAPTER 18

Snow began to fall around three o'clock on Christmas Eve. Reid watched the darkening sky with a growing sense of anxiety. His first wife had been killed in a snow-related car accident. He wanted Kate home, and he wanted her home now.

He was about to call her when Jack walked into the stables, where Reid had been mucking stalls as an excuse to stay away from the house while Kate, her sisters and mother were out.

The kids had been playing football all afternoon, while others took long walks or watched Christmas movies or helped with the baking going on in the kitchen. Everyone seemed happy, or at least it seemed that way to him.

He eyed Jack cautiously, never sure what to say to him. "Feel like a ride, Jack?"

"No, thanks. Horses were never my thing. The girls have been crazy about them since they were little. Especially Kate."

"She's an amazing rider."

From his stall, Thunder whinnied, seeming to approve of Reid's assessment. "That'd be Thunder—her horse. He knows her name and always has something to say when he hears it."

Jack walked down the row of stalls to make Thunder's acquaintance.

"That's Kate's daddy, boy. Be nice."

Thunder stood perfectly still as he and Jack sized each other up.

Reid produced a couple of sugar cubes from his pocket and handed them to Jack. "Butter him up."

"Thanks." Jack held out his hand with the sugar resting on his palm.

Thunder never blinked as he scooped up the sugar with his tongue.

"I think he likes you," Reid said.

"That's good." Jack turned to face him but didn't say anything.

Reid continued to rake, refusing to be cowed in his own home. "Something on your mind, Jack?"

After another long silence, Jack said, "I'm never, *ever* going to introduce you as my son-in-law."

Reid stopped raking and tightened his lips to hold back laughter he knew Jack wouldn't appreciate. "Fair enough. As long as you don't expect me to introduce you as my father-in-law."

"Please don't."

Reid finally gave in to the need to laugh and was relieved when Jack joined him. "I'm glad we got that resolved."

"There's something else... That day when you came to my office... I told you I'd think about what you asked me. And I have. Thought about it. A lot."

Making an effort to hide his anxiety, Reid propped his arm on the closest stall and waited to hear what Jack would say.

"I'm fifty-six years old, and I'm still learning things."

"Right there with you."

Jack gave him a wry smile. "The thing I've learned this week is that I shouldn't make judgments or reach conclusions without having all the information."

"How do you mean?"

"Now that I've seen you and Kate together, as a couple, I understand it better. I can see that you love her."

"I do. Very much so."

"You'll take good care of her."

"Always."

"Then you have my blessing."

Reid shook his hand. "Thank you, Jack. That means a lot to me, and it'll mean everything to her."

"Do me a favor, will you? Let me tell her?"

"Whatever you like."

"They're back," Jack said, nodding to the open barn door, where Kate's Jeep was visible.

Reid expelled a deep sigh of relief inspired by multiple events as he accompanied her father out to greet the women.

Kate saw them coming toward her together and looked at him with questions in her gorgeous blue eyes.

He kissed her and took note of her pale complexion. "You look tired, darlin'."

"I am."

"Feeling okay?"

"I was a little dizzy earlier, but I'm good now."

"You haven't been dizzy before."

"Who's dizzy?" Jack asked.

"Kate is," Reid replied, never taking his eyes off her.

"How come?" Jack asked.

"*Why* did I think I could keep this a secret?" Kate moaned.

"Keep what a secret?" Jack asked, looking to the others for info.

She turned to face her father. "Dad, you're going to be a grandfather in June."

Jack looked like he'd been hit by a stun gun. "Oh. Wow. A grandfather." He glanced at Reid, who wondered if their fragile accord would be undone by this news.

"Are you going to faint, Jack?" Clare asked her ex-husband, her voice laced with humor.

"I don't think so, but thanks for asking." He reached for Kate, who stepped into his arms. Jack closed his eyes as he hugged his daughter. "Congratulations, honey. You'll be a wonderful mother."

"Thank you, Dad." Kate had tears streaming down her face, and her hair was covered in snow by the time her dad let her go.

Reid slipped an arm around her shoulders. "Let's get you inside and out of the cold."

Kate's arm encircled his waist and she leaned her head on his shoulder. Jack stayed back to help Clare and the girls with some bags they had in the car.

"Did I see you two coming out of the stables together?" Kate asked.

"You did."

"And?"

"And I think it's all going to be fine, darlin'. Your daddy and I have come to an understanding of sorts."

"Is that right?"

"It is."

"When will I hear about this understanding of yours?"

He helped her out of her coat and hung it next to his in the mudroom. "As soon as he sees fit to tell you."

"Is this some sort of guy thing?"

Reid propelled Kate through the kitchen and into their room, closing the door behind them. "I can understand how you might think so, but he specifically asked if he could be the one to share the details of our understanding with you. Since our agreement is rather, shall we say, *fragile*, I'd intend to respect his wishes."

"You do know I have ways of torturing information out of you."

"Which is why I was afraid to tell you there was information to be had."

A fit of laughter overtook her as she fell onto the bed.

Delighted by her amusement, he stretched out next to her, propping his head on his upturned hand. "Have mercy on me, will you, please?"

Kate reached for his free hand and linked their fingers. "He took the news about the baby well."

"I noticed that. I take it you told your mom and Maggie, too."

"I had to when the dizzy thing happened."

"What's up with the dizzy thing?"

"No idea. It came on out of nowhere. I was fine one minute, and the world was swimming the next. Reminded me of when I had pneumonia."

"Should we call the doctor?"

"I don't think so. It only lasted a second."

"You're sure?"

She nodded, gazing up at him with love in her eyes. He'd never seen her looking so peaceful or serene. "What?" he asked, smiling at her.

"Everything. It's perfect."

"Yes, it is," he said, leaning over to kiss her as her phone chimed with a text.

"I need to check that. We do have a houseful of guests."

"Who can fend for themselves for five damned minutes while I kiss my fiancée."

"You can kiss me around the clock when we get back to St. Kitts." They were going for three weeks to close on their new house and to honeymoon in the sun.

"I'll hold you to that."

"I really wish you would." She withdrew her phone from her pocket. "It's from Maggie. She wants to talk to us for a minute." Kate sat up and texted back, telling Maggie to come to their room.

Reid groaned and rolled onto his back. "So no more kissing?"

"In a minute."

A knock on the door preceded Maggie into the room. "I'm so sorry to bother you guys."

"It's fine," Reid said, waving her in. "Do you want me to go so you can talk to Kate?"

"No, I want to talk to both of you about the project. The women and kids."

"What about it?" Kate asked.

In a rush of words, she said, "I want to be your director." For Reid's benefit, she said, "I double-majored in social work and sign language. I did a yearlong internship in a homeless shelter in the city. I understand the issues and the challenges. I know how to help them. And I want to be here, with my sisters." Looking at Kate now, she said, "I really miss you guys." Maggie stopped talking and took a deep breath. "I know it's a lot to ask, but I'm dead serious about this. I'll give it everything I've got. I promise."

Kate glanced at him, seeming astounded by her sister's speech. "We need to talk it over."

"No, we don't," Reid said. "As far as I'm concerned, the job is yours if you want it."

Maggie gasped. "You mean it?"

"If Kate agrees," Reid said, looking at her. "We were hoping to find someone who'd be passionate about it."

"I agree," Kate said, drawing a scream of delight from her sister. "You're sure you want to leave New York?"

As Maggie nodded, her eyes flooded with tears.

"What is it, honey?" Kate took Maggie's hand and urged her to sit between them on the bed.

"There was a guy in New York, but it's over now. I could really use a change of direction as well as scenery. And if I have to translate the details of one more disgusting murder, I might commit one."

Kate laughed and hugged Maggie. "We'd love to have you here with us. Wouldn't we, Reid?"

Seeing Kate surrounded by the people she loved warmed his heart. "Absolutely."

"Thank you," Maggie said, wiping her tears as she stood. "I'm sorry to barge in on you guys. I'll let you get back to whatever you were doing."

Kate poked her sister in the ribs, making her laugh.

Maggie left the room, closing the door on her way out.

"Well, we can check interviewing for a director off our to-do list," Reid said.

"Are you sure you're okay with Maggie doing it?"

"If I wasn't, I wouldn't have said I was. One thing you need to know about me, darlin', is I never say anything I don't mean."

She lay back on the bed and held out her arms to him. "Can we do some more of that kissing stuff we were doing before?"

"By all means."

Christmas Day passed in a whirl of food and presents and laughter and music. A foot of snow fell overnight, delighting the younger members of the family, who spent most of the day outdoors. A snowman was built and everyone but the seniors participated in a massive snowball fight after dinner.

Kate was completely exhausted but happier than she'd ever been in her life. She'd waited all day for a moment alone with her dad, but he'd been outside with the twins for most of the day. She hoped they'd get a chance to talk before the wedding tomorrow.

They were gathered by the fire in the great room, relaxing after the busy day when the jingle of bells outside had the kids running for the windows.

"Oh wow," Rob cried. "It's a horse and sleigh! Two of them!"

Kate looked at Reid, who shrugged, but his mysterious smile gave him away.

"Who wants to go for a ride?" he asked.

"I do!" Olivia and her twin, Owen, said in stereo.

"We do, too," John said, pushing and shoving his twin Rob to get to their coats first.

"How fun," Andi said. "Count me in."

"Me, too," Frannie said, grabbing Jamie's hand and dragging him off the sofa.

"Each sleigh can take ten at a time," Reid said. "So we can go in shifts."

As everyone suited up and rushed out the door, Kate went up on tiptoes to kiss Reid. "Thank you."

"I thought it would be fun."

"Hey, Dad," Ashton said. "Can I reserve one of the sleighs after everyone else has had a ride?"

"Sure. We have them until midnight."

"Great, thanks."

"Any specific reason?" Reid asked his son in a teasing tone.

"None of your business," Ashton said with a good-natured smile. "Kate, could I borrow you for just a minute?"

"Um, sure."

"Don't keep her too long, son."

"I won't."

Kate followed Ashton into the kitchen, wondering what he might have to say to her. They'd gone out of their way to be polite to each other in the weeks since she and Reid had been home, but they hadn't spoken one-on-one.

"I wanted you to know that I'm going to ask Jill to marry me tonight."

"Oh! That's amazing! Do you think she knows?"

"No, I'm quite certain it'll be a total surprise to her."

"Wow, I'd love to see that. It's really hard to surprise her. She's always one step ahead of everyone."

"Don't I know it. The thing is… I can almost guess exactly what she's going to say when I ask. That we can't upstage you when you're getting married tomorrow."

"Oh please! Tell her there's no one in the world I'd rather share the stage with than her. She knows that."

"I had a feeling you might say that. I'll tell her."

"Good luck. For what it's worth, I hope she says yes."

"You do? Really?"

"Yes, really," Kate said with a laugh. "She lights up when you're around. I've never seen her look at any guy the way she looks at you."

"That's good to hear. I'm a little nervous that she might say no."

Kate took pity on him and squeezed his arm. "She won't."

"Um, listen, Kate… I told Jill this, but I should tell you, too. I'm sorry about what happened way back when. I have a lot of regrets about that time, what I said to you that day in the parking lot and the role I played in breaking up you and my dad. He's so happy since you guys have been back together. Seeing him happy makes me happy, too. I wanted you to know that."

"And I'd like you to know that other than the bumps at the end of our friendship, I always thought you were a great guy and a good friend. I'm thrilled that you might also be my brother-in-law."

"Sounds a lot better than stepson, huh?"

Kate tossed her head back and laughed, and then she hugged him. "Much, much better. Thank you for apologizing. I'm so sorry we lied to you. That never should've happened, either."

"It's all in the past now. Let's leave it there."

"Deal."

"Can I ask you something else?"

"Sure."

"I sort of thought my dad might ask me to stand up for him tomorrow, but he didn't."

"You've been pretty cool about us being back together. He didn't want to push his luck with you."

"Huh," Ashton said, rubbing at the stubble on his jaw. "I didn't think of it that way."

"You were his first choice, though. You have to know that."

"He should really have his first choice on such an important occasion, don't you think?"

Kate smiled at him. "I couldn't agree more."

"I'll take care of it." He leaned in to kiss her cheek. "Enjoy every minute tomorrow. You're getting the very best man I've ever known."

Touched, Kate said, "Thank you."

They returned to living room, and Ashton joined Jill on the sofa.

"So he told you his big news?" Reid asked.

Kate looked up at him. "How long have you known?"

"A couple of days. He asked me not to tell anyone, but I was dying to tell you. I'm glad he did."

"It was nice just now with him. Felt like old times. I love them together.

"So do I." Reid glanced at his son and Jill, their heads bent close as they whispered to each other. "He hasn't left her side all weekend."

"Except to sleep. Maggie told me he hasn't been staying at Jill's while she's been there."

"No, he wouldn't. That doesn't surprise me."

"You Matthews men are extremely *old*-fashioned in your beliefs."

"Did you just call me old, darlin'? The night before our wedding?"

"I don't know what you're talking about."

He leaned in to press his lips to her ear, making her shiver. "The other sleigh is ours after everyone else is done."

Kate snuggled into his embrace, delighted by him, his surprise and the possibility of her sister's engagement. This was shaping up to be the very best Christmas ever.

"Are you warm enough?" Ashton asked Jill as he tucked a second blanket around her.

"Yep. Are you going to join me, or am I going alone?"

His heart raced with nerves and excitement. What if she said no? What would he do then? He pushed those negative thoughts out of his mind and settled in next to her. The full moon cast a bright glow over the snow, making it glisten like thousands of tiny crystals.

Jill raised the blankets to invite him in, and Ashton slid closer, putting an arm around her.

"There," she said. "Now, it's perfect."

"Yes, it is." He turned to her, loving how cute she looked with a knit hat pulled down over her ears and her nose pink from the cold. As the sleigh jarred forward, sliding silently through the snow, Ashton kissed her. He'd intended it to be a quick kiss, but after three nights without her in his bed, he was aching for much more.

"I've missed you," he said many passionate minutes later.

"I've missed you, too. I've gotten used to sleeping with you."

"Please don't break the habit."

"I won't. Maggie is going home the day after tomorrow, and then I'm all yours again."

"I like the sound of that. All mine."

She put her arm around him and rested her head on his chest. "Mmm."

"I want you to be all mine forever, Jill." The words were out of his mouth before he had time to consider the carefully worded proposal he'd been practicing for days.

She raised her head and met his gaze. "You do?"

He nodded. To hell with carefully worded. "I love you so much. These last few weeks, when we've finally gotten to be together, have been the best of my whole life. I never want what we have to end. Will you make me the happiest guy in the world and marry me, Jill?"

Her face was a study in dismay, which was not at all what he was hoping for. "You can't ask me tonight when my sister is getting married tomorrow!"

"I knew you'd say that, so I talked to Kate about it."

"Wait—*you* talked to *Kate*?"

"Yes, and I told her you'd be worried about us getting engaged the night before her wedding, and she said—I'm quoting here—'Tell her there's no one in the world I'd rather share the stage with.' She also said—and this is me being extremely self-serving—that she hoped you said yes. I suspect that was mostly because she'd rather I be her brother-in-law than her stepson, but that's another story."

Jill laughed through her tears.

"And your dad gave me his blessing, too."

"He did? You asked him?"

"Of course I did," he said, indignant that she would even ask. "I'm a Southern gentleman, darlin', and there're rules for these things." He tugged off his glove with his teeth, retrieved the jeweler's box from his coat pocket and opened it so she could see the two-carat diamond ring he'd picked out for her. He'd suspected that anything bigger would've been too much for her. "What do you say? Should we spend the rest of our lives together?"

Jill looked at the ring and then at him.

Ashton thought he would die as he waited for her to say something—*anything.*

"Yes. Yes, we should."

Somehow he managed to hide his overwhelming relief from her, but his hands trembled as he pulled off the glove on her left hand and slid the ring onto her finger. "Let me see." He held up her hand to use the moonlight to gauge how the ring looked on her. "Perfect," he said, kissing her hand and then her lips.

"I love you, too," she said, making his heart dance with joy.

He hugged her tightly and kissed her again, lingering this time. "That's the best gift anyone has ever given me."

"This reminds me of the night we took Thunder for a ride in the snow," Kate said as she and Reid skimmed over the snow in the other sleigh. The cold air had reinvigorated her after the long day, and she was thrilled to be cocooned with Reid under the blankets.

"I know you would've preferred to take Thunder tonight, but I really don't want you riding while you're pregnant."

"How will I go *nine months* without riding?"

"You can do it, darlin'. For the baby."

"Yes, I can, but it's not going to be easy. And I'll get fat as a house without the exercise."

"I won't let you get fat. I'll take you for long walks on the beach in St. Kitts and more long walks through the woods when we're here."

"What if I do get fat?" she asked playfully. "Will you still love me then?"

"I'll love you no matter how fat you get, no matter how many wrinkles line your sweet face, no matter how gray your hair gets or how many warts pop up on your nose."

Kate laughed at the visual he created. "So you're picturing a fat, wrinkled, gray-haired witch of a wife?"

"I'm picturing you, round with our child, glowing with excitement and love and anticipation. I can't wait to see that. I can't wait to watch our baby be born and watch you feed him or her." He rested a hand on her still-flat belly. "I can't wait for every minute of it."

She was deeply moved to hear him speak with such excitement about their child. "I can't believe that this time tomorrow we'll be married. What a long and winding road it's been to end up exactly where we belong."

"Thank you, darlin', for choosing me when you truly could've had anyone you wanted."

"I chose the only one I've ever wanted."

He captured her lips in a sweet, soft kiss that had her clinging to him, wanting so much more.

"Tomorrow," he said. "Tomorrow, we'll have everything." He kissed her again. "I'm going to take you home now and tuck you into bed, and then the next time I see you, you'll be coming toward me as my bride, and I'll be the luckiest, happiest guy in the entire world at that moment."

"I don't get why you can't stay with me tonight."

"Because it's bad luck to see the bride before the wedding, and I'm not doing anything to tempt fate when she was kind enough to bring you back to me."

"I don't want to sleep alone."

"I'll ask Maggie to come sleep with you."

"I want you and no one else." Kate knew she sounded like a petulant child and didn't care. She hated the idea of even one night without him.

"You have me, and this is the last night you'll spend alone. I promise."

A short time later, the driver pulled up to the house, which was dark except for a single light still shining in the living room. Reid walked her inside and waited until she was ready for bed.

True to his word, he tucked her in and then sat on the edge of the bed to look down at her.

"I don't want you to go," Kate said.

"I'm not going far."

"Where will you be?"

"In town at the Hermitage. That's where we're going tomorrow night, too."

"We're not staying here?"

"No, we're not spending our wedding night with your entire family."

Kate smiled at the forceful way he said that.

"Your mom wants to come back in the summer after the baby is born, and I told her we'd love that," Reid said.

"I would love that. I'll need her here to tell me what to do."

He leaned over to kiss her. "Close your eyes and go to sleep. Dream about tomorrow and all the other tomorrows we'll have together. When you wake up, it'll be our big day."

"I love you," she said.

"I love you, too. Now close those magnificent blue eyes."

Kate kept her eyes closed when he kissed her once more and got up to go. She opened them to watch him leave the room. Staring into the darkness, she heard his car start and the crunch of snow under his tires.

He was only gone a minute when she reached for her phone.

"You're supposed to be sleeping, darlin'," he said with a chuckle.

"I can't sleep without you."

"Yes, you can."

How fitting, she thought, to spend the last night before their wedding the way they'd spent so many nights in the past. "Can I keep you company while you drive into town?"

"Only if you promise to sleep the minute I'm there."

"I promise. Do you want me to sing for you?"

"I'd love that."

So she did.

***

Jill and Maggie woke Kate at ten the next morning, thirty minutes before the hair-and-makeup people she used on tour were due to arrive. For this special occasion, she'd agreed to let the professionals have their way with her.

"I can't believe I slept so late!"

"You needed it," Maggie said as she handed her sister a mug of coffee. "Here is your one serving of caffeine for the day."

As much as she wanted and needed the coffee, Kate's stomach turned at the smell. "Can't do it, Mags." She handed the mug back to her sister. "Sorry."

"That's okay. How about some tea and toast?"

"That'd be great, thanks."

"Coming right up."

"Are you okay?" Jill asked when she and Kate were alone.

"I'm fine, just the usual nausea. How about you? Any news to report?"

Jill blushed and smiled as she held out her left hand to show Kate the ring.

"It's gorgeous. Congratulations!" She hugged Jill. "Do you love it?"

"I do. He did great."

"How was the proposal?"

"Lovely and perfect. Thank you for what you said about sharing the stage. I would've turned him down if he hadn't told me that."

"You would've broken his heart if you turned him down."

"I'm glad I didn't have to."

"When's the wedding?"

Jill rolled her eyes. "Can we please get through yours before we talk about mine?"

"I suppose so."

"Reid gave me this yesterday and asked me to give it to you this morning." Jill handed her a small box, wrapped in silver paper with a card attached.

"This isn't fair! We agreed to skip Christmas presents for each other with everything else going on."

"I don't think it's a Christmas present."

"Oh." Kate opened the envelope first. On an embossed cream-colored card bearing his initials, he'd written, "Something new for the big day. I can't wait for today, tomorrow, the next day and all the days after. With all my love, Reid." She tore the paper to find a black velvet box. Inside were teardrop diamond earrings.

"They're gorgeous," Jill said.

"I can't believe he did this," Kate said, reading the note again and wiping away tears. "We said no gifts."

"A man can buy his new wife a wedding gift if he wants to. It's in the rule book."

"But I didn't get him anything."

"You're giving him everything, Kate, and he knows that. That's all he wants."

"Have I thanked you for supporting us even when it wasn't cool to support us?"

Jill smiled. "I support *you*. That's what we do for each other—what we've always done for each other."

"And what we'll always do."

"Right. All this wedding stuff will never change that."

"Did Maggie tell you her news?"

"It's all she's talked about this morning. I'm so excited that she'll be coming to Nashville and for such a good cause."

"Are you guys talking about me?" Maggie asked when she returned with the tea and toast.

"We sure are," Kate said. "We're so excited that you'll be living close by. The Harrington girls, back together again."

"I'm not sure which part is more exciting—the job or being with you guys."

Jill checked her watch. "You'd better eat up and get in the shower, Kate. You don't want to be late for your own wedding."

Kate managed half the toast and a bit of the tea. It came rushing back up while she was in the shower, the first time she'd actually vomited since she'd been pregnant. She turned off the water, wrapped her wet hair in a towel, pulled on a r obe and sat on the closed toilet for a long time, taking deep breaths to get the nausea under control. Figures it would be worse today than any day so far.

"Kate?" Jill asked through the closed door. "Are you okay?"

"Come in."

"What's wrong?"

"Sick."

"Oh no."

"It's better now."

"Do you want to lie down for a bit?"

"Do we have time?"

"No, but we can make time."

"Maybe for a few minutes."

Kate stood, and the whole world tilted, her brain spinning with the most intense dizzy spell yet.

Only Jill's arms around her kept her from falling. "Let's get you back into bed."

"Why does this have to happen today of all days?"

"Because that's the way it goes."

Jill guided her back to bed and pulled the covers up and over her. "Rest for a while. I'll take care of everything. Don't worry."

The nausea was so severe that Kate didn't dare speak. Over the next hour, she was aware of her sisters, mother and stepmother coming in to check on her as she floated between sleep and wakefulness. And then she was fully awake, staring at the ceiling and waiting for the nausea to attack again. When it didn't, she sat up slowly and sat perfectly still at the edge of the bed. So far, so good.

Jill came in and was surprised to see her sitting up. "How're you doing?" Her hair had been corralled into an elegant French twist, and her makeup was done.

"Better, I think. You look great."

"Thanks. Perfect timing. Everyone else is ready. It's your turn, if you're feeling up to it."

A burst of excitement and adrenaline propelled her off the bed and into the bathroom, where she brushed her teeth and hair and pinched some color into her pallid cheeks.

She joined the others in the great room, which had been transformed for a wedding with fifty chairs arranged in a half-circle in front of the fireplace. "Sorry I slept through all the work, guys."

"Are you feeling better, honey?" her mom asked, concern etched into her face.

"Much better and ready to get married. Where do they want me?"

"Upstairs," Jill said, leading the way. "Let's go make you into a bride."

Two hours later, Kate stood before a full-length mirror in one of the upstairs bedrooms, assessing her appearance from all angles. Not bad to say she'd been crippled with nausea only a short time ago. Before she donned her dress, she'd eaten a plain turkey sandwich that had gone down well. She prayed it stayed down.

The dress was made of cream-colored silk that pooled at her feet. She hadn't wanted a train or veil, settling instead for the Harrington family's diamond tiara that her grandmother, mother and aunt had worn at their weddings.

Taking a gander at her elaborately braided and arranged hair, she wondered how she'd ever find all the strategically hidden bobby pins that had been used to hold it together. She'd probably still be finding them in a year—a thought that made her giggle with excitement and nerves. How much longer?

Jill and Maggie came in a few minutes later, wearing matching red silk dresses that they had chosen for themselves and carrying bouquets made of red roses and white lilies for all of them.

"That color reminds me of Frannie and Jamie's wedding," Kate said of their dresses. "You guys look amazing."

"So do you," Maggie said. "Gorgeous."

"Thank you. I don't look too pale, do I?"

Maggie took a close look at Kate's face. "Nope. Just right."

"Good. Reid will zero right in if I'm too pale. Is he here yet?"

"For a while now. He and Buddy are using your room to get dressed."

"Is Ashton with them?"

"No, but he's here."

Kate wondered when he planned to make his move. The room was soon full of mothers, grandmothers and junior bridesmaids, all of whom would be escorted downstairs by a male member of the family. Kate had invited only her closest friends in the business, the members of her band and a couple of people from Long Road Records. Reid had also only invited a few friends, hoping to keep the wedding small and intimate.

As far as Kate knew, the media hadn't caught wind of the fact that they were being married today, and she hoped it stayed that way. Jill planned to release a single photo from the wedding once they were well on their way out of town.

Twenty minutes later, Buddy appeared at the door looking handsome in a dark suit with a red tie. "Wow, kid," he said when he saw her. "You clean up real good."

"Same to you," Kate said, amused by him as always. "Thanks for doing this."

"I gotta be honest, sweetheart, I feel a little weird doing something your own daddy ought to be doing, especially when he's here."

"I couldn't agree more, Buddy," Jack said from the doorway, his eyes fixed on Kate. "Would you mind if I took over?"

"Not at all," Buddy said gallantly. He kissed Kate carefully on the cheek and left her alone with her dad.

"Do *not* make me cry," Kate said as she blinked back tears. "No matter what you do, don't make me cry."

Dashingly handsome in a dark gray suit and cranberry tie, Jack laughed. "I haven't said a word."

"I know you. You're going to say something, and it *will* make me cry."

"I'll say only that you're stunningly beautiful, I love you and I'm happy for you—and Reid. I've waited your whole life for this moment, and there's no way in hell anyone else is walking you down those stairs but me."

She fanned her face with her hand, fighting an epic battle against the gigantic lump in her throat.

"Are you ready?" he asked, extending his arm.

"I need a minute."

"Take all the time you need."

"Now I need a tissue."

He withdrew a handkerchief from his pocket and handed it to her.

Kate dabbed carefully at her eyes, surrounded by the familiar scent of his cologne on the linen cloth. "Nothing you could've said or done would've made me happier today than having you give me away," she said as she tucked the handkerchief back in his pocket and curled her hand into the crook of his elbow.

"I'm sorry it took me so long to come around."

"All that matters is that you got here in time."

"Shall we?"

"Yes, please. Let's go."

Minutes before he was due in the great room, Reid wrestled with an uncooperative cufflink.

Buddy came to the rescue. "Allow me."

"What're you doing down here? You're supposed to be with Kate."

"Her daddy relieved me."

"Did he? Oh, that's great news."

Buddy finished with the cufflink and took it upon himself to straighten Reid's tie. "He took his own sweet time getting onboard, didn't he?"

"Doesn't matter now. He's here, he's giving her away and that's all I care about."

"Ya look real good, not that you don't always. Goddamned ageless freak."

"I love you, too," Reid said with a laugh.

"I do love you, brother. You know that, right?"

"That's one thing I've never doubted in my entire life."

"Mama loved the corsage you sent her."

"She's the closest thing to a mother I have left."

"It was a nice thing to do. Made her cry."

"Aww, isn't she sweet?"

Ashton came into the room, carrying a white box. "For the groom."

"Need me to put that on for you?" Buddy asked. To Ashton, he said, "I had to dress his ass."

"One cufflink," Reid said.

"I'll take care of it," Ashton said. "In fact, Buddy, I know you're the one he actually asked, but if it's all the same to you—"

"Say no more. It's a good thing my ego is nice and healthy, because it sure is taking a beating around here."

"Second time he got fired today," Reid told Ashton.

"You could do with a little humility," Ashton said to his godfather, who guffawed and flipped him the bird on the way out of the room. "I hope that was okay," Ashton said as he pinned a white rose to Reid's lapel.

"It was more than okay. As much as I love Buddy, there's no one I'd rather have stand beside me today than you."

"I had a feeling that might be the case." He brushed some lint off the arm of Reid's dark suit. "I was hoping you might return the favor next summer."

"Really?"

Ashton smiled and nodded. "I asked her last night, and she said yes."

"Aw, son, I'm so happy for you." He drew Ashton into a hug, mindful of not crushing the flower.

"Thanks, Dad. Check us out—marrying sisters."

"That'll give the tabloids something to talk about."

"Let 'em talk. Happy birthday, by the way. I meant to say that earlier."

"Thanks. Just what I needed—to get even older, today of all days."

Ashton laughed.

"But it made sense to do it when her family was going to be here anyway." Reid paused and glanced at his son, so young and handsome with his whole life before him. "Listen, son, I have a favor to ask of you."

"Sure. Whatever you need."

"It's kind of a big deal."

"Okay…"

"So, you know, Kate doesn't like to talk about the fact that she'll probably have a lot of years without me."

"I don't want to talk about that, either. Especially not today."

"I know, but here's the thing… She's pregnant with a baby we both want very much."

"Oh. I wondered if you guys would have kids."

"I know it's a lot to lay on you when you've been my only child for so long—"

"In case you failed to notice, I'm a big boy now, Dad. I think I can handle it."

Reid smiled, amused and moved by Ashton's support. "If the day comes when I can't be there for them—"

"I will be. As of today, they're both family to me. You don't have to ask."

Reid hugged him again. "Your mom would be so proud of you. I sure am."

"I never get tired of hearing that."

"We should probably get out there so Kate doesn't think I stood her up."

"We can't have that."

Reid gestured for his son to lead the way and followed him out of the bedroom. In the great room, every seat was taken and a hush fell over the guests when he and Ashton walked to the front of the gathering and shook hands with Reid's longtime friend, Superior Court Judge William Branch, who was officiating.

Buddy's girls were first down the stairs. They were beautiful in fancy red dresses and were accompanied by Kate's brothers Rob, John and Nick. Eric and Max had begged to be left out of the wedding party, and Kate had reluctantly agreed.

Next came Maggie and then Jill, who shared a private smile with Ashton as she took her place across the aisle from where they waited for Kate.

She appeared at the top of the stairs on the arm of her father, looking radiant and happy and absolutely gorgeous.

Ashton nudged him. "Breathe."

Until that moment, Reid hadn't realized he was holding his breath. It wasn't the first time she'd taken his breath away and he'd wager it wouldn't be the last. And then she was there before him, looking up at him with those dazzling blue eyes. He shook hands with her father, who took a seat in the front row between his wife and Kate's mother, both of whom extended a hand to him.

"Happy birthday," Kate said with a smile.

He leaned in to kiss her. "Best birthday of my life."

"Not yet," Judge Branch said to laughter from the guests.

Since nothing else about their relationship had been traditional, they'd decided to go with traditional vows that they recited with prompting from Judge Branch. Rings were exchanged, and then the judge was pronouncing them husband and wife, and Reid was kissing her, his wife. Kate… At long last, his wife.

Only when he felt her fingertips on his face did he realize he was crying—and so was she. He gathered her into his arms and held on tight while she did the same. When he released her, her smile reassured him and the squeeze of her hand in his grounded him.

Surrounded by family and friends, they received congratulations, hugs and kisses. And Kate never let go of his hand.

At her request, Buddy and Taylor sang their blockbuster duet, "My One and Only Love," while Reid and Kate had their first dance as Mr. and Mrs. They toasted their wedding as well as Jill and Ashton's engagement and Maggie's new job. Waiters circulated with an endless stream of hor's'doeuvers and champagne.

They posed for countless family pictures with the photographer Kate had hired to document the day.

After they cut their cake, Ashton clinked a spoon against a crystal champagne glass to quiet the gathering. "Tradition dictates that the best man say a few words about the bride and groom," he said when he had their attention. "And I couldn't miss the opportunity to roast my dad a bit."

"Oh great," Reid said to laughter.

Ashton smiled. "Just kidding about the roast, but I do want to say that no kid could've asked for more in a father than what I had with mine. He was mom and dad to me and managed to fill both roles effortlessly, even though I know how hard it must've been to raise me on his own. Since I've been grown up, he's filled the roles of best friend, fishing buddy and occasional drinking buddy. My dad and I have a good time together, and we always have. Kate, I want to welcome you and your *extremely* large family to our family. I've never been a part of a Christmas quite like this one, and I hope it's the first of many that the Harringtons and Matthews will spend together. Help me to congratulate Reid and Kate. May today be the first day of a long and happy life together."

"I'll definitely drink to that," Kate said, touching her crystal glass of ice water against his glass of champagne.

"Hear, hear," Reid said, kissing her.

At six o'clock Reid told her it was time to head into town. While Kate was looking forward to some alone time with her new husband, she wasn't ready yet to say good-bye to her family, who'd be heading home in the morning. The time together had gone by far too quickly in Kate's opinion.

"We'll do it again next year," Andi assured her with a hug. "Dad and I will host."

"And back here again the year after?" Kate asked.

"Sounds like a plan to me," her mom said. "You we were a wonderful hostess and a beautiful bride. None of us will soon forget this Christmas."

"Thank you, Mom."

Kate was in tears by the time she said good-bye to her dad and Aidan, Jamie, Frannie, her grandparents, the Booths and all the kids. Last in line were her sisters, who waited patiently for Kate to get to them.

"Thanks for all you did to make this happen," Kate said to Jill when she hugged her. "I'll be right there for you when it's your turn."

"I know that. Go be happy. That's how you can thank me."

"And you," Kate said to Maggie. "We'll be seeing you soon, right?"

"I'll be back as soon as I can give notice at my job and pack up my apartment."

"We'll look forward to that. Plan to stay here until the house is ready for occupants."

"This was the best Christmas ever," Maggie said. "For once, no one was missing. Thank you for that."

"My pleasure, honey." She hugged her younger sister for a long time. "Hurry back."

"I will."

"Ready, darlin'?" Reid asked.

"I need to get my bag."

"Jill already put it in the car."

"Of course she did," Kate said with a smile for her endlessly efficient sister who draped a fur-lined cape around Kate's shoulders. Kate turned to face the family that had gathered to see them off. "Thanks for being here, everyone. You'll never know how very much it meant to me."

"Wait," Maggie said. "Let us go first."

The entire family trooped onto the front porch ahead of Reid and Kate.

"Okay," Maggie called to them. "We're ready!"

As Reid and Kate walked onto the porch, they were showered with fragrant rose petals.

"Don't tell me you guys tied cans to my car, too," Reid said as he brushed a petal off Kate's forehead.

"He wanted to," Ashton said, pointing a thumb at Buddy, "but I intervened."

"Thank you, son," Reid said, hugging him. He reached for Kate's hand. "Shall we?"

Kate nodded and took his hand to go down the stairs. He tucked her into the sleek silver Mercedes sedan he'd bought a couple of weeks ago. In the biting cold, Kate was immediately grateful for the heated seats.

"Goddamned Buddy," Reid muttered.

"What?"

He glanced up at the rearview mirror. "Look."

Kate spun around and laughed when she saw the words "Just Married" written on the back window in white foam.

"He better not have gotten any on the paint, or I'll have to kill him."

"I won't let you kill him. But you have to laugh—one of the biggest names in country music writing on a car with shaving cream."

"Ha. Ha."

"Come on, it's funny."

"If you say so."

Kate took a last look back at the family that was waving them off. "I can't believe it's over. I already miss them."

"Don't forget you're married to a pilot now, darlin'. You can see them any time you want to."

"Thanks for the reminder. That makes me feel better." She looked over at him as he drove down the long lane from her house to the main road. "Can I ask you something?"

"Sure, you can."

"How are we going to get into the hotel without attracting a mob?" They were still dressed in wedding attire that would surely create a stir in the hotel.

"Have you no faith whatsoever in your new husband?"

"I'm very sorry. I didn't mean to insult you."

He took her hand and brought it to his lips. "I'll forgive you if you put your head back, close your eyes and relax."

"I can do that." Her eyelids felt like they weighed a hundred pounds. The next time she opened her eyes, Reid was lowering her onto a bed in a room that glowed with candlelight. "How did we get here?"

"It was magic."

"Mmm. It's been magic from the very start." The combination of the silk dress and the soft brush of the fur lining in the cape made her skin tingle. She held out a hand to him.

"Be right there. Let me get rid of my coat." He discarded the coat and kicked off his shoes before joining her on the bed.

"I can't believe we're really married."

He reached for her hand and kissed the rings on her finger. "Believe it."

"I keep waiting to wake up to find out it was all a dream. It wasn't a dream, was it?"

"It was a dream come true, baby." His phone chimed with a text, but he didn't move. Rather, he ran his fingers over her arm, raising a trail of goose bumps.

"Aren't you going to check that?"

"Wasn't planning to."

"What if it's Ashton and he needs you?"

"He doesn't need me tonight."

"Just check it, will you?"

"I will if it'll make you feel better." He rolled onto his back and pulled the phone from his pocket.

"Who's it from?"

"Mari."

"Oh." Kate regretted pushing him to look at it. "What does it say?"

Sighing, he said, "Dear Reid, I know today is your birthday, so I hope you're doing something fun. I wanted to tell you how sorry I am for everything that happened after we broke up. I'm ashamed of my behavior as well as the trouble I caused for you and Kate, and I'm hoping you can find it in your hearts to forgive me. Wherever you are and whatever you're doing, I hope you're happy. Sincerely, Mari."

"Wow. How do you feel about that?"

"It's nice of her to apologize, but I don't want to think about her tonight. I don't want to think about anything or anyone but you."

"You should drop the complaint against her."

"After all the trouble she caused for you with that video?"

"Let it go. She can't hurt us anymore, and we have nothing to gain by hurting her."

"She ripped up my son's baby picture."

"Don't you have others?"

"Yes, but that was one of my favorites."

"Let it go."

"Do I have to?"

Kate bit her lip to keep from laughing and nodded.

Begrudgingly, he keyed in a text and showed it to her when he was done. To Ashton, he'd written: *See to dropping the charges against Mari, will you? She apologized, so Kate says I have to let it go. Thanks.* "Happy now?"

"I'm very happy now, but I could be even happier."

"Is that right?" He tossed the phone onto the floor and turned over to face her. "What can I do for my lovely wife?"

She tugged at his tie, pulling it loose and going to work on his shirt buttons. "You've been holding out on me."

"Have I?" He smoothed a hand over her silk-covered hip, drawing her in closer to him.

"Uh-huh."

"It wasn't for lack of wanting you."

"No?"

His lips hovered a fraction of an inch above hers. "I've been dying for you, missing you, wanting you. Like I did for all the years you were gone."

"I'm here now, and I'm all yours."

He made fast work of helping her out of her wedding dress, his eyes popping—as she'd hoped they would—when he encountered the garter belt and thong combination she'd worn under it. "Are you trying to kill me on our wedding night?"

Kate laughed and pushed his shirt off his shoulders.

With a hand under her, he released her sheer, strapless bra, pushing it out of the way so he could feast on her breasts.

She gasped and arched her back to get closer to him. "Reid..."

"What, honey?"

"Don't go slow. Not this time. I need you."

He freed himself from his pants, pushed the thong aside and entered her in one swift stroke.

"*Yes*," Kate said on a moan.

He propped himself up on his elbows and gazed down at her. "Is that what you wanted?"

"*Yes*. You're what I wanted. I wanted you so badly for so long."

Gathering her close to him, he kissed her without breaking the intense eye contact. "I wanted you just as badly."

Kate wrapped her legs around his hips, making him groan and throb inside her.

He moved slowly and deliberately, letting the anticipation build until Kate almost couldn't bear it. And then he began to move faster, gripping her shoulders as he pushed her harder and higher, higher than she'd ever gone before.

"Kate, God, I love you. I love you."

The words, uttered gruffly against her neck, shattered what remained of her control. She cried out as the shock waves consumed her entire body. She came down from the incredible ride to find one hand fisted in his hair and the other clutching his backside.

Reid rode the storm of her climax and then let himself go, too. Afterward, he rested on top of her, breathing hard. "I'd hoped to show a bit more finesse the first time I made love to my wife, but you've got me feeling like a randy teenager with my pants around my knees."

Kate laughed at the disgusted face he made. "I adored the way you made love to your wife for the first time."

"I'll do even better the next time," he said with a kiss. "And the time after that."

"I can't wait to see how you top this."

"I can't wait for everything."

"Me too." She brushed the hair back from his face and brought him down to her for more of the kisses she loved so much. "Thank you for giving me the life I've always wanted but didn't know how to find without you."

"Believe me, darlin'," he said with a sexy grin as he pressed his hips tighter against her, "it was absolutely my pleasure."

Kate held him as tightly as she could, delighted to have found her way back to him and content to know they had the rest of their lives to spend together.

***

ACKNOWLEDGMENTS

Thank you to all the readers who asked me to finish Reid and Kate's story. Back in 2005 when I wrote *Marking Time*, it never occurred to me that readers would want them to end up together. Boy, was I wrong about that! I've never gotten more mail about any story than I did about theirs. I hope you're pleased with their second act. Returning to the *Treading Water/Marking Time* world was like spending time with precious old friends. Most of you know that Jack Harrington was my very first fictional character, so it was a great thrill for me to bring him back in *Coming Home*. I enjoyed the themes of forgiveness and redemption in this book, as well as the growth the characters experienced in the decade between *Marking Time* and *Coming Home*.

A special thank-you to my editor Linda Ingmanson, who is so very good to me by making time for me whenever I need her. Linda, you've become a wonderful friend since we've begun working together, and I couldn't do what I do without your support. Linda introduced me to proofreader extraordinaire Toni Lee, who is the last set of eyes on every book. Thank you to my writing pal Cheryl Brooks for the information she shared with me about aging horses. A great big thank you to my beta readers Ronlyn Howe, Kara Conrad and Anne Woodall, always the first to read my books and provide invaluable feedback and suggestions.

Thank you to Chris Camara and Julie Cupp, my former and current coworkers, whose faithful assistance allows me to write more. As always, thank you to Dan,

Emily and Jake for supporting my writing career and to Brandy and Louie for being my office mates during the day. Finally, to my wonderful, faithful, lovely readers—there are simply no words to tell you what each of you means to me. Your e-mails, participation in the reader groups, your comments on Facebook and Twitter, and your enthusiastic appreciation for my books makes me smile every day. Thank you, thank you, thank you.

xoxo

Marie

OTHER TITLES BY MARIE FORCE

Other Contemporary Romances Available from Marie Force:

The Treading Water Series

Book 1: Treading Water *(Jack & Andi)*

Book 2: Marking Time *(Clare & Aidan)*

Book 3: Starting Over *(Brandon & Daphne)*

Book 4: Coming Home *(Reid & Kate)*

The Gansett Island Series

Book 1: Maid for Love *(Mac & Maddie)*

Book 2: Fool for Love *(Joe & Janey)*

Book 3: Ready for Love *(Luke & Sydney)*

Book 4: Falling for Love *(Grant & Stephanie)*

Book 5: Hoping for Love *(Evan & Grace)*

Book 6: Season for Love *(Owen & Laura)*

Book 7: Longing for Love *(Blaine & Tiffany)*

Book 8: Waiting for Love *(Adam & Abby)*

Book 9: Time for Love *(David & Daisy)*

Book 10: Meant for Love *(Jenny & Alex)*

Book 10.5: Chance for Love, *A Gansett Island Novella (Jared & Lizzie)*

Book 11: Gansett After Dark *(Owen & Laura)*

Georgia on My Mind

True North

The Fall

Everyone Loves a Hero

Love at First Flight

Line of Scrimmage

The Erotic Quantum Series

Book 1: Virtuous *(Flynn & Natalie)*

Book 2: Valorous *(Flynn & Natalie)*

Book 3: Victorious *(Flynn & Natalie)*

Book 4: Rapturous *(Addie & Hayden)*

Book 5: Ravenous *(Jasper & Ellie)*

Book 6: Delirious *(Kristian & Aileen)*

Book 7: Outrageous *(Emmett & Leah)*

Romantic Suspense Novels Available from Marie Force:

The Fatal Series

One Night With You, *A Fatal Series Prequel Novella*

Book 1: Fatal Affair

Book 2: Fatal Justice

Book 3: Fatal Consequences

Book 3.5: Fatal Destiny, *the Wedding Novella*

Book 4: Fatal Flaw

Book 5: Fatal Deception

Book 6: Fatal Mistake

Book 7: Fatal Jeopardy

Book 8: Fatal Scandal

Book 9: Fatal Frenzy

Book 10: Fatal Identity

Single Title

About the Author

Marie Force is the *New York Times* bestselling author of contemporary romance, including the indie-published Gansett Island Series and the Fatal Series from Harlequin Books. In addition, she is the author of the Butler, Vermont Series, the Green Mountain Series and the erotic romance Quantum Series. In 2019, her new historical Gilded series from Kensington Books will debut with *Duchess By Deception*.

All together, her books have sold 7 million copies worldwide, have been translated into more than a dozen languages and have appeared on the *New York Times* bestseller list 29 times. She is also a *USA Today* and *Wall Street Journal* bestseller, a Speigel bestseller in Germany, a frequent speaker and publishing workshop presenter as well as a publisher through her Jack's House Publishing romance imprint. She is a two-time nominee for the Romance Writers of America's RITA® award for romance fiction.

Her goals in life are simple—to finish raising two happy, healthy, productive young adults, to keep writing books for as long as she possibly can and to never be on a flight that makes the news.

Join Marie's mailing list for news about new books and upcoming appearances in your area. Follow her on Facebook at *https://www.facebook.com/MarieForceAuthor*, Twitter *@marieforce* and on Instagram at *https://instagram.com/marieforceauthor/*. Join one of Marie's many reader groups. Contact Marie at *marie@marieforce.com*.

CPSIA information can be obtained
at www.ICGtesting.com
Printed in the USA
LVHW011712030519
616576LV00010B/290/P

9 781942 295280